THE FINISHER

BOOKS BY PETER LOVESEY

THE SERGEANT CRIBB SERIES

Wobble to Death
The Detective Wore Silk Drawers
Abracadaver
Mad Hatter's Holiday

The Tick of Death
A Case of Spirits
Swing, Swing Together
Waxwork

THE PETER DIAMOND SERIES

The Last Detective
Diamond Solitaire
The Summons
Bloodhounds
Upon a Dark Night
The Vault
Diamond Dust
The House Sitter
The Secret Hangman
Skeleton Hill

Stagestruck
Cop to Corpse
The Tooth Tattoo
The Stone Wife
Down Among the Dead Men
Another One Goes Tonight
Beau Death
Killing with Confetti
The Finisher
Diamond and the Eye

THE HEN MALLIN SERIES

The Circle

The Headhunters

THE PRINCE OF WALES MYSTERIES

Bertie and the Tinman
Bertie and the Seven Bodies

Bertie and the Crime of Passion

OTHER FICTION

The False Inspector Dew
Keystone
Rough Cider

On the Edge
The Reaper

THE
FINISHER

A PETER DIAMOND INVESTIGATION

Peter Lovesey

Published by
Soho Press, Inc.
227 W 17th Street
New York, NY 10011

Library of Congress Cataloging-in-Publication Data

Lovesey, Peter, author.
The finisher : a Peter Diamond investigation / Peter Lovesey.
Series: The Peter Diamond series; [19]

ISBN 978-1-64129-288-7
eISBN 978-1-64129-182-8

Subjects: GSAFD: Mystery fiction.
PR6062.O86 F56 2020 823'.914—dc23
2020007211

Map illustration © Jacqueline Ruth Lovesey and Saffron Olivia Russell

Printed in the United States of America

10 9 8 7 6 5 4 3 2 1

*For my mapmakers, Saffron Russell
and her mother, Jacqui Lovesey, in gratitude*

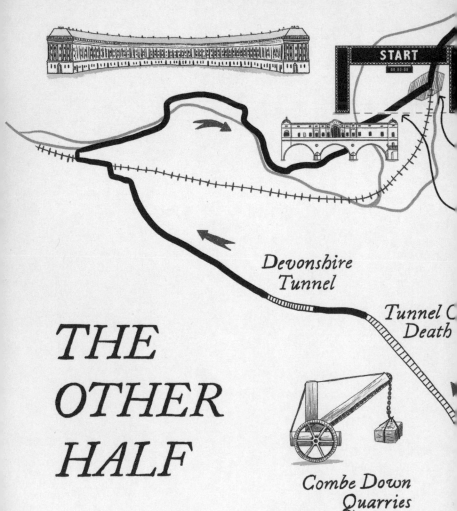

CITY *of* BATH

START

Devonshire
Tunnel

Tunnel C
Death

THE

OTHER

HALF

Combe Down
Quarries

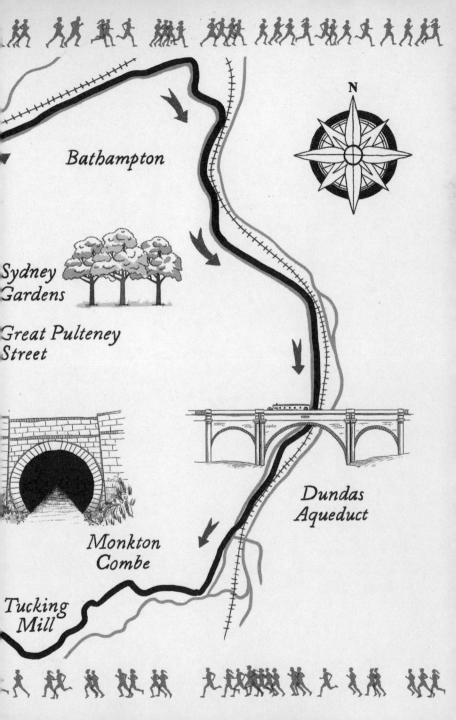

Bathampton

Sydney
Gardens

Great Pulteney
Street

N

Dundas
Aqueduct

Monkton
Combe

Tucking
Mill

1

The city of Bath isn't all about Roman plumbing and Georgian architecture.

It offers unrivalled facilities for getting rid of unwanted corpses. Beneath the creamy, sun-kissed squares, crescents and terraces is a rat-infested underworld undreamed of by most visitors, a dark, dank warren of cellars, vaults, culverts, sewers and drains. And the surrounding hills are riddled with miles of mines, quarries and tunnels, all but a few disused and some no longer mapped or remembered.

The Finisher got his reputation by completing the job. He had no wish to be investigated, so he left no clues. He preyed on the losers. "Defy me and you're finished," he would say. "I'll finish you myself and you won't be the first." He wasn't bluffing. He'd killed at least once before. His victim simply vanished from the scene. It was a deliberate act of terror and it worked. The select group he informed about the murder said nothing for fear they would be next.

His method of killing was simple and left nothing to chance. After a short moment of violence, life ebbed away in a series of satisfying, calm exhalations, each softer than the last, until they stopped.

The easy part.

Murder is only the beginning.

Killers throughout history have faced the problem of

how to dispose of the body. Landru tried with a large stove, Haigh an acid bath and Christie home decorating; all three were caught. It's almost impossible to leave no trace. What is more, there isn't much time for clever stuff. Burial is a favoured method but is hard work. Just to conceal the volume of a body requires shifting large amounts of earth, which is why so many murdered corpses are found in shallow graves. The other drawback is that the disturbance of the ground is obvious. Immersion in deep water involves transport and navigation and the use of weights to keep the body from rising to the surface. Dismemberment is messy and multiplies the task. Dropping the victim into unset concrete is said to have worked, but can be difficult to arrange unless you're a construction worker. Even then, your mates may well ask questions. For the same reason, feeding body parts to pigs is risky because someone is sure to notice.

Through the blessing of geography, the Finisher didn't need to use any of the flawed methods listed above. He'd given thought to the problem of disposal. He knew what to do.

He lived in Bath.

2

In Concorde House, northeast of Bristol, where Bath's Criminal Investigation Department had been put out to grass for reasons of economy, Detective Superintendent Peter Diamond, the senior man, walked in with a large roll of laminated paper, unfurled it and pressed it against the wall.

"Help me, will you? Drawing pins, anybody, at least six."

"What's this, guv?" Keith Halliwell, his deputy, asked.

"What does it look like?"

"A wall chart?"

"Top of the class." Diamond looked over his shoulder. "Someone must have pins."

"Blu Tack would be better for the wall," Sergeant Ingeborg Smith said.

"Sod the wall," Diamond said. "My arms are aching."

Ingeborg took some Blu Tack from her drawer and went to help. The chart, as wide as Diamond's reach, was soon in place.

Constable Paul Gilbert stepped up for a closer look and ran a finger down one of the columns. "It looks like a staff planner."

"You'll go far," Diamond said. With undisguised pride, he told the team, "The entire year at a glance."

No one else looked enthusiastic.

"If you don't mind me saying, it's hardly cutting edge," Ingeborg said. "The software on Office is better than this."

Diamond was unmoved. "You can't stick software on the wall where everyone is going to see it. We want the top brass to know how busy we are, don't we? I've started filling it in. Feel free to add significant dates using one of the wet-wipe pens. We'd better agree on a colour coding. I've bagged red."

"This is to impress Georgina?" Halliwell said.

"Or the Chief Constable, the Police and Crime Commissioner or any of the inspectorate passing through. We don't want them thinking we're overstaffed."

"What does the *H* stand for?" Gilbert asked. "Holidays?"

The letter *H* was all over the chart.

"Optimist," Inspector John Leaman said.

"It's not important," Diamond said.

This satisfied nobody.

"Is H one of us?" Halliwell asked, turning pink.

"And who might that be?"

Smiles all round.

"Actually," Diamond said, "it's for home."

"Days off?"

He shook his head, chastened at how slow they were for a bunch of detectives. "Home matches. Rugby fixtures when Bath are playing at the rec. Significant dates, I said. Get it?"

"We can put in stuff like that?"

"Birthdays, anniversaries, dental appointments, just as long as it gets filled in. This is smoke and mirrors, understood?"

Finally they got it. Wet-wipe pens were put to good use in the next hour. The planner changed from largely white to an abstract expressionist masterpiece. How disappointing that it wasn't noticed by the Assistant Chief Constable, Georgina Dallymore, when she looked in.

Blinkered, it seemed, she marched straight past and into Diamond's office.

He looked up from his coffee.

Georgina was in uniform as always. She must have put on her jacket in a hurry because one of the silver buttons was in the wrong hole. She tightened her black tie. "Peter," she said in a tone of doom, "you will have seen the latest directive from the Home Office."

Most directives came from Avon and Somerset headquarters. This had to be serious.

"Where, ma'am?"

"On your computer, forwarded from me two hours ago."

His PC was in sleep mode. He touched the keyboard and play resumed of a clip of the gunfight from *High Noon*. He reached for the mouse and tried to access his emails. The music got louder.

"For heaven's sake," Georgina said. She reached for the top of the monitor and pressed the off button. "I'll save you the trouble. The threat level from terrorism has been raised from substantial to critical."

He sat back in the chair. "Why is that?"

"It's not for you or me to ask," she said. "New intelligence, no doubt. To quote from memory, all police forces are instructed to put security measures in place to ensure that there is a heightened presence, overt and covert, at major public events."

"Overt and covert. Typical Whitehall-speak."

She ignored that. "Covert means plain clothes. That's you."

He made a covert change of emphasis. "We don't do major public events. We're more dignified in Bath. Antiques fairs won't be a target for terrorists."

"You've forgotten something."

"The Jane Austen Festival?"

"The Bath Half."

A half was a measure of beer to Diamond. He frowned.

"Don't be obtuse," Georgina said. "The long-distance race. You know perfectly well what I'm talking about."

He did now. The Bath Half Marathon, known affectionately as the Barf Arf, was undeniably major, one of the most popular road races in the country, through the city streets over a flat, fast course favoured by runners wanting to achieve fast times. More than twelve thousand took part and three times as many cheered them on. If you hadn't signed up six months ahead, you could expect to go on a waiting list.

"That counts as major, I guess," he conceded.

"It's huge," she said.

"But it's on a Sunday."

"Immaterial. You must bring in everyone for this."

"I'd love to," he said, "but don't count on it. I'll need to check the planner. When is it—March? Heavy month."

"The *planner*? Since when have you planned anything?"

He ushered Georgina out of his office and into the CID room where the wet-wipe ink was barely dry on the new chart.

Her face was a study in disbelief. "What on earth . . . ?"

He ran a finger down one of the columns. "March, we said. Generally the third Sunday, is it not?" He touched the little square too heavily and smudged the letters into a blood-red fingerprint. "Oh fiddlesticks, can't read it now. Good thing we're colour-coded. Wouldn't you know it? Red is me. What was I down for on the third Sunday?"

"Whatever it was, it's got to be cancelled." Georgina moved closer and peered at what remained. "It looks like the letter *H*."

"That'll be the Saturday."

"It overlaps two squares."

"My clumsy lettering—or the whole weekend is spoken for."

"Not anymore," she said. "There are red *H*'s all over the thing. What do they stand for?"

"Headquarters," he answered without pause or guilt.

Georgina's cheeks turned the colour of the smudged square. She had always treated police headquarters as if it were the holy of holies, but lately, knowing that the position of Deputy Chief Constable was vacant and needed to be filled soon, she scarcely dared speak its name. "Is there something you haven't told me?"

He nodded. "This puts me in a delicate position."

"I can't think why."

"I'm not authorised to confide in anyone else."

"Oh?"

"Nothing personal, ma'am. One of those need-to-know situations." He let that sink in before adding cheerfully, "But don't worry. I can tell headquarters this date is out, cancelled on your orders."

"Don't do that," she said in alarm. "Headquarters has priority here. We can manage without you, even if I have to wear plain clothes myself."

He picked up one of the pens. "I'll write it in again, then."

Simple as that. So simple that he felt a stab of conscience. Did he really want to excuse himself from duty on the day? He'd feel a right shit when everyone else gave up their Sunday. Why had he done this? Mainly out of mischief. His superior always sounded so superior that she brought out the rebel in him. Now he'd need to find a way of telling her.

But Georgina hadn't finished. She was still studying the planner. Nothing was said for some time. She took a step back with arms folded before leaning forward and staring at an empty square. "I see that Sunday April nineteenth isn't marked."

He checked. "Correct."

"So you're available. That's the date of the Other Half." Caught.

The Other Half had been thought up a few years ago by some people who applied too late for the Bath Half. They'd had the good idea of organising a little brother to the main race on a different Sunday over a more challenging route mainly along towpaths, footpaths and disused railway tunnels. The modest numbers of the first year had grown to over five thousand starters.

A major public event, undeniably.

"Give me your pen," Georgina said. "I'll put a large *O*, for Other."

3

At a sensitive time in her youth, Maeve Kelly was told by her mother, "There are sporty girls and there are curvy girls, my darling, and you were born curvy. You'll never be much of an athlete but in the game of life you'll come out the winner."

So what in the name of sanity was this curvy girl doing running along Great Pulteney Street in Bath kitted out in expensive sports gear?

Fate had fixed it. Fixed Maeve as well. Overnight she'd become a plaything of the gods, as deserving of our pity as any hapless heroine in a Thomas Hardy novel.

First, her favourite aunt had collapsed from a sudden cardiac arrest while on a Mediterranean cruise. The steward who had saved the old lady's life using CPR had learned with a British Heart Foundation kit. A fully recovered Aunt Jayne was so grateful that she made a large donation to the BHF and sent each of her family and friends a present of a CPR kit and a bright red baseball cap with the BHF logo.

Maeve never wore hats of any sort and gave her baseball cap to Trevor, who worked with her as a teacher at Longford Road Primary School and wore a cap indoors and out because he hadn't much hair. Trevor didn't seem particularly grateful. He didn't even try the thing on. Possibly he felt the colour didn't suit him. Or perhaps he felt Maeve was mocking his baldness. Anyway, he arrived next day with a bag that he left on her desk. She guessed he felt a return gift would excuse his behaviour.

The bag contained a Toby jug. She stared at it in disbelief. What would a fun-loving modern woman, 32, want with a sodding beer mug in the form a seated old man wearing a three-cornered hat? It was more of an insult than a peace offering. The thing was obviously second-hand and Maeve suspected Trevor was glad to offload it. She knew some people collected Toby jugs in the characters of well-known figures, but this thing wasn't recognisable as anyone famous. It was the plain old Toby.

When asked, Trevor said the jug had belonged to his grandfather and had become a bit of a joke in the family, an unwanted gift handed from one person to another, and he'd decided the joke had gone far enough and he was giving Toby to her and if she wanted she could donate it to the BHF.

Thanks a bunch, Maeve thought. You don't have houseroom for the thing anymore and you can't be bothered to take it to a charity shop yourself, so you dump it on me. Now I'm lumbered with the job of finding the nearest BHF shop and handing it over.

She wasn't one to hang about and mope. Sooner begun, sooner done was her philosophy, so she checked the location of the shop and went there after school. On the way to Green Street on her bike, with the bag dangling from her handlebars, she braked sharply when a car came too close. The bag banged against the bike frame and split and the jug fell on the road and smashed. Toby was just a bad memory now, emphatically beyond repair.

Cursing the motorist and Trevor at the same time, she got off and started removing bits of china from the road. People helped her pick up the biggest pieces and put them in her backpack. And then her conscience got to work. She decided she'd better continue her trip and make a donation to the charity.

In the shop, she told the assistant what had happened and asked if she had any idea what a Toby jug was worth, common old Toby with a black three-cornered hat and gripping a small jug himself. The woman took her responsibility seriously. She found a website that was a valuation guide on her phone.

If the figure had been in bold colours, it could have been antique and Victorian Royal Doulton.

Gulp.

Much relieved, Maeve showed the woman a large shard that was definitely not in bold colours but more of a dull biscuit shade. Then, horror of horrors, the same article went on to say that biscuit-coloured jugs were mostly pre-Victorian and could be Staffordshire pottery of high value. There were other checks you could make.

Horrified, she took what was left of the jug from her backpack and spread the pieces on the counter.

"If the moulding is thin," the woman read from her phone, "the piece is likely to be pre-Victorian."

Thin it most certainly was. Hollow legs were another sign of age. Maeve picked up an unbroken fragment of leg that you could see through. The clincher was the maker's name. She fitted two shards together and made the name R Wood. The website informed them that there had been three generations of eighteenth-century potters called Ralph Wood. The first was believed to have made the original Toby jug. If hers had been made by him it would have been worth a fortune. Even later Ralph Wood jugs had fetched four-figure sums in auctions.

"Oh my God!" Maeve said.

Her negligence had robbed the charity of a heap of money. She'd been expecting to empty some loose change from her purse into the collection box on the counter. Now it seemed paltry.

The woman in the shop was sympathetic. "It was your property at the time, dear, not ours. If you'd knocked it off the shelf here in the shop and broken it, that would be another matter."

"But it wasn't mine. It belonged to someone else. I was bringing it here. I'm sick to the stomach. I don't know what to do."

"Don't take it to heart. Accidents happen."

"If I'd known it was worth all that money, I'd have wrapped it up properly."

"Go home and forget about it, my dear. As far as I'm concerned, it never happened."

But Maeve couldn't dismiss it. She lay awake that night wrestling with her conscience. Morally she should do something in reparation, but she already owed money to the bank and needed every penny to pay her rent and basic living expenses.

She couldn't ignore the whole incident as the woman had suggested. She imagined Aunt Jayne shaking her head at that and saying, "I wouldn't be alive without the Heart Foundation. You must do something, my dear."

She also felt she ought to tell Trevor how much his donation had been worth, and how she had smashed it to bits.

Trevor never did learn the truth.

After a week in her private hell, Maeve thought of a way out. Charities get their income mainly from shops, legacies and fundraising. She would become a fundraiser. She would collect a thousand pounds for the BHF. But how? Rattling a tin wouldn't be much use. She'd find some personal challenge and ask people to sponsor her for this good cause.

And that was how she took up running. She'd watched several Bath Halfs and been moved by the interaction between the cheering crowd and the runners of all shapes and sizes, so happy to achieve their goals. Thanks largely to that well-meant and oft-repeated advice from her mother, she'd grown up thinking the only sport open to her was strutting her stuff in clubs and parties. She could dance the night away, so why shouldn't she take up running? She went online, discovered she was already too late to enter, so signed up instead for the race called the Other Half, stumped up the registration fee of twenty pounds and became a BHF runner without needing to tell anyone her real reason for doing this.

Then reality kicked in. A BHF *runner*. She hadn't run anywhere in years. She didn't even walk much. A stroll to the corner shop was the extent of her daily exercise.

Late that evening she made a start. Couldn't call it training. She tried jogging along the canal path in soft boots, leggings and a loose top with the hood up, like a teenager up to no good.

After fifty steps she stopped and thought about walking. Wasn't there something called race-walking? She could be a BHF *walker*. Come on, she told herself. This can only get better. You're not decrepit, even if your body tells you otherwise.

That night she didn't lie awake thinking about the Toby jug. Exhausted, muscles aching, she slept at once and deeply, cancelling the backlog of restless nights, and woke up at seven as stiff as a frozen fish. But she forced herself to go out again. She had to get into the habit of moving those protesting legs.

Each outing was a struggle. She dreaded meeting someone she knew, so she would only ever venture out soon after dawn or at dusk. Her movements amounted to little more than a shuffle and her breathing was so noisy that the bird life along the canal took flight with terrified squeaks. The pain of shifting her unfit body for pathetically modest distances was far worse than she had expected. Hidden nerves and sinews announced themselves with alarming cricks and cramps. And as each fresh day dawned, she felt like a felled tree.

One morning she saw a man walking towards her along the towpath with a dog off the lead. Scary. Some dogs will attack a runner or cause a trip just by being playful. She glanced left and right for an escape route. Left was a patch of stinging nettles. Right was the canal. Compelled to keep going, she eyed the dog and the dog eyed her. She couldn't tell what breed it was, just that it was short-haired, medium-sized, brown with black smudges and frisky. It trotted towards her and hesitated, as if weighing her up as a challenge, barked and ran past. She was thanking her lucky stars until she heard snarling and felt the touch of teeth on her heels. The dog had chosen to attack from the rear. She squealed in alarm, made a swerve and almost lost balance. The dog's owner shouted and the dog ran to him, and he knelt and grabbed it by the collar.

All her attention had been on self-preservation, but when the man looked up and said, "Sorry," and their eyes met, she realised she knew him.

The deputy head, Mr. Seagrove.

Mortifying. And he was plainly as mortified as she was. Too breathless to say anything in response, Maeve raised a heavy hand and hobbled past.

That wasn't the end of it. At school later in the day Mr. Seagrove came to her in the staffroom practically wringing his hands and apologised profusely. He asked if she was in training for something and when she owned up to the Other Half, he offered to sponsor her.

Her first backer—but how embarrassing.

He insisted on signing up for twenty-six pounds, two for each mile, and from this moment there was no escape. On hearing of that handsome endorsement, Mrs. Haliburton, the head, couldn't offer less, and soon the word passed around the staffroom and someone suggested pinning a sponsorship form to the noticeboard. The pledges mounted steadily through the week. Even Trevor's name appeared, giving Maeve another stab of guilt. She hadn't told him the real reason for her conversion to athletics.

The pressure was on with a vengeance. She'd been trying not to think about the prospect of running thirteen miles, but the people at work kept asking how far a half marathon was and those who already knew would say something like, "Rather you than me. That's a hell of a long way."

Worse still, she hadn't yet managed as much as half a mile without stopping to walk some of the way. She was measuring her progress by counting the strides she made. The number was too pathetic to think about.

She persevered and life got busier. As well as putting time aside for what she laughingly called her training, then recovering and showering afterwards and washing sweaty garments, she needed to get organised about the fundraising. Someone told her to get social media working for her. She joined one of the biggest websites that make this possible and spent most of a weekend creating her own page and personalising it with photos, text and links, being as honest as possible without mentioning the Toby jug.

Having gone public, she couldn't avoid telling her family. Her brother Dave thought the idea of his sister running anywhere so hilarious that he signed up for fifty pounds and threatened to put it on film, but her overprotective mother was strongly against it. Older brother Jim stumped up ten pounds but Ma refused to encourage what she called a lunatic act. By contrast, Aunt Jayne, who had started all this, phoned to say how overjoyed she was. "I'm so proud of you, my dear. Little did I think when I sent you that silly red cap that it would come to this."

Tell me about it, Maeve was tempted to say.

"I'd be joining you if only my cardiologist would allow it," Aunt Jayne went on. "How much have you raised so far?"

"Just over two hundred."

"I'll double it. Send me a form and I'll make sure my book group chip in as well. They're not short of a few pounds. They all had BHS caps from me and I know for a fact that two at least have been seen wearing them. My medical emergency was a wake-up call to them all."

Each new pledge sealed her fate more firmly. One of the kids in her class asked if it was true that she was going to run a marathon and some of the others wanted to know what a marathon was. A good teacher never misses an invitation to explain something, so she found herself relating the legend of the messenger Pheidippides bringing the news to Athens after the battle of Marathon, saying, "Rejoice, we conquer," and then expiring. Seeing the children's troubled faces, Maeve realised she'd got carried away with the story. She should have left out the last bit. "I'll be all right. Mine will only be a half marathon," she was quick to add, as if it was as easy as getting on a bus.

The next morning, three different parents phoned and offered to sponsor her. Two were under the impression she would be running from Marathon to Athens, but they still agreed to back her when she put them right. This thing was taking off without much effort on her part. Well, the fundraising was. The foot-slogging was another matter. She dreaded any of her sponsors seeing her dismal progress along the canal path. She was running in short bursts interspersed with walking, and there wasn't much difference between the walking and the running.

She admitted in the staffroom that she hadn't improved much since starting and she was beginning to think she was physiologically incapable of running more than a few yards at a time. Amid the sympathetic voices only one had any practical suggestions and that was Trevor, the Toby jug man. Allegedly a maths specialist, he'd ended up teaching most of the PE in the school because with his solemn delivery he wasn't much good as a classroom teacher. Typically of him, he'd mugged up on methods of exercise. He asked about her training runs and said it sounded as if she was hitting her lactic threshold. Those short bursts of running flooded the body with lactic acid, which resulted in the fatigue and stinging sensations in her legs. With practice, her system would compensate and allow her to move with less discomfort into a different gear that regular runners take for granted. There would always be a lactic threshold if she pushed too hard; she had that in common with every Olympic athlete who sprinted at the end of a race. "Don't give up," he said. "Your body will understand what you're asking it to do and will adapt. Keep a diary and you'll be encouraged by the improvement. Make a note of how you feel and what you achieved. Weigh yourself regularly, too, and keep a record of the pounds you shed and how much less you're carrying."

"What do you mean—the pounds I shed?" she told him. "I'm a size twelve. That's not obese. It's not even big."

Typical bloody man, analysing it all and talking down to her like one of the kids in the reception class, but he hadn't meant to sound as pompous as he did and he may have had a point. The science was a comfort.

Buoyed up by the thought that nothing was seriously wrong, she went for an evening run that didn't go any better, but she consoled herself thinking of all the Olympic athletes battling with the same lactic threshold she was. "We're all in this together, kiddos, and you'd better watch out. I'm on a learning curve."

One day in the staffroom, Trevor asked how the training was going.

"Can't complain," she said. "No, that's a lie. I can complain and I do, every step of the way, but I haven't given up yet."

"Would it help if I followed you on my bike?" he said.

"I could look at your action and maybe give you some tips on style."

The thought of it! "I'm not ready for that, Trevor. If I ever get to the point of worrying about style, I'll let you know."

As her daily stint got more ambitious, kit became an issue, and not just because she could scarcely move around her tiny house for soggy, washed garments hanging from chairbacks and door handles. She was starting to suffer discomforts that would only be remedied by proper running shoes and a sports bra. Secretly she wondered how liberating it would be to run in shorts and a top. The sensation of fresh air against her limbs would be too good to miss—when she felt brave enough.

A visit to a shop called Runners Need was a revelation. Buying trainers isn't a matter of deciding which colour you like and trying them on. She was filmed running on a treadmill and had her foot plant, stride and running pattern analysed by the young assistant dressed in sports kit and cap. Predictably she was a special class of runner requiring special shoes—and the bra wasn't cheap either. The hell with the overdraft.

There were hidden costs as well. Against all expectation, her appetite had increased. She was packing pasta at an alarming rate and raiding the fridge for snacks. The food bills went up and so did her use of electricity and water for showers and laundry.

On a sunny morning five weeks into her practice runs she had a surprising experience when instead of forcing herself forward she began to move freely. The effect didn't last more than a hundred yards, but for Maeve it was a boost, a glimpse of what might be possible. Trevor would say her metabolism had started to adjust to the demands she was putting on it. Her own reaction was less clinical. There's an old saying: it's dogged as does it.

She had just over six months to become a runner.

Because the race was in April, her serious training would have to be through the winter. Getting out in freezing weather would need true dedication.

Early in November her mother phoned. "Are you still planning to do that dreadful marathon, dear?"

"It's a half marathon, Ma."

"Whatever it's called, it's a lot of running."

The thought crossed Maeve's mind that her obstinate parent had softened her heart and was planning after all to sponsor her.

Not so.

"I've been thinking about Christmas."

"Already?"

"You know how difficult it is buying presents for people. When the time comes, I can never think what to get. How would you like one of those trays with a cushion attached that sits on your lap when you have a meal in front of the television?"

Mother, you slay me. "I don't get much time for TV these days. When I'm not preparing lessons, I'm out on a training run."

"Now the evenings are drawing in, you won't be able to run."

Try and stop me. "What I'd really like is a nice warm top and leggings and I'll be ready for anything."

Smart thinking, an invitation to her mother to show that she cared while sticking to her principles. A date was made for a shopping expedition to London and she was taken for lunch at Selfridges, lectured on the perils of heart strain and taken to the in-store Sweaty Betty, where she ran her finger-tips over a mind-boggling array of tops and finally chose some powder blue thermal tights and a matching hoodie. Mother couldn't understand why the tights had reflective panels; she still believed nice girls weren't ever on the streets after dark.

Maeve didn't like to look at the price labels, guessing

the gear must have cost as much as ten padded trays. Then her mother had to be persuaded not to visit the stationery department and buy Christmas wrapping paper. When the need was explained, she handed the gift over for immediate use, but not without saying, "If you come to your senses and give up the whole idea of running before Christmas, you can still wear it to go shopping. People do. I've seen them."

Maeve was starting to believe in herself as a runner. When another jogger approached, she would raise her hand in recognition. And with the more professional image came the acceptance that she must demand more from herself. The diary confirmed it. Instead of "I managed a full two minutes of running" she was writing: "Half a mile twice over. Quicker recovery."

When Trevor next enquired how the training was going she surprised him by saying she had improved her high-intensity endurance performance. He was speechless.

"But it's not pretty. I wouldn't want you or anyone else to see me," she added in case he once again brought up the suggestion of following her on his bike.

Katie, who had the classroom next to hers, later said, "What is it with you and Trevor? He tries so hard and you give him the frost each time."

"I don't want him hanging around me, that's all."

"I've seen the way he looks at you."

"Yes, and it makes me squirm. If you want to make a play for him, Katie, feel free. You'll be doing me a good turn."

Half miles grew into miles. The training changed in character when she knew she could keep going for a respectable distance. As a change from the towpath run, she started touring the streets, smartphone in hand, using an app called MapMyRun. Bath's streets aren't level like the canal path, so this was a fresh challenge. Going downhill, she discovered, wasn't the treat she expected. Her already sore shins and toes took more punishment than they did on the climbs.

One late November evening cool enough for gloves, she decided she needed a boost and she knew a way of getting one that didn't involve caffeine, chocolate or alcohol. Using her app, she planned a two-mile training run that would take her along Great Pulteney Street, where the Other Half was going to start and finish that third Sunday in April. Pounding the roads can get you down unless you find ways of stimulating the brain. Many runners carry smartphones with a punchy playlist and she'd found this helped—except when the cable got entangled with her clothes. Fortunately she had a fertile imagination. She would have no difficulty picturing the finish line at the climax of her run, thirteen miles behind her and just the final yards to cover.

This was a treat she'd saved up. Never mind that she had run little more than a mile. All along the approach roads she was telling herself to stay strong. She pictured the noisy spectators urging her on as she braced herself for the last strides to the finish, powered more by adrenalin than any vestige of stamina. "Come on, Maeve, you can do it," she gasped. "Go, go, go."

She made the last turn. In reality, she was running on the pavement, but on the day she would be in the middle of the road and in her mind's eye she could see the finish, the red towers with OTHER HALF emblazoned across the gantry. The fantasy knew no limit. She had found undreamed-of reserves of energy and worked her way through to the elite group and outrun them all in the last mile, men and women, and was about to break the tape, the fun-runner turned champion.

"Help!"

A voice had penetrated her daydream, a voice demanding to be heard, more of a scream than a request.

For God's sake. I'm about to make history.

"Please, please, please!"

Give me a break, will you?

4

Maeve couldn't ignore the voice. She hated putting a stop to her fantasy, but the appeal for help was real. This could only be someone in trouble.

She slowed right up and jogged on the spot, wondering if her brain was playing tricks. She could see nothing except the stone façade of the elegant terrace that lined the left side of Great Pulteney Street, the arched doorways and windows, the fluted Corinthian columns.

The shouting had come from close by, so she stopped moving altogether and stood listening.

Another yell told her someone had to be there, so she stepped right up to the wrought-iron railing in front of the nearest house and stared up at the balcony.

Nobody was up there.

"Down here."

The voice was coming from below ground level. Maeve peered over the railing into the shaft of the basement. Two wheelie bins and a heap of rubbish.

Feeling stupid, she said hello to the wheelie bins.

One of them moved. It almost tipped over. The rubbish heap came to life and a face tilted upwards.

Maeve asked. "Are you in trouble?"

The response was a sound of impatience, a snort. Was this a mental-health issue? Whatever the explanation, nobody should be in a place like this on a cold November evening.

"I'm coming down." She found the gate and pushed it open. The bolt was already drawn. At the foot of the steps the talking heap made room. Not easy. This big blonde woman could have made two of Maeve.

She was dressed, like Maeve, in black jogging gear, leggings and a long-sleeved top. Her white Nike trainers looked as if they'd come straight from the shop.

"Did you fall?"

A grunt that could have meant anything. Close up, Maeve could see a trickle of blood running from the edge of the woman's mouth down her jawline. "Have you had an accident?"

"Accident? Of course I have accident. What you think I do here?" English wasn't her first language for sure.

"Do you live here?"

The woman peered around her, as if deciding. "No."

"So where do you live?"

"Russia."

"Okay," Maeve said with the patience acquired from extracting the truth from muddled five-year-olds. "What I meant was here in Bath."

"On Sydney Place."

Maeve often ran past there. Not far from where they were. Top of the street, facing Sydney Gardens. Top address, too. Jane Austen and her family had once resided there. If that was this woman's home, she was likely to be one of Bath's super-rich, a Russian oligarch, or married to one. But what was she doing in the well of someone else's basement? That might be too much to discover just now.

"Can you stand?" Maeve was hoping so. She wouldn't care to lift this amount of poundage without a hoist.

"Now I try."

"What's your name?"

"Olga."

"I'm Maeve."

"You bloody English—so polite. I am here in stinking hole in ground and you want to introduce."

Olga took a grip on the handrail, braced and didn't succeed. She sank down again and shook with laughter. The whole manoeuvre had been comic and she knew. At the second try she got upright and gave a grunt of triumph but didn't look capable of climbing the steps.

"Nice work," Maeve said. "Put your arm over my shoulder, and we'll see if we can do it together."

Physical contact with a stranger is always difficult. Olga hesitated, so Maeve took hold of her left arm and showed what she meant. The feel of a flabby bicep against the back of her neck was not the best sensual experience she could remember. Then the pressure. A sack of potatoes wouldn't have been any easier.

"Let's go, then. I've got you."

She put her right arm around Olga's side. You couldn't call it her waist.

"Is it your leg?"

"What is this bloody silly question—is it your leg?" Whatever the injury might be, big Olga wasn't showing much gratitude. "Leg is mine, not some other person."

"I'm asking if you can use it."

"Okay, I try."

Maeve had been assuming this woman was middle-aged. Close up, it was clear she wasn't much over twenty-five. And pretty. Large blue eyes, classic nose and a finely formed mouth framed by dimples.

By treating each step as a one-time challenge and then struggling to recover their balance, they reached street level. Conquering Everest couldn't be tougher.

"Sydney Place, you said?"

Maeve had hoped for easier movement up here. Now it

became obvious from regular thumps against her hip that Olga's left leg could barely hold her up. Oh, for a wheelchair.

"How did this happen? Did you fall?"

No answer. Olga could be forgiven for putting all her concentration into getting along the street.

The two women were similar in height, which was a good thing. About the only good thing. Maeve was going to feel the after-effects of this unusual muscle activity tonight and tomorrow. She would end up with a limp of her own.

"Let's rest at the next streetlamp."

She extricated her aching shoulders from the yoke that was Olga's arm and propped her against the lamppost. The relief was bliss. She wriggled her shoulders and stretched her arms.

A car approached and she noticed Olga turn her head, following the movement until the tail lights vanished around Laura Place.

"Are you frightened of someone?"

Olga didn't even nod her head. Didn't need to. The answer was in her eyes. Domestic violence, maybe? Would she be better off in a women's refuge?

"You definitely want to go home, do you? I'm not trying to force you."

Several firm nods.

"Let's move, then. Not far now."

They started again and got to the top of the street and crossed to the side of Sydney Place facing the mature trees of Sydney Gardens, as elegant a terrace as any in the city.

"You'll have to tell me which house."

Olga pointed.

The far end. Sod's law.

When they finally reached the arched entrance lit by an overhead lantern, each grunting with the effort, Olga produced a key and unlocked the panelled front door. She turned to face Maeve and said, "Thank you. Goodbye."

She was effectively barring the way, making clear she wouldn't be inviting Maeve inside, and she was of a size to insist.

Have it your way, lady, Maeve decided. An offer of a drink or just a handshake wouldn't have come amiss.

She was on the point of saying a cool "Okay" and turning away when she noticed something else. The light from the lantern above them was revealing a raw, red line around Olga's neck.

Olga must have noticed the shocked stare because she clapped her hand over the marks.

"I think you should call the police."

The whites of her eyes doubled in size. "No. No need police."

"Who did this—someone you know? I'm trying to help you, Olga."

Without warning, the resistance dissolved in hot tears and huge, convulsive sobs that would have moved anyone to sympathy. Automatically Maeve reached out to grasp the jerking shoulders. Olga responded with a bear hug, pressing her face into Maeve's chest and practically wrestling her to the ground without meaning to. She was saying something repeatedly. At first it was too muffled to hear, then the words made sense. "You stay, you stay, you stay."

Maeve was tugged inside the house and the door slammed.

Aware only that some powerful conflict had just been resolved, Maeve was expecting to be released, but Olga kept hold of one of her hands and led her through a dark hallway to a room where she put on the light.

This woman of contradictions was over her tears already.

"Now we drink tea," she said in a tone that brooked no refusal. "You sit."

Good suggestion. A chance for some calm conversation— if that was achievable.

This was a kitchen unlike any Maeve had seen before, designed to make the best use of the large, high-ceilinged Georgian room that must have once been fitted with a range, deep stone sinks, and banks of wooden cupboards and shelving. The original cook and maids would have been wide-eyed at the twenty-first-century version. For a start, it was voice-controlled. Olga spoke some unrecognisable words and triggered the sound of running water inside the white island at the centre. A section of the flat surface tipped downwards and, in its place, a jug of hot water and two mugs popped up.

"You like English breakfast?" she asked Maeve. "Bloody thing can only use teabags."

"Fine."

While the brewing was in progress, Maeve marvelled at the ingenious use of the space above their heads. A selection of ovens that looked to be specifically for microwaving and baking pizzas and bread were fitted into a false ceiling, each ready to descend by some miracle of engineering and presumably function at the voice command.

The mugs were filled with steaming tea. Milk didn't seem to be automatic and had to be collected from a double-door fridge behind her.

"We take to sitting room," Olga announced, distinctly more commanding in her own home. "Stools too high for me right now."

"I'll carry the mugs," Maeve offered, thinking of the limp, "unless they transport themselves."

Olga didn't get it. The hi-tech kitchen had long ceased to be a novelty for her.

The sitting room couldn't have been a bigger contrast. Small and cosy, it was furnished in the style of the early nineteenth century with what might well have been a genuine Sheraton sofa and matching armchair with reeded mahogany legs and square-shaped seats and backs. The walls were papered to halfway in faint satin stripes. An oil painting of a vase of roses hung above a fireplace with a grate containing ash of recent use. Olga gestured to Maeve to sit on the sofa.

"This is a joy," Maeve said.

"Joy—what is joy? I call it guest room. In beginning was for housekeeper."

"The real guest room would be upstairs, I expect?"

Olga nodded. She squeezed herself into the seat of the armchair. The mahogany creaked, but the workmanship was equal to the challenge. "I like sitting room here. I chill here."

Her limited English gave force to everything she said, probably more than she intended. Maeve decided on some direct talking of her own.

"What were you doing in that basement in Great Pulteney Street?"

Olga rolled her eyes. "Look at me."

It wasn't an answer, so Maeve waited.

"Am I fat woman?" No beating about the bush.

"That's not a word I'd use."

"In Russia we have many words. All mean same." She grasped a bunch of flab at her waist and shook it as if she was trying to rip it away. "Fat belly, fat arms, fat legs, fat arse."

What could anyone say to that? Maeve gave a sympathetic smile, as if excess flesh was a problem for everyone.

Olga smiled back. "Bath is strange place. Many peoples by day. Nighttime I go out. I see no one."

"At this end of town, you mean? You've got a point. There's not much here in the way of nightlife."

"Not many peoples see me, thank God."

"So you like it quiet?"

Her eyes slid upwards in self-mockery. "Fat woman on street in tracksuit."

"You're trying to lose weight?"

"Trying, hoping, praying." Olga laughed again. "I have treadmill downstairs. Exercise bike. Weights." She pulled a face. "Boring."

Maeve agreed with that. She didn't have her own gym in the basement—she didn't have her own basement—but since going into training she'd tried hotel fitness centres and hated running on a bloody belt. And the music was always crap. "So you go out for a run?"

Olga made a fart sound with her mouth. "For walk."

"And something really bad happened tonight?"

The hand started moving to her neck again, but stopped. "All quiet on street, like I say. Long line of cars, cars, cars. I am walking past." She swung her arms to demonstrate.

"Serious walking," Maeve said to show she was following this.

"And then suddenly"—she snapped her fingers—"this guy get out of car and stand in front. I stop. He has hand on my chin like this." She mimed the action, showing how her jaw had been forced upwards. "He is strong bastard. I am frightened. Bite my tongue. He pull gold neck chain. Zap—is broken."

"That's awful."

"I am wearing rings, such fool." Something Maeve couldn't have failed to notice, a glittering display of afflu-ence that would have appealed to any mugger. "Yes, I know what you think. I try to get away. Down steps, falling"—she clapped her hands—"where you find me." The simple sen-tences had conveyed the incident vividly. She'd suffered a terrifying attack.

"Olga, you should report this to the police. He mugged you. He'll do it to someone else."

She shook her head and glared. "No police."

"Why not? They could get your gold necklace back."

"Not important."

"I expect it was valuable." Worth a small fortune, judging by the house and its contents. "The mugger shouldn't be allowed to get away with it. Unless he's caught and locked up, you won't feel safe at home or in the streets. What was he like—young?"

Olga treated the question as if she was playing chess. She made a countermove. "You want cake, biscuits? I have."

Maeve could be firm, too. "Would you recognise him again?"

She was too smart to fall for that. "So you are runner?"

"Me? Only a beginner. I signed up for the half marathon a few weeks ago and now I'm trying to get myself fit. Do you live here alone?" It was worth underlining the danger of a repeat attack.

But for some reason Olga was laughing at the question, laughter fit to ring the great bell of Moscow. "You think?"

"I'm asking. Do you?"

"Sometimes I think so, too. My husband, Konstantin, he is in Qatar five weeks. Before that, Kuwait one week. Much travel."

"And you don't go with him?"

She laughed again. "Too hot for fat woman."

"Wouldn't your husband want you to report the mugging?"

"To police?" She pulled a face and made a pushing gesture with her right hand that said husband Konstantin would want the forces of law and order kept at arm's length. It begged the question how he made his money.

Maeve tried another tack. "How did you hurt your leg? Was that in the attack?"

"My fault. I fall down steps."

"Whilst trying to escape from the mugger?"

"I think he is running after me, but he is not. Next I hear car drive off."

"Don't you think you should get yourself checked at the hospital? You could have broken a bone."

"Hospital, no way. Questions, questions, questions."

"You've done nothing wrong. You're a victim."

"Please, no more." Olga reached forward. "Give me hand." She grasped Maeve's fingers and squeezed them gently. "You are such help to me. If you want, we can be friends. Meet again, yes?"

The slap of trainers on tarmac was a return to normality for Maeve. She was on her way back to Larkhall, finishing her interrupted run. The episode with Olga had been so bizarre that it was already starting to seem like fiction. Yet her aching shoulders and hip testified that it must have happened, that she'd brought different sets of muscles into play. She wasn't running freely. Now that she thought about it, everything was aching from her toes upwards. Not for the first time she wished she could look forward to a bath at home instead of the feeble shower that dribbled lukewarm water over her. There was a strong appeal about the idea of soaking in hot water and easing the tension from her body. But her mood wasn't totally down. Olga had been entertaining company, full of contradictions, obstinate, outspoken, vulnerable and lonely, and all of this graced by self-mockery and that lovely infectious laugh.

They'd agreed to meet again. First, Olga had offered the use of her "boring" basement gym. Maeve had turned that down straight away. Nothing could take the place of real running on solid roads.

They'd settled on a lunchtime walk in Henrietta Park as soon as Olga was fully mobile again. Walking was Olga's way of slimming. It would be slow going for Maeve, but it would do her no harm.

That evening she smothered her sore shoulders with an ointment called Cold Comfort that was supposed to take away muscle pain. Her running guru, Trevor, wouldn't have thought much of it. He'd prescribe stretching or something equally painful.

While the stuff began to work, she reflected on this latest unexpected twist in her life. In truth, the incident hadn't been entirely outside her control.

She could have ignored Olga's cries for help, but if she'd run on, nothing would have eased her conscience. Certainly not Cold Comfort.

I did the right thing, she told herself.

Didn't I?

5

At eight on Sunday morning when the door was unlocked as usual and everyone trooped upstairs and along the street to where the silver van stood at the end, engine humming, Spiro stepped out of line and ran.

Jesus, did he run!

Powered by terror, he dashed up a street he didn't know in a city two thousand miles from home.

He had been warned he would be crazy to try, but if he didn't escape now he'd end up like the others, a zombie. You don't know how well off you are, Spiro, they had said, with a job to go to and a bed to sleep on. Yes, he'd said, a stinking, low-paid, seven-day-a-week job and a mattress on the floor in a poky, windowless room shared with five others. Better than what you left behind, they'd said, which was true. But at least he'd had his freedom then and spoke the language and knew where he was.

Both of his parents had been killed in the Kosovo conflict in 1999, when he was eleven. In shock, he'd been sent with hundreds of others to an orphanage in Tirana. When he was fourteen the law required him to leave and fend for himself. The youth unemployment rate in Albania was about the highest in Europe and there were only part-time labouring jobs to be had, which is a major reason why two-thirds of the population have left the country. For the next fifteen years, Spiro had lived hand-to-mouth, job-to-job, in growing despair. He had been homeless and skint and supposedly in the prime of life when he'd got the offer of free passage to a new life in Britain with steady employment and lodging provided.

Spiro wasn't daft. He knew this was a racket and meant travelling in a container with ex-prisoners and alcoholics and being classed as an illegal immigrant when he got there. He knew the living conditions would be basic and the work menial and underpaid and he could be deported at any time. Like the others on the trip he had hopes of surviving undercover for long enough to find a way of staying on.

His new existence in England was modern slavery, so deal with it, he had told himself. He expected hardship at the beginning. What he hadn't foreseen was the psychological effect. The real need to escape was the gnawing realisation that he, too, was becoming a zombie.

After seven or eight weeks of drudgery—he was losing count—he had felt himself falling into the trap of mind-less obedience. He was becoming conditioned just as they were, but he had always prided himself on being a thinking man. A few more days of the same numbing routine would do his brain in.

So he made his dash for freedom and sanity.

The gangmaster, the one the workers called the Finisher, didn't immediately react. His back was turned while he counted twenty-three shambling, half-awake men into the van that transported them to the private recycling plant on the edge of the city. Getting them to squat and squeeze together in the limited space was always a slow process. He would only react when he realised the count stopped at twenty-two.

An all-out, do-or-die sprint.

Spiro was now twenty-nine, stocky, stronger than most of the others. He had once been a passably good runner, but he was out of condition and couldn't last long at this speed. Even though his legs and back had been toughened by the long hours of standing, picking trash from the belt, the muscles needed for running hadn't had any use in years. Desperation was driving him. A bullet in the back was a possibility. He didn't know for certain whether the Finisher was armed. That pig had never produced a gun, never needed to with the wimps he managed, but an enforcer without a weapon is hard to credit.

Hoping to God he had a few seconds in hand, Spiro was going like a bat out of hell and saving nothing for a longer effort. Fear was fuelling him, fear and self-preservation.

From deep in his panic-stricken psyche, the rational part of his brain insisted on being heard. Running flat out, eyeballs bulging, can only get you so far, Spiro. Soon you'll be unable to go another step. Get a sense of where you are and where this mad dash is taking you.

The block of terraced buildings to his right had ended— he must be on the edge of town. About fifty metres ahead was a row of swaying poplars, and, beyond, more trees filled the landscape and stretched away to a distant hill.

Too distant.

Across the street was a waist-high stone balustrade overlooking some sort of public park with well-kept lawns and paths. His first thought was to climb over and out of sight, but a glance between the bellied pillars told him he'd kill himself because the ground was so far below. Instead, he pressed on, up the street, towards those poplars, willing his aching legs to support him long enough to reach the trees.

The early morning traffic cruised by, most of it facing him, coming into the city. A man out running was nothing remarkable, even a man wearing T-shirt and jeans and moving as jerkily as a seven-legged spider. This was a time of day when fitness freaks took to the streets.

He had come to a stretch where the street narrowed and the long line of the balustrade was interrupted by a four-square stone building that might have been a toll collector's booth in times past. The door looked as if it hadn't been opened in years and weeds were growing on the roof. He realised he was about to cross a bridge. Large lanterns on wrought-iron columns and plinths were built into the balustrade.

A glance to his right showed him a broad, silver band of water fringed by trees and—man oh man!—a path along the riverbank about eight metres below street level. The path to freedom. Find a way down there, Spiro, and you might actually make it.

But his stride was shortening with every step and he was hurting. His breath rasped and his thighs had turned to lead. Keep going, he told himself. To stop will be suicidal. Somewhere ahead will be steps or a ramp.

At the far end of the bridge was another booth-like structure matching the first, except for one thing. Where the other had the closed door, this had an open entrance.

A chance to step out of sight and catch his breath—but at serious risk. He'd be trapped here if he was found. He was so spent by this time that he had no choice. He'd collapse if he went any farther.

A gap in the traffic allowed him to hobble across the street for a closer look.

He stepped inside and was elated to discover he was at the top of a spiral staircase, steep, narrow and dark, with grimy paint flaking from the wall, but surely the way down to the river. Boosted by a fresh adrenalin rush, he took a deep breath and started the descent, gripping the handrail, trying to ignore the spasms of different leg muscles in play.

But fortune is fickle.

He was almost at the bottom when he heard the sound he least wanted to hear, the rapid, purposeful slap-slap of rubber on stone above him. He was not alone. He groaned in despair. To have come this far.

He wouldn't make it now.

He'd be as obvious on the riverbank as in the street he'd just left. In fact, an easier hit, invisible to the passing traffic.

With the Finisher so close behind, what could he do? Stand his ground and fight? No chance. He was a physical wreck. Jump in the river where less of his body would be exposed?

No other choice.

Emerging into daylight, he dashed across the path—and was forced into a split-second adjustment because a large longboat was moored alongside a jetty in the shadow of the bridge. A railed-in ramp and landing stage.

THE AVON RIVER PARADE BOAT:
TRADITIONAL SUNDAY ROAST

Most of the words meant nothing to him, but the tables with furled parasols on the open deck suggested this was some kind of eating place.

A floating restaurant.

Nobody was aboard this early and a locked gate barred entry to the vessel, so instead of jumping straight into the river, Spiro took a leap and hit the upper deck with a thump like a beer keg striking a cellar floor.

Now what?

There was a cabin below, but no way into it. A tiny fore-deck and a poop at the stern end offered no cover at all. In the split-second left, he got out of sight the only way he could. He climbed over the rail on the far side.

This longboat was designed with maximum width for the cabin. All it had along its side for a foothold was, in effect, a rub rail. But there was enough purchase for his feet. By flattening himself against the outer bulkhead of the cabin, he became a far-from-secure limpet attached as much by will-power as muscle and hoping to God he was hidden from view.

He heard the footfalls on the lowest steps of the spiral staircase and then the lighter sound of the shoes on the tarmac footpath. The pursuit paused.

Heart thumping, he waited.

How smart was the Finisher? How keen? How scared? He'd be in deep shit with his superiors if one of his charges escaped. But would he risk leaving the other twenty-two unsupervised for long? The most optimistic hope was that he'd see nothing, give up and go back to the van.

What Spiro heard next crushed that hope. It was almost certainly the crack of gunfire. A shot echoed off the stone walls of the jetty. Then another. And another, as if the firer was discharging at random.

Gulls took to the sky and screamed and circled overhead.

The sound of gunfire is deceptive. Survivors of mass shootings sometimes say they thought at first it was some other sudden noise, like a car backfiring or a firework. This was no car and no firework.

So the arsehole was armed, just as Spiro had feared, and had no qualms about causing injury. Killing, even.

But who was he firing at? Some bystander he'd mistaken for Spiro?

It would be suicidal to check, so Spiro hung on grimly and waited for the shooting to stop. He hadn't been count-ing the shots, but the number easily went into double figures. Several more and then silence.

As if he wasn't in enough trouble, a fresh problem hit him now. Cramp in his left leg, the tell-tale tightening of the muscle before it hardened and locked. The pain at the back of his thigh became excruciating and he had no room to stretch. He tried hanging onto the bulkhead with one hand and massaging his leg with the other and almost fell off.

Change position, he told himself. But how? This was the only possible stance, legs astride and feet bent along the ridge of the rub rail while the upper half of his body was hunched to keep out of sight.

You need to stretch, Spiro.

In the end, the urge to stop the pain topped everything, even the high risk of showing his head and shoulders. He braced and straightened.

For a few insane seconds he stood like a proud man facing the firing squad, resigned to what would happen. Nothing did, except the blissful, merciful inrush of blood to his leg. The spasm eased and he was still alive. With a view of the entire riverbank, he could see no one.

Any confidence was short-lived. The crack of gunfire started again. He ducked and only just hung on to the boat. Steady reports followed at short intervals, as if the shooter was taking aim.

But not at Spiro.

He'd noticed a subtle difference in the sounds. A stone wall about two metres high bordered the path as far as he could see and the firing was going on behind it.

Could it be a shooting range?

He tried to force some sense into the chaos that was his brain. The gunfire was definitely contained behind that wall.

He risked another look above deck. There was still no one in sight, aboard the boat or along the path.

Safe to move? He thought so. Over the rail he climbed and stood stiff-legged for a moment before crossing the deck and lowering himself to the landing stage.

Still alive.

The Finisher must have given up the chase and returned to the van. With the immediate danger past, Spiro could get his thoughts together. The shots from behind the wall continued, but he was no longer concerned. They sounded less menacing now, and he was sure he could hear voices coming from the same place, good-humoured, relaxed voices.

He moved a short distance up the path to where he could look over. Then he understood. Across a freshly mown playing field was a white building emblazoned with the words BATH CRICKET CLUB.

Bath Klub Kriket in Albanian. Spiro understood.

Bat on ball.

He knew little about cricket except that it was a summer game, but he could see for himself the source of the "gunfire." In the foreground just below the wall were a number of tall, open-ended cages of netting attached to steel frames. Inside the nearest was a man standing on matting, holding a bat and swinging it at a hard, red ball bowled with force by another man. The crack of bat striking ball would have fooled anyone nervous of being shot.

The relief that surged through Spiro was a liberation. For the first time in months, he smiled. He could start getting his life back, making decisions for himself. His mistake had been laughable but was excusable. Plus, he'd learned where he was. Even with his narrow schooling under the former communist regime in Albania, he'd heard of Bath, the spa city in England developed by the Romans and rebuilt by the British into one of the architectural marvels of Europe. Here, surely, would be civilised people who would help him survive.

He watched several balls being struck hard into the netting. The sight of young men out early practising a summer game on a cold morning in winter was itself inspiring. He had no identity here, no passport, no funds, but he would find work for a fair wage, the means to exist and fit in and maybe—one day—join in their sport.

Then a hand clasped his shoulder from behind.

"Te gjeta, Spiro," said the voice in Albanian.

I found you.

6

The body was unlikely ever to be found. No one had any reason to go down there. The Finisher had no conscience about what he'd done. He didn't allow morbid thoughts to burden him. The act of murder had become necessary. End of story.

Now is now and then was then.

The final stage in getting away with murder is that you do nothing different. You carry on living at the same address, rise at the same hour, eat the same food, use the same shops, meet the same people and give the impression you're no different from any of them.

Normal life resumed. He lived at a good address and had a reasonable income, enough to indulge himself when he wished and others when he chose. The others he indulged were always women and Bath was the ideal place to meet them. He loved their company and they responded to him, his good looks, his sense of humour and infectious laugh, his delight in everything they said and his interest in their stories. He never forced the pace. They relaxed with him over tea and cake, coffee and biscuits or gin and lime—whichever they preferred. Carrot juice and a high-calorie protein bar for one fit lady.

He didn't need to go far. Gorgeous women were every-where in this enchanting city: students too deep in loan debt to enjoy the best time of their life; tourists on short visits wanting to pack as much pleasure as possible into a few hours; over-thirties starting to lose confidence in their pulling power; fitness fanatics desperate to be told they glowed with health; bored housewives thinking there must be someone better out there; and trophy wives of the ultra-rich, only too willing to be unfaithful with someone more their own age.

And so to bed, as the diarist said.

But it isn't as straightforward as that.

Where to meet them? This city was stiff with coffee shops, tea rooms, restaurants, pubs, parks, galleries, museums, gyms, thermal spas, nightclubs and a bewildering choice of tourist attractions from the Roman Baths to the Jane Austen Centre. He would join a guided walk, hop on a tour bus, take a river trip or simply stroll up Milsom Street, where they did their window shopping. If you can't make out in Bath, you must be Godzilla.

He wasn't short of experience, and that helped. He could read the signs, so he didn't waste time and money on unresponsive dates. He knew the chatlines that worked and he used them. Relationships weren't for him. He was a one-night-stand man (in fact, a one-afternoon man, because he had other things to attend to at nights). Always on neutral ground, hotel rooms he paid for. No strings. He would say, "That was sensational." But never, "When can we meet again?"

He wasn't deceitful. He told them they were amazing, sexy, irresistible, like no one else he'd ever met, and he believed it at that moment, and they could tell and they lapped it up. He said nothing about future plans. You don't, before you've got to know each other. After sex, he was generous enough to confirm that they'd been amazing, sexy, irresistible and like no one else he'd ever met, and that was it. They couldn't possibly top such a high, so the best thing was to leave it there. No exchange of phone numbers. In the nicest way he knew, he would let her know that the experience had been a one-off.

Finish.

The majority understood. A few had to be told he didn't do second dates. Some got emotional, which was a pity. You can't predict how everyone will react.

After that, there was a small risk of being recognised by one of them when he was with somebody else. It had to be factored in and it had happened more than once. His way of dealing with it was a quick, faint smile of recognition and then back to full-on charm with his new companion. It worked.

Now is now and then was then.

7

The year had turned and the days were lengthening. You wouldn't notice, but they were. Maeve was still training in darkness, thankful for the reflective patches on her leggings. She'd got over the feeling that if she hadn't broken that sodding Toby jug she could be sitting at home with a glass of wine going through a favourite box set on TV. Running had become a mission. Not only was she helping heart patients, she was doing her own heart a power of good and her skin felt and looked positively peachy.

She was in danger of turning into Little Miss Perfect.

She'd given up the canal runs altogether. Bath's streets had plenty of variety and were well lit. She'd mapped out routes that would stretch her ability as the weeks went by, for she'd found a pace that suited her and she could keep going for up to half an hour. Trevor's advice about weighing herself regularly had been helpful. She was shedding pounds. Already it amounted to more than two kilos, hugely encouraging when she thought how liberating it was not to be carrying the equivalent of two bags of sugar around all day.

This wasn't to say that the runs were easy. Her body still told her many times over she wasn't meant for this and reminded her of her mother's advice about curvy girls. Then there were nights when it was really cold and gloves and a bobble hat made no difference. The temptation to take a break was overwhelming, but she wasn't going to give Mother the chance to say, "I told you so, dear. You'll never be an athlete."

On the positive side, the friendship with Olga was a definite support. In her own way, her new Russian friend was as committed to self-improvement as she was.

Maeve joined her one Saturday in Henrietta Park, Olga's favourite place, its two-kilometre footpath around the central lawn making it ideal for anyone doing laps. She was amused to see how the big woman stepped out purposefully with chin up like one of the Young Pioneers, her wobbly arms angled and swinging across her chest.

Olga had recovered from the mugging quite quickly and wasn't deterred from going out. She was incapable of running, but she walked, and it was no-nonsense walking. She told Maeve she, too, was weighing herself regularly. She kept a diary and logged every outing. She still sported the rings and a new gold chain, but wisely did most of her walking by day.

She was clearly well-known in the park, greeted with waves and smiles by many people they passed. Some even knew her name. However, she wouldn't stop to talk. This was serious training.

"You're amazing," Maeve told her. "I'm almost running to keep up with you."

"You can run if you want," Olga said. "No one to see. Trees say nothing."

Maeve stepped out and swung her arms and hips in the same way as Olga—at the cost of some dignity.

"You've never explained why you're doing all this walking."

"Not true. First time we meet I tell you."

"To lose weight?"

"Lose fat, get fit. Here is tree looking at us," Olga said, pointing to their left. "Purple sycamore."

"You know your trees, then?"

"Oak, birch, golden elm. They watch us."

"You think so?"

"Next I like best of all, from Russia. Caucasian maple."

As if in tribute to Olga, the ground around the tree was carpeted with red leaves.

"You've lost weight, that's obvious. But is that the only incentive?"

"I do not understand."

"What's the reason behind it, Olga? Are you doing this to surprise your husband when he gets back from his travels?"

"Him?" she said and vibrated her lips.

"I've never seen anyone so serious about training as you are."

"I am Russian." That, apparently, said it all.

Maeve had a wild thought. "You haven't secretly entered the Other Half like me?"

The now-familiar chesty laugh erupted. "First lady walker to win."

"You could walk all the way at this pace and be ahead of some of the runners by the finish."

"Of course."

"But you'd tell me if you were in the race?"

"Don't ask stupid question, Maeve."

"If you're not training to race, I'm starting to wonder if you have a secret lover."

"You think?" More laughter.

The reaction encouraged her to tease Olga a little. "With Konstantin away from home so much, it wouldn't surprise me. We have a saying: when the cat's away, the mice will play."

A frown. "You think I am mouse?"

She seemed to have taken it as an insult, so Maeve laughed to show she was joking. "Far from it. All woman, definitely."

But the mood had changed. "I tell you something. I am Olga, right?"

"That's what you told me."

"My mother and father called me this name."

"Same for me," Maeve said. "That's what happens."

"My mother she is Russian, but I am born in Ukraine. They choose Olga after famous lady, Olga of Kiev. You know?"

"I can't say I do."

"She is princess and saint, more than thousand years ago."

"Nice to be named after a saint."

Meant as a compliment, this cracked Olga up so much that she had to stop walking and lean against a tree, shaking with laughter. "Saint Olga is killer. Many, many times killer."

"How was that?"

"She is married to Prince Igor."

"I've heard of him."

"No, no, no. Prince Igor of Kiev, very strong leader, he conquer tribe called Drevlians. When Igor go to collect tribute, Drevlians make revenge. Take two birch trees like this." She pointed upwards with both hands. "Tie ropes high up and bend, bend, bend right over, fix to Igor's feet. Trees spring back and Igor is two piece."

"Torn apart? What a horrible way to die."

"So Princess Olga hate Drevlian tribe."

"Who wouldn't?"

They started the striding again, and Olga continued the tale.

"Now she is widow, with three-year-old son who will be next ruler of Kievan Rus', but, until boy is grown-up, Olga is ruler. You understand?"

"We'd call her the regent."

"Okay. She is regent. But smart-ass Drevlians have plan. There is Drevlian prince called Mal. If Mal marry Olga, then Mal becomes ruler of tribe as he is man."

"Same old same old."

"What is this same old?"

"Never mind. Did she marry Mal?"

Olga's dimples creased a little more. "Drevlians send twenty guys to sweet-talk her, twenty cute guys who are clever with words. What does Olga do? Drop them in ditch and fill with earth."

"Buried them alive? Ouch!"

"There is more. Olga send message to Drevlians. She can marry Prince Mal if they send more cute guys to travel with her."

"As escorts?"

"Yes. They send and she is charming. Tells cute guys they can use her bath house. In Russian, *banya*. They are dusty from long journey. They go in. Olga locks *banya*, burns it down with Drevlians inside."

The strong story came over vividly in the pidgin English. The image of the trapped Drevlians was far more compelling than the scene they were passing, the stretch of lawn rising to Henrietta Mews and the high backs of Great Pulteney Street.

"How this woman ever got to be a saint I can't imagine."

"Ha. Is nothing yet. She travel to Drevlia with army for great funeral feast for husband Igor. Much drinking. When Drevlians are drunk, her men kill them. Five thousand die. Later, she burn down Drevlian capital city Iskorosten. Many more dead. End of Drevlian tribe. Kaput. Finish."

"She ordered all this? She's a mass murderer. How on earth did she get to be a saint?"

"Smart lady, she take Christian faith, baptise in Constantinople. This is big, big deal, new thing for Rus'. Olga tell all her peoples you better go Christian."

"Or else . . . ?"

More hearty laughter. "Many do. But her own son is not baptise. He is not Christian."

"I sense more trouble," Maeve said.

Olga shook her head. "Olga is Christian now. Commandment of God: no killing."

"Thou shalt not kill. That must have reined her in a bit."

"She is patient. She speak to grandson, Prince Vladimir. You better become Christian when you are ruler. And Vladimir has good sense and all of Kievan Rus' goes Christian."

"Thanks to Olga's persuasive powers."

"She is first saint of Russian church. All Russians know her."

"And you're Olga as well? I'd better not mess with you."

Olga laughed again. "Don't even think." And she lifted her chin a fraction higher. "Don't call me mouse again."

Maeve decided against explaining the cat and mouse proverb. She didn't want to cause more offence than she already had.

The Olga of Kiev story had to be a mix of folk history and myth, but Maeve had the strong impression that every gruesome detail of it mattered profoundly. Olga identified with her namesake, and not just her evangelism. She was not unwilling to be associated with the violence. Underlying it all was the message that anyone who took her for a softie, or, worse still, a laughing stock, would come to regret it.

Her own training progressed well. After Trevor the PE teacher had told her about the lactic threshold, she'd done some internet research of her own on the science of running and she could easily have talked back to him about oxygen debt, the same peril under another name. For a few days he didn't pester her about the running because he didn't spend much time in the staffroom and, when he did, he sat in a corner using his laptop. She heard he was flat-hunting with the aim of moving closer to the school.

She was happy progressing by trial and error, learning how to avoid the mistake of demanding too much and having your muscles scream that you should stop. The key was to find a pace she was comfortable with. Steadily she increased the length of her runs, always allowing for the extra effort of coping with Bath's hilly terrain. She even mapped out a route that took her some of the way up the stiff climb of Lansdown on evenings when she was feeling especially good. Setting goals and achieving them gave her more than mere confidence. It was the antidote to long-held insecurities, those setbacks in her romantic life and her day job that could bring on depression.

Unsurprisingly there were runs that didn't go to plan. More than once she tripped on uneven paving and fell. She was so bruised one time that she took two days off to get over it. She got lost a few times in streets that looked different from the way she'd pictured them. There was a night when a power failure put out all the streetlights. Another time a dog waited behind a certain fence for her to approach and then flung itself at the woodwork, ferociously barking, and gave her the fright of her life. There was a skateboarder who cut across and missed her by a whisker. And groups of small boys on street corners shouted comments about her boobs. Yes, even in genteel Bath.

More than once on a night run, she was sure she could hear the steps of another runner behind her. In a race you can't object if others use you as a pacemaker. You'd do it yourself to keep going. A training run was altogether different. The mysterious follower didn't try to overtake, but kept about twenty-five yards behind for ten to twenty minutes of the run. She tried glancing over her shoulder and couldn't see anything. Was it an echo of her own footsteps? She didn't think so, but she didn't care to stop and find out. The experience was scary enough for her to change her route next time, only for it to happen again on different streets. Did runners have stalkers? She kept herself from panicking by rehearsing things she'd say if ever the stupid jerk got close enough to hear them.

Strangely, the calamities she most feared hadn't happened. She hadn't had an elastic failure while out training and she hadn't yet had urgent need of a bathroom. Maybe those horrors were waiting to happen on the day she finally ran in the real thing. Thirteen-and-a-bit miles still seemed about as likely as shaking hands with the Venus de Milo. The most she had managed by the end of January was five.

But the training diary was testament to genuine progress. She recorded her daily mileage, the time taken and the route. She weighed herself every three days and saw the improvement there. And there was another, more pleasing measure. She found she could fit into favourite dresses she'd despaired of wearing again. They'd only survived being taken to the charity shop because she couldn't bear to part with them.

In the staffroom at work, she was often asked how the training was going and she didn't give much away, except to confirm that she hadn't stopped altogether. As most of them were sponsors, she couldn't clam up completely. Angie, who taught the year threes, said one lunch break, "You're looking great on it. How much weight have you lost since you started?"

She knew precisely how much and didn't want to boast. "The thing is," she said in all truth, "I have no control over which parts of me are changing shape. I've always wanted slim legs, but they're getting chunkier, if anything."

"Don't worry. That will be muscle."

Trevor couldn't resist chiming in. "You won't change your body shape however hard you train. You're a mesomorph on the cusp of being an endomorph. Heavy thighs, sturdy calves."

Whereupon the entire staff of Longford Road Primary stopped what they were doing and stared at Maeve's legs.

"Go on," Angie said with a giggle. "Give us a twirl and we can get a proper look and make up our minds."

"Get a life, the lot of you," Maeve said with a smile. Before she'd grown confident from her running, she would have turned crimson and left the room.

Instead, it was Trevor who walked out as if he was upset.
He didn't even rinse his mug in the staff kitchen.

"What's his problem?" Angie said.

Katie had the answer. "He didn't like everyone goggling
at Maeve. He thinks he owns her, poor sap."

Maeve smiled, shook her head and said nothing.

"Is that why he moved to a new flat?" Angie said.

"What's that got to do with it?" Katie said.

"Only that his new place is in Bella Vista Drive. Isn't that
where you live, Maeve? You've got a new neighbour now."

One midweek run early in March brought an unexpected
breakthrough. She was listening to the Take That album
Odyssey, a compilation of their biggest hits, on a stretch
of London Road she generally avoided because of traffic
fumes, when she became aware that she'd covered the last
mile and a half without any recollection of doing it. What a
boost. She felt strong and was still going steadily and here
she was almost at the big intersection with the A4. I need
to be more ambitious, she told herself. I can be running
seven or eight miles at a stretch. On the way back she took
a detour and managed six for the first time.

She had to share the good news with someone who would
understand, so she texted Olga. Back came a quick reply:

How much kilometre?

About ten, I think.

Wow. Next thing is marathon.

Hold on. I'm only doing a half. Can we meet Saturday?

Sunday is better. After church, Olga go walk in park,

12:30. Konstantin he is doing business stuff.

Maeve had forgotten Konstantin, the husband, existed, he'd been away so long. And it was unexpected to learn that Olga was a churchgoer. She had never mentioned religion before. It would be Eastern Orthodox. She checked online and much to her surprise there was a church called St. John of Kronstadt that had a foothold in the Anglo-Catholic church opposite the fire station near Cleveland Bridge. They celebrated Vespers there on Saturdays at 5 P.M. and the Liturgy at 11 A.M. on Sundays. She'd passed the building regularly on her runs. It turned out that they had their own convent and a chapel on Lyncombe Hill. Who would have thought it?

Olga had never said much about Konstantin and Maeve hadn't pressed her. The impression she'd got was that he was more of a meal ticket than a soulmate, but she could be wrong.

This Sunday on a crisp, bright morning before the frost had disappeared, the big Russian was well into her laps in Henrietta Park, hot breath leaving a trail in the air like a steam engine and arms going like pistons, but she wasn't panting. She looked to have lost at least ten pounds in recent weeks.

Maeve stepped in beside her with a word of greeting and tried to keep up.

"It's no use," she was forced to say. "You've speeded up since I last joined in. I can't walk at this pace. I'll have to run to keep up."

"Okay with me," Olga said. "Cycle if you want."

Maeve started jogging beside her. "Was Konstantin pleased when he saw how much weight you'd lost?"

"He is not interest, selfish pig," she said. "Work, work, work and himself running."

"Is he a runner?"

"Long-time runner. Marathon two hours twenty-five minutes."

"That's awesome, Olga. It's almost world class. When does he train?"

"After work. Even in Qatar, temperature thirty-five, forty, he run."

"I'm impressed. You didn't tell me. I feel very inferior talking to you about my modest efforts."

"In marathon world, he is nothing. Rubbish."

"I wouldn't say that."

"I can say." She returned a wave from one of her admirers. "All this training and he does not go faster. Two hours twenty-five I put on his gravestone."

Maeve felt some sympathy for Konstantin.

Olga hadn't finished putting him down. "Everyone else get better. You go more kilometre. Me, I burn much fat. Stupid prick Konstantin train and train and stay same." Whatever deficiencies she had in English grammar, she was well equipped to badmouth her husband.

"So why does he do it?"

"Good question."

"I expect it's the joy of running. When I started, I didn't want to go out at all, but now I'm beginning to get pleasure from it."

Olga's tone became friendlier. "This I like to know, how you start."

"There's no mystery to it. I'm doing it for charity." The full story was too complicated to explain. Trying to describe the Toby jug and why it was such a loss would take the rest of the morning. "If I can run the half marathon it will help the British Heart Foundation."

"Nice. I like Turner, Gainsborough, Constable."

Maeve had to think about that. Then she laughed. "Heart, not art." She pointed to her chest. "Medical research."

Smiling, Olga said, "British *Heart* Foundation?"

"You've got it. I've been raising funds, so I can't give up."

"How much you raise?"

"So far? Almost a thousand pounds."

"So, thousand. I tell Konstantin and we give five hundred."

Maeve's legs almost folded under her. "But Konstantin doesn't even know me."

"I tell him tonight. He can afford, capitalist pig. Run many marathons, never for charity. You take cheque?"

"That would be wonderful. If you're serious I'll bring a sponsorship form next time I see you." Stunned by the amount, she continued jogging in silence for some distance. She couldn't peel off and walk away directly after such a generous pledge, but what could she say next? A remark about the weather would seem ungrateful.

She thought of something. "Now that I've told you how I started, how about you, Olga? I know you're in serious training to lose weight, but what's behind this big change in your life?"

"You want me to tell?" Olga gave one of her chesty laughs.

"Is it funny?"

"I think so. Big joke. Is for Konstantin."

"You're doing it for him?"

Another burst of laughter. "He think so."

"But you aren't?"

"One time before he go to Qatar he say I am elephant woman, fat cow, good for nothing. Too much eating, not enough exercise."

"That's so unkind."

"But he is right."

"Not anymore, he isn't."

"So I tell Konstantin I need personal trainer and"—she snapped her fingers—"he find."

"You have a personal trainer?"

"Sure. Don't you have?"

Maeve thought of Trevor. She refused to call him a trainer. He was the self-appointed consultant she didn't like to consult because it might encourage him to come calling. "No, I do my own thing. But good for you, getting organised. You go to a gym now?"

"Jim? Who is this Jim? My trainer, he is Tony."

"Misunderstanding. Tony it is. I mean, where do you see him?"

"Come to house, Monday, Thursday, downstairs in exercise hall, make me fit."

Exercise hall? Maeve was reminded that her new friend lived on another social plane.

"Is he any good?"

Olga's shoulders started shaking, the beginning of another bout of laughter. "He is good, yes. Very, very good. Like film star. Dark hair, nice teeth, sexy eyes. Gorgeous. Touch me and I want to grab."

"Oh, my."

"Cute little bum I could bite."

"Yikes."

"Now I do everything Tony say. Everything. Take walks, eat no cake, chocolates, pasta, and he is big smile."

"Pleased with you?"

"You bet."

"Has it gone any further?"

"Has what?"

"Like kissing?"

"Sod bloody kissing. One day soon, please God, Tony get close, measure waist and we . . ." She raised both arms, puffed out her chest and shouted a word in Russian that Maeve had no difficulty understanding.

This time it was Maeve who was laughing.

"You tell no one, eh?" Olga said, turning to give her a sudden, ferocious look.

8

Spiro swung around.

"You?"

Big surprise.

Huge relief.

He wasn't eye to eye with the Finisher, as he feared, but another of the work party.

Murat. Tall, shambling, soulful Murat, the giant of the gang and the most often picked on for poor work even though his was no worse than anyone else's. Being two metres high makes you stand out.

In Albanian, Spiro said, "You nearly gave me a heart attack. I thought you were the gangmaster."

Murat shrugged his broad shoulders. He'd been a wrestler in the old days, but there wasn't much muscle left on him after months of underfeeding and hard labour.

"How did you find me?" Spiro asked.

"Followed you."

"Oh, Christ."

"You ran, so I did."

"He'll kill us both. You know he killed Vasil." Everyone knew about Vasil, the only other idiot to try to escape. They were told repeatedly that he was dead.

"Vasil wasn't smart," Murat said. "He got caught before he'd gone a few steps. You're smart."

"Smart? I'm fucking crazy to try. Did he see you go?"

"Sure."

How could he sound so complacent?

Some quick thinking was wanted here. "We've got to hoof it, then, and fast. Why don't you go that way, under the bridge, and I'll head in the other direction?"

Murat blinked and didn't appear to grasp the logic.

"He can't follow us both. One of us gets away, see?"

Murat took a few seconds to ponder the plan. He seemed to have an inkling who was the more likely to get lucky. "I'm coming with you. Then we both get away." His faith in Spiro's competence would have been touching if it weren't so dangerous.

"No way," Spiro said. "I'm going alone."

There wasn't time to stand arguing. Spiro started running again as well as he could, southwards along the tree-lined towpath beside the river, hoping to shake off Murat. However, the big man followed close behind, breathing heavily. Neither would keep this up for long. The best hope was that the Finisher would give up before they did, but that wasn't likely. Two escapees were seriously bad news for him. He, too, would be in deadly peril if word got back to the high-ups.

Four minutes on, they reached the cover of a railway bridge. In the shadow of the arch, Spiro leaned against the grimy stonework and tried to collect his breath.

Murat said, "I don't see him. I think he lost us."

"You're a fucking optimist," Spiro said. "Likely as not, he'll have used a car and be waiting for us round the next bend."

"He didn't see which way we went."

"He's only got to ask. A guy your size followed by me is going to be noticed. That's why we should split up."

Murat was having none of it. "I'd be lost. I don't know where we are."

"And you think I do? Ever heard of a place called Bath? That's where we are, and I only know because I saw it on the side of a building. I've no more idea how to survive in it than you have."

"We need a map."

"Great! Show me one."

"Or a phone."

"For Christ's sake, Murat. We're runaways."

"Bikes."

"Now you're talking, but where do we find one—or two, since you insist on trailing after me?"

"Station."

Spiro was all ears now. Maybe, after all, Murat wasn't the dimwit he seemed. People left their bikes in stations and rode on trains, didn't they? As if to endorse the point, a train thundered overhead.

Spiro stepped out from under the bridge for a better view. On the opposite side of the river was the long, low roof of a railway platform.

"Do you see what I see?"

"Yeah."

A station would be a risk. People came there in numbers and would surely notice two shabby fugitives looking for bikes to steal. On the other hand, the Finisher wouldn't want to create a violent scene in front of witnesses.

"So how do we get there?"

"Bridge."

They were standing under a bridge, but it was the mainline bridge with no path for pedestrians to use unless they wanted an early death.

"There must be a passenger bridge for everyone who lives this side."

They moved on and saw what they hoped for, partially masked by a huge, softly swaying willow tree: a narrow iron structure painted green that crossed the river to the back of the station. People were using it. A man was walking his bike across.

"We could take him and grab the bike," Murat said.

"That's a sure way to get arrested. We act like everyone else, right?"

So they walked. And when they reached the bridge, they crossed with other pedestrians as if they used it every day. The movement of people took them into a long, broad tunnel that was likely to bring them out to the station front.

"Look at this," Spiro said. He couldn't believe his luck. "Beautiful."

Along the right side of the tunnel was a row of at least fifty cycles shackled to iron stands embedded in concrete. As easily as this, they'd found where the bikes were parked.

"Keep walking," he muttered to Murat. "Pretend you're not interested. Right through to the end."

When they reached daylight and the station forecourt and looked around, they were in the city, with several streets ahead of them and traffic moving in all directions.

"Don't stop," Spiro said.

"Aren't we going back for a bike?"

"They're locked to the stands, all the ones I saw."

"What do we do—take a taxi?"

This may have been meant in jest. Spiro couldn't tell. "Are you carrying cash, then?"

He knew the answer. Their so-called earnings amounted to peanuts.

Spiro said, "What we need to do is get hold of a pen, a simple ballpoint pen."

"What for?"

"I'll show you when we've found one."

They crossed and started up the busiest road. A sign said it was Manvers Street.

Spiro had lived off his wits before ever coming to this

country. He knew a few wrinkles and the ballpoint trick
was one.

They didn't have to go far before noticing a place called
the One Stop Shop. From the front it appeared to be some
sort of citizens' advice bureau with counter spaces, meeting areas and enquiry points. Fertile ground for discarded
ballpoints.

They marched in like house owners coming to enquire
about the council tax.

"The police are here," Murat said from the side of his
mouth.

"Where?"

"Left."

Spiro glanced at two bored-looking uniformed officers
seated behind a steel-framed space in the wall looking as
if they'd serve you a burger and fries if asked.

"So what? We've done nothing wrong."

"We don't have any papers."

"Relax. We're safer here than we were outside." Murat's
anxieties were working wonders for Spiro's nerves. He
moved about as if he had plans to redesign the entire
premises, while in reality looking for a pen. At last, he found
a wastepaper bin containing two common Bics, presumably
no longer functioning. He picked up both.

"Let's go."

"Where to?"

They returned to the station and the bikes in the tunnel
and Spiro walked its length again with Murat at his side.
"This works with U-locks, preferably old ones."

About five of the locks looked easy picks in every sense.
"Anyone coming?"

"Nobody behind us."

Spiro had his sights on a drop-handlebar city bicycle
secured to the rack with two sturdy but basic U-locks. He
took one of the Bics from his pocket, removed the cap

stop at the end with his teeth and spat it out. The open end fitted snugly into the keyhole. He pushed it home and twisted hard until the bar of the lock snapped open.

"Easy as that?" Murat said in admiration.

Spiro freed the second lock, securing the back of the frame to the stand, and the bike was ready to move.

"Shall I pull it out?"

"Not before we're ready. You want one, too. The next lock I can open is near the other end."

They had to wait for a couple of students to pass through the tunnel. The main rush seemed to be over.

"Can you get me one for long legs?" Murat said.

"You're lucky to get anything."

The second lock was harder to jemmy, even when using the second pen. Spiro cursed a few times. "It would work better with some cuts in the pen but not having a knife . . ." He shook the lock and tried again. "No joy."

"Shall I have a go?" Murat offered.

"Be my guest."

Murat twisted hard and the pen's casing splintered and snapped. "Fuck."

"Great. You've busted it."

"Cheap goods."

"They're the ones that work. Can you chew the other end off with your teeth?"

"I'll get a mouthful of ink."

"It's up to you. My bike is ready to go."

Murat jammed the ballpoint end of the pen between his teeth and bit hard. The cone at the end separated from the rest and dropped on the ground with the ink tube, but the casing held steady, leaving a serviceable tool.

"Try it," Spiro said.

This time the trick worked. Murat removed both locks and liberated the bike, a Dutch roadster with high handlebars and a basket.

"It's a girl's bike."

"Quit complaining."

"The ink tastes horrible."

He had a tongue like a chow, but Spiro didn't tell him.

Obeying the sign, they wheeled their stolen bikes across Halfpenny Bridge, mounted and pedalled shakily along the towpath.

"Where to?" Murat asked.

"God knows," Spiro said.

9

Spiro and Murat cycled frantically along the towpath. The need to survive dominated everything. Escaping from the work party had been only a first step. The dread of recapture and death wouldn't go away. If the Finisher didn't catch them himself, he was sure to call in reinforcements. A pack will hunt down its prey and show no mercy. The stress was as unrelenting as the mind-numbing grind of forced labour had been. And their leg muscles weren't used to hard pedalling. After little more than an hour, they had left the city behind, but exhaustion forced a stop. They lifted the bikes over a gate, gulped water from a cattle trough and sheltered under a hedge.

After a while they got back on and rode again. Progress through the rest of the day was in stages and the stages got shorter as weariness took its toll. They didn't speak much. By early evening they were done for. It was obvious that they needed to rest up and recharge.

They slept rough in a field. In the morning they were damp, shivering and hungry. The sensation of liberty was good, but the sensation of hunger was not. Where do you find food and drink when you have no money and you're illegally in a foreign country, at risk of being slung into jail and sent back where you came from? Putting as much distance as possible between themselves and the Finisher had seemed the obvious thing to do, but where were they heading? They needed food and that meant getting closer to people again. Without a map they had no idea how far off the next town would be.

"You know what?" Spiro said to Murat. "I think we should turn back."

"You're mad."

"I thought you knew that already. I've had experience back home of living rough. The easiest place to survive is where other people are, not out here in the country."

"We can find stuff in the fields," Murat said.

"Like what—sheep and cows?"

"Rabbits."

"How do we catch a fucking rabbit? And if we do, how can we cook it when we haven't got a fire? The town we left was filled with rich people. You saw the posh houses they live in. They throw out good food and clothes. There were shops and hotels and restaurants that have to get rid of food they can't use."

"We can find another town if we keep going."

"As good as Bath? No chance."

"It's too dangerous. He'll find us there."

"Not if we're clever. He'll be thinking like you—that we're miles away already. You saw how busy the streets were. We'll be lost among the crowds."

"You might," Murat said. "I stand out."

"There are people of all sizes. That's the point. Anyone spots us here in the open sees a tall guy and a squib. In the town you'll be one of hundreds. You want breakfast?"

"Yeah."

"Okay, catch your rabbit. I'm going to cycle back the way we came and see what I can find."

"I can't manage on my own."

"Your choice, my friend."

Murat chose. Together they started back in the direction

they'd come from, but using roads rather than the river-bank. Spiro said it would be a more direct route.

Late that morning in a lay-by they got lucky and found fresh food in a litter bin. A driver had cleaned out his car and binned some apples and a sandwich still in its pack.

Spiro was triumphant. "What did I say about breakfast?"

"This is lunch."

"We'll call it brunch. See the sell-by date? This hasn't been in the bin more than an hour or two."

They shared. Not much, but enough to stave off the worst pangs.

"Smoked salmon and cucumber," Spiro said. "You'd better get used to posh food. They eat well in Bath."

He had been right. This route was more direct, but busy, and when they saw the first road signs for Bath he got nervous of being spotted, so they took a detour up a quieter road.

"Up" was the operative word.

After toiling uphill for about fifteen minutes, they were rewarded with a view of the entire city sited mostly in the loop of the river in a vast bowl enclosed by more green hills. Stone terraces commanded the slopes, gleaming in the morning sunlight. No high-rise buildings here. The tallest were the spires and towers of churches. Clusters of trees poked above blue-grey slate roofs. Surely this was a place big enough to hide in.

"We did the right thing," Spiro said.

"Prove it," Murat said. He wasn't thinking about their safety anymore. Hunger had taken over again.

They rode boldly into town like gunmen in a Western and freewheeled the last part. Spiro was making the decisions. He said they should head for the station and return the bikes to where they'd found them because it would be easier to suss out the centre of the city on foot. No one challenged them and they were rewarded for their honesty. In a bin attached to the wall they found half a banana and most of a sliced loaf, perfectly clean. An elderly woman saw Murat up to his elbows in the bin and took out her purse and handed him a piece of paper with something printed on it.

"What's this for?" he asked in Albanian.

The woman smiled and spoke in English and made a gesture as if she was forking food into her mouth with both hands.

Spiro held out his hand. "Some kind of voucher," he told Murat after inspecting the slip of paper. "Put it in your pocket."

"A banknote would be better."

"Quit moaning."

While scavenging for food in a bin behind a supermarket that evening, they found some broken boxes and packing material that would come in useful for bedding. A loaf past its sell-by date was another good find. They took their prizes to a multi-storey car park. After dark there were still lights left on, so they found a shadowy corner. Outside it started raining heavily, but they were dry.

"Let's eat," Spiro said, and tore the wrapping from the loaf. He divided it and handed his big companion the larger portion. "I wouldn't call this stale." He took a bite. "Not bad at all."

He noticed Murat mouth some words and cross himself before starting to eat. "Are you Christian?"

Murat nodded.

"This must be bread of heaven, then," Spiro joked. "The Lord looks after his own. Lucky I was with you."

Murat smiled and said nothing.

A little later, after most of the loaf had been consumed, Spiro said, "I'm atheist. How long have you been a Bible-basher, then?"

"Almost all my life."

Spiro frowned. Murat was at least forty. He would have grown up when Enver Hoxha was head of the communist state and ruthlessly suppressed every form of religion, declaring Albania the world's first and only atheist country. Every church, mosque and place of worship in the country was demolished early in his forty-year regime. Anyone suspected of practising religion was liable to imprisonment and torture. Only after Hoxha's death in 1985 had the persecution stopped.

Murat explained. "My parents were believers. I was secretly baptised into the Orthodox faith in a farm building by a brave man, an ordained priest from Greece, who was later arrested and murdered. I was given a Turkish name so nobody would suspect I was Christian."

Spiro understood. Many people had been ordered by the state to change to non-religious names in those days.

"I grew up in a family that secretly observed the church festivals and took communion with a few others. I was too young to know much about it. I have a faint memory of an Easter celebration in a cellar with liturgical music played on a wind-up gramophone. When I was four, my mother and father were denounced by neighbours and taken away. I remember that vividly. My sister Elira and I were sent to orphanages, different ones, and taught that all religion is dangerous superstition. I accepted this as truth and came to believe my parents had been bad people. Later, after everything changed, I met Elira again. She hadn't allowed herself to be brainwashed. She put my head right and told me the truth about our family."

"Did your parents find you?"

"They died in prison. I try not to think about them."

"Sorry."

"I pray for them. I still believe, but I haven't been to church for a long time."

He had related the facts of his personal history without a trace of self-pity. The suffering this quiet man had endured must have been beyond words.

They wrapped themselves in cardboard and slept fitfully.

By stages in the days that followed, they learned more about living on the street in this city. They were wary of joining other rough sleepers or using drop-in centres. Spiro warned Murat that it wasn't wise to become part of the homeless community. "That's too bloody obvious. If the Finisher comes looking, he's sure to check that lot first."

Instead, they watched the street dwellers from a distance and learned how they coped. There was a lot of sitting or lying on the pavement and some begging, but Spiro noticed they all had water and saw where it came from. Certain shop windows had blue stickers in the shape of drops of fluid, with writing on them. If you took an empty bottle in, you could get it refilled with tap water. The idea was to cut down on the number of plastic bottles, an eco-friendly scheme the two newcomers were happy to support.

Better still, they discovered how to use the food vouchers the old lady had handed them. Free soup, sandwiches and cake were on offer to the homeless each evening in the Cattle Market and there was another charity handing out food in the car park at the back of Waitrose. Spiro and Murat felt safe using these open-air facilities. Existing like this wasn't comfortable or easy and couldn't last indefinitely, but it was better than sorting rubbish ten hours a day, seven days a week. When they'd learned some English and found casual work paid at a fair rate, they would begin to think about what happened next.

Once the basics of survival were overcome, the biggest problem would be communication. Albanian has obscure origins and bears no obvious resemblance to any other language, even those of neighbouring countries, never mind to English.

Murat was better than Spiro at picking up a smattering of English. He had an ear for sounds. He listened and repeated the words and was good at remembering them. "What are they talking about?" Spiro asked him one evening at the food van when everyone seemed more animated than usual.

"Something about goody bags."

"What's that?"

"I'm not sure."

Spiro set his logical mind to work. "I know what good is and I know what a bag is. Maybe they're saying where good bags can be found."

"Instead of plastic?"

He shrugged. "It's only a suggestion. Listen up, Murat, and they might say more."

"They seem to be talking about stuff inside the bag. I'm hearing water, biscuits, granola, bananas and chocolate. They could be the goodies."

"Is all this being given away? Where?"

"Wait." Murat tried speaking some English to a homeless man who seemed to be the main bringer of the good news. After much nodding, pointing and repetition he came back to Spiro. "It's not till Sunday morning and thousands of these bags will be given out."

"That's an exaggeration. I can't believe thousands. There aren't thousands living on the streets here."

"Hold on. I may have misunderstood." Murat went back to his informant and a longer consultation took place, punctuated with much gesturing, nodding and pointing. "It's true," he told Spiro. "Five thousand and they're given to runners."

"What do you mean, runners? People on the run like you and me? I keep telling you there can't be that many."

"No, Spiro. Ordinary runners doing it to get fit, like we see every day on the streets. There's a big road race here on Sunday and they get given goody bags after they finish. Some of them aren't interested in the food in the bag, so it's a great place to be for handouts."

"Okay, it's making sense. Where does this happen?"

"The runners' village."

"Get away," Spiro said. "They don't have their own village."

"On Sunday they will and that's where they collect their bags when they finish the race. They get a T-shirt and a medal. They always keep the medal and most keep the shirt, but not all of them want the bag."

"So where exactly is this runners' village?"

"A sports field over that way." He pointed. "It's just big tents."

Spiro's interest in all this evaporated. "I know where you mean and I'm not going there for biscuits and bananas. I wouldn't go there for a five-course dinner. They can keep their fucking goody bags."

Murat understood why. He'd pointed in the direction of the no-go area east of the city where they'd been detained all those months. Neither of them wanted to see that house again, ever. But the goody bags had a strong pull. "It could be all right, Spiro."

"No."

"It's going to be busy with all those runners milling around."

Spiro ignored him.

Murat wasn't giving up. "We won't be noticed. I'm up for it if you are."

"Fuck off."

"Safety in numbers."

"You were the guy who didn't want to come back to Bath at any price. Now you're saying we show our heads where we were last seen."

"I get hungry, Spiro."

"Go there if you want, but if you tell anyone I'm hiding up here, you're a dead man."

10

Five thousand men and women were jammed shoulder to shoulder in Great Pulteney Street. Here they started and here they would finish.

If they survived.

This was the worst time, waiting for the start. The tension showed in a variety of ways: muscles twitched, hands were rubbed together, hair was tugged, scraped and smoothed, watches checked many times over, water bottles upended. Some stared fixedly ahead and some tried joking with the people around them.

In the runners' village at the Sports Centre, North Parade Road, marshals with loudhailers had been issuing instructions for the past hour. People were graded by ability and sent to the start by different routes. The white pen was for the elite group, the ones who took the front position and already stood with fingers poised on their own stopwatches. Green was for those with some experience who weren't expected to challenge for a top-fifty finish. Orange, by far the largest, filtered by way of the riverside path and Grove Street, where most were waiting, was for the tenderfoots, starters who might never have tried such a distance. They would probably walk some of the way.

The last ten seconds were counted down to 11 A.M.

The hooter blared.

The elite runners led the charge. The white pen emptied like rice from a packet and the greens were close behind. The winner would finish in little more than an hour.

That first dash towards Sydney Gardens at the top of the street was thrilling to watch, cheered by hundreds crushed into the space along the sides. Sydney Place was closed to traffic, so they headed straight across the road, through the entrance to the gardens and around the Holburne Museum to the central walk, where lines of marshals kept control.

The route took them over the bridge across the railway cutting, heading for the canal path and south, right through the tunnel under Cleveland House, where tolls were once collected from the barges through a hole in the roof. From here they would follow the Kennet and Avon Canal until it merged with a stretch of the old Somerset Coal Canal. Ancient canal paths and disused railways made up much of the Other Half course.

All who came after the elite runners passed at a slower tempo, competing mainly with themselves. A personal best or the triumph of finishing at all was their aim. They didn't worry about starting some minutes after the hooter. They all had timing chips fastened to their shoelaces that emitted a unique code when the shoes passed over the antennas sheathed in the rubber mat that was the start line. Everyone from the winner to the wackiest fancy-dress runner would be timed.

The prizes weren't huge. The first male and female finishers would each get a thousand pounds. Others who placed in the first five would get scaled-down sums. There was a similar prize list for the best British finishers, so in theory a Brit might win in each category and earn two thousand. The big beneficiaries were the charities. Among them, they would scoop a cool two million. Their main outlay was a T-shirt for each supporter. Some proud wearers of the shirts would have spent more time getting sponsors than getting fit. When they suffered, as they would, they had the consolation of knowing it was for a good cause.

Back at the start, screams of excitement were heard as the first of the orange pen crowd finally got their adventure under way, multicoloured, dazzling to watch. The tension of the long wait evaporated. This group had the biggest spread of age, shape and ability and was the most fun. Among them were the fancy-dress entrants, the pirates, pantomime horses, fairies, carrots, bananas, spacemen, dinosaurs—and at least one policeman carrying an old-fashioned truncheon.

For the real police, all leave was cancelled. Aside from enforcing traffic diversions, they needed to be alert for every kind of crime from theft to terrorism. Any event that attracts large crowds brings concerns. The 2013 Boston Marathon bombing was a recurring nightmare. Officers were deployed along the course in what the Deputy Chief Constable described as overt and covert roles.

Difficult to tell whether Detective Superintendent Peter Diamond, on duty in the gardens, was overt or covert. If he had been in the race, you would have taken him for one of the jokers in fancy dress. He might have stepped out of a 1940s film, a sleuth on the trail of Sydney Green-street. The gabardine trench coat and dark brown trilby, his so-called plain clothes, weren't plain at all in twenty-first-century Bath.

Diamond had watched too many half marathons to get much pleasure from the day. They had been fixtures here longer than he had. Running had never appealed to him. Sitting was more his thing, several hours every day in a comfortable chair. When necessary he would stand up. He'd even amble short distances. But he had never understood why joggers put themselves through such discomfort, let alone did it in competition. At an earlier stage in life he had played rugby for the Metropolitan Police and twice a week had been forced to trot a few training laps around the Imber Court pitch, always without breaking sweat. He didn't want to shed much weight. Poundage was needed in the scrum.

Cheering from the museum end signalled the first sight of the leading group. The central walk through Sydney Gardens was wide and straight, so this was a good viewpoint.

"There's your winner," Diamond told DC Paul Gilbert, who was with him mainly to allow for occasional tea breaks in the museum's garden café.

"Who's that, guv?"

"The black lad in fourth place. He'll be a Kenyan or an Ethiopian. They're natural runners. Look at him, scarcely breathing. They live at altitude, you see. Less oxygen. Makes them work harder at their running, so when they come down to sea level, they can beat anyone." He made common knowledge sound like revelations from on high, and no one had better say so.

Gilbert studied the smooth action of the black athlete.

"He'll be a professional," Diamond added. "They use this as a training run."

Gilbert waited for the race leaders to get closer before saying, "I know him."

"Watched him on TV?" Diamond said.

"I was at school with him."

"Come off it. You're a local lad."

"So is he. Harry Hobbs from Midsomer Norton," Gilbert said.

"Get away. Are you sure?"

"Hundred per cent. He always won the cross-country."

"It must be in the blood, then. Kenyan parents."

"Birmingham, he told me. He's third-generation British."

Diamond didn't pursue the point. He'd reached the limit of his expertise on distance running. And genealogy.

Seconds later, the scene was transformed by the colours

of a thousand runners in close order funnelled between the lines of watchers. Seen in close-up, the flickering pattern could almost have triggered a seizure.

They were moving with ease and the mood was boisterous. Not for much longer. The serious stuff began now, the grind along lonely stretches out in the country, on footpaths across fields and through the mile-long Combe Down Tunnel, once a feature of the Somerset and Dorset Railway, known locally as the Slow and Dirty. Out on the course they were truly in need of the goodwill of spectators.

"Would you credit it?" Diamond said suddenly, breaking the spell. "What's that dickhead doing in the race?"

The dickhead was a dapper, dark-haired man of about forty-five, below average height and as slim as the silver birches he was running past. Dark blue headband with white polka-dots. Yellow T-shirt, blue shorts and trainers. Gold chain bouncing on his chest. He was running with a blonde woman in a British Heart Foundation shirt. From her expression, he was trying to chat her up and not succeeding.

Gilbert had never seen either of them before.

"Tony Pinto," Diamond said as if everyone in Bath should know the name. "He's evil."

People nearby turned to see who had spoken. If Gilbert hadn't been outranked, he'd have told Diamond to keep his voice down.

"He's supposed to be banged up. I put him away for a fifteen stretch soon after I got here."

"How long have you worked here, guv?" Gilbert asked. "He must have served it out."

Diamond wasn't listening. The sight of Tony Pinto fit, flash and at liberty was too disturbing. "And not a grey hair on his head."

"What did you get him for?"

Diamond was still getting looks and now it dawned on him that he was causing a distraction. "Step back a bit."

They found a less crowded spot in front of a bank of roses. "Well, you know Bog Island?"

Gilbert nodded. Every copper knew Bog Island, the paved triangle in the middle of the huge road junction opposite Terrace Gardens.

"And how it got its name?"

"The underground toilets."

"Right, but you've never been down there, have you?"

"It's been locked up for years, hasn't it, locked up and condemned?"

"Like Pinto should be."

Gilbert looked at his boss. Was that what he'd been leading up to, a tired old quip?

But Diamond was singing the praises of Bog Island. "It was a palace in its time. When the council first extended Pierrepont Street and linked it with Orange Grove, they decided to excavate and put in a public convenience worthy of the handsome city this is. This was in the 1930s, when they still liked to do things in style. Coloured tiles, brass fittings, skylights, big glass cisterns overhead, no expense spared. Male and female attendants, dressing rooms, a left-luggage room, bathrooms and all the usual offices. It was such a showpiece that about forty years ago it became a drinking club."

"What—while it was still a toilet?"

"Give me strength. Of course not. It was a change of use. What do you call it?—a relaunch. Then it was opened as a nightclub."

"How do you know all this, guv?"

"I support the rugby club, don't I?"

Diamond had this habit of making unrelated statements, challenging his listener to find a connection. Gilbert had learned that the only solution was to keep your mouth shut and wait for the follow-up.

"Bath RFC bought the place. Well, three of the players

did, Roger Spurrell and two others. Spruced it up and called it the Island Club. You'll have seen the archway over the entrance."

Two handsome archways, in fact, with the club's name picked out in ironwork. You couldn't fail to notice them if you came by, one over the ladies' side, the other the gents'.

"It became the hot spot in town because it had a late licence at a time when most places closed at eleven. Anyone who played for the first team got in free. You went there and rubbed shoulders with your heroes. Great nights, they were. They cleared the floor one night and one of the All Blacks performed the haka."

"Were you there?"

"Wish I was. Bit before my time, the 1980s. That was when Bath RFC started dominating British rugby."

Gilbert knew about Diamond's passion for the oval-ball game, but he couldn't see what Bog Island had to do with a crook called Tony Pinto who was already across the railway bridge and out of sight.

"By the nineties, when I came to Bath, the place was on the slide. The rugby lads had sold up and left." Diamond shook his head and sighed. This could become a lament. "The Island Club got to be a student dive, more of a pulling club than anything else. The new owners packed in the punters, two hundred or more on Wednesdays, their big night, and didn't do enough in the way of maintenance and it smelt like the public loo it was originally. What with the heat and sweat of the dancing, drips of condensation and God knows what else falling from the ceiling, it got dangerous in the end. Subsidence. Health and safety was an issue. The council closed it down, but not before Tony Pinto became a regular."

"What was he up to? Drugs?"

"Picking up girls. Nothing criminal in that, you're going to tell me. The thing is, Pinto wanted a different one for sex each time. Once he'd had them, he dropped them, and he had the gall to go back to the same club and look for more."

"Fuck 'em and forget 'em."

"Crudely, yes. He was in his twenties, a few years older than the students, good-looking, well turned-out, not short of money, and they fell for it."

"Didn't they spread the word about him?"

"One in particular did, a second-year called Bryony Lancaster, barely nineteen. She went all the way with him one night and was shocked when he ignored her the next time and chatted up some other girls. While he was buying drinks she went over and warned them about him. Pinto didn't make out with anyone that night and he found out why. He waited outside for Bryony and went to work on her face with a knife. She was scarred for life. Her upper lip needed stitching together and there were two long slashes on her right cheek."

Gilbert's eyes squeezed shut. "That's horrible."

Diamond didn't need telling. He looked away, remembering. Runners streamed past and didn't register on his attention. "If you'd met her, as I did, you'd know how horrible. Unsurprisingly, she was traumatised. I couldn't get a proper victim statement from her, even weeks afterwards. She wouldn't speak about her attacker."

"Weren't there witnesses?"

"Nobody came forward. We made the usual appeals for help and got nowhere."

"Who reported it?"

"A taxi driver who came along later found her near the cab rank and saw she was in trouble. Good man. He called 999 and our people were first at the scene, followed soon after by the ambulance. I was put on the case next morning and hit a problem right away. No one was talking other than that cabbie."

"Too scared?"

"The girls who could have shopped him were. Like I said, we got nowhere with our witness appeals, so our best hope was finding the exact spot where the knifing took place. It's an area without much cover."

"The Parade Gardens?" The obvious place to go for outdoor sex. The gardens just across the street from Bog Island, more than two acres of them, fringed by trees and bushes, sloping down to the river.

"That was my first thought. They're kept locked at night, but there was an emergency exit from the club, a tunnel that gave access to the gardens."

Bizarrely, the talk of the knifing and its aftermath was being punctuated by screams, cheers and yells of encouragement as the crowd spotted runners they knew.

"Did you search there?"

"The gardens? Of course. Found all the junk you'd expect in a public park, but no weapon and no evidence of a recent assault."

"I can't think where else it could have happened."

"There are rows of shops facing two sides of the island. I had them searched minutely and eventually got a result. A small bloodstain on the tiled floor of a shop entrance in Terrace Walk."

"Bryony's blood?"

"Yes, and only thirty yards from the club exit. He must have forced her across the street. She professed not to have any memory where the attack had happened, but I have my doubts about that."

"She could have blocked it out, guv."

"It amounts to the same thing. She was terrified of being attacked again. When forensics went to work, they found another smear of blood on the shop door itself and a thumbprint."

"His?"

Diamond nodded.

"Bit of luck."

"We didn't call it that after fifteen days of searching."

"Wasn't there any CCTV footage?"

"Fifteen years ago in Bath? You're joking. And this was way before phones had built-in cameras. The next time the club opened, we had our people there. I wasn't expecting the knife man to show, and he didn't, but some of the regulars—blokes, exclusively—recalled seeing this guy they'd noticed in the past chatting up the talent. A loner, they said. Nobody knew him by name. It took some hard questioning to get a reasonable description. People's memories aren't all that reliable."

"In the dark, half pissed."

"There speaks a hardened clubber. Time went by and the ACC scaled down the hunt, which really hacked me off. This was personal for me." Even now, all those years on, Diamond's voice thickened with emotion. "I had teams planted in clubs all over Bath and Bristol and there were suggestions from on high that they were having a good time at taxpayers' expense. Ridiculous."

"But you caught him?"

"Julie did. Julie Hargreaves, one of the best detectives I ever worked with. Pinto had stopped going to the Island. He was on the pull at another club, Chemies, in Seven Dials. Julie saw what he was up to and we collared him as he was leaving with some tanked-up young woman."

"He matched the description?"

"More important than that, his thumbprint matched the one from the crime scene."

"Did the victim ID him?"

"Bryony? No. She wasn't up for it and I wasn't going to put her through more pain. The mental scarring was as bad as the physical. Worse, I'd say. She wouldn't testify in court and I think she was right. Any cross-examination would have destroyed her. It's the same dilemma we have in rape cases."

"Getting a conviction must have been hard."

"We got a confession."

Gilbert's eyebrows shot up.

"Don't ask."

11

Murat, being so large and seriously undernourished, might have had more need of food than Spiro. On the day of the race, he set off for the recreation ground. Those goody bags had preyed on his mind. He offered to bring one back for Spiro.

Spiro told him not to bother and gave the impression he would have nothing to do with the race. But he'd secretly gone to the trouble of getting a free newspaper with a map of the course, which he'd torn out and put in his pocket. After his foolhardy companion had departed, he planned to visit the drink station along the route. There, he'd pick up some bottled water just to demonstrate to Murat that there were safe ways of doing things.

He needed to borrow a bike again and this time he didn't have to use the ballpoint-pen trick. As if it was fated, some trusting person—probably one of the runners caught up in the bonhomie of the day—had left a shining blue roadster unlocked in a stack of bikes to the left of the station entrance. Spiro, an avowed atheist, turned his face to the sky, crossed himself and rode off through the tunnel. Like any law-abiding Bathonian, he dismounted and walked the bike over the footbridge they had used before.

The map unfortunately didn't show contours and he wasn't pleased to find, once he was back in the saddle,

that the direct route was by way of a road called Widcombe
Hill. The climb was so stiff that he had to get off the bike
and walk. He watched a few serious cyclists in helmets and
skinsuits battling with the gradient and knew it was not
for him. Even when he'd walked for ten minutes and the
slope eased enough for him to use the bike again, grateful for the gears, there was plenty of hill remaining. This
was strange because he was supposed to be on his way to a
drinks station beside a canal, which to his logical thinking
ought to be on even ground.

Not wanting to go back and look for an easier route,
he pressed on until the road levelled out and took him
past a university campus. The board beside the road told
him he was on Claverton Down. The English language was
hard to fathom. He thought he'd learned the meaning
of the word "down" but in Albanian it would definitely
be "up."

In a few minutes he started descending and was rewarded
for all the thigh-straining as the bike picked up speed down
a hill called Brassknocker. He had to go into bottom gear
and use the brakes to keep control. But the view of the
valley ahead when he descended the last section told him
he'd arrived. He could see a fine old limestone structure
with three arches carrying a canal over a river, so this had
to be Dundas Aqueduct as marked on the map. People were
standing looking down from the balustrade to where the
runners would pass under the arches. Many more spectators
had lined the sides of the canal. The drinks station was in
a visitors' car park stretching between the aqueduct and
the spur of the disused Somerset Coal Canal.

Spiro dismounted to cross a main road and wheeled
the bike into the area where hundreds of bottles were
already set out on trestle tables and thousands more in
packs formed walls behind. He parked against a tree where
he could keep an eye on the bike (you can't trust anyone)

and watched what was happening. The race should have started, but apparently no runners had come through yet. Some volunteers were picking up red sleeveless jackets from a stack behind the tables and putting them on, so Spiro did the same and instantly became a drinks marshal, or whatever they called themselves. Simple as that.

He could have picked up a couple of bottles and left, but having come this far he had an interest in seeing the runners come through.

Cheers and clapping greeted the leaders when they showed, a group of three men of colour who already had a fifty-metre lead over the rest. Taking his cue from the other volunteers, Spiro held out a bottle for one of them to grab, but none of the trio took one. Only four miles into the race, top athletes would be used to going farther without drinking.

When the others started coming through, the take-up was more encouraging. Some took a few gulps and slung the bottles aside and others splashed the water over their heads and shoulders to cool down. These were still the elite runners racing it out rather than the vast majority who would be satisfied to finish at all.

Soon enough the charity people in their shirts of many colours arrived and the demand was more than gratifying. All Spiro and the other volunteers could do was push rows of bottles across the tables for hundreds of hands to grab. He enjoyed being a giver rather than a taker for a change. For ten to fifteen minutes the demands of the job couldn't have been greater and for a while afterwards there was no let-up. Luckily, everyone seemed to be in a good mood, pleased to have reached this point and united in their wish to keep going to the finish. The inevitable pushing, bumping and splashing prompted only apologies and smiles. Mass participation was bringing out the best in everyone.

As more passed by, the occasional runner would find time

to make a joke or say a few words to the marshals. Mostly Spiro got the gist of what was said and responded in English with, "You're welcome," mimicking the others. He was still busy, but the flow eased enough for him to marvel at the spectacle, the unbroken multicoloured ribbon of jogging figures spread along the towpath as far as he could see.

Then, without warning, the joy went out of it. For about the twentieth time, Spiro turned to collect three more of the packs of twenty-four, move them to the table and rip off the plastic holding them together. He reached for a stray that was rolling off the table, caught it neatly, handed it to the waiting runner and his blood ran cold.

He'd locked eyes with the one man he was here to avoid.

The Finisher.

Maeve's half marathon was unlike anything she'd imagined in her training run daydreams. The real thing was noisier, friendlier, more inspiring and more emotional. The temptation in this early part of the race was to get excited and go too fast, particularly with so many people packing the sides of the course yelling encouragement and reaching out to the runners to catch high fives. Most of them were from Longford Road Primary, going by the repeated shouts of, "Go, Miss Kelly," which was lovely and embarrassing at the same time because everyone else in the race was plain Tom, Dick or Harriet and didn't get the same support. Amused looks were exchanged by other runners when she waved back like the Queen, but what else could she do? She was Miss Kelly to the parents as well as her class and it was lovely that so many had come to cheer her on.

She kept reminding herself that the hard part was ahead and she needed to save some energy for later. Be responsible, Miss Kelly. You're not doing this for yourself. Thousands of heart patients are relying on you to get round. You're lucky enough to have a good ticker, unlike them. The final sum in sponsorship topped two grand, so you'd better not mess up like you did with the Toby jug. Everyone, the kids, parents, teachers, neighbours, family, friends, will want to know if you finished the race and you mustn't let them down. Aunt Jayne, Mr. Seagrove, Mrs. Haliburton, Trevor, Olga, Mother. You'll face them all when this is over and you must be able to say, "Yes, I did it."

The weight of so much expectation almost brought her to her knees. She was still the wrong shape for running, in spite of all the training. It helped that many of the others she'd joined in the first-timers' pen were similarly handi-capped and more so. Thank God she hadn't committed to running the thing in a gorilla suit or with a polyester Royal Crescent draped around her shoulders. She'd done everything humanly possible: got the kit, done the mileage, eaten the carbohydrates and smeared Vaseline over every bit of her body capable of chafing. She'd listened to Trevor, her distance-running guru, and taken his advice.

Everything humanly possible? Well, almost.

When lecturing her on the importance of the last three weeks before the race, Trevor had talked about tapering, which she took to mean slimming.

"For pity's sake, Trev," she'd told him. "I'm happy with the way I am now. I've lost almost twenty pounds."

He'd shaken his head. "That isn't tapering. You're on a countdown now. You don't want to be tired on the day. You ease up gradually on the workload, reduce the mile-age, possibly do some fitness walks instead of runs. You want to be fresh and full of energy when you get to the start line. I've written down some guidelines for you. Then your nutrition needs adjusting. Keep up the proteins for the time being, but two or three days before the race you must carb-load. Bread, pasta, rice in bulk, to be stored as glycogen in your muscles and liver."

"Trevor, I just want to get to the end of the race. I'm not aiming to win it."

He didn't seem to have heard. "Avoid caffeine and alcohol. Then you'll feel more relaxed and sleep better. You're sure to be nervous, but coffee and cocktails aren't the answer. Herbal tea is good."

On the day before the race she'd touched base with a guy who knew about running from personal experience. In a small bar on Wellsway, they'd discussed her race strategy and he'd talked a lot more common sense than Trevor and with humour. Alcohol? He recommended it. Between them they'd got through a bottle of the house red and Maeve laughed at his stories of athletes famous and infamous. When he suggested they capped a fun-filled session with some action of their own in a room upstairs, she was surprised, flattered and didn't object. The sex wasn't the greatest—passionate while it lasted, fast and furious, meriting a six or seven at most, but better than herbal tea. Trevor's list of things to avoid hadn't included a shag. He just hadn't thought of it, wrongly supposing she was as single-minded as he was.

After Sydney Gardens, excited onlookers lined the road all the way to the humpback bridge at Bathampton. There the support thinned and Maeve was thankful for a quiet stretch southwards along the canal towpath—quiet, except that she was doing it with five thousand others, most, it seemed, ready to chat along the lines of, "Your first time? Mine, too. And the last. My feet are killing me already."

They progressed through the spectacular Limpley Stoke valley, but she wasn't in this to admire scenery. She'd needed more elbow room and was getting it now. The conversation dwindled and was replaced by the muffled drumming of footfalls.

A cyclist came by, steadily overtaking runners. "Have a heart, mate, and give me a lift," someone shouted, but there was no comeback from the rider, intent on getting through on the outside without hitting anyone. Presumably he was someone's trainer. All the elite runners had trainers and called them coaches. He'd have some catching up to do if he wanted to get through to the leaders. Maeve had a mental map of the route and was looking forward to slaking her thirst at the Dundas Aqueduct.

"Take water at every opportunity," Trevor had advised. "Dehydration is your biggest enemy."

She wasn't worried that Trevor hadn't been much in evidence today. He must have felt no more needed to be said. She'd seen him from a distance with his bike in the runners' village before the start and for once he'd been looking the other way. Even in the Longford Road staffroom he had this habit of gazing at her in the way a racehorse trainer studies a filly entered for the Derby, assessing her haunches for excess fat—of which there was still too much—and planning how to get her race-ready. He would never say she was flabby or overeating. Instead he'd tell her, as he had a week ago, that she might care to go to the swimming pool and practise walking in water.

Isn't that what they do with horses? She hadn't taken up the suggestion. She had the feeling Trevor would insist on watching, getting an eyeful of her less-than-svelte figure.

She was gasping for a drink of water. Overindulgence in cheap Merlot and sex the day before? No way, she told herself. I can cope with alcohol. The running is making me thirsty. All I need is to recharge. Happily, plenty of hydration was on offer when she jogged into the aqueduct car park. Red-jacketed marshals at tables were making sure everyone could grab a bottle.

"Can I?" she asked the guy when she reached for a spare one. He was trying to manage two tables with armfuls of packs.

"Help yourself. I don't think I'm winning here. There was

someone next to me until a few minutes ago. He vanished just when it was getting really busy."

She moved on herself, making way for other thirsty people. She noticed some queueing to use a portaloo, jogging on the spot, either to keep the muscles supple or from pressure on the bladder. She wondered if the missing marshal was inside. It wasn't only the runners who sometimes needed a leak. Personally, she was blessed with excellent plumbing aided by the drying effect of that wine.

She guzzled most of one bottle, rejoined the race and splashed the last part over her head. Personal grooming be damned.

The race left the towpath and followed the track bed of a former railway, now a leafy lane leading eventually to the village of Monkton Combe. Maeve knew from her training runs what to expect—the nearest thing to a theme park, starting with mouldering evidence of an industrial past, the source of Bath's wealth, remnants of railways, dried-up coal canals, blocks of Bath stone and a mill that over the years had processed fuller's earth and flour and also served as a yard for sawing stone. All this was climaxed by the tunnel of death, the mile-long excavation underneath Combe Down. On a November day in 1929, locomotive 89, a heavily overloaded steam engine hauling thirty ten-ton wagons of coal, had been straining to make the 1:100 rise through the dark, unventilated tunnel. So slow was progress that the driver and his fireman were overcome by carbon monoxide fumes emitted from their own funnel. They collapsed in the cab. Driverless, still at a crawl but fatally out of control, the train chugged into daylight and on through another tunnel, the Devonshire, before picking up terrifying speed down the hillside, at least sixty miles an hour before it reached a set of points in the goods yard at Bath station and was derailed and overturned, crushing a goods inspector who was waiting to see the train in. The trucks concertinaed. Hot coals were flung into nearby homes. It was remarkable that only three men were killed.

This would be Maeve's first time through the tunnel of death. In training, she had approached the entrance a number of times and avoided going in. The interior had been spruced up and given some lighting in recent years to become a cycleway, but it still felt spooky to anyone who knew the story. She would make sure she stayed close to the runner ahead.

12

While the five thousand were driving their protesting bodies along the roads and footpaths south of Bath, Diamond and young Gilbert enjoyed coffee and cake at the Holburne Museum and then took a gentle stroll to Great Pulteney Street. It was sensible to be posted somewhere near the finish, so they found a position fifty yards short of the big red gantry that stretched across the street. News of the leading runners was being relayed over the public address, but the two CID men didn't pay much attention. For them this was a lazy Sunday, an agreeable way of earning overtime.

The finishing straight filled up and the marshals in their high-visibility jackets took control. Some of the crowd were getting updates by phone from the runners themselves. The sense of anticipation was rising.

A bigger buzz of excitement suddenly spread along the lines. An hour and twelve minutes was showing on the digital display on the gantry and shouts had been heard from the top of the street. Shortly after, a runner appeared. He had a clear lead.

"Told you, didn't I?" Diamond said.

Harry Hobbs, the black guy Gilbert had been at school with, was about to finish first.

If Diamond expected to be congratulated, he was

mistaken. Gilbert cupped his hands to his mouth and yelled, "Up St. Mark's!"

To whoops and screams of encouragement and near-delirium from the public address, Hobbs sprinted the final yards and breasted the tape in record time. "And what's more," the announcer added, voice breaking with emotion, "Harry is one of ours, a local lad, from Midsomer Norton."

Some forty yards behind, the next two were in a sprint for second place. Both were black. Diamond wasn't getting caught out again. He didn't venture an opinion on their countries of origin. "Daniel Wanjiru and Martin Maiyoro, both of Kenya," came the announcement.

More elite runners appeared soon after, with quite long gaps between small groups going at a pace Diamond couldn't have kept up with for more than a few yards, even in his rugby-playing days. After crossing the line, they were wrapped in tinfoil blankets and escorted away by volunteers.

Paul Gilbert's attention was on his old school chum, being photographed with the Kenyans. "Remember why we're here," Diamond said, feeling the need to reassert himself. "Keep an eye on the crowd. It only takes one idiot to spoil the day for everyone."

Three more minutes and at least five hundred runners passed before it happened. A ripple of amusement animated the crowd. The two officers leaned in for a better view.

"That's all we need," Gilbert said.

A pair of streakers had joined in. Stark naked, male and female, they were dodging among the toiling runners doing dance moves and star jumps and jiggling their loose bits.

Pleased with himself, Diamond said, "Not one idiot, but two. I wasn't far wrong, was I?"

"Nothing much to boast about," Gilbert said.

He was given a sharp look. "What do you mean?"

"The bloke, guv. If I was him I'd keep it covered up."

A sniff. "Haven't you noticed? Modest guys like you

and me are always surprised at what other people think is special."

"Had we better stop them?"

"How?"

"Well, bundle them off the course and get them covered up."

"What with?"

"My jacket for the woman."

"And my hat for the man, I suppose? No, thanks."

"Isn't it our job to deal with them, guv?"

"You can if you want. I've got bigger fish to fry."

Gilbert glanced at him uncertainly.

"The terrorist threat."

"Right."

"Anyone can see those two aren't armed."

Having got their few seconds of attention, the streakers discovered they were unpopular. Someone in the crowd threw a water bottle and hit the man's back and he collided with a runner and fell heavily. He was hauled up by a marshal and led away. No one in the crowd wanted to come into contact with bare flesh, so there was no need to ask them to make room. The woman tamely followed and the show was over.

By this time, hundreds more runners had plodded into view. Diamond was still alert, but—if truth were told—not expecting a terrorist. He was keen to get a second look at the ex-jailbird, Tony Pinto. He wanted to be sure he could trust his own eyes. Had it been a lookalike, or had he truly seen that sicko up to his old game of chatting up a pretty woman? If so, why wasn't he having a tougher time, as most prisoners do when they are released? How had he got fit enough to run a half marathon? How could he afford the race fee and the smart running kit?

These weren't idle questions. He meant to follow them up at the first opportunity.

More than an hour went by and the crowd along the finish was still enthusiastic. Every runner was getting cheered and some had joined the supporters to look out for friends. Humanity at its most positive.

But Diamond was weary of scrutinising the finishers. He'd not seen Pinto or the blonde he had been running with. It was well possible that the woman had run by unnoticed, but he doubted that he'd missed the scumbag he'd once arrested, interviewed and charged.

More of the fancy-dress people were coming past now. When last seen, Pinto had been running strongly enough to have finished well ahead of that lot.

Maeve had survived the tunnel of death and a second, shorter, railway tunnel, refuelled at another drinks station, and was starting to believe she would finish the race. She was on a high, literally. The worst was over and all that was left was a steady downhill jog into Oldfield Park and from there into the heart of Bath. She turned a corner, heard a shout of, "Here she is!" Then "Miss Kelleeeeee!" and saw at least a dozen hands reaching to be high-fived. Buoyed up, confident and tearful, she slowed to make sure she didn't miss one. The human contact after so long with her own insecurities and fears was as good as an injection of energy. Someone thrust a bottle of water at her and she grabbed it, gulped and got into her stride again.

Her first glimpse of the abbey was another thrill. She started striding faster, overtaking runners she'd trailed for the past hour and still finding the strength to wave back each time someone urged her on. Where had this come from? For so much of the race she'd feared she wouldn't finish, yet here she was, going better than she had all afternoon. All those hours of pounding the streets in every extreme of weather were repaying her. The tumbles, the

snarling dogs, the rainstorms, the sore nipples, the sensible
eating, the proper kit—and the laundering it required—
and the battles to push back the dreaded lactic threshold.

Another pocket of Longford Road kids screamed, "Go,
go, go, Miss Kelly!" and behind them she saw the deputy
head, Mr. Seagrove, waving his cap and shouting with them,
in spite of the fact that twenty-six pounds had gone from
his bank account. And she felt a lump in her throat when
she reminded herself of all the other generous people who
had sponsored her. And the one who hadn't, her mother,
unwilling to encourage such madness, but as a concession
funding the expensive kit.

"Shall we call it a day, guv?" Gilbert asked. "Some of them
will be crawling in for hours yet."

"You can if you want," came the answer. "I'm going to
watch a bit longer."

"An hour and forty minutes."

"Is that all?"

"Since the winner finished. This lot are taking almost
three hours for a thirteen-mile run. Some people could
walk it in that time."

"Look, I said you can knock off."

"I'm thinking your guy dropped out. Blisters or something."

"He's not my guy. He's a serpent."

"He'd have passed us by now."

"No way of telling, is there?"

"Later on there is. The list of all the finishers."

The frustration was all too evident. "I'm not completely
clueless about what goes on. I trust my own eyes better
than a results sheet."

"Masses of them have come through already. It would
have been easy to miss someone."

"Bugger off and leave me in peace."

Paul Gilbert obeyed orders.

The crowd had thinned to little more than a single line each side of the street. There were long gaps between the pathetic also-rans coming in. The guy with the mike had given up commentating and put on a loop of "We Are the Champions."

How many times Maeve had crossed the Avon in this mind-numbing foot slog she didn't know, but at Pulteney Bridge she was over for the last. Then up Argyle Street towards the fountain in the middle of the road and already she could see the dreamed-of scarlet gantry across Great Pulteney Street, the finishing straight. It was a riot of balloons, flashing cameras, blaring music and red-shirted marshals ready to assist.

Her vision blurred as tears streamed down her face, and they weren't tears of joy. Each step punished her badly blistered feet and brought sharp pains in her shinbones, knees and pelvis, but the thirteen-mile torture was almost over.

With a cry of triumph, she reached the line. She had an overpowering urge to hug somebody, her mother, her friend Olga, even po-faced Trevor. None of them was there, so she settled for a hapless marshal, who didn't seem to mind the sweaty embrace.

"Well done, love. You deserve a medal and there's one waiting for you with your goody bag."

"*No time for losers,*" for the umpteenth time. Diamond's head ached from the music and his feet were hurting, although he hadn't run a step. He was getting hungry. He looked at his watch. Gone 3 P.M. Four hours since the start.

An ostrich with swollen ankles hobbled by.

Time to call it a day.

That evening, Diamond drank more beer than was good for him and watched TV with his long-term friend Paloma in her house on Lyncombe Hill. A crime drama was on. He had a feeling he'd watched it before. He may have dozed through some of it. When the commercials came on, he said, "I lose patience when the detective has that light-bulb moment and doesn't share it with anyone else."

"Dramatic licence," Paloma said. "It's the signal to the viewers to make up their own minds. People enjoy that. And they stay tuned to find out if they're right." She spoke from experience of looking at hundreds of scripts and screenplays. She had a successful business in TV and film, providing images for costume dramas.

"I've usually sussed it out already."

"Clever old you. What's bugging you tonight?"

"A blast from the past." He didn't often talk about work issues, but the Pinto case was done and dusted. No harm in sharing it with Paloma. It had made the headlines before he knew her.

After she'd listened, she said, "You let him get under your skin."

"He got under Bryony Lancaster's skin with a Stanley knife."

"But it wasn't murder, Peter. They're not going to lock him away for life. Sometimes we all have to move on."

"The girl still has her scars."

"Have you seen her lately?"

"Not for a long time."

"She could have had cosmetic surgery."

"She'll carry the mental scars for the rest of her life."

"You can say that about anyone touched by a serious

crime." She took a deeper breath and released it before adding, "Admit it, you're scarred mentally and so am I. There are times when it still hurts badly, but we don't dwell on the past and I daresay Bryony doesn't."

He knew exactly what she meant. Her son was still serving a life sentence for murder. She visited him regularly and never spoke of what was said between them, if anything. The strain showed for days afterwards. "Do you think I should warn her Pinto is out of prison?"

"Why?"

"It could come as a horrible shock. It shocked me."

"I wouldn't. He's not a threat anymore. He's probably more scared of meeting her than she will be of him."

"He didn't look scared in that race today. He was as cocksure as ever."

"Are you a hundred per cent certain it was Pinto?"

"Ninety-nine and counting. Most of us have a double somewhere in the world, I've heard." He hesitated and grinned. He'd seen a chance to lighten the mood. "All right, I'll say it for you. Two of me would be hard to take."

"Doesn't bear thinking about."

The commercials had ended. Diamond watched the screen to the end of the show without taking anything in. He couldn't shift Tony Pinto from his thoughts. "Why do people do it?" he asked Paloma when she'd switched off the TV.

"Do what?"

"Run. I can't see the attraction."

"All sorts of reasons. It's the most basic of actions. Cavemen had to run to survive. If you're the right shape and good at it, you'll probably feel the urge to show your paces."

"Me?"

"Not you specially. You have other talents."

He lifted his glass. "Here's to those, whatever they are. What I'm getting at is Pinto's reason for doing the Other Half. Was he in it for the glory of sport or to pull girls?"

"From all you've told me, it was the latter."

"In which case, he didn't need to complete the run if he made a hit already."

"I see what you're getting at. They may have quit the race for a bit of how's your father. Does it really matter?"

He ducked that question. "She didn't look as if she was enjoying his company."

"The woman he was running with? What age would she be?" Paloma was a couple of moves ahead in this verbal chess game.

"I'm not much use at ages. Thirties, maybe."

"And how old is Pinto?"

"Forties."

"Old enough to know what they're doing, both of them."

"Agreed." By now he knew what was coming.

"So they're grown-ups. Forget them."

"I can't forget he's violent."

"Did the woman finish the race?"

"I didn't see her—but there were hundreds in British Heart Foundation shirts and I wasn't looking for her particularly."

"You won't know her name, so you can't check whether she finished."

"She'll have been wearing a number. There's such a thing as CCTV."

"And who's going to scroll through hours and hours of video? You fall asleep in twenty minutes watching *Midsomer Murders*."

He didn't answer. She was right. He ought to let go.

After a pause, Paloma signalled a personal announcement by steepling her hands in front of her chin. "I'd better own up. I've taken up running myself."

He jerked forward and stared at her, fully alert now. "You're kidding."

"I'm not. I was getting breathless walking up the hill

from the station. I decided to do something about it, so I bought myself some trainers and now I pound the streets of Lyncombe Vale every other day. It's doing me good. An inch off my waistline. Haven't you noticed?"

"What time do you do this?"

"After I finish work and before I cook the meal. It's a fascinating time. People are turning on the lights but they haven't pulled the curtains. I see inside front rooms I'll never visit. You'd never believe what some folk get up to at five in the afternoon."

She was making light of this, but he disapproved and needed to let her know without getting heavy about it. "You want to be careful."

"Looking in people's windows?"

"No. Running through dark streets."

She laughed. "Don't go all protective on me, Peter Diamond, or I'll throw you out. I don't need looking after. If you want to join me, that's another thing, but a moment ago you made your views on running very clear."

"Can't you do Pilates or something?"

Paloma's steely look left him in no doubt he was out of order. "This is my choice, Peter. I enjoy it. Don't glare at me like that. I won't be entering marathons in the hope of meeting some sex-starved guy just out of prison."

"If you mean Pinto I should bloody hope not."

"He doesn't sound like any girl's dream date."

"I've looked into that man's eyes and seen something I never want to see again."

"I'm forewarned, then. But the chance of him ever crossing my path is remote."

Unusually for him, Murat was bragging. "I could have filled a sack with all the goodies I was offered. It was like Christmas Day. You should have been there." He tipped the contents of one of the bags on the ground between his own blow-up bed and Spiro's. "Help yourself."

"I'm not hungry."

They were at their latest sleeping quarters in the Parade Gardens under the colonnade that stands below the busy street known as Grand Parade. This prime location had become their private shelter after they had discovered a simple way into the gardens when the main entrance was locked. The inflatable beds had come from Argos, nine pounds ninety-nine each (the cash donated by a German tourist who took pity on them and may not have appreciated the value of a twenty-pound note) and the blankets from a stack left out for the refuse collectors by an old people's home—courtesy of something overheard by Murat in the queue for charity bread and soup.

"Don't be so sniffy, just because you were wrong," Murat said. "I can't eat them all. At least have some of the water."

"I've got my own fucking water."

"Be like that, then."

After a pained pause, Murat started up again. "I know you didn't like me taking the risk, but honestly, Spiro, if you'd been there you would have seen how safe it was. They'd finished their race and they wanted to talk about it to anyone who would listen. Real excitement. Sweaty people with smiles on their faces. Long time since I've seen anywhere as noisy as that."

Spiro wasn't listening. Murat's experiences at the recreation ground were of little interest to him and he had no intention of sharing the trauma of his own terrifying showdown with the Finisher. Nothing could be the same again. What was done was done.

He was here tonight out of loyalty to Murat. Their shared experience as fugitives had forged a bond between them. He'd come to appreciate his big companion's personal qualities, his openness, his trust, his simplicity in the best sense of the word, and his bravery. You can't abandon a mate as staunch as that without warning him. All those months in the work party had taught him little about Murat or any of the others. The last few days had restored his trust in human nature. Here was one truly good, sweet guy who hadn't been crushed into despair or cynicism.

"First thing tomorrow I'm leaving," he said. "I thought you'd want to know."

"Why?" Murat said on a shocked, high-pitched note. "Just when we're getting settled."

"It's not safe to be in Bath any longer, that's why."

"Has something happened?"

He sidestepped the question. "My mind is made up, that's what's happened."

"Because of me?" Murat asked. "You think I'm too much of a risk after what I did today?"

"It's not you. Get that out of your head, Murat. We disagreed, but that's history now. I shouldn't have ranted at you like I did. Like you say, your visit to the athletes' village turned out all right. We've moved on from there. The truth is that I'm the problem here, not you."

Murat shook his head.

"Really," Spiro said. "I'm a marked man now and I'm getting the hell out of here and so must you. They'll be onto you next. But this time we're splitting and no argument. I'm going alone."

13

Next morning in his office at Concorde House, Diamond put everything on hold while contacting the probation service about Pinto. As he expected, he was put on hold himself several times over while various jobsworths passed the buck. Sheer dogged persistence got him eventually to someone called Deirdre who knew about the case. And even she declined to say whether she was Pinto's probation officer.

"He was given parole at the end of last year after serving twelve years of a fifteen-year sentence."

"But is he safe to be at liberty?"

"Why are you asking?"

Too direct, it seemed. He was on the wrong foot already. Dealings between the probation service and the police can be a minefield. "I take an interest because I headed the investigation."

"I see." Spoken in a voice that was jamming on the brakes.

"Seems like yesterday to me," he said, and meant it. "I was shocked to learn he's out."

"After twelve years?"

"For what he did? Doesn't seem long to me."

"Twelve years is a long time to be locked up, Superintendent."

"And he's judged to be no danger now?"

"Low risk. There were positive reports all round. He was visited regularly in prison. He'll be on probation for at least six months and if he breaks the rules of his order he'll be back inside."

"But you can't monitor him twenty-four seven."

Her tone was as dry as the dust on his keyboard. "If there's anything we should know, you'd better tell me. Has he come to your attention in some way, Superintendent?"

"Saw him out yesterday, and that's the first I knew of it. A real blast from the past. He's a reformed character, is he?"

"That's a phrase I wouldn't use about any offender. We can supervise and support up to a point, but there can never be certainty they won't reoffend."

"He was running a half marathon when I spotted him. Did you know about that?"

"I didn't. It's not a crime, is it?"

"I'm surprised a man so recently out of prison is ready to enter a long-distance race. He looked tanned, fit and well capable."

"There's nothing remarkable in that. He saw out his sentence in Berwyn."

"Does it matter where he was?"

"In this case, yes. The so-called super-prison opened a couple of years ago."

"I may have heard of it. Where?"

"Wrexham, in North Wales. Pinto was one of the first to be sent there."

"Super in what sense?"

"There's been a lot in the media. It's huge and well equipped and the emphasis is firmly on rehabilitation."

He resisted the impulse to say something sarcastic. "How do they achieve that?"

"By treating the inmates as human beings," she said loftily, as if she was speaking to a Neanderthal. "They're allowed laptops, TV and phones. Prison officers knock on the doors of cells before entering. That sort of thing." .

"Better than most of them get at home."

"You're right about that."

"And are there sports facilities?"

"That's what I was coming to. I haven't visited yet, but I'm told they're amazing—a gym with all the latest exercise machines, sports hall, football pitch and so on. If he's any kind of runner, he'll have used the treadmills for sure."

"By choice?"

"I expect so."

"Not the treadmills I'm thinking of, then."

She mellowed enough to manage a faint laugh. "Definitely not."

"Sounds like he worked on his tan while doing laps of the football pitch, or lounging out there."

"It's no holiday camp. I may have given the wrong impression. They've already experienced the problems endemic in the system."

"Such as?"

"Drug use, fires, dirty protests, assaults on staff."

"Some people never change. How many inmates are there?"

"The building is designed to take over two thousand."

He whistled.

"But they're not up to capacity yet."

"Even so. *Two thousand*?"

"The biggest in Europe, I'm told. Two to a room, and that's unpopular. They have to shower and use the toilets in full view of each other."

"You said 'room,' I noticed."

"They don't call them cells, just as the wings are called houses."

"What do they call the governor—headmaster?" She wasn't in tune with his humour so he moved on quickly. "So Pinto had at least two years in this enlightened set-up?"

"He was coming to the end of his sentence and he behaved well at his previous prison."

"Does that entitle him to an extra handout?"

"What do you mean?"

"How much did he get on release?"

"The usual. Forty-six pounds to tide him over until he qualifies for the job-seeker's allowance—and that can take weeks, as you know."

"The reason I ask is that he was expensively kitted out when I saw him. The trainers he was wearing will have cost at least ninety."

"He may have private means. Who knows?"

"Shouldn't his probation officer know?"

"Not if it's legal."

"Does he have a job yet?"

"There's no record of one, and I've answered enough of your questions, Superintendent."

"Do you have an address for him?"

"I'm not at liberty to reveal it."

A red mist blocked his brain. Through it he heard a faint note of reason pleading with him to rise above his fury and stay in control. "What's the problem?"

"It's MAPPA."

"Who's she when she's at home?"

"The multi-agency public protection arrangements."

An acronym, for crying out loud. She was talking about an extra level of bureaucracy. "Aren't you part of this?"

"We're represented. And so are the police and other agencies. All the details of MAPPA offenders are held in a secure database called VISOR."

He wasn't going to ask what that stood for. He was picturing a committee of Home Office eggheads with no other job but thinking up sets of letters that resembled words.

Deirdre added, "I would need to consult the probation service offender manager before I could reveal the address and that would be at his discretion. They have strict guidelines."

"I'll save you the trouble," he said. "I'll get it from the police member now I know we're represented on this quango."

"Suit yourself."

"When's Pinto's next appointment with you people?"

"This afternoon. But if you think we're going to turn him over to you, you've got another think coming."

The famous Diamond charm hadn't worked its magic on Deirdre.

He checked the Other Half website and found a report of yesterday's race, but only the top ten finishers in each category were listed. A complete result list would appear later, he learned. He phoned and asked if they could supply him with a list of all the runners who started. When they said it couldn't be done because there was a huge amount to be sorted out on the day after a major half marathon, he was tempted to pull rank and say it was an urgent police matter, but good sense prevailed and he held off.

He'd already walked on eggs, pressurising Deirdre, and now he'd been on the point of doing the same with the race organisers. His hunch that Pinto had been up to no good had better be well-founded. If the high-ups got to hear he was using his rank to extract information about an ex-offender purely on his intense dislike of the man, he'd be in serious trouble.

Unrepentant, he used his rank to start another line of enquiry. He called Paul Gilbert in. "You remember Pinto, the ex-con I told you about, the guy we saw in the race?"

"Of course I do, guv."

"He's due to meet his probation officer this afternoon. You'll be doing a recce outside their office at the Old

Convent in Pulteney Road. Watch him go in and wait for him to come out. Then follow him back to wherever he lives. I need to know his address."

As if she'd got wind of all this, Georgina Dallymore, the Assistant Chief Constable, presently stepped into his room wearing her fault-finding look as domineeringly as her silver-trimmed uniform.

"What are you doing?"

"Working, ma'am."

"What on?"

"Borrowed time."

"You're not dying, are you?"

Did he detect a note of optimism? He gave her an answer that stretched the truth by a few hours. "I was negotiating the overtime allowance with Inspector Walker, of uniform. He owes me some. A lot of my detectives were on duty yesterday keeping an eye on the Other Half."

She blinked, baffled. "Husbands and wives?"

He'd had a tough morning, but he enjoyed that. "Runners. Thousands of them in the half marathon."

"That other half. I understand you now. And did it go smoothly?"

"Smoothly as these things can. Some of them looked anything but smooth at the finish."

"I was at morning service in the choir." She planted herself in the armchair in the corner, always an ominous move. "I don't suppose you've had time to read the latest bulletin from ROCU."

"As in 'We will . . .'?"

"Be serious for once. The Regional Organised Crime Unit."

Was he being victimised or did he have a persecution complex? "In that case, no, I haven't."

"They're recommending the greater use of unmanned aerial vehicles."

Flying saucers crossed his thoughts but he kept them to himself. "Now you've lost me altogether."

"Drones, Peter."

"Ah."

"For surveillance. Wiltshire Police have won a special award from the Home Office for technical innovation. They have a team of five ready to attend incidents."

"Five drones?"

"Pilots."

"You just said they were unmanned."

"The pilots control the drones from the ground."

"Five policemen doing nothing but playing with drones? How can Wiltshire justify that when my team and I are doubling up on marathon duty?"

"They're specials."

"We all like to think we're special, ma'am."

"Special constables. Local enthusiasts recruited for their skills. All volunteers."

"Something for nothing, then?"

"I wouldn't put it so crudely. They get expenses."

"Cheap at the price."

"And that's a cheap comment. I'm surprised you haven't thought of this. It would be a boon to your activities, making searches of dangerous environments, looking for weapons, stolen property, fugitives on the run. Frankly I was disappointed to learn that Wiltshire are ahead of us. If an incident happened today, we'd have to enlist their help."

"Good thing, too," Diamond said, quick to see an opening. "We're always being encouraged to share with other forces."

Georgina wasn't impressed. These days, she was taking every chance to buff up her reputation. There was still a vacancy for the job of Deputy Chief Constable of Avon and Somerset. She turned her head to gaze out of the window at the empty sky over the Avon portion of the empire. "I want a drone team of our own. We must embrace the new technology. We have vast areas of countryside to police. This is an essential aid."

"The eye in the sky."

"You've got it."

"I haven't yet."

"See that you do, Peter. Make enquiries locally. Find the enthusiasts and recruit them. Reliable people, of course."

"Where? The Drones Club?"

She frowned, uncertain if she was being sent up. "If one exists in Bath, yes."

"I'm sure it must, ma'am."

After she'd gone, he kicked the wastepaper bin and made another dent in it. Typical Georgina, wanting something for nothing. But on reflection he started to see that drones might be of use. They would have been helpful on Sunday, patrolling the Other Half when it was out in the country. He called out to DCI Halliwell. "Keith—I've got a job for you."

14

"Would you believe it?"

"What's that?" Sergeant Ingeborg Smith asked. She'd come into Diamond's office late in the afternoon and found him staring fixedly at his computer screen, a rare occurrence.

"A waste of space I put away years ago."

"In the headlines again?"

"Let's hope not. I was sure I spotted him running in the Other Half on Sunday. Paul Gilbert and I waited ages at the finish just to be certain, but we missed him."

"Perhaps he dropped out."

"No. I've just downloaded the complete results and he finished after we gave up and left—in four thousand six hundred and twenty-seventh place. It's here in front of me: Tony Pinto. He must have walked in, or crawled. Time four hours, twenty-three minutes, twenty-six seconds. So I wasn't wrong."

"Not much of an effort for a half marathon," Ingeborg said. "I'd have given up well before then. Do you think he walked literally? It's average walking pace, about three miles an hour."

"He ran at least some of the way. He was going at a fair lick when he passed us."

"I expect he broke down at some point and needed to recover."

"Or was otherwise occupied. When we saw him he was chatting up a blonde in a red T-shirt."

"What are you suggesting, guv?"

"I thought it was obvious."

"They took time out for sex? Why not say it, then?"

"Because I'm an officer and a gentleman."

"Ho ho ho."

"Pinto was always a randy sonofabitch. The course is out in the country, over footpaths and through tunnels for much of the way. It wouldn't be hard to find a secluded spot."

"As long as it was consensual, I don't see a problem with that."

"When I saw them, it didn't look consensual. She wasn't enjoying his company. Hard to be certain when two people run past you, but he was doing all the talking and she was unimpressed."

"I still don't see the problem."

"He has a record of violence."

"What sort of violence?"

He explained about the knifing of Bryony Lancaster.

Ingeborg heard him in silence apart from several sharp, horrified breaths. Their conversation had got serious.

"I'm not assuming it happened a second time," Diamond went on. "He had no grudge against this woman as far as I know, and runners don't normally carry knives, but for my peace of mind I'd like to know if she finished the race."

"So would I," she said, fully alert to the danger. "You've got the results in front of you."

"I don't know her name. I was so shocked to see Pinto at liberty that I didn't even make a note of her number."

"But you remember what she looked like?"

"Blonde, thirtyish, with a good figure."

"That's all?" Ingeborg's eyes rolled upwards, leaving no doubt what she thought about male perceptions of women.

As it happened, she, too, was blonde, thirtyish and with a good figure.

"She was wearing a cap with a ponytail poking out of the back of it. That's how I knew she was blonde."

"T-shirt?"

"Red, with the heartbeat logo so many of them were wearing."

"The British Heart Foundation. We're getting somewhere."

"It's a long way short of identifying her."

"You carry a phone. You should have taken a picture of them."

"To me, Inge, a phone is a phone."

She let it pass. "We need CCTV footage. Then we can get the number she was wearing."

"I thought of that, but we're talking about five thousand runners. I don't know if I'd recognise her."

"You'd recognise Pinto and she was with him. Where were you when you saw them?"

"In Sydney Gardens, soon after the start. No cameras there."

Ingeborg was already committed to the cause. "May I see what you've got on your screen?" She didn't wait for an answer. She was round his side of the desk and leaning over his shoulder. "I thought so. They give a split time for each runner at ten K. They're able to do that electronically as they pass over the mat. His time is fifty-eight twenty. That's reasonable going. He was definitely running at that stage. We have two ways to go here. Either we ask if they had CCTV at the ten-K point, which is quite possible, or we see if we can get the names of everyone who passed there within a few seconds either side of Pinto's time. Let's do both. I can get in touch with the organisers."

He was swept along by her positivity. "Okay, but don't

be too obvious about it or I could be accused of running a witch hunt."

After she'd returned to her desk, he had a twinge of unease. This had started as a personal quest, a visceral reaction to what he'd seen, but already he'd shared his misgivings with others—Paul Gilbert, Paloma, Deirdre and now Ingeborg—and everything up to now was supposition. Keeping a lid on it would be difficult.

Images of the race were already posted on the website, so he studied them keenly. Finding one of Pinto and his companion was a long shot that had to be tried. Most could be eliminated at a glance. The first batch were the elite runners, wearing three-digit numbers. Pinto's number had been 2714. Actually there weren't many shots from the middle section of the race and none that were helpful. The picture-takers had chosen instead to feature the fancy-dress people, among them, the ostrich with lumpy legs.

One batch of photos featured the railway tunnels, back views of runners entering and sinister-looking silhouetted figures chasing their shadows towards the next dim light. Pity any woman who found herself in there with Tony Pinto for company. Combe Down tunnel was a mile long.

Ingeborg returned, eager to report.

"I'll give you the bad news first. No video camera at the ten-K mark. Plenty of people were there taking pictures of their own and there may be something helpful, but we can't build up our hopes."

"The good news?"

She put a sheet in front of him. "Never knock computers again. A click of the sort function and we get a list of everyone's time in sequence as they crossed the ten-K line. Pinto's was fifty-eight twenty, so I homed in on that and got the runners just before and after."

He glanced at the names:

2618	Polly Perez	Shelter	SF	58:09.6
2800	David Smith		VM45	58:11.0
2589	Amber Jackson	WWF	VW40	58:11.2
2612	Phil Spenser	WWF	VM45	58:12.0
2645	Belinda Pye	BHF	SF	58:19.8
2714	Tony Pinto		SM	58:20.0
2817	Paul Davidson	Oxfam	JM	58:21.0
2629	Adrian Hardaker		VM40	58:59.6
2736	Susie Bingham	BHF	SF	59:03.8

"Top of the class, Inge. You seem to have found her. Pinto in close attendance."

"They crossed almost together."

"I can understand the names of the charities and I can believe Pinto wasn't sponsored. What does the SM stand for if it isn't sex mad?"

"Senior male, between twenty and forty."

"Which is untrue. He lied about his age. He wouldn't want to be known as a veteran. So we have a name for the blonde: Belinda Pye."

"And we can't rule out Susie Bingham," Ingeborg said. "Even forty-three seconds behind, in a BHF shirt, she could still be your woman."

"Let's concentrate on Belinda first. Put my mind at rest and tell me she finished the race."

"I haven't checked yet."

"Do it, then. I'm still on the website."

She took the mouse. "It should be simple. We can sort by name. Oh, Jesus."

The data on the screen was clear.

2645   Belinda Pye   BHF   SF   58:19.8   DNF

"Is DNF what I think it means?" Diamond said.

"I'm afraid so."

His skin prickled all over. "Get onto the organisers. They must have a contact number for her."

Ingeborg snatched up his phone and got through to the Other Half office. Diamond switched to speakerphone.

No messing. Ingeborg said straight away that she was from the police, enquiring about a runner giving cause for concern. She insisted on knowing the name of the man she'd reached—always a wise move. Apart from assisting communications, it didn't allow them to retreat behind their organisation.

Brian Johns was as helpful as he could be, allowing that Belinda Pye was only a name to him, too. He confirmed from the records that she was a non-finisher. There had been no reports that she was an emergency for any reason. More than a hundred had failed to finish. It was a demanding course and some entrants weren't well prepared. Most who dropped out made their own way back to the start with the help of friends or volunteers, collected their bags from the baggage tent in the runners' village behind the Sports Centre, and left.

"So you'd know if Belinda didn't collect her bag?"

"There are always some bags people don't bother to collect after the race for a variety of reasons."

"Obviously you know who they belong to."

"They're all marked with the race numbers."

"Can you check whether Belinda's was collected?"

"If it wasn't, it will be stored by now. The tent is taken down overnight."

"It's important, Brian," Ingeborg stressed. "We need to know urgently."

"I'll get someone onto it and call you back."

"Hold on. We also need all the information you have on her: full name, contact numbers, address. What else do you ask for?"

"They're required to supply an emergency contact name and phone number."

"Good. That, too. Bring everything up on your system and forward it to us now, please."

Brian Johns hesitated. "These details are given to us in confidence. She isn't under investigation, is she?"

"If she were, we'd need them anyway. As it happens, we're concerned for her well-being."

"She isn't in hospital?"

"Not that we've heard. Would you do this directly, please? I'm Detective Sergeant Ingeborg Smith." She told him her email address and direct line.

"With any luck," she told Diamond when she'd ended the call, "we'll be able to phone her shortly and make sure she got home safely."

"I'm trying to get Pinto's address as well." He hadn't heard anything yet from Paul Gilbert, but he had to admit to himself that the priority now was Belinda, as Ingeborg's next statement made clear.

"Not if she's okay, guv. He'll be in the clear."

"There's that other woman in the BHF shirt," he reminded her. "Susie Bingham. We haven't checked whether she finished the race."

"Let's do it, then."

They returned to the results. Susie Bingham had recorded a time of just under three hours for the full distance.

"So Susie is okay. We can eliminate her," Ingeborg said.

"Not yet. We may need to interview most of these runners, particularly those coming behind. If Belinda retired from the race, they may have seen the incident."

She nodded. The boss was covering every angle, as he should. She checked her phone for messages. Nothing yet from Brian Johns. "Anything else we should be doing?"

"See if she's on Facebook or Twitter or any of those."

"That will be easier when we know where she lives."

"Bath, I'm assuming."

"It's not so simple. People travel quite long distances to join in races like this one. Here we go—a message from Brian."

The email undermined Ingeborg's last remark. Belinda Pye had an address in Spring Gardens Road, Bath.

"You know where that is?" Diamond said, but not in a told-you-so way. "Right on the riverbank, on the other side from where the nick was. If I remember right, it's nineteen-sixties terraced housing. Try her mobile first."

She touched in the numbers. "I'm getting unavailable."

"Is there a second number, a landline?"

"No."

"So what's this other number?"

"That's the friend she had to nominate in case of emergencies."

"This is an emergency."

"Okay." Ingeborg dialled it up and listened. "Busy."

"Ask for ringback. What's the friend's address? Is that in Bath as well?"

"St. Michaels Road, Twerton. Bella Kilbury."

"Still busy?"

"Hang on, it's dialling." She nodded to him as she started the call. "Ms. Bella Kilbury? This is Bath Police, Sergeant Ingeborg Smith, with an enquiry about Belinda Pye, who I believe is known to you. She nominated you as the go-to person when she entered for a half marathon here in Bath. Does that make sense?" She gave the thumbs-up to Diamond. "Have you spoken to her since the race? . . . I see . . . We'd like to know a little more about her. She lives in Spring Gardens Road, I believe."

From the lengthy gap in the conversation, Bella Kilbury was talking freely about her friend. Ingeborg didn't need to prompt her much.

"No, it's a routine enquiry, but we may need to get back to

you . . . Can you give me Belinda's email address? . . . Thanks. You've been helpful." She ended the call and turned to Diamond. "They went through university together. Belinda is thirty-two, works in IT, mostly from home, which is a rented bedsit in a private house in Spring Gardens Road. She took up running about a year ago because she felt she spent too much time in front of the computer. She decided to enter the Bath Half to give her an extra incentive, but applied too late, so signed up for the Other Half. Managed to get in as a BHF runner and raised most of the sponsorship money over the internet. She's quite shy and confessed to Bella that she didn't want to ask people face to face. No current boyfriend. Extremely conscientious. An introvert, according to Bella, but a lovely character when you get to know her. She asked Bella's permission to name her as the person to reach in an emergency, but said she didn't want Bella to turn up to cheer her on. That's a measure of how shy she is."

"I'm getting the picture. Did you ask about her hair?"

"The blonde ponytail?" Ingeborg said. "Stupid. I should have done."

"I don't like this," he said. "The nervous woman under pressure from a predator like Pinto. She'd find it difficult to shake him off."

"Any woman would, from what you've told me."

"Yes, but some might enjoy the attention."

"Not many, from a skunk like him."

"Don't be so sure. He had a technique that worked."

"Once."

"Once was all he needed."

He needed to visit Spring Gardens Road, leaving Ingeborg to deal with any more information coming in from Brian, the Other Half man. There was still a chance Belinda might be back in her bedsit and getting over the bad experience of the day before. He had to keep reminding himself that his worst fears about her fate were speculation. He was always warning the team about making unsafe assumptions.

The drive down Pulteney Road, with the Sports Centre to his right, made him aware how close Spring Gardens Road was to the open area that became the runners' village on the day of the half marathon. Belinda wouldn't have needed to store her bag in the tent provided. She could go straight from home to the start. If she chose to wear an extra layer she could do what many others did and use an old, unwanted sweater that one of the charities would gratefully collect and recycle.

The street was right beside the Avon, facing the post office sorting office. The houses were terraced and built in the same unattractive yellow stone used for his old workplace in Manvers Street.

He noticed the twitch of a curtain at a downstairs window before he rang the bell. The occupant wasn't quick in coming to the door and when she answered it was from behind a safety chain.

"I don't buy anything at the door." The voice was thin and elderly and came from halfway down the narrow space. She must have been under five feet tall.

"Madam," he said. "I'm not a salesman. I'm from the police."

If these were meant as reassuring words, they had the opposite effect. She slammed the door hard and he heard a bolt being forced home.

He stooped to raise the flap on the letterbox. "You're not in trouble. I'm here about Belinda, your lodger."

No response, so he tried again.

"I don't want to force the door."

After more seconds passed, he heard the bolt withdrawn

and the latch turned. The slit between door and frame reappeared, but she left the safety chain on.

"I need your help. Is Belinda in there with you?"

"No."

"Was she here last night?"

"No."

"I need to know she's safe."

"Go away."

"I'm not going anywhere until I get what I came for. I've reason to be worried about her. Here's my ID. Can you see?" He held it at what he thought was her level. "Superintendent Peter Diamond. What's your name, ma'am?"

"Mrs. Hector."

"Let's do this in a civilised way, Mrs. Hector. I can call for assistance, but you don't want a police car outside and you don't want your door knocked down with a battering ram."

She closed the door again, but this time to free the safety chain. Revealed, she stood defiantly in the doorway with arms folded, a wisp of a woman in apron and slippers, short as a broom handle and not much broader. "This is not a council house," she said. "It's privately owned by Mr. Patel. I'm allowed to have a lodger."

"I believe you, Mrs. Hector," he said, understanding her behaviour better. There was an issue over subletting that he didn't want to go into. "My only concern is Belinda and what happened on Sunday. Did you know she was in the half marathon?"

"Of course I did. I went to watch her. They came down Pulteney Road."

"You saw her run past?"

"I clapped and gave her a cheer when she came by. I don't know if she heard me. Someone was talking to her."

"A man? Blue headband, yellow shirt and blue shorts?"

"That was him."

"And did you notice whether she was talking back to him?"

"Belinda?" Mrs. Hector said with disbelief. "She's shyer than a limpet. She wouldn't talk to a strange man if her life depended on it."

"I'm glad to hear it. This man isn't nice."

"He looked all right to me. A bit of a lad, is he?"

"He's more than that. And did you see the finish as well?"

"No. I went shopping. It was going to be a long race. She could have been hours. I'm not all that interested in sport."

"Did she come back here after it was over?"

"I've no idea. She can come and go. She has her own keys."

"Did she sleep here last night? Surely you'd know?"

"I don't spy on my tenants."

"Do you have more than one, then?" Maybe that was what was making her so jumpy. He couldn't believe this small house had more than two bedrooms.

"Of course not. I was speaking generally."

"She's the sole occupier of the room?"

"Didn't I just say?"

"Have you seen her at all since the race?"

"No. Why are you asking me these questions?"

"I told you. The man she was with is known to us. We're concerned about Belinda's safety. It's important to know whether she came back here. Is it possible she returned and got changed and went out again?"

"She could have. I wasn't here all afternoon."

"Would she tell you if she was going to be out all night?"

"I expect so. I don't think it's ever happened."

"May I see inside her room?"

"Certainly not."

Faced with a denial like that, Diamond needed a Plan B. "I don't want to alarm you, Mrs. Hector, but it's not impossible that what's behind that door is a situation you might find distressing. Wouldn't you rather I took a look inside than you?"

She turned ashen. "What are you saying? Is she dead?"

"I don't know, ma'am. I honestly don't know, but it's my job to find out."

"You've frightened me now."

"I didn't mean to," he lied.

"I won't want to be alone with a dead body in my own house."

"Which is why I must go up and check."

"You'd better." She stepped back and made way, adding, "You can see for yourself, only one lodger lives here."

Mrs. Hector handed Diamond a key and remained in the hallway with the hem of her apron tugged up and gripped between her teeth.

Belinda's was the first door at the top of the stairs. He unlocked it and let the door swing open. In truth, he wasn't expecting to find a corpse. If Belinda was dead, she was likely to be miles away, lying unseen in scrubland along the Other Half course.

What he found was a neat, uncluttered bedsitting room that looked as if it hadn't been used for days. Quilt four-square on the bed. Pillow plumped. Desktop empty except for a small row of books and a closed laptop. TV, armchair and upright chair. Small fridge and microwave with a few food items on the top. He opened the fitted wardrobe and found a line of clothes on hangers and some pairs of boots, shoes and trainers.

So tidy it was soulless.

The lack of any personal touches was more sinister than if the place had been strewn with signs of habitation. Belinda Pye wasn't here. She hadn't been here for some time. Whether she would ever come back was an open question.

"Is she in there?" Mrs. Hector's anxious voice from downstairs.

"No, ma'am, I'm happy to tell you she isn't."

Happy? How can I be happy? he thought. Belinda was

last seen running with Pinto beside her. She'd failed to finish the race and she hadn't come home.

Normally when searching, he would have opened drawers and examined the laptop for clues about the young woman's lifestyle and contacts, but in this case it would be an invasion of privacy that wasn't justified or necessary. The situation was clear. If she was anything, she was a victim, almost a random victim. Pinto was the aggressor.

He closed the door and returned downstairs.

"Is she going to be all right, then?" Mrs. Hector asked.

"I can't say until we find her. She may be okay, but we don't know why no one has seen her. Did she have any callers, friends or family?"

Mrs. Hector shook her head. "She liked to be independent."

"If she comes back—" he started to say.

"I hope not," she cut him short. "I'll have a heart attack."

"Don't be like that. Let's be positive. When she appears, ask her to call Bath Police right away. She had to give the race organisers the name of someone to contact in an emergency and she named a friend called Bella Kilbury, who lives in Twerton. Ring any bells?"

"Means nothing to me. What shall I do about the room?"

"Do nothing until you hear from us."

He left that house more uneasy than when he'd arrived.

15

Diamond's fears for Belinda were built on the flimsiest of foundations—a single sighting in the park—but they were as strong as the building he worked in. That inner voice of his was insisting he must see this through, or he'd have regrets for the rest of his life. The next obvious move was to visit Tony Pinto, only there were sound reasons not to. The creep would be sure to complain to his probation officer that he was being victimised. Without real evidence, the whole thing could backfire.

Before driving off from Spring Gardens Road, he looked at his phone. Ingeborg had texted to say that the check of runners' unclaimed bags had proved negative. No surprise, that. More concerning, she was not responding to emails or answering her phone.

A voice message asked him to contact DCI Halliwell.

"Keith, you wanted me."

"Guv. It's just to tell you I followed up on the drones and we're in luck."

"Are we?" He couldn't raise any enthusiasm. He'd forgotten about the pesky drones.

"Ever heard of The Sky's No Limit? It's a family firm based here in Bath. Brother and sister with degrees in engineering build and fly the drones and their father manages the business side. They're at Claverton, near the university."

"Handy."

"They're good. They've won loads of international awards with their UAVs."

"You've lost me already, Keith."

"Unmanned aerial vehicles. I spoke to the father and they don't mind helping the police as long as it's ethical."

"What does he mean by that?"

"They're Quakers. They live by certain principles."

"How did you answer that?"

"I said it was about making searches, like for a lost child."

"Sounds ethical to me."

"Yes, he'd heard about them being used to spy on people in protest marches and he doesn't care for that. I told him we'd draw up some guidelines."

"Smart thinking. Will he be tricky to deal with?"

"I don't think so. Once we'd got that settled, he was fine."

"Did you offer to appoint them as special constables?"

"I wasn't sure how he'd take it, so I didn't. He might not want to be identified with our lot."

"You surprise me. So how did you leave it?"

"He'll talk to the others and fix a time when we can see the drones in action."

"Where?" An idea sprouted in Diamond's brain.

"Up at the campus site on Claverton Down."

"Which part?"

"The playing fields."

"That's no use."

"Why not?"

"It's a billiard table. We want to give them a real test. Combe Down is the place. Plenty of scrub and uneven ground, trees, old quarries, the canal. Let's see how they perform over difficult terrain."

"They won't want to damage their drones."

"They're no bloody use to us if they can't work in testing

conditions. Get the demo sorted for as soon as possible. I'll
be there and I'll make sure Georgina is as well."

He still hadn't found where Pinto was living. Posting
Paul Gilbert outside the probation office all afternoon had
not worked. Paul had called to report that he'd waited
and seen nothing of the guy. The safest bet would have
been to try contacting the police delegate to the MAPPA
committee, but going through official channels would be
a giveaway that he was hot on the trail of an allegedly
reformed ex-con. He called Brian Johns, the helpful guy
from the Other Half team, and listened patiently to the
speech about confidentiality.

"I appreciate where you're coming from, but I really do
need to know. It's a police matter."

"Yes," Johns said, "but there has to be some overriding
emergency. I gave you the details of that woman—I forget
her name . . ."

"Belinda Pye."

". . . because she didn't finish the race and there was
concern about her."

"Correct, and now I'm concerned about another runner
called Tony Pinto."

"Did he finish?"

Finished Belinda, if my worst fears are right, Diamond
thought. "One of the last, I think, but we need to contact
him urgently."

"Is it a medical emergency?"

"It may well be."

A sigh. "Wait a moment." A few seconds passed. "All
we have for Pinto's address is a post office box number.
There's a mobile number."

Diamond noted them. Should have expected this, he
thought. The far side of the moon is easier to reach than
bloody Pinto.

With no confidence of a result, he tried the mobile number.

Unrecognised.

The box number would be impenetrable without legal documentation. For the present, Pinto's privacy was safe.

Spiro felt bad about abandoning Murat. The desolation on that already troubled face would stay in his memory forever. The plain truth was that Murat now had a better chance of remaining free if he was unaccompanied. Whether he could survive alone on the streets was another question. He wasn't streetwise or independent-minded. He didn't want to make decisions for himself. He was loyal, truthful, uncomplaining and willing to learn, but alone with his memories he would be a tortured soul.

"I've been thinking about your situation," Spiro said when they were both in their blow-up beds. They generally exchanged a few words before sleeping. "Maybe after all you should stay on in Bath. You're much better than me at picking up the language and you make friends and blend in." He was speaking as much to his own conscience as to Murat. "You'll get to know some of these guys we see every night at the food van. They aren't all druggies and alcoholics. They can tell you're no threat to them. They'll show you what's safe to do in this town and what isn't."

"If it's okay for me, why can't you stay here as well?" Murat asked.

"Me, I'm a marked man now. I don't think I said before. I was unlucky. I was recognised. The Finisher knows I'm here. I'm getting out."

"Him?" Murat said, and he rolled over to look at Spiro. "How can he know? Did someone tell him?"

"Something like that." Spiro didn't want to revisit the moment, even in his imagination.

"But nobody in this town knows who we are," Murat said. "I haven't told a soul."

"I'm not blaming you. It's my own stupid fault. The wrong place at the wrong time. Say your prayers and go to sleep."

Some minutes later, Murat started up again. "Where will you be if I want to link up with you later?"

"How would I know? Anything could happen."

"Where are you heading?"

"Shut the fuck up and get some sleep, man."

They were the last words spoken between them. Spiro would be burdened by guilt, but he knew what would happen if he gave even a hint of his plan to Murat.

Before dawn when Murat was mumbling in his sleep, Spiro got up, stuffed a few things into a carrier bag and left. He didn't take the inflatable bed or the blanket, figuring they would come in useful to Murat as goodwill offerings to other rough sleepers.

In fact, he returned to the railway station where a few bikes had been left in the racks overnight, helped himself to his best ride yet, a Claud Butler with a wide spread of gears and semi-slick tyres, and was out of Bath on the Kennet and Avon Canal towpath before Murat would be awake. This time he headed in a new direction out of town, the way the runners had gone in the half marathon, a winding route that almost turned back on itself to bypass the hills to the east, but one that should be quiet at this time of day.

He was going nicely when the rain started after only about thirty minutes. He didn't intend to get soaked, so he vowed to take shelter under the next bridge he reached, a huge four-arched construction that turned out to be an aqueduct allowing the canal to pass over the river and the railway. This, he realised with a shock, was the scene of his nerve-shattering experience the day before: the Dundas Aqueduct. He'd approached it from another direction.

Quick change of plan. He'd take the drenching and ride on. There was no reason why the Finisher should be around today, but this place gave Spiro the creeps.

At intervals along this canal, longboats were moored, apparently privately owned. Some were people's homes and some looked as if they hadn't been used in months. He had the wild idea of boarding one and seeing if he could get the engine working. He knew how to hotwire a car, so why not a boat? He could take the bike on board and make slower but less obvious progress and he'd have a roof over his head at nights. There might even be food inside.

An attractive idea, but he felt a visceral need to put quick miles between himself and Bath.

By mid-morning he was as wet as any of the ducks in the canal, yet starting to feel safer. He'd reached a place called Caen Hill and was looking downhill towards a town called Devizes. So how did the canal continue to function? By means of a flight of sixteen locks, side by side, enough to test the patience and arm muscles of anyone using a longboat. Spiro, freewheeling, sped by them all and congratulated himself on resisting his earlier temptation to become a bargee.

How would he survive in the longer term? He liked what he'd seen so far of England. The people, the down-and-outs he'd met, were mostly all right and less nosy than Albanians. What he would need was a job that paid a living wage, cash in hand and no questions asked. Not easy, but not impossible. He'd learned a few skills back home. He could clean cars but, from all he'd seen, the car-cleaning was monopolised here by immigrant groups who made sure the work was shared only by people of their own nationality. Cleaning shop windows was more open to private enterprise, but first you needed the bucket, squeegee and a portable A-frame ladder. Every job brought its own problems.

Near Devizes he found a board with a map of the canal. Miles of it were left to travel before it joined the River Kennet and a town called Reading. At the speed he was going he'd be there by nightfall.

* * *

Diamond drove back to Concorde House through a thunderstorm while asking himself how a prisoner on parole could find thirty pounds a month to pay for a box number. The money this man was lashing out was a mystery in itself.

In the CID office, he was greeted by Keith Halliwell with the news that The Sky's No Limit were willing to demonstrate their latest UAV at Combe Down on Wednesday morning. The rough terrain would be no problem.

He bristled at the use of the acronym. "What are you on about?"

"The drone, guv."

"Call it that, then, so people can understand. Will it have a camera attached?"

"I didn't ask."

"We're not interested in a flying display. Get back to them."

This sounded like a putdown, and Halliwell's face showed it, but an order was an order. He reached for the phone.

After Diamond went upstairs to tell Georgina about Wednesday, there were mutterings in the team. Halliwell, clearly bruised, shook his head. "I don't know what's got into him. First he wants the show moved to Combe Down and I fix that and now he wants a drone with a camera. I wish he'd make up his mind."

"I can tell you," Ingeborg said from across the office. "It's on the marathon route and he thinks there could be a body up there. The woman he saw running with Tony Pinto didn't finish the race and no one has seen her since."

"Doesn't mean Pinto clobbered her. It's supposition."

"It's more than that for him. It goes deep. He was telling me what Pinto did to that girl Bryony."

"I know," Halliwell said. "I was here at the time and the scarring was horrible, but you can't let a thing like that take root in your brain. You move on. Christ only knows we've seen some evil bastards over the years. What's so different about this one?"

Paul Gilbert had just walked in after his frustrating afternoon. "It was the shock of seeing Pinto at liberty chatting to a woman like old times, like nothing had happened."

"Maybe," Halliwell said, "but Pinto is basically a lech. He likes one-night stands. He's not going to change. Cutting Bryony Lancaster was an exceptional act."

"I don't believe I'm hearing this," Ingeborg said.

"What I'm saying is that he doesn't routinely attack women. He did it once and paid the price and there's no certainty he'll do it again."

"Oh, come on. Get real, Keith. All she did was warn other women about him. For that, she gets her face slashed with a Stanley knife. The guv'nor says he's evil and I'm with him."

"And I'm not here to argue Pinto's case, but there's such a thing as redemption."

"A leopard can't change its spots."

"No point in reasoning with you, then."

That evening, Diamond visited Paloma in her house on Lyncombe Hill and told her about the drone demonstration.

"Have you seen one of them close up?" he asked. "You might like to come along."

"Normally I would," she said, "but my neighbour Miriam had to go off to Liverpool in a hurry this morning, poor soul. Her mother's had a massive stroke. I'm keeping an eye on things for her."

"Round the clock?"

She smiled. "In a way, yes. I'll show you." She walked through the sitting room to the patio door and opened it. Out in the garden under an apple tree in blossom was a small brown and white dog with floppy ears. "That's Hartley. I'm in charge of him as well."

Hartley lifted his head, barked several times, scampered across the lawn and allowed himself to be fussed over, or, to phrase it accurately, demanded to be fussed over. "Friendly little guy," Diamond said, straightening up. "A beagle, isn't he?"

"Yes. He's a charmer, but he needs watching in the house. Miriam warned me not to leave him alone because he's very destructive. He chewed through several of her shoes, a Persian rug and an electric cable. The cable is worrying. I've got so much electrical gear."

"You could bring him to the drone show. Up at Combe Down he won't get bored."

"He'd eat the drone."

He laughed. "I'd enjoy that."

"I suppose I could keep him on the leash."

"Bring him, then."

She didn't answer immediately. "Why are you doing this? Does it have something to do with that man who was released from prison?"

"Pinto. Yes and no. The interest in drones comes from Georgina."

"She's forward-looking."

Piqued, he said, "It's not her idea. She got it from another police authority."

"Fair enough. Henry Ford didn't invent the motor car."

"Are you comparing Georgina Dallymore to Henry Ford?"

"Okay, Amelia Earhart might fit better. Georgina is smart enough to embrace the new technology. That's how she gets ahead."

"I wouldn't call it new," he said. "I was flying remote-controlled model aircraft when I was a boy. That's all it is."

She smiled at his reluctance to give any credit to Georgina. "A moment ago I asked what's in it for you?"

"The half marathon went over Combe Down. Pinto

finished in a very slow time, but the woman he was pestering didn't and she didn't go home that night. It's a wild, overgrown stretch. Need I spell it out?"

"Do you know who the woman was? Does she have a job?"

"Computer stuff. She works from home."

"He's never killed anyone, has he?"

"Not that we know about. I'm sure he's capable of it."

"How can you be sure?"

"I spent more hours with the scumbag than I want to remember. How he got paroled, I don't know."

"There could be an innocent explanation."

"Like what?"

"Let's go indoors." Paloma picked up a stuffed toy and threw it for the dog before quickly ushering Diamond inside and closing the patio door. "Like they knew each other before the race and ran it together until she got blisters. He stayed with her, but in the end she couldn't manage another step and told him to finish the race alone, which he did."

"And then?"

"He went back for her and took her to his place where they spent the night together."

Fitted the facts, he couldn't deny, and maybe was more realistic than his own theory. Gut instinct told him not to be swayed. "We'll see. How about Wednesday, then? Will you be coming?"

"I'll let you know. I need to see how much work comes in."

"Do you good to get out." He added casually, as if it was an afterthought, "Are you still running?"

"Of course. I enjoy it."

Before he left home in the morning, he phoned the CID room to see if there was any news of Belinda.

Nothing.

He tried the landlady, Mrs. Hector, at the risk of alarming her even more. She said she'd left the chain off the door all night in case Belinda returned, but she hadn't. "I got almost no sleep and when I did my dreams were horrible."

He called Deirdre at the probation service. She didn't sound pleased.

"What is it now, Superintendent?"

"You told me Pinto was due to meet his probation officer yesterday afternoon. Did he show up?"

"Why are you asking?"

Why was he asking? He was always being told to watch his high blood pressure. He could *feel* it right now. "It's a simple question. I told you my concerns about him."

"He missed the appointment. I'm not surprised."

So casual. "Why not?"

"If he ran in that half marathon on Sunday, he's probably exhausted."

"Have you checked? Has anyone checked? Isn't it normal to check if your clients, or whatever you call them, miss their appointments?"

"He's been reliable up to now. I expect we'll hear from him. I don't understand why you keep calling us."

"Because I'm a lot more concerned now. When I saw him in the half marathon, he was running beside a woman who plainly wasn't amused by what he was saying. I checked with the organisers and she didn't finish the race. She hasn't been home since."

"I expect there's an explanation."

"That's my fear."

"An innocent explanation is what I mean."

"I thought so." He let the silence speak.

"Are you telling me my job, Superintendent?"

The "my" didn't escape him: almost an admission that Pinto was on her caseload.

"If there isn't anything else . . ." She wanted to end this.

"The name of the woman was Belinda Pye and she lived in a rented room in Spring Gardens Road."

"I'm sure there's no need to speak in the past tense, Superintendent."

"I wish I could be sure, ma'am."

16

Hartley the beagle was enjoying Combe Down more than anyone, straining at the limit of his retractable lead. He'd met and greeted all the humans and now he was into serious exploration. Paloma was finding him difficult to control. Already he'd collapsed the drone's stand by catching one of the legs with his lead. Good thing the drone hadn't been in place yet.

The so-called pilots from The Sky's No Limit, a likeable duo called Noah and Naomi, had come early to set up. Conditions were difficult for them in a keen east wind, even without an excited dog.

When Paloma succeeded in getting Hartley back on a short leash, he protested by barking.

And continued.

Paloma shouted to Diamond over the din, "This was a mistake."

"The mistake was mine."

"I'll take him for a run and try and tire him out." She must have anticipated this because she was wearing tracksuit and trainers.

"You might miss the drone flight."

"It won't break my heart."

Diamond watched them head away across the field. He

was starting to regret this adventure. "Bleak spot," he said to Halliwell.

"You chose it, guv," Halliwell reminded him.

"Can't argue with that. I wish they'd get on with it."

"We can't start without the ACC. Where is she?"

"Georgina? Probably gone to the wrong place and wondering where we are."

"Did you give her coordinates?"

"Do I look as if I'm capable of giving anyone coordinates? I offered to meet at the Hadley Arms, if that's what you're getting at, but she said she'd find her own way here. She thought I was touting for a drink."

"Were you?"

"It crossed my mind."

They were south of the village, at the top of a steeply sloping uneven field off Summer Lane that would be a good testing ground for the drones. The hazards included trees, stone walls and bushes.

"Did your Other Half come through here?" Halliwell asked.

Diamond was fazed for a moment.

"The runners."

"They did, but no one will have seen them." He could be enigmatic, too. "They will have gone beneath us."

"Yes?"

"The route goes through Combe Down tunnel, which passes under the village."

"Why are we up here, then?"

"Put yourself in Belinda's shoes, if you can, with a berk like Pinto running beside you for mile after mile, trying to chat you up."

"I'd tell him to get lost."

"You might, but she wouldn't. She's painfully shy, according to her friend Bella and her landlady. He was still at her side when they went through the ten-K mark."

"Where's that?"

"Monkton Combe, near enough. She'd know the tunnel is ahead and a mile long and she wouldn't want to be in there with him. I think she'd quit the race before she got there and head this way along one of the footpaths towards the village."

"He'd follow her, wouldn't he?"

"If I know anything about him, yes."

"I'm with you now, guv. If he attacked her, it would be somewhere out here. We know he finished the race about an hour later than the people he was running with. Plenty of time to carry out an assault and maybe silence her forever, not wanting another long spell in prison."

"Some big assumptions there, Keith."

"Isn't that what you're thinking?"

"Broadly, yes. It's my duty to think the worst and hope for the best."

"If there's a body in the fields, the drone might spot it."

"Possibly. But don't hold your breath."

"Does Georgina know why we finished up here?"

"No—and don't you tell her."

They went to see how the preparations were going. The drone, a strange-looking silver contraption made of some alloy material and with four propellers, was on its stand and the operators were testing the electronics.

"No pressure, but how much longer?" Diamond asked.

"We want to make sure everything is right," Naomi told him. "Didn't you say someone else is coming?"

"The Assistant Chief Constable, yes."

"And the other lady, with the dog? Is she coming back?"

"I hope so. But don't let that hold you up."

"We were wondering if you were planning to test us out, using the UAV to find them."

"Hadn't thought of that."

"We have a thermal imager with us."

"A heat-seeking device?"

"Yes. The heat-sensing camera would show the location of a living person, say if they'd had an accident and were lying somewhere in the open."

"I hope it hasn't come to that." Diamond weighed his options. "What if the person we were looking for is dead?"

"Pessimistic."

"Hypothetically, I mean."

"We'd need to use normal imaging for that. There's a technique using NIR—near infrared—for detecting decomposition, but we don't have the equipment. It would probably find a body in a shallow grave. Would you like us to show the heat sensor at work? It will almost certainly pinpoint the position of the lady with the dog."

He pictured Paloma's annoyance at having the drone hovering above her like a hungry falcon. "No, thanks. We'll settle for a straightforward aerial view. Can you do that?"

"With an optical camera. Certainly."

"And can we cover the area fully?"

"If that's what you wanted, you should have said." She made him feel like a five-year-old. "We'd use a grid system to make a search."

"Let's try that."

"Can't be done today. This UAV uses a lot of battery power because it's a quadcopter. If I'd known you wanted a systematic search, we'd have brought a fixed-wing drone."

A gleeful smile spread across his face. "Like the model planes I flew as a boy?"

"No," Naomi said. "These are far more sophisticated. I expect yours were driven by elastic."

"Excuse me, they had little motors."

"Simple two-stroke glow engines using methanol or nitro-methane?"

"I couldn't tell you, but you could get high on the fumes."

"And do yourself untold damage. Didn't anyone tell you the fuel is toxic?"

"I survived."

"These days you'd wear a gas mask."

"Health and safety," he said in a tone that left no doubt what he thought.

"As a policeman, I thought you'd know better than that."

"I was talking about my childhood."

"And I'm talking about UAVs that are battery-powered. And they don't fly in circles on control wires. They use satellite navigation."

"It's another world." He stared across the field at a substantial female figure in uniform complete with the policewoman's bowler hat heading rapidly towards him, every stride eloquent of displeasure. "That's my boss. I'm not her blue-eyed boy by the look of her. Do me a favour and get the thing in the air as soon as possible and she'll be off my back." He turned away and went to meet Georgina.

"Nice timing, ma'am," he said before she got a word in. "We're almost ready for liftoff."

"I've been driving round this godforsaken village for the past hour," she said. "Your directions were useless. Is your phone switched off?"

It was. He dug deep for an excuse. "Were you trying to reach me? I didn't want to cause a problem for the drone pilots, messing up their signals. Is yours turned off?"

Georgina looked ready to implode. Good thing she was as ignorant of the technology as Diamond was. She took her phone from her pocket and switched it off. "I doubt if it makes a jot of difference."

"Drones are like dormice, sensitive creatures," he said with no authority whatsoever.

She returned to the attack. "It was no thanks to you I saw the cars at the side of the road and recognised yours."

"The unwashed one. But you haven't missed a thing. Naomi and Noah are still setting up. Do you want to meet them?"

Somehow, he'd succeeded in deflecting the worst of the onslaught.

The next ten minutes were passed in what Noah insisted on calling the cockpit, the space in front of a screen protected by a sunshield—although there was little sun today. The brother and sister went to a lot of trouble to explain how the drone could work in a variety of conditions and how simple it was to operate. Georgina mellowed and made approving murmurs. Introducing drone technology to Avon and Somerset would look splendid on her CV.

Finally, the object of all this attention took to the air with a vertical take-off and hovered twenty feet above them.

"That's you," Georgina said to Diamond.

"What?"

Unlike him, she was looking at his on-screen image on the tablet Naomi had put in front of them. "A bird's eye view you never thought you'd see. Doff your hat to the future of policing, Peter."

He didn't want his baldness brought to stark attention, so he kept his trilby on and showed two fingers to the future instead, and watched himself on the screen.

Georgina was handed the remote control.

"Try it," Naomi said. "It's child's play."

Georgina bridled at the way the invitation was phrased, but allowed herself to be shown the basics, working the two sticks on the transmitter to achieve changes in movement using gyro stabilisation. Naomi spoke about roll, pitch, yaw and throttle as if they were as familiar as bread and butter. The drone responded well.

"Can I send it down the field and back?"

"Farther, if you like."

Naomi showed how it was done and the flying machine headed off at speed.

"How do I stop it hitting the trees?" Georgina said in some alarm.

"Don't worry. It has its own collision avoidance system. Sensors detect any obstacles and adjust the movement."

"Clever. Let's bring it back. Are you following this, Peter?"

"You bet I am." He was enjoying the interplay of pride and panic on Georgina's face as she played with the new toy.

Naomi said, "Watch the screen, Mr. Diamond."

"Isn't he paying attention?" Georgina said, still working the sticks. "Careful, Peter. I may be handing the controls to you."

"I wouldn't, if I were you, ma'am. You're coping brilliantly. I'm sure to crash it."

Naomi said, "It's smarter than either of you. It won't allow that to happen." For someone promoting a product, she wasn't doing well. Without intending to, she had this unfortunate knack of belittling her potential customers.

But Diamond didn't complain. Machines in general got the better of him, most recently an electric toothbrush Paloma had suggested he should try. With no electric socket in the bathroom for the charging stand, he had plugged it into the nearest one outside the door, low down near the skirting board. On the second morning, he'd forgotten it was there, stepped on it and snapped the brush into two pieces.

"If you'd been watching the screen as I said," Naomi told him, "you'd have seen the lady with the dog who was here earlier."

He was fully alert now. "In the field? I can't see her."

"The eye in the sky did. The ground dips quite steeply. She's definitely coming this way." She took the remote back from Georgina, put the drone into reverse and restored first Hartley to the screen and then Paloma, who looked up and raised her arm. It wasn't clear whether she was waving or flapping her hand in protest.

"Magic," Diamond said. "Can you do some more sweeps of the whole field? Let's suppose you were searching for a, em—" He stopped himself saying the word on his lips. "—lost child."

"No problem."

The drone travelled across the field and back again several times.

This time Diamond followed the progress on screen and saw nothing but grass and clumps of weeds. Duller than watching CCTV footage.

"I don't want to do this indefinitely," Naomi said. "We'll soon run out of power."

"I don't need any more convincing," Georgina said. "If you're willing to work with the police, we can discuss the arrangements."

Naomi looked relieved. She brought the drone back and allowed it to hover above them. Then she slowly cut back the throttle and let it descend. The landing was perfect.

"Nicely done," Georgina said. "I couldn't manage anything as complex as that."

"Nonsense. It's simple, and you work the transmitter like a professional."

"How kind." Georgina basked in the praise. "But when we ask for your help, you'll be here to work the controls yourselves, I hope?"

"That goes without saying. This little beauty is our livelihood."

"One thing, ma'am," Diamond said to Georgina. "When you sign up to this, be sure to include the model aircraft in the deal."

"The fixed wing UAV," Naomi corrected him.

He didn't argue. He'd sighted Paloma's head and shoulders coming up the slope. In seconds she was fully visible and so was Hartley.

He stared at her and felt the hairs rise on the back of his neck.

She was carrying something red.

He left the others and started running towards her.

Hartley barked.

"Is this what you were looking for?" Paloma asked when he got near enough.

"What is it?"

"Hartley found it," Paloma said. "I had to fight him off to stop it being chewed to shreds."

She handed him a red T-shirt with the British Heart Foundation logo and a race number fixed to it with safety pins.

17

"Can you remember her number?" Paloma asked Diamond.

"I don't need to," he said, all fingers and thumbs trying to unfix the safety pins. "I know what's behind this."

On the backs of their race numbers, all competitors were required to enter their names, addresses and the contact details for next of kin to be notified in an emergency. Anyone with an existing medical condition such as epilepsy, diabetes or heart problems was required to mark the front with a large black cross using a felt-tip pen.

Paloma suddenly said, "Hartley, no!"

Concentrating on what he was doing, Diamond had allowed the shirt to dangle too close to the small dog. It had sunk its teeth into the cotton and was trying to drag it away. There was a ripping sound.

"No, damn you," Diamond shouted, clinging on. "Get off."

"He's tearing it apart," Paloma said.

She grabbed Hartley and picked him up. Keith Halliwell had joined them and, between them all, they managed to prise the strong jaws apart and rescue what was left of the shirt.

Belinda Pye's name, with the Spring Gardens Road address and Bella Kilbury's details as next of kin, were marked on the reverse of the number in small, neat lettering.

This altered everything.

Diamond took out his phone and called the CID office. John Leaman was the senior man on duty. In a crisp exchange Diamond said what they'd found and asked for assistance: a search team of at least ten, crime scene tape, rakes, sieves, evidence bags and a sniffer dog because there was a chance of more of Belinda's clothes being found.

"Where exactly are you, guv?" Leaman asked.

"Didn't I just say?"

"Combe Down, but where on Combe Down?"

He'd never been good at giving directions. He called to Halliwell for help.

"I don't know which field you ended up in," Leaman was saying.

"Hang on."

Paloma was using her phone to get a GPS reading.

He read out the coordinates. "And send any of the team who are there." He pocketed his phone and told Paloma she'd better show them where Hartley had found the shirt.

"Do you want to tell your boss?"

"Not now. This is my call."

Diamond went silent. Seeing the name in what was surely Belinda's own handwriting and handling the shirt that she'd worn didn't just confirm his gut fear that something had gone badly wrong. It brought him closer to the shy young woman so much in his thoughts.

"Should you be holding the shirt?" Paloma asked. "Don't the forensic people do tests to see if they can find traces of the attacker?"

"Bit late to get fussed over that. They'll find traces of us both. And Hartley."

"I had to wrestle it from him twice over," she said.

"Where did he find it?"

THE FINISHER ■ 149

"Hidden under the hedge at the bottom of the field. It was screwed up into a small bundle, but he dragged it out and I saw what it was."

Behind them, the drone show was over. Georgina was deep in discussion with Naomi and Noah about the immense potential of UAV-assisted policing. After all the hype, she would be mortified that a dog had found the piece of vital evidence. That revelation could wait.

With Hartley tugging at the leash, Diamond, Halliwell and Paloma started across the field towards the hedge.

His mouth pinched tight, Diamond gripped the rolled-up shirt in his fist and prepared himself mentally for what else they might find along the hedgerow. In his mind was an image of violent death.

Paloma tried to strike an optimistic note. "She may still be alive."

Halliwell said, "You think so?"

"If she was trying to escape an attack, she would have come this way, heading for the village."

"Without her shirt?"

"I don't know what else she was wearing. It was a colder day than this when the race was held. I still put on several layers when I go for a run."

"Why would she take it off, then?"

"You're confusing me with all these questions."

"Where would she be if she didn't go home?"

"She'd knock on the door of the nearest house, I should think."

"She won't still be there three days later."

"She'd call someone she knows and ask them to collect her."

Halliwell's voice showed he wasn't convinced by any of this. "So you think she's with a friend? Bella—the one whose name we have—doesn't know where she is."

"I'm trying to imagine what I would do." She looked to

Diamond for support and got none. He wasn't listening. Emotionally he was back with the young woman he'd seen on Sunday running beside Pinto, transparently unhappy with the attention he was giving her and unable to do anything about it. Her fate was already decided and she didn't know. Diamond had seen the tragedy coming and couldn't do anything to stop it.

Paloma was trying to be more positive, but only Halliwell was hearing her words. "It could be a mistake to assume that she's dead just because of the shirt. I couldn't see any signs she was attacked. I know it's red, but surely blood would show up in some way?"

"A darker stain." Halliwell was nodding. At least they could agree on something.

"And if there was a struggle, you'd expect the shirt to get torn. The fabric looked intact before Hartley got his teeth into it."

"It's almost in pieces now."

"That's my fault, trying to tug it away from him. God knows what your forensics lot will think when they examine it."

"They'll be told about the dog," Halliwell said.

"Anyhow," Paloma said, "in her situation, I'd run for it, try and get help."

They were almost at the lowest point of the field and Diamond was still deep in his private hell, cursing himself—but for what? His impotence in the face of evil? The wind across the vast down was stiffer and a huge mass of purple cloud had blotted out the sun. In the valley to the south a few streetlights pinpointed villages like Southstoke and Midford that had been reduced to dark smears in the grey terrain. Somerset, his county, with its cheerful name, had the capacity to be as bleak as any place on earth in conditions like this.

Sensing the negativity in his thoughts, Paloma turned

to him. "No one who saw Pinto running beside her could have done anything to prevent it."

Diamond looked straight through her.

She didn't give up. "Even someone who knew the man's record. He'd served his time in prison and he was free to do as he wanted. The parole board must have made a judgement that he wasn't dangerous."

Halliwell took up the theme. "If anyone is responsible, they are."

"That's putting it strongly," Paloma said.

"It's the truth."

"They get advice from experts, but the decision is always going to be subjective. You can never be certain how another human being will behave."

The whole of the brown hedgerow was in their view, stretching across two hundred yards or more, an unusual sight in this area where drystone walls bordered most of the fields. Mainly a tangle of hawthorn and bramble with young trees sprouting higher in places, the thicket was starting to come into leaf.

Diamond snapped out of his brooding. Decisions needed to be made. "Where exactly was the shirt?"

Paloma pointed. "See where that gate is in the far corner? About thirty yards to the left."

"You said it was hidden. What did you mean by that?"

"Hartley dug it out from under a lot of leaves. I don't think it was visible."

"We must look for more clothing. Keith, start at the far corner and work your way along. I'll check the part where the shirt was."

"How about me?" Paloma asked.

"Keep the pooch at a safe distance."

"He's the one who found the shirt."

"We'll get a trained sniffer dog."

"Do you mind? That's a real snub to Hartley."

"He'll have to live with it. If more of her things are scattered along there, I'd rather they weren't chewed to bits—or worse."

"Or worse? What's worse?"

He looked away, in no mood for levity.

"Oh, I get you, spoilsport." Paloma smiled, trying her best. "All right. Come on, Hartley. You can spray all the rest of the field as your territory."

Diamond was already marching off to the place where the shirt had been found. He'd not go too close for fear of corrupting a crime scene, but he wanted to see if more items of clothing were scattered nearby. He'd rather know now than have them brought to his attention by the search team.

He saw at once that this job wouldn't be measured in minutes. A hedge acts as a windbreak and collects all manner of lightweight material, mainly its own leaves, but also anything blown across the land: scraps of sheep wool, feathers and paper and plastic evidence of the human users of the field. The leaf mould provides a habitat for shrews, voles, mice and hedgehogs as well as millions of insects and invertebrates. The person who had stowed the shirt away had apparently rolled it up and tucked it into this ecosystem. If other items were to be found, the entire length of the hedge and the adjacent one needed to be raked.

That could wait. When the search team arrived, he'd spread them in all directions to look for a body.

Uncertain of what lay on the other side of the hedge, he stepped up to the gate and let himself into the next field. A surprised sheep raised its head, stared, then turned tail and ran towards the rest of the flock when he moved on for a better view.

From a distance, a resting sheep could be mistaken for a human figure dressed in white. He had to go closer to some to make sure they moved.

Sheep, all of them.

Part of his brain had heard most of what Paloma had been saying and he replayed it now and found it unconvincing. He couldn't share her optimism about Belinda's fate. There was no denying some of the clothing had been removed and hidden from view. Would she do that herself? His own scenario of a violent sexual attack was far more realistic. Factor in her disappearance and it was likely she had been killed and her body disposed of, but where? Pinto would have difficulty moving it far, and there was always the risk of local people witnessing him.

To get a better sight of the rest of the field, he moved to the centre, where he'd noticed a patch of ground that hadn't been grazed. As well as a small crop of briars with some well-established blackthorn and hawthorn, there were large embedded pieces of limestone too massive for any farmer to remove. Now he understood why this island of thorns had been allowed to thrive in the centre of the field.

Some of the stone projected waist-high and would give a better view of the entire area. He heaved himself up on to one of the slabs.

And the view didn't interest him any longer.

Hidden under brambles between the slabs of stone was an iron grille coated in rust. What he'd found was an old ventilation shaft.

He was reminded that Combe Down wasn't just an unremarkable name for an unremarkable village. It was the source of Bath's magnificence. Beneath him was a deep bed of Jurassic stone, the most valuable in Britain, used for the historic buildings of Bath and Bristol and throughout southern England as well as for parts of Buckingham Palace and Windsor Castle.

He swung his legs over the steep side of the slab he was on and slid down to the level of the grille, wanting to check if anyone had recently lifted it. He swore as the thorns scratched his legs, and when he got a foothold along the edge and crouched, he was pricked in his backside. For every action there is said to be a reaction and in this case it was painful.

The shaft gaped wide enough to dispose of a body, but the iron cover looked immovable, fixed in place like prison bars. Beneath it was a black void. He dropped a large stone and heard it hit the bottom. Maybe twenty to thirty feet in depth, he thought.

Nothing suggested the cover had recently been opened. You'd need a crowbar to move it. The surface rust was powdery and some fell through when he touched it.

He doubted whether anyone else had explored this relic of the mining industry in years.

Stone extraction had really taken off in the early eighteenth century, when Ralph Allen had started quarrying in earnest, having realised the potential of the vast deposits of oolitic limestone at Combe Down. Such had been the demand that more than forty quarries eventually joined the Ralph Allen workings and the ground beneath the village became honeycombed with shafts and tunnels, so intensively that no one could map them with total accuracy. Eventually this led to serious problems of subsidence because the workings were relatively shallow and the supporting columns had been shaved by locals wanting the stone for private use. A four-year infilling programme using foam concrete had been undertaken to stabilise the inhabited part of the village and completed in 2009. Outlying workings remained untreated and, in some cases, unlocated.

His legs and buttocks itched from the scratching and his hands looked as if they'd been steeped in henna, but he wasn't discouraged as he hoisted himself back over the stones and prepared to rejoin the others. He'd learned something useful. The unique character of Combe Down meant any killer had opportunities of disposal all over the area. One ventilation shaft had proved negative. More needed to be examined.

The drone team had packed up and gone by the time he had toiled up the side of the first field. Two police vans were parked at one side and about twenty bobbies in uniform were being issued with rakes. The section of hedge where the shirt was found was already marked off with do-not-pass tape. A dog and its handler were checking the leaves at the far end.

"Hold on," he said. "First things first. I want all the surrounding area checked for a body. Leave the rakes for later."

While the sergeant in charge was dividing the men into smaller groups, Diamond found Halliwell. "Does Georgina know about this lot?"

A smile and a shake of the head. "She left with the others before the vans drove in. The young couple offered to show her around their workshop, or whatever it's called."

"They're brother and sister," he pointed out testily. "She's out of it, then, off my back for a while. Did Paloma go, too?"

"A few minutes ago. The dog got excited when it saw the uniforms."

"Noisy?"

"Worse than a pack of hounds."

"I can imagine. Did you find anything?"

"Under the hedge? Nothing of interest."

"Where's the nearest house from here?"

"Beechwood Road or Summer Lane."

"We should knock on doors."

"In case anyone saw anything?"

"Or heard. That's not a job for uniform. How many are coming from Concorde House?"

"I think Inge and Paul."

"They'll do." He went back to check on arrangements with the sergeant in charge of the search team.

Two hours later, all the nearby fields and several small wooded areas had been walked by the searchers, but without any result. A lunch break was called and Diamond was approached by the same sergeant who, it soon became obvious, was angling for a move to CID.

"Mind if I make a suggestion, sir?"

"Fire away."

"Speaking as a humble copper—"

"Spare me that. What's on your mind?"

"Are you sure this is the place, sir?"

"What do you mean—am I sure? It's where the shirt was found."

"Yes, but I was wondering, if I may be so bold, if the attack happened somewhere else."

"I don't follow you."

"You said the shirt still had the victim's number on it and that's why the perp rolled it up and buried it under some leaves."

The *perp*, for pity's sake. Diamond was tempted to tell this sycophantic creep he watched too much American TV. "No argument with that. Her name and address were written on the back."

"So he'd be an idiot to stick it under a hedge at the crime scene. He'd move on somewhere else."

"Fair point." Annoyingly, it was bloody obvious. And by implication, Diamond was an idiot, too. "You're telling me the rest of her clothes are on another part of the down?"

"I wouldn't presume to tell you your job, sir." He wasn't just a groveller. He was so servile he could double up as a butler.

"You're not the first. I agree with you. We should be searching the whole of Combe Down."

"Between here and the old railway tunnel."

"That's still a lot of ground. Can you conjure up another box of bobbies?"

"Me, sir?" The sergeant smiled.

No prizes for guessing what the answer would be if he asked the chief inspector for reinforcements. Police resources were so stretched that the only way a full-scale search could happen was by going public and asking for civilian help. He wasn't ready for that. "You've just condemned your mates to raking all the leaves on Combe Down."

He phoned Ingeborg and asked how the doorstepping was going. She told him no one so far had seen or heard anything.

"That's Summer Lane?"

"A good stretch of it."

"When you finish, start at the bottom end of Beechwood Road."

"Are you kidding?"

"No."

He called Paloma and apologised for the way the morning had turned out.

"That's all right," she said. "Hartley got his walk, but he was threatening to take over by the end, so we beat a retreat."

"You missed the drone."

"It didn't miss me. I was well and truly under its beady eye. It's going to be a useful aid, I'm sure."

"That's a matter of debate. My money would be on Hartley or one of his four-footed friends."

"Preferably a silent one."

"That would help, yes."

"Did you find anything else?" she asked.

"Nothing of Belinda's, but the morning wasn't wasted." He told her about the ventilation shaft. "Someone must have mapped all the shafts on Combe Down. I'm going to check them personally—the likely ones, anyway."

"How will you know if there's a body down there?"

"The cover will have been disturbed. It should be obvious. The one I found is rusted in. Hasn't been opened in years."

"You're confident you'll find her?"

"I can't give up."

"Wouldn't it be simpler to question Mr. Pinto and find out what happened?"

"Maybe after we identify his DNA on the shirt. It's all about doing things in the right sequence. The case could go belly up if I flout the rules."

"And have you told Georgina what's going on?"

"She'll know by now. She has her finger on the pulse, as she likes to say, even though I keep my wrists covered."

Paloma laughed. "You have pulse points in other places, you know."

"Like my groin? No, thanks."

As it turned out, Georgina had already found a pulse and it felt like the jugular. She phoned him about 2 p.m. and said, "You'd better have a good explanation, Superintendent. I hear you've got twenty officers and a dog searching the fields. Why wasn't I informed before I left?"

He was expecting this. "Couldn't interrupt your business with the drone people, ma'am. I could see it had reached the delicate stage."

"What do you mean by that?"

"Haggling over fees."

"I don't haggle."

"Pardon me."

"We were having a civilised discussion."

"Way above my head."

"Don't soft-soap me. I'm totally aware of what went on behind my back."

In that case, he thought, give me an ear-bashing and leave me to get on with my job.

"You found a T-shirt belonging to this woman Belinda Pye."

"The dog did." He was tempted to add that this counted as a result, but Georgina wouldn't appreciate having it pointed out. "Belinda was last seen alive in the company of Tony Pinto, a violent character recently released—"

"I know all about Pinto," she butted in. "You had him put away twelve years ago for cutting a student's face and now he's out you think he's turned to murder."

"He's missed his regular meeting with his probation officer. I phoned them this morning. He'll have gone into hiding somewhere."

"But you haven't found a body yet."

"It's a big area. I believe Belinda left the half marathon before they entered the Combe Down tunnel. The crime scene may not be in the same field where her T-shirt was found."

"You want to search the entire down? That's going to take an army, not twenty bobbies and a dog."

One of Diamond's best talents was his ability to get inspiration when he most needed it. "There is a better way, ma'am."

"Oh?"

"Using a drone."

There was a satisfying silence from Georgina's end. He pictured her face going through a series of expressions from denial to self-doubt to curiosity to compliance, each with a deeper flush of her cheeks, like a speeded-up sunset. She said, "Oh," once again, this time with relish.

"Not the drone they demonstrated this morning,"

Diamond said. "The fixed-wing job with more battery power, capable of staying in the air much longer. More efficient than people tramping the fields and far more economical."

Georgina said, "Mm," as if she'd just bitten into a chocolate.

"Naomi and Noah will be back like a shot for a real challenge," Diamond pressed on. "They'll welcome the chance to show it off, and if they make a find, you can bet your life your initiative will be held up as an example to every police force in the land." He was tempted to add that she'd be a shoo-in for the vacant position of Deputy Chief Constable, but there was no need. Georgina was ahead of him.

"You may be right about this," she said. "You're still in my bad books, but it's an opportunity and we'll embrace it. Yes. I'll call The Sky's No Limit and tell them we have a major challenge for them."

He phoned Ingeborg next.

"You can take a break from knocking on doors. Find me someone on Combe Down with expert knowledge of the old stone mine workings. I'm interested in shafts where a killer might dispose of a body."

"I thought it was all infilled with concrete," she said.

"That's the main area where the housing is. The outlying parts are still riddled with tunnels. I found a shaft this morning, but the cover hadn't been moved in years. There are sure to be more."

"I'll make enquiries, guv."

"Don't tell anyone why," he said. "I'm out on a limb with this."

18

The terraced cottage was one of the eleven stone dwellings in De Montalt Place built in 1729 for the foreman
and staff who had started serious quarrying in Combe Down.
Originally they were the only dwellings. The entire village
had grown up around them.

The man at the door couldn't be as old as the cottage,
but he was running it close. He must have cultivated the
white beard since his youth.

He sounded confused. "You're not the young lady I spoke
to on the telephone a few minutes ago."

Not a good start.

"Sorry to disappoint," Diamond said. "That will have been
Ingeborg, one of my team. I'm Peter Diamond." Automatically he held out his hand and quickly drew it back. The
old man needed both the walking sticks he was leaning on.

"Seymour Ramsay. Forgive me. She sounded so charming on the phone."

"She is, most of the time."

"You don't mind dogs, I hope?"

On cue, there was a yap from inside.

"I'm used to them."

"Come in, then, Mr. Diehard. We'll talk in my living
room."

Seymour pushed open a door with one stick and revealed

a room more like a museum than a living room. Where most people had ornaments, there were stonemasons' tools and lamps. They were ranged along the mantelpiece and suspended from the beams. The walls were hung with geological maps and photos of groups of quarrymen. Picks, saws and crowbars filled the spaces above and below. Even the fire irons beside the slow-burning stove looked as if they would be more useful below ground.

Another yap—not enough to be called a bark—drew Diamond's attention to a chair in the corner where a wire-haired fox terrier reclined on a plump cushion. Diamond went over and allowed the moist nose to inspect the back of his hand.

"He's called Patch, for the obvious reason," Seymour said. "He only moves when absolutely necessary because one of his forelegs is missing."

Diamond winced.

"He moves better than I do," Seymour added. "There's a saying among vets: 'Dogs have three legs and a spare.' I understand you want some information about the quarries, Mr. Diehard."

"Peter will do. In actual fact, the mines interest me more than the quarries."

"Mines?" He sounded as if he'd never heard of them.

"The mines underneath us."

"They're all known as quarries here, above ground or below. Coffee or tea?"

It was hard to imagine how Seymour would manage a tray with hot drinks.

"Had one before I came, thanks. It's about a missing person, a young woman from Bath who was in the half marathon on Saturday. She seems to have run off course and hasn't been seen since." All of which was true without going into suspicion of murder.

Seymour was still wanting to be hospitable. "Do sit down,

Peter. Move Patch off the chair in the corner and bring it closer to where I sit by the fire."

"He looks too comfortable."

"He won't mind. Put his cushion on the floor and he'll know what to do."

Tough, but it was this chair or squat on the floor. Fortunately, Patch seemed to have been through this indignity before. He hopped off, surprisingly sure-footed, waited for the cushion to be repositioned and settled on it without objection.

"Was the lady runner seen in Combe Down?" Seymour asked when Diamond was sitting facing him.

"Not to my knowledge. But it's the obvious place to make for if she couldn't face running through the old railway tunnel."

"A panic attack?"

"Possibly."

"But if she'd entered the race she must have known it included the tunnel."

"She may have been put off by someone seen running with her, getting too familiar for comfort."

"That sounds more likely. And you're wondering if she is lost in one of the quarries. Is that it?"

"That's exactly it. I know most of them were filled in some years ago."

"There's only one left in business."

"Some abandoned workings outside the village weren't given the treatment, isn't that so?"

"They weren't judged to be a danger to anybody's property. I'll show you on a map if you wish." He pointed to one hanging on the wall. "Take it down and bring it over here."

Diamond unhooked the framed map of Combe Down and handed it to Seymour. "I'm interested in any that lie to the southeast, above where the railway tunnel entrance is."

"The obvious one would be Jackdaw." His arthritic

forefinger touched a point on the map. "The entrance was here, through an inclined shaft in Kingham Field. It was certainly one of the larger quarries because you can still see the grand arched portal opposite Lake Cottage, just off Summer Lane. The way in was blocked off years ago, before my time, with backfilled spoil, but it must have been a major source of stone. Some of it was used in the building of the railway tunnel."

"Really?" Diamond leaned forward for a closer look.

"But the full extent of the Jackdaw workings is unknown. They must have been extensive. Back in the 1980s when some foundations were being laid near Monkton Combe Junior School, the workmen broke through to a tunnel believed to be part of the Jackdaw complex."

"How far from the entrance is that?"

"More than a furlong."

Diamond didn't think in furlongs.

"About two hundred metres."

He didn't think in metres either, but he let that pass. "It also looks close to the disused railway. That's the route the runners took."

"Down in the valley. If your missing lady found her way into the Jackdaw workings she had some uphill running to do first." There were no blind spots in Seymour's thinking. He was visualising this.

"Agreed, but we found her running vest this morning in a field near Summer Lane. An underground quarry on that scale must have had some ventilation shafts."

"Very likely."

"Do you know of any uncovered ones?"

"For Jackdaw? No." It was a negative, but there was some reserve in the old man's tone.

Diamond waited.

"Most of them have been identified and covered or filled in, but there could be others. A shaft was discovered by accident only three years ago. It's a bit of a mystery which quarry it belongs to. Possibly a previously undiscovered one."

"Where's this?"

"In the woods near Kingham Field. There was a quarry opened there in 1810 by William Smith, the father of English geology, but that one was short-lived and to the best of my knowledge was not below ground."

"You said 'discovered by accident'?"

"Literally so—and the accident was to an individual not a million miles from here. If Patch could talk, he'd give you his first-hand account."

Hearing his name, the fox terrier lifted his head from the cushion and stared in their direction.

"He's only here by adoption, you see," Seymour said. "He belonged to a local lady, Miss Wayland, and in those days he had four legs and was taken for regular walks off the lead. He'd wait if he needed to cross a road. He's very obedient. One afternoon in the woods above Tucking Mill, he caught sight of a fox and did what fox terriers are bred to do, chased it until it went to earth somewhere. In his excitement he'd left Joyce Wayland far behind. She was in her sixties and not all that agile, but she did all she could to find him, calling his name until her voice ran out, unfortunately with no result. He'd vanished."

Patch still had his ears pricked as if he knew his story was being told.

"She returned home, expecting him to find his own way back. He didn't. She spent a sleepless night worrying about him. Next morning she was dreading what she might discover, but she retraced her steps and still couldn't find him. In the afternoon, others volunteered to help and eventually someone heard a faint whimpering from below ground. Patch had fallen through a small hole obscured by thick fronds of bracken and was unable to get out."

"He'd found the quarry?"

"Yes. He was nine metres down and was helpless on the stone floor. He'd broken a foreleg, hadn't you, poor old fellow?" Seymour turned to look at Patch and got some vigorous wags of the tail in response.

"How did they get him up?"

"A young lad from the village offered to go down on a rope ladder. He's well-known to be sympathetic to animals. He has more time for dogs than he has for people. He managed to get Patch into a sling and they hoisted up the cause of all the fuss, distressed and dehydrated, yet overjoyed, of course. Sadly, the leg was so badly fractured that it needed to be amputated. Dogs are very adaptable, as I was saying, and he was able to cope."

"Was it a ventilation shaft he'd fallen through?"

"It was. And none of the mining engineers who have inspected it since can say for certain whether the tunnel was joined to an existing quarry, like Jackdaw, or was another one altogether. The locals have no such problem. They call it Patch Quarry and I think the name will stick. It was quoted in an article about Combe Down in the Bath Geological Society journal, so he's earned himself a place in the history books."

"A celebrity."

"Don't praise him too much, or he'll demand a better home."

"And how did you come to adopt him?"

"That's the saddest part of the story. The stress of the whole incident seemed to have been too much for Joyce Wayland. Three weeks after, she suffered a sudden heart attack and died. She was a great loss to the village, active in all sorts of ways."

"So Patch was homeless?"

"When nobody came forward to take on a three-legged dog, I offered, knowing he was unlikely to want long walks, and we could hobble along as two old cripples together. The arrangement has worked up to now, although I've got slower as he has speeded up. I think I benefit the most. Use it or lose it, they say, don't they? He gets me out of here twice a day. Just as important, I needed company."

"He looks contented, too. Tell me about the tunnel he fell into. Has anyone been down since?"

"If they have, I'd be surprised. It's considered dangerous and a cover has been placed over the shaft. It was probably abandoned before 1850. Most of them were."

"Did the boy who rescued Patch say anything about the state of it?"

"We didn't get much from him. You know what teenagers are like."

"There must be a proper entrance like the one you were talking about."

"Jackdaw? Not necessarily. Some of the smaller mines were only accessible by ladder down a shaft."

"How did they get the stone up?"

"With horse-operated cranes."

"Bigger than a ventilation shaft, then?"

"Certainly, but it will have been filled in, or covered, for safety reasons."

"May I have a look?"

Seymour handed the framed map across.

Diamond studied the relative positions of the railway tunnel entrance, the field where Belinda's shirt had been found and the copse where Patch had fallen down the shaft. The placing was close enough to bear out his theory. "I must see this for myself. Do you know of anyone who'll take me down?"

"Into the tunnel?"

"I'll wear a hard hat."

"You'd need more than that."

"Whatever, I'm serious."

"What would be the point? The young lady won't have fallen down the same shaft as Patch did. I told you, it's been capped."

"If the workings are any size, there must be other shafts, even though no one has found them above ground. The obvious way to locate them is to look from inside the tunnels."

"There's some logic in that. When would you hope to do this?"

"Today, if someone can escort me. What happened to the boy who rescued Patch? Is he still around?"

"He's a young man getting on for eighteen now, works as a farmhand. Comes here sometimes and takes Patch out."

"How do I contact him?"

"If there isn't an animal in trouble down there, he won't be interested."

"Could be a woman in trouble."

"That won't impress him."

"Will a twenty-pound note?"

"That's another matter. I'll see if I can find his phone number."

In the large town of Reading, Spiro felt more confident and safer. He'd spent the first night sleeping rough under a bridge and become cold and depressed and loathed the place, but during the next day he sold the bike for fifty pounds to a teenager and his young brother, all done with sign language. He bought fresh, dry clothes from a charity shop and treated himself to fish and chips and suddenly Reading was the next thing to heaven.

Later in the day, he sat in a window seat in a coffee shop in Broad Street watching a bearded guy across the street who was lying propped against the door of an empty shop with a blanket over his legs. On the pavement, where passers-by would notice, was an open guitar case and occasionally some sympathetic shopper would drop a coin into it. No other bedding was visible in the doorway, no cardboard, and no guitar, for that matter. The usual thing for any street person who possessed a guitar was to earn some cash by busking. Had the instrument been stolen, Spiro wondered, or was the case only ever used for begging? Of more immediate interest, did the guy know of a place to doss down at night?

Late in the afternoon, Spiro returned and the doorway was still occupied by no-guitar man. As dusk approached and the streets emptied, the guy got up, stretched, pocketed his takings, zipped up his collection box, slung it over his shoulder and walked up Broad Street at a surprisingly brisk rate, as if he was going somewhere. Spiro had to trot to keep up, hopeful that he might be led to a food van of the sort he and Murat had found essential to survival in Bath.

No-guitar man turned a corner, reached a roundabout, used the crossing and started up another street. The shops gave way to messy industrial units, tool-hire places and scrap yards. Here on the fringe of town there was no sign of a food van.

Abruptly the man dodged the traffic, crossed the street and walked into a pub. Disappointing. He'd be spending his day's takings in there, Spiro decided. This wasn't what he'd hoped for. But something struck him as unusual. Typical of other pubs he'd seen, this one had the hanging sign of a coat of arms where it could be seen as you came along the street, but the building wasn't covered in boards advertising the treats inside, only some big lettering that he supposed was the name of the place. A stark, white exterior. No boxes of geraniums or hanging baskets. Then he noticed an A-board near the front door.

He went over—and of course couldn't understand what was written on it.

He was about to move on when a young woman came

out of the pub, treated him to a warm smile and spoke to
him. She was inviting him inside.

Spiro spread his hands and shrugged and managed to
let her know he didn't speak English.

She took that as a done deal and opened the door for
him, so he went in and was even more mystified. The bar
had no pumps for serving beer and there wasn't a single
bottle on the shelves behind.

His new friend said, "Tea or coffee?" and even with his
limited English Spiro understood and chose tea. Behind
him, at tables, customers were drinking from mugs, not
glasses. No-guitar man was eating a sandwich.

She didn't want payment for the tea, which was the usual
coarse brew the English served everywhere. Spiro was used
to Albanian mountain tea, known as ironwort, velvety on
the throat and subtle in flavour, taken without milk, but he
appreciated the kindness. He took his to an empty table
and watched what was going on and by degrees decided
this must be an alcohol-free pub that catered for homeless
people. Even more remarkable, he could overhear Albanian
being spoken at another table.

The dialect was Gheg, making them northerners. Spiro
was a Tosk speaker, but it didn't matter. He tuned in and
knew what was being said by the man and woman, both
about his own age. Mostly the woman did the talking and
she was on about food, some meal she'd enjoyed the night
before, and how she'd slept like a baby afterwards. Places
were mentioned and Spiro hoped he would remember
them because it seemed churches were open where Christian people served meals and supplied beds for the night
to unfortunates like himself. His good opinion of Reading
was being confirmed.

Tempting as it was to go over and speak to the Albanians
in his own language, he resisted. There were sure to be
questions. He remained terrified of word getting back to

the Finisher. Instead, he swallowed the rest of his tea and
went back to the hostess or whatever she called herself
and spoke the name of one of the churches he'd heard was
a good night shelter. She understood at once and produced
a town map to show him where the church was.

Revived (the tea had its merits if you could stomach it)
and confident, he left the pub and strolled back in the
direction of Broad Street. Plenty of the evening remained
before he needed to claim his bed for the night, but as he
would be a first-timer, he resolved to get there early and
make himself known.

He was vaguely aware of a few people on the corner
across the street and didn't take much interest who they
were until one of them called out to him, not by name,
but in a tone that left no doubt he was being addressed.
What a friendly town this was.

Or was it? He started to walk on.

A second shout came, less friendly. Spiro glanced over
his shoulder and recognised the teenager who had bought
the Claud Butler bike. Strange. The kid had got a bargain.
What had he got to complain about? But the shout hadn't
come from the kid. An older guy, around forty, in leather
and jeans, was creating this scene and he looked as if he
wanted a fight and was big enough to win one. He had a
phone in his hand and was speaking into it. He broke away
from the kid and his mate and started running towards
Spiro. Maybe he was the kid's father, angry that his son had
been involved in receiving stolen goods. Or he could be a
mugger who thought the fifty pounds hadn't been spent yet.

Spiro didn't wait to find out. He started running, too,
sprinting flat out up the street, then around a side turning towards Broad Street, where he would feel safer if only
because it was a main thoroughfare, sure to be equipped
with CCTV. His legs ached and his backpack was bouncing against his spine, but he kept going at the best speed

he could manage, hoping his pursuer would give up. He glanced over his shoulder and he was definitely putting distance between himself and the guy.

Most of Broad Street is pedestrianised. Reach the red-brick section, Spiro told himself, and you should be safe. He was going to make it and he reckoned he had fifty metres in hand over the mugger. He took another look over his shoulder and saw no sign of him.

Nasty. He'd made the mistake of thinking everything here would go his way. Never let your guard down when you're living rough or some evil-minded schmuck will try it on. He slowed to a walk, like other people around him, and gave his legs and lungs a chance to recover.

He was spent, so exhausted he didn't react to the police patrol car moving straight up the walkway with siren blaring and lights flashing. Didn't show much interest when it screeched to a stop and two officers jumped out. Had no thought that they'd come to arrest him. Only when he was wrestled to the ground, had his face pressed to the bricks and felt himself being handcuffed did he understand he'd been nicked.

19

Diamond's guide forced a path through a clump of waist-high bracken and stopped.

"Are we there?" Diamond asked. He was eager to get underground. If the drone was still at work and located him, there would be questions to answer. Although daylight was coming to an end, he was conscious how much he stood out in the caving gear, a borrowed yellow oversuit, hard hat, boots and knee and elbow pads.

The animal-loving young man called Stanley was more interested in his mobile phone than anything Diamond was saying. He'd scarcely spoken a word except to confirm that he'd accept the twenty-pound fee. Privately Diamond already had him down as Stroppy Stan.

"I said, are we there?"

"Yep." Stanley stooped to unfasten the padlock on the grille.

"Wait," Diamond said. He wanted to check for any sign that the ironwork had been tampered with.

He found nothing obvious.

"Okay. Carry on."

The grille was not much larger than a manhole cover. The hinge groaned like a soul in torment when it was lifted and bits of rust and dirt dropped off, confirming nobody had moved it in recent weeks. If Belinda's body had been hidden in Patch Quarry, this was not the shaft the killer had used.

But it was the only known way to get in.

Stanley unfixed a rolled-up rope ladder from his backpack.

Diamond gave it a look of distrust. "That's how we get down?"

"Unless you want to jump."

To be fair, the ladder looked well-built, with rigid metal rungs and wire rope sides.

"Is this what the miners used?"

"Quarrymen."

To hell with the terminology. "I'm saying they wouldn't go down on a rope ladder."

"Wouldn't go down here at all."

"That's why I asked."

"Ain't the entrance."

"I know that. It's for ventilation, or light, or something. I was expecting a more solid ladder."

"You was wrong, then." Stanley rigged the eyelets of the ladder to the grille and let the rest of it clatter into the void. "Want to go first?"

"Maybe I should."

"Turn on your light."

They both had LED lights attached to their helmets. Diamond switched his on, knelt over the space and put a tentative foot on a rung.

"You'll be arse over tip if you do that," Stanley told him.

"What's wrong?"

"Grip the sides and reach down lower with your foot, as low as you bleeding can."

He tried what was suggested and was suspended over space for a few alarming seconds while he jiggled his foot against the loosely swinging ladder, trying to feel for a rung. Once he'd made contact and trusted the alloy with his weight, he was grateful for the walls of the shaft stopping the ladder from swinging out of control. Fully committed now, he gripped the rung close to his chest and was more in control. Hand under hand he descended, trying to ignore the cobwebs he was disturbing. He was starting to think he would survive this when a worrying thought intruded.

"Does it reach right to the ground?"

An unsympathetic answer came from above. "Dunno, mate. You'll find out soon."

Maybe Stanley had a grudge against the police.

Diamond hadn't wanted to look down. He took a deep breath, gripped the rungs harder and lowered his head until his lamp showed what was beneath him, mercifully only a short space between the bottom rung and the floor. He was shaking when he stepped off, grateful for the firmness of the stone. "Made it."

His guide followed almost at the speed of gravity.

They were standing where Patch the terrier had spent a painful night, in a large cubic space cut symmetrically from the limestone. By mining standards, they were still uncomfortably close to the surface. Only about six metres of solid material was above their heads. How much of that was earth, clay and sandstone and how much solid stone was a calculation he preferred not to make at this stage.

"Which way?" Stanley said.

"I was hoping you'd tell me. Have you been down here since you rescued Patch?"

"No."

A fine guide he was.

A choice of three tunnels, two of which would involve some stooping. The other had a rail track partially covered by dust and fine rubble.

"The main one," Diamond decided.

They started along it, adjusting their strides to the positioning of the sleepers, Diamond leading, his boots crunching fine particles of limestone and creating an echo. "How far do the tunnels usually run?"

"Mile or more."

Not what he'd wanted to hear. He'd pictured something on a small scale where they could make a thorough search.

"And these rails were for trucks to shift the stone, right?"

"Obvious, innit?"

They hadn't walked for more than three minutes when the tunnel opened to a space as big as a village hall, the roof supported by massive columns of the original bedrock. You could have seated a hundred people here. Amazing to think it had been created by extracting numerous blocks of stone using basic hand tools of the sort in Seymour's cottage. In fact, there was still a heap of chain lying at one end with a saw beside it unlike any Diamond had ever handled, almost two metres long with a vertical pole handle. Propped against the wall was a crowbar similar in size. Tools on that scale wouldn't be taken to the surface each day. Their presence after probably a hundred and fifty years was humbling, a privileged link with the quarrymen who had toiled down here all their lives.

"Frigbob."

Diamond gave Stanley a glare. "What did you say?"

"The saw. Stone-cutters called them frigbobs." This was the first unsolicited information the young man had provided.

"Got you. It looks frigging hard to use, for sure."

"The weight of it helped to make the cut. That and water from a drip can."

"I noticed some timber props holding up the roof back there. Tree trunks basically."

"Wasn't so scientific in them days," Stanley said.

"There must have been accidents."

"Plenty."

Diamond approached one of the columns and peered at some names and dates scraped into the stone. "Graffiti."

"That's nothing."

"I'd call this one something. '1858. Elvis.'"

Stanley's lip curled. "Says who?" He came closer and shone his lamp on the carved lettering. "Ellis."

"If that's Ellis, he did a poor job on the second *L*."

They moved on down the main tunnel, with Diamond increasingly aware that even if Belinda's body was down here the odds against finding it were heavily loaded. "I'm looking for more shafts. They'll only be found above the really big spaces like the one we just came through, I suppose?"

"Rooms," Stanley said.

Seymour had talked about rooms and Diamond hadn't fully understood. "So I'm thinking we're doing the right thing following the rail tracks. Let's go as far as this main tunnel takes us. The smaller ones don't interest me. What was that?" His head lamp had flickered as if it was on the blink, literally. Troubling. He didn't want to lose his light source. "There it goes again."

"Bats."

"Are they common underground?"

"Thousands."

He thought about bats and their feeding habits. "They live on flying insects, don't they? They must know ways out of this place." He didn't get an answer, so he continued thinking aloud. "They wouldn't be here if there weren't ways up to the surface. They'll know shafts nobody has mapped."

"No use to thee or me," Stanley said. Giving encouragement wasn't included in his fee.

"There must be shafts up ahead. I haven't noticed any except the one we came down." Diamond quickened his step, hoping they'd come to another room. The tunnel had been straight up to now, but it curved to the left a short way ahead.

Disappointment awaited. They rounded the bend and

were confronted with a huge heap of rubble that had covered the rails and blocked the tunnel.

"Hold it," Stanley said. "Could be a roof collapse."

Diamond halted. They both turned their beams upwards and examined the surface above them for tell-tale cracks. There was nothing obvious.

"Don't move from here," Stanley said, taking charge. He edged along the right-hand wall towards the obstruction. Most pieces of the displaced stone weren't large. He picked some up and held it in his palm. "Spoil."

"Too small to be of use?"

A nod.

The rubble wasn't from a rock fall. It was unwanted pieces of stone dumped in the most inconvenient place.

Diamond swore and said, "Why here, in the main tunnel?"

Stanley stepped up to the pile and started skirting it, using his hands as well as his feet, and squeezed between the loose stone and the wall until he was out of sight. Presently he called out, "Gully."

"What?" Diamond called back.

"Dead end. They hit a gully. Quarryman's bleeding nightmare."

The seam of oolitic limestone had come to an end because a ravine lay across the intended route of the tunnellers. The action of water over millions of years had penetrated the beds of clay and ruptured the Jurassic layer.

Stanley wriggled back into view. "They couldn't get no further, so they used this end as a spoil heap."

"We came all this way for nothing?"

"What do you want to do?"

"Got no choice." Frustrated, Diamond fell into Stanley's laconic style of speech. He turned and trudged back the way they had come.

This expedition seemed to be ill-fated. The scale of the task was massively bigger than he had imagined. He was unused to the clothes, uneasy with the environment and he had small confidence in his companion.

"I've lost my bearings," he said to Stanley. "Do you have a sense of where we got to?"

"Dunno what you're on about."

"What's above us now?"

"Woods and fields."

"Still south of the village?"

"Maybe."

"We're going which way—eastwards?"

"I'm not a bleeding compass."

"Anyhow," Diamond said. "We'll soon be back where we started." And after a few more minutes of walking they returned to the open area Stanley had called a room.

They stood in silence while Diamond considered the limited options.

One of the lower tunnels led off at an angle to the one they'd explored. "I wonder where this goes."

"How would I know?" Stanley said.

"I'm thinking it might link up with another truckway."

"You tell me."

Diamond had heard enough of this negative stuff. "What's your problem, Stanley? Everything I've had from you since we started is a downer."

"Waste of time, innit?"

"You'll be paid. Lighten up, man."

There was no reply.

"I'm going to see where this one leads," Diamond said. "Are you coming?"

A shrug.

"I'm going to have a go."

"Your choice."

Stanley had made it obvious he wasn't keen. He didn't

say whether there were dangers, or he simply considered
it a waste of energy.

Diamond wasn't being put off by a stroppy teenager.
"Come on, then. I'll go first."

Stanley's face was a mask of indifference.

Diamond dipped his head and stepped inside.

They soon had to bend their backs and watch for pro-
jecting stone. The cut-through wasn't as smooth as in the
main tunnel.

"Is it my imagination or is there some movement of air?"

He got no answer from behind. Only the crunch of
Stanley's boots told him anyone else was with him.

The posture was a strain, not only on his back but on
knees and thighs. It came as a relief when the gap ahead
narrowed so much that they were forced to go on hands
and knees. He'd needed some convincing earlier to wear
the knee and elbow pads. "I don't know how far I can go
like this."

The narrow sides had one good effect: his headlamp
lit up the cream-coloured stone with dazzling intensity.
He didn't like to think about the view Stanley was getting
behind him. It was unlikely to make misery-guts any more
companionable.

"I'm going to pause a moment," Diamond said. "This is
hard work." He squirmed into a position where he could
sit with his knees up and give Stanley a change of view. "I
would say there's definitely some cooler air coming towards
us. There must be a reason why they cut this tunnel. Surely
it wasn't just for the stone."

"Crawl space," Stanley said, still insisting on the quarrymen's jargon.

"Crawl space to where?"

He hadn't expected an answer and he didn't get one. His
hand touched a small object with a smooth curved surface.
He picked it up. "Hey, a candle stub. Seymour told me

about these. Imagine working down here by candlelight. How long ago since this was last alight? A hundred years? Two hundred, more like."

Stanley was unmoved.

They sat for some seconds in silence.

"Seymour has an iron candlestick he showed me," Diamond said. "It had a spike where they hammered it into the stone where they were working."

More seconds passed.

"Must have been a bind having to change them each time they burned through."

Stanley unzipped the front of his oversuit and took out a phone.

"You're an optimist," Diamond said. "You won't get a signal down here."

The young man stared at the blank screen as if it was a comforter. Or a way of blocking out Diamond.

"Better move on, hadn't we, before our headlamp batteries run out?" Diamond said. "The ghosts of the old quarrymen would enjoy that."

On hands and knees again, and some of the way on elbows, they progressed by stages. He could definitely feel a draught against his face, giving hope of connecting with a full-sized tunnel ahead. He still felt responsible for Belinda, promising himself the least he could do was to find her body. Rational thinking should have told him he was blameless, but the psyche doesn't operate rationally.

And gradually the sides got wider and forward movement was easier. "We're getting somewhere, Stanley."

Aching in every sinew, but encouraged, he continued to crawl and squirm until—thank Christ!—he saw an opening ahead. "We've made it, Stanley. There's a big space. I can see a room with rail track running through it."

The beam from his lamp revealed more as he got closer: two huge pillars supporting the roof; a hand crane with the chain and hook dangling; some blocks of stone with lewis pins attached, ready to be hoisted; and, on the rails, a flatbed trolley that had waited to be loaded for at least a century and a half.

Howard Carter could not have felt better than this the day he unsealed Tutankhamun's burial chamber.

Diamond rested on chest and belly for a moment and gathered strength for the last few seconds of moving like a lizard. A short way ahead was space to crouch and beyond that the bliss of being fully upright.

"Still with me, sunshine?"

No reply, which was what he expected from Stanley.

He looked over his shoulder for the glow of his companion's lamp. Stanley wasn't far behind.

He wriggled some more, got to his haunches, paused, braced and straightened.

Too much. His hard hat clunked against the roof and gave him a moment of dizziness, no more. Without head protection he could have injured himself and it would have been his own fault for misjudging the height.

He was telling himself it was a lucky escape when there was a grating sound from above and a section of the roof detached itself and dropped in front of him, raising dust. He stepped back, but not enough to avoid a second fall, a boulder the size of a football that bounced off the other debris and onto his right boot.

First, his foot registered only numbness and then the pain stabbed in, pain more severe than anything he could remember.

He passed out.

20

"So how did you get out of the mine?" Paloma asked.

"Quarry," he said.

He was in bed in a side ward of the trauma and orthopaedic unit at the Royal United Hospital and somewhat sedated, but not enough to let mistaken terms get by. His right foot was cocooned by a metal blanket support that made a large hump in the bedding.

"Have it your way," Paloma said. "Ingeborg called it a stone mine when she phoned me."

"She doesn't live on Combe Down."

"Stop being so grouchy and tell me what happened."

"Grouchy I am not. The last person who called me that got kicked off my team."

"You won't be kicking anybody in your present state."

He managed a grin. "What did you ask me?"

"How you got out."

"The lad who was with me. I don't know how he coped. We had no chance of getting help from above ground. Phones wouldn't work. We had to get back to where we started. Young Stanley dragged me most of the way. I used my good foot and my hands as much I could, but it was basically down to him that I got back to the shaft where we started. I'm no lightweight, as you know."

"Then—when you reached the shaft—you still had to get to the surface."

"Right. There was no way I could get up a rope ladder. Stanley knew what to do. He went to the top and used his phone to call 999. Don't ever let me complain about modern youth. That kid is a hero, a bloody hero."

"Have you paid him yet?"

"Jesus—I haven't." He clapped a hand to his head and raised a flurry of limestone dust.

"How much is he owed?" Paloma asked when she'd wiped the worst of it off his forehead.

"Twenty. Make it fifty. Would you tell Keith Halliwell? He'll make sure it's done."

"How did they get you out?"

"The air ambulance came. It was after dark and the entrance to the shaft was in the middle of a wood, so they landed the helicopter in the nearest field. I don't know how they knew where to come."

"Stanley, I expect."

"It would be, yes. You wouldn't know it, talking to him, but he's a bright lad. He will have used GPS to tell them where to come."

"Good thing you weren't on your own. You'd never have known what to do. So they lifted you?"

"Bosun's chair. Two paramedics brought it down the shaft. They gave me a painkiller, made me as comfortable as they could and hoisted me up like Patch the dog."

Paloma frowned. "Did you say a dog was down there or are you feeling woozy?"

"Another time, another story."

"And what's the prognosis?"

"Several broken bones. Do you know how many bones there are in a human foot?"

"Tell me then."

"I was told, but I can't remember. They had to cut the boot off to get at the foot, it was so swollen."

"I expect the boot was some protection."

"That's for sure. The foot would have been mince-meat without it. They X-rayed me, of course, and I'm going for surgery later. Then I could be wearing a cast for up to three months, like a character out of a Charlie Chaplin film. What's funny about men with their legs in plaster?"

"I couldn't tell you," she said, "but I'm creased up picturing it."

"Traitor."

"Careful what you say. You're going to need help from me."

"What with?"

"Driving."

"I thought you were here to cheer the patient up. Hadn't thought of that. What a drag."

"Don't fret. I'll make sure you get to work. You won't want to stay at home."

"Speaking of home, could you look in and see Raffles? I'll be here overnight and maybe longer."

"I already fed him."

"You're an angel."

Paloma smiled. "I don't know what they gave you, but it's having some unusual effects."

"I'll be more like my old self when it wears off."

"I'll stay well clear, then. And to think all this happened because you wanted to get one over Georgina."

"Untrue."

"It isn't. You had high hopes of succeeding while the drone didn't."

"They didn't find anything, did they?"

"I've no idea. Your CID people will know."

186   ■ PETER LOVESEY ■

He turned his head to look at the door. "Why haven't they been to see me? Are they waiting outside?"

"Peter, it's nearly midnight. Get some rest now and catch up with everything after the operation."

After a night in a cell at Reading Police station, Spiro had worked out what must have happened. No one here spoke Albanian, of course, and much time had been used the evening before trying to question him in English. He'd answered in Albanian and there wasn't much overlap except that they kept using a word that sounded worryingly like the Albanian *imigrim*. They searched him and took away the little money he had left and his backpack. They went through some formal procedure, reading from a printed card. He was photographed, fingerprinted and had a DNA sample taken from his mouth. But at least they didn't beat him up. In fact, they removed the handcuffs and gave him coffee.

The explanation became more clear when he had time to himself to go over events. The mugger hadn't been a mugger at all but a policeman in plain clothes. The police had been suspicious of the kids in possession of a valuable Claud Butler bike. They'd checked the stolen property index and found it had been reported stolen from outside Bath station. To save their skins, the kids had cooperated and agreed to help a detective track down the thief. Once the police had the description of an unshaven man in shabby clothes who spoke in sign language, it didn't require much detective work to deduce that he was a foreigner, a down-and-out and possibly an illegal immigrant. The obvious place to find such a man was the converted pub, so they'd put it under observation.

The rest was obvious.

Quite early in the morning, he was given more coffee and a surprisingly large breakfast of eggs, bacon, beans and a sausage before being taken to an interview room where an Albanian-speaking interpreter was seated beside a man he introduced as an immigration officer. Spiro refused to say how he had entered the UK or where he had been living. He was told he'd committed several offences including theft and evading arrest, and he was believed to be an illegal immigrant and would be taken to Campsfield House, an immigration detention centre in Oxfordshire.

His world imploded.

Diamond slept well for five hours and then had some worrying dreams of being underground again, but alone. He was relieved when some of the early activity in the corridor outside woke him up. He was hungry. He hadn't eaten for about fourteen hours.

"How are you today?" a young nurse said when she came in with a face flannel.

"Ready for breakfast," he said. "Is it the full English?"

"No such luck," she said. "You're the first op this morning. No food or liquids."

"So they'll give me an anaesthetic?"

"You wouldn't enjoy it without."

"Will I enjoy it at all?"

"You'd better speak to the anaesthetist about that. She'll be along presently to discuss the options with you."

More strange thoughts buzzed around his head while he was recovering consciousness. Uncertain at first where he was, or where the questions were coming from, he understood enough to confirm that he could feel no pain before drifting off again, reliving the rides in the bosun's chair and the helicopter and wanting, for some reason, to tell these well-meaning people that he hadn't completed his mission underground and needed to go back. There was unfinished business down in the tunnels and nobody believed him.

If he concentrated better, he could go below ground again. It was a matter of willpower, finding the shaft and reaching down as far as possible with his foot. But his leg wouldn't seem to function.

"How are you now, Peter?"

That voice again.

"You're in the recovery room. We'll soon have you back in the ward. Is there any discomfort?"

Only in my brain, he thought. I should be below ground, not here.

"Still rather dizzy?"

What do you expect, when I've been hauled up spinning from a hole in the ground and loaded into a helicopter?

"You'll soon come round. It doesn't take long."

He had a strong sense that coming round, as she put it, would be a mistake. He was leaving something behind, something that mattered hugely.

"Where's Stanley?"

His words weren't heard. The owner of the voice had gone away. And his grip on events underground was going away as well. He needed desperately to hang on.

"Peter, you're shouting. Are you hurting?"

"I can't stay here. Got to go back."

"Can you open your eyes?"

"No." He squeezed them in case she tried to force them open to check whether he was bluffing.

The steps went away again.

All this mental effort to reach the shaft entrance and he was stuck above ground, unable to move his bloody leg.

"I'm going to give you some oxygen, Peter. You'll feel so much better."

Would that give him back some movement? Unlikely.

He felt the pressure of the mask against his face.

"There. Eyes open."

Defeated, he obeyed.

The light was dazzling. He blinked.

"Well done. You'll be pleased to hear that your operation was a success."

Back in the side ward, he was made comfortable, as they put it, with a drip feed through a catheter taped to his hand. He was told there was a bowl within reach in case he needed to vomit. Where have you been all my life? he was tempted to ask the nurse, but she might not have appreciated sarcasm and anyway the words refused to come.

The depressing reality of his situation closed in. Stuck in bed with his leg fastened in some way he couldn't see but could feel, he wouldn't be going anywhere without assistance.

Pinpricks of sensation returned to the injured foot. The next few hours wouldn't be a joyride. But he could move his hands and they'd given him a buzzer to call the nurse if necessary.

He should be thankful to these health professionals for what they were doing.

He pressed the buzzer.

The same nurse returned and she had an expression that said she hadn't expected the call to come this soon. Certain patients take advantage and Diamond already fitted the profile.

"Yes?"

"Am I allowed visitors?"

"When you're well enough, yes. You'll want to get your head clear before you start seeing people."

"It's clear already."

"The anaesthetic won't wear off for a while. You don't want your nearest and dearest seeing you in pain."

"I'm not asking for my nearest and dearest. I need to see some people from work."

"You won't be capable of holding a staff meeting, if that's what you mean."

"Do you know who I am?"

"It says Peter on the notes, but to me you're the right foot in side ward two."

"I'm the head."

She laughed. "Oh no, definitely the foot."

"Head of CID."

"Head or foot, we treat every patient the same."

"It's imperative that I speak to some of my team. I have vital information to share with them."

"You may think so, Peter, but you could be mistaken. Anaesthetics can do strange things to the brain. My advice is to wait a while. For the next few hours you'll be in no state to receive visitors. Tomorrow, perhaps."

"Tomorrow is too late. Have you got my phone?"

"The hospital doesn't allow phones on the wards. There are certain areas where it's allowed, but not here."

"How do I get there?"

"Get where, Peter?"

"To those certain areas?"

"You're not going anywhere. Relax and get some rest." She moved off.

The pinpricks were becoming needle pains. If he asked for help, they'd give him extra medication that would make him even more helpless. He needed to think clearly. Was it a drug-induced fantasy, the vital development he wanted to pass on to the team? He didn't think so. He had a clear image in his brain of what he'd witnessed underground.

He pressed the buzzer.

She was back, and she wasn't smiling. "This had better be serious. I have other patients in my care."

"If I was dying—" he began.

She closed him down. "That's absurd. You're a foot case. You're not dying."

"I'm saying I'd be allowed visitors if I was dying. I'm expected to recover, so there's even more reason to invite visitors."

"It doesn't work like that."

"I know. I'm talking about my friend Paloma, who was here the other night."

"All in good time."

"Do you have her phone number? She's the nearest I've got to next of kin. Well, I have a sister, but she lives in Liverpool."

"You're recovering. You're not dying."

"Would you ask Paloma to visit?"

"If she calls to enquire about you, we'll ask her to come in as soon as visiting is permitted. Does that put your mind at rest?"

"Not really, if I'm honest. When vomiting ends, visiting starts. Is that it?"

"In a nutshell, yes."

"Except this is a sick bowl."

She shook her head and marched out.

He'd tried everything he could think of. Charm, wit, invention.

Soon the pain in his foot took over from everything else. When another nurse came to take his blood pressure, he asked for something to ease the soreness. And two hours passed like two minutes. They woke him up to get him to exercise the ankle joint. It reduced the risk of clotting, they said.

After that, he slept again.

The anaesthetist came by and so did the consultant.

"You may be slow to heal, Mr. Diamond."

"Why is that?"

"The nature of the injury. Several bones were severely damaged. I did the best I could. Be patient, wear the post-operative shoe, do the physiotherapy, and we'll see how you are in a few weeks. Oh, and stay out of dangerous caves."

"Quarries."

"It was a quarry? I stand corrected." The consultant turned to the sister beside him. "I don't think he heard that. Look, he's drifted off again."

21

"**D**id the drone find anything at all?"

Diamond wasn't interested in the drone. He asked the question to demonstrate to his deputy, Keith Halliwell, that he had a grasp of life outside the orthopaedic ward. Over the past twenty-four hours he'd got accustomed to being treated as a basket case. He was sometimes accused of being a grouch. Couldn't usually understand why. In here, he knew what they meant.

Halliwell shook his head. "Too many trees. Drones can't see through trees. When are you coming out, guv?"

"Today, if I have any say in it. They got me out of bed first thing this morning and walked me in the corridor outside. I've done that twice, with some help. Paloma was here at nine. That's halfway through the day in hospital. I was already thinking about lunch. Anyhow, she's offered to do the caring when I'm released. I get the feeling the hospital won't object if I discharge myself. They'll be glad to be shot of me."

"Paloma called me at the office. Said you wanted to see me."

"Correct. Did she give you the message about Stanley, the lad who was with me when I did this?"

"Sending him fifty? I did. He should have got it by now. That was yesterday."

Irritated, Diamond said, "I know it was bloody yesterday. My head is straight now. I'm off everything except ibuprofen if I need it. Do I sound as if my head's clear?"

"Clear as a bell."

"Because we have a problem. When I was below ground with Stanley, I saw something that needs to be acted on. Shortly before the accident we wriggled through a tunnel, really narrow. We had no choice, because the main tunnel had come to an end. I suppose this cut-through was only about forty to fifty metres, but it took a lot of effort."

"To dig?"

"To crawl through, dumbo. But you do have a point. I was thinking if they took the trouble to dig the thing, it ought to lead somewhere. And I was right."

A nurse appeared at the end of the bed.

"Not now. I've got a visitor," Diamond said.

"Have you exercised the foot today, Peter?"

"Don't you people talk to each other? I walked up the corridor twice. I'm not interrupting my conversation to do it again."

"I'm not suggesting you get out of bed. It's important that you move the ankle joint. You can do that while you're talking to your visitor. Both feet, please."

After she'd gone, he said to Halliwell, "See what I'm up against?"

"Don't mind me, guv. Wriggle your ankles as much as you like."

"They call me Peter. Did you notice? Not Mr. Diamond. It's all part of the brainwashing. You feel five years old. Where was I before she interrupted?"

"Down the tunnel. You were saying it led somewhere."

"Right. To a room."

"In the mine?"

Diamond looked as if someone had given his injured foot a twist. "Quarry."

"A room in a quarry?"

"A big space, big enough for a crane and a trolley on rails and horses to work it. I could see all this ahead of me. That's where I was heading when I hit my helmet on the roof and brought down the lumps of rock. Idiot me—I was too excited."

"Anyone would be," Halliwell said.

"Yes, but there was something else. When the quarrymen cut these rooms, they leave massive pillars, ten feet wide at least, to support the roof. One of them was there in front of me. And in that microsecond before I hit my head, I had a view of the floor beyond the column and there was something down there, Keith. A body, in running shoes."

22

"He's coming in," Halliwell told the team at Concorde House. "He persuaded them he's fit to leave hospital and he'll be in first thing tomorrow. He wants us all here."

After a stunned silence, DI John Leaman said, "I bet they were glad to be shot of him."

"He can't drive with an injured foot," Ingeborg said. "How's he getting here?"

"Paloma."

"He might listen to her. She'll tell him it's too soon."

"He's dead set on it."

"Why? What's on his mind?"

Halliwell shared Diamond's story of the body in the quarry and Leaman said it was unlikely and probably wishful thinking. "He's obsessed with this idea that the woman is down in the stone mine. They'll have given him some kind of anaesthetic for the operation and he'll have imagined it."

Some of the others agreed. One of the civilian staff spoke about the anaesthetic-induced fantasy she'd once experienced of finding Satan in her bed. "It was horribly real at the time. I can still picture it and now I never get into bed without putting on the light first."

To the credit of Bath CID, no one followed up with a lewd comment.

"Getting back to the boss, whatever it was, he's convinced it happened and he wants action," Halliwell said, doing his duty as deputy.

"Sending some of us down the mine so we all end up in hospital? Count me out," Leaman said.

"It's blocked. The roof fell in," Paul Gilbert said.

"He'll think of something. He always does."

"And he's usually right," Ingeborg said. "I say we should take him seriously."

Diamond's entrance on crutches at 8:30 next morning was watched with misgivings by the team. His office chair had been wheeled into the CID room. Helped by Paloma, and clearly awkward with the crutches on the shiny floor, he came to rest on the padded seat with a thump and a swear word while Halliwell held the back to stop him from rolling. If anyone had expected the big man to look pale after his ordeal, they were mistaken. He was rosebud pink from the effort.

A second chair was supplied as a foot rest.

In the circumstances, a round of applause might have been nice. It didn't happen. They were all too suspicious about what he was planning.

Paloma said something to him and left.

He cleared his throat. "I told you we were looking for Belinda's body when we last met. And now I know where it is—down the quarry where I copped my broken foot." He paused as if to check whether anyone was smiling at his misfortune. They weren't, so he grinned instead. "And now someone has to go down and deal with it."

All that could be heard was the faint hum of car tyres on the motorway to the north.

"I've given plenty of thought to this. God knows, I've had time to think."

John Leaman was rash enough to interrupt. He, too, had had time to think, and it wasn't in his nature to hold back when something unwelcome was in prospect. "Isn't this a job for the professionals, guv?"

"Who do you mean?"

"Cavers. If any of us tried, we'd do no better than you." Leaman sometimes spoke good sense and today he was speaking for the team, but he was incapable of being tactful.

Diamond grasped the chair arms as if he was about to stand up. On finding he couldn't, he said with menace, "Where did I go wrong, then? Tell me, John. We're all listening."

Leaman eyed the surgical boot. "Causing a roof fall and getting injured."

"If I'd left it to the professionals, we wouldn't know Belinda was down there."

"Can we be certain she is?"

Everyone except Leaman winced. Some looked down to avoid eye contact.

Diamond said, "You've got my word she's there."

"I'm not calling you a liar."

Mercifully, this went unheard by Diamond. He talked through Leaman's words. He was down in the quarry again. "We crawled through this small connecting tunnel and it opened up to reveal a room, a quarryman's term for a really large space where they loaded the stone onto trucks. I didn't get in there because of what happened, but before my foot was crushed I caught sight of her legs. Flat to the floor. She was mostly concealed by a pillar, but her shins and feet were visible and she was definitely wearing trainers, modern running shoes with the Adidas logo. Is that good enough for you?"

Not for Leaman. It turned him into counsel for the prosecution. "What if you imagined it?"

"I didn't imagine anything. I saw for myself."

"Before you came in, some of us were saying anaesthetics can do strange things to the brain. Really vivid images."

"This was the day before I *had* the bloody anaesthetic. I was down the tunnel."

"When the rock landed on your foot, did you pass out?"

"Momentarily. It doesn't alter anything."

"It does if it affected your memory."

"I was conscious again almost at once."

"And what did you say to the guy who was with you?"

"What's he got to do with it?"

"He's the only independent witness. Did you tell him you'd just spotted a body?"

"Listen, I was in extreme pain. I was thinking I could die down there."

"So you didn't?"

Diamond was being skewered by one of his own team.

Ingeborg said, "Get real, John. The boss was in agony."

Leaman wouldn't be deflected. "What was his name? You remember that?"

"Of course I bloody do. He was Stanley."

"Did Stanley see anything for himself?"

"My arse," Diamond said and stopped Leaman in his tracks. The words were literally meant, but they came out as a rebuke.

The team waited for a second eruption, but it didn't come.

"He was behind me. And, no, we didn't discuss it while we were struggling back to the shaft. Even if I'd been out of pain, Stanley isn't the sort you share your discoveries with. I'm not sure I'd want to share anything with him, but he saved my life. And now, if you've had your say, John, we'll move on."

Shot to bits, Leaman nodded and went silent.

"The problem is this," Diamond said to everyone, back in charge. "The only way we know is where I went, down a ventilation shaft in a spinney southeast of the village, along a main tunnel with a rail track for a few hundred yards, no more, and then on hands and knees through a smaller one that is now blocked."

"And dangerous," Ingeborg said.

"True. But it led to a room in another main tunnel. The distances wouldn't be huge above ground. If I can work out the direction we travelled we might be able to pinpoint the position."

"Didn't you have a compass?" Halliwell asked.

He shook his head. "Stanley had his phone, of course, being a teenager. No use at all underground. With hindsight, a compass would have been sensible, but I didn't think of it."

"How would this have helped?" Ingeborg asked.

"Pinpointing the position above ground? Well, it's obvious, isn't it, how the body got down there?"

"Through a shaft?"

"All these tunnels needed light or ventilation or a means of extracting the stone. Find the right shaft and we've got our crime scene."

She picked up her mobile and started scrolling.

"You won't find it there," Halliwell said. "Patch Quarry is unmapped, isn't that right, guv?"

"Yes," Diamond said. "But I'm thinking we may have linked up with another quarry."

"Is there one nearby?"

"Seymour, the local expert, talked about one called Jackdaw."

His memory was functioning well enough.

Ingeborg said without looking up from her screen, "The approximate area is southeast of Combe Down, above Midford and Tucking Mill, right?"

"Correct."

"There's a steep-sided valley to the south called

Horsecombe Vale, so there can't be any underground workings there. Where's the entrance to Patch Quarry, guv?"

"In a wooded area below Summer Lane. It's just a hole
in the ground with a grille over it."

"Jackdaw isn't far off."

"I'm trying to recall what Seymour told me about Jackdaw. He knew of a blocked-up entrance in a field—Kingham
Field—a proper arched entrance, suggesting it was a major
quarry that you walked into rather than using a ladder,
but no one seems to have kept a record. Some workmen
drilling foundations in the late 1980s some distance away
broke through to a section they thought must be a part
of Jackdaw."

"The Brow," Ingeborg said, still using her phone. "The
work was going on near a Grade Two listed Victorian building called the Brow. It will have been filled in, surely."

"But not the entire workings, if they extended some
way," Diamond said.

"Should we go back to Seymour?"

"He told me as much as he knew, and no one is better
informed." He sat back in the chair and folded his arms.
"There's no ducking it. This calls for another search."

You could have filled a removal van with the unease in
the room.

"Above ground?" Halliwell said.

"Of course." This eased the tension appreciably. "Didn't
I make that clear? We want to find a shaft down to Jackdaw
Quarry. We'll get help from uniform again."

"Will the ACC play ball?" Halliwell asked. "She wasn't too
pleased the last time we borrowed some bobbies."

"Because I didn't consult her," Diamond said. "It's all
about protocol and her self-esteem. I'll do it by the book
this time."

* * *

He insisted on being driven to Combe Down to supervise the search. "I'm not missing the action," he told Ingeborg when she said that crutches wouldn't work well in a field. "Besides, I promised Georgina I'd make sure the extra men were used properly." By toeing the line he'd lulled his reluctant boss into parting with fifteen bobbies and a vanload of search and rescue equipment.

"I don't suppose she knew you were going to be there in person."

"If you're unwilling to drive me, I'll go in the van." He tried—how he tried!—to be civil to Ingeborg because she was always civil to him, but he was starting to feel as if no one believed him.

They assembled at the side of Summer Lane, close enough to Kingham Field to get a sight of the one-time entrance to Jackdaw, much of it infilled and overgrown, but with about a metre and a half of the stone arch exposed.

The location would have given breathtaking views down the escarpment to Wellow Brook if there hadn't been so many tall trees coming into leaf. This side of the village was more wooded than he'd appreciated. In one way, this was encouraging: there was a chance of finding overgrown shafts. But a proper search was likely to take days rather than hours.

"How did this lot find us?" Ingeborg asked.

About a dozen of the local youth of both sexes had appeared on foot along the lane and were clearly heading towards the police vans. Half of them were using their phones. The others were giggling or guffawing, except one who saw Diamond and gave a nod.

"That's Stanley and his friends. I invited him along and he said he'd bring some support. It's only thanks to him that I'm here at all. I won't introduce him. He's antisocial."

"Really? He doesn't seem to be short of friends," Ingeborg said.

"Could be me who's antisocial, then."

She looked the other way.

Sticks, spades and cutting equipment were unloaded.

Everyone was asked to gather round the back of the search and rescue van, for it now contained Diamond, sitting in state between the open doors. "Not too close," he said. "Keep away from my foot." He thanked everyone for coming and set the parameters for the search, a northeasterly trek towards the top with everyone spaced at intervals of about five metres on the open land and two metres in the wooded sections. "It's not a fingertip search, so we can move at a moderate walking pace. You're looking for a hidden shaft, about the size of a door. It will be covered with a grille or a lid of metal or wood probably coated with leaf mould and hidden by brambles and bracken, so you'll have to force a way through. I suggest you thump the ground ahead of you with your stick and listen for the sound it makes. Anything suspicious, tell the head honcho, DCI Halliwell. I'll be here waiting for a call."

They spread across the field, about thirty searchers altogether, including Stanley's volunteers and most of the team from CID, apart from John Leaman, who had stayed behind to man the office. The mood was cheerful. For the police it was a change from routine duties, and for the youths "a bit of a giggle" being on the side of law and order.

Satisfied that everything possible was being done, Diamond heaved himself fully into the van and got his legs into a level position. He wasn't in severe pain, but the foot was reminding him that he should, perhaps, have spent a few more hours in professional care.

The first call from the search team came after forty-two minutes. "It's impossible to hold the line, guv," Halliwell told him. "We can do it crossing fields, but the woods make all kinds of difficulties."

"Fair enough. You can't walk through trees."

"It's the other stuff. Bits are impassable, really overgrown, so we have to scythe it down or go at it from another angle."

"If it's all that overgrown, you can leave it. The shaft we're looking for must have been disturbed not long ago for the body to have got down there."

"He'll have covered his traces if he's got any sense."

"Do the best you can," he said. "Are the teenagers still interested?"

"Can't fault them so far. Stanley doesn't say much, but he's well in charge. They listen to him."

"Like I should have done. All kinds of difficulties, you said. What else is there?"

"You talked about forcing our way through bracken and brambles but we're dealing with big patches of stinging nettles."

"They grow fast this time of year."

"Some of us have sore hands to show for it."

"In a good cause, Keith. How far have you got?"

"Five hundred metres, no more." Halliwell's voice changed. "Hold on. Someone's found something. I'll get back to you shortly."

Diamond could hear faint shouting over the phone. The frustration of not being close to the action was hard to endure. He pressed the phone closer to his ear. Then it clicked off.

Almost five minutes passed before the line was active again.

Halliwell said in a disappointed voice, "Badger sett. One of our guys found quite a large hole and Stanley took one look and said badgers. We found more burrows, so he's right. We're moving on."

Diamond sighed and opened an Ordnance Survey map to get a sense of where the search had reached. It was large-scale, showing footpaths, bridleways and trails, and it gave a good idea of the area including the Combe Down railway tunnel way underneath where he was now, but it didn't show any of the quarry locations. He'd need the sort of hand-drawn map old Seymour Ramsay had hanging on the wall of his cottage. He could remember the two named quarries south of Summer Lane, where he was now. To the west of Jackdaw was Vinegar Down, one of the oldest. They'd reach that if they went much farther.

His phone chirped again. "We may have found something," Halliwell told him. "It's definitely man-made. Stone, rectangular, about the size you said, on the edge of the same wood where the badgers were. We're removing earth and dead leaves right now. Ingeborg is sending you a picture."

"Have you given it a thump to see if it sounds hollow?"

"Too much muck for that. Check the photo. She's sending it now."

Technology had its advantages, he had to admit.

This was promising. Enough earth had been cleared to show the stone sides of what appeared to be a shaft a good two metres in length. The width was less than the opening he'd used with Stanley, under a metre, but it might well have been the difference between shafts meant for light and ventilation.

"I like the look of this and it's in the right area," he told Halliwell over the phone. "Get the opening clear and we'll send someone down."

"There seems to be an obstruction, guv."

"Don't force anything, then. There could be traces left by the killer. Is it boarded over?"

"It's stone."

"Are you sure?"

"Down about the length of my forearm. I'm not sure now if it is a shaft we found. Stanley is coming over. He'll know."

There was a pause for the verdict. Stanley was unlikely to say much, but his opinion was worth having.

"He says it's not a shaft, guv."

"What the fuck is it, then?"

"A coffin."

"A *what?* You just told me it's stone."

"A Roman coffin, but without the lid. Apparently, it's not unusual here. Ten or more have been found over the years. There was a Roman settlement up here. A villa was excavated in the eighteen-hundreds. The locals often turn up coins and bits of pottery. The south-facing slope we're on would be ideal for a vineyard."

"Did Stanley tell you all this?"

"No, his friends. He took one look at it and said 'coffin.'"

To the point, as usual.

"Pity. Keep going, then. Things can only get better."

He didn't hear what Halliwell said to that. The phone went dead.

When the next call came, his hopes weren't high. He guessed the search team would be needing a break. The sun was up and getting warm for April.

"What is it this time, Keith? An alien spaceship?"

"What?" The voice wasn't Keith's. He hadn't checked to see who the caller was. "This is John Leaman, from Concorde House." Solemn John Leaman, the most literal man in the team.

"Got my wires crossed. Sorry, John. What's the latest from the hub?"

"You're not going to like this, guv."

"Georgina on the warpath?"

"No."

A rising note in the response told him that whatever bad bit of news he was about to hear wasn't necessarily bad news for Leaman. The man couldn't wait to pass it on. He was positively smug. "Let's hear it, then."

"A call came in just now from a Mrs. Hector."

He knew the name. He had to dredge deep in his memory. Still couldn't grasp it. His life experiences were mapped in his brain as pre- and post-anaesthetic and Mrs. Hector was pre-. Registered there, but hazy.

"Belinda Pye's landlady," Leaman reminded him.

"Got you. She remembers something?"

"No." Leaman was enjoying this. "Are you sitting down?"

"I've got no choice. Spit it out, man."

"Mrs. Hector says Belinda is alive and well. She returned to her room this morning."

23

Chew on that, Leaman might have added, if Diamond hadn't blasted him with a fusillade of questions, none of which he answered.

"How's that possible? . . . What did she say? . . . Where has she been? . . . What happened to her? . . . Does she have any idea of the trouble she's caused?"

"That's all Mrs. Hector said."

"You didn't fucking ask?"

"I didn't take the call myself. It was made to the One Stop Shop down in Bath."

"I've got thirty people searching for her body."

"I know."

Even a man with the limited social skills of John Leaman understood that this was not a moment to brag that he'd warned about anaesthetics and wrong conclusions.

In imminent danger of bursting a blood vessel, Diamond spoke his anxieties aloud. "Until I've seen her, spoken to her . . . No, it's got to be true. It can't be a hoax. I've messed up big time. Better deal with this right away. I'll be back as soon as I can. We all will. Do me a favour, John, and say nothing to anyone until I get there."

Having ended the call, with thoughts of disciplinary hearings bombarding his brain, he tried to devise some

form of words that would break the news gently to Keith
Halliwell and the team.

There was no ducking it.

But before he made the call, the phone went again and
this time it was Halliwell and the gloom had gone from his
voice. "Better news, guv. We've moved on to a place the
locals know as Shepherd's Field and this is the real deal at
last, definitely a shaft and clear signs that the undergrowth is
disturbed and the iron cover was moved recently. Ingeborg
is sending a picture. Have you got a pen? I'll give you the
map reference."

"Keith."

"We can't claim any credit for finding it," Halliwell
motored on. He'd missed the note of caution in Diamond's
voice. "The shaft was known about already. But the turf
at one side has been disturbed, so we're quite excited,
here. You'll see in the picture. Hold on. Ingeborg wants
to speak to you."

"No, stay on the line. There's something I must—"

Diamond's *mea culpa* was drowned by Ingeborg's excited
voice. "Have you looked at the pictures, guv?"

"Before you say any more—"

"Don't worry. We're treating it as a crime scene, mark-
ing it with do-not-enter tape. Keith has already sent for a
SOCO team. If they drive to the end of Beechwood Road
they'll be reasonably near. Shepherd's Field, it's called."

"For fuck's sake, listen to me, Inge."

She went silent. He'd never sworn at her before. Never.

"Belinda is alive. She turned up out of the blue today
and is back in her bedsit in Spring Gardens Road."

"What?"

"Somewhere along the line I made an almighty miscal-
culation. Can I speak to Keith again?"

He couldn't hear the exchange of words before Halliwell
came on. His ears were ringing. He was still punch-drunk

from the blow he'd been given by Leaman. Paloma, the medics and his own team had all warned him about the tricks anaesthetics play on the brain and still, stupid arse, he'd insisted he was right.

Belinda's corpse had been an illusion.

"Is this true, guv?"

"I'm sorry, but it is." He repeated the little he'd learned from the call. "Obviously I screwed up and I'll take what's coming to me, but I'm going to have to ask you to tell everyone the search is over and why. Thank Stanley and his friends and get all the police back to normal duties as soon as possible. I don't know who you spoke to about the SOCO call-out, but cancel that as well."

"Okay, guv." Halliwell muttered something inaudible. Then, "Ingeborg wants another word."

"Put her on."

Her voice was sympathetic now. "Guv, think of it this way. Belinda is safe and that's brilliant news, something to rejoice over. You did the right thing, pulling out all the stops to try and find her."

"That's a way of looking at it, Inge. Thanks."

"What will you do now?"

"Keep my head down."

"That won't work for long."

"I know. I'll travel back with you lot and then get someone to drive me out to Spring Gardens Road. I want to hear Belinda's story before the sky falls in."

He chose to be driven back to Concorde House in the same search and rescue van he'd used as his temporary headquarters. The ride wasn't comfortable, but he didn't want the palaver of moving to the people-carrier on crutches, struggling up the steps to sit among a bunch of complaining bobbies. Instead he propped his back against some

first-aid packs and slipped his injured foot into a space
between two rolled-up stretchers. The van hadn't gone
far over the bumpy field when he regretted the absence
of springs underneath him. The bundle of used police
tape fell from a shelf and spread over his thighs as if to
remind him what a fiasco this search had been. He let
it lie there.

Back in Emersons Green, he disentangled himself and
prepared to move again. He wouldn't risk going inside
the building and meeting Georgina. With difficulty, he
transferred to the passenger seat of Ingeborg's small car.
Not much was said on the drive into Bath. She enquired
about his foot and he lied and said he'd forgotten he had
one. But when they reached Belinda's digs, he needed the
strong arm of the law—Ingeborg's—to help him get vertical.

"Shall I come in with you?" she offered when she'd
handed him the crutches.

"Good suggestion. Stop me strangling her."

Little Mrs. Hector had seen them coming and had the
front door open, in contrast to their reception last time.
She was back in her apron and slippers as if they were her
uniform. "What's happened to you, poor lamb?" she asked.

He glanced at Ingeborg to see if she was in difficulty,
but the remark had been directed at him. He hadn't been
called a lamb in forty years.

"Long story," he said.

"You look dreadful."

"That's what all the girls say, and they can't get enough
of me. Is she inside?"

"She hasn't left her room since she arrived, except to
go to the bathroom. I hope you didn't mind me phoning
in. You asked me to tell you if she was back."

"Public-spirited of you, ma'am."

"She's never going to tell you herself, so it was up to me."

"Did she say anything?"

"When?"

"When she came in."

"We didn't speak."

"Why was that?"

"I was in bed, petrified. You told me she was dead."

He felt the chill of Ingeborg's disapproval. "I don't remember using those words. I said we were concerned for her, that's all."

"When a policeman comes knocking on my door, what else am I to think?"

"So she arrived first thing today and let herself in?"

"She has her own key. She went straight up to the room."

"You haven't even seen her?"

Her eyes switched to full beam. "God almighty, do you think it's someone else?"

The possibility hadn't crossed Diamond's mind until now. Was this the twist that could yet salvage his career?

Too much to hope. Face it, he thought: nothing has gone right since I started on this quest. I'm screwed.

"No, I believe it's Belinda. Let's hope so, for her sake. Would you ask her to come down?"

"Certainly not."

Thrown by her refusal, he waited for more.

"It could be a stranger."

"We're the police, Mrs. Hector. You're perfectly safe."

"I'd rather you went up. Oh." She looked at his crutches. "Would the young lady like to go?"

"Detective Sergeant Smith. What a good idea." He glanced towards Ingeborg. "See what you can do."

Mrs. Hector batted her eyelashes at Ingeborg. "How brave. The first door you come to, my love."

Diamond asked, "Is there somewhere we can have a quiet chat with Belinda?"

"You can use my front room." Mrs. Hector opened a door off the hall. "It's not as tidy as I would like."

While Ingeborg went upstairs, Diamond looked into the front room, which was dominated by a large-screen TV blaring out some noisy show about family feuds. Mrs. Hector's armchair was squarely in front of it and some upright chairs would be available if the newspapers and magazines were removed from them.

"This will do nicely."

"It will if your sergeant can tempt her down," Mrs. Hector said, gathering newspapers to free up the chairs. "Don't get up your hopes. She's a very private person."

He could have said that a locked door was no barrier to the police but he thought better of it.

Although the sound of Ingeborg's knocking travelled downstairs, the words she spoke couldn't compete with the TV volume. "Would you like to make a cup of tea?" Diamond suggested to Mrs. Hector. "She might come down for that."

This had the double advantage of occupying the landlady in the kitchen and enabling Diamond to pick up the remote and silence the TV. Now he could hear Ingeborg saying, "You're not in any trouble, Belinda. We just need to ask you a couple of questions. Everyone has been worried about you."

There didn't seem to be a response.

"It's essential that we speak to you, not just for your own sake, but for other women who may be harassed or stalked."

A socially responsible point he wouldn't have thought to make and so much better coming from a female officer as empathetic as Ingeborg.

But she wasn't succeeding. The persuasion had to be raised a notch. "It's just me and my boss downstairs and he's a teddy bear, really. He's been so worried since you went missing."

A lamb and now a teddy bear. He could almost be convinced it was true.

"We know you didn't finish the race on Sunday and we have a good idea why that was. You'll be doing a service to vulnerable women. Believe me, Belinda, if we don't get your help, there's a real danger of worse things happening."

The sound of a key being turned in a lock was testament to Ingeborg's strategy. Diamond limped out of sight, into the living room, more Quasimodo than teddy.

Soft steps on the stairs. No words other than a murmur of thanks from Ingeborg.

Then Belinda was in the doorway, brushing back dishevelled hair, a slender young blonde woman in a grey tracksuit, her eyes red-lidded, cheeks lined with tension. Without any doubt, she was the woman he'd seen in the half marathon getting full-on attention from Tony Pinto.

On first seeing the figure hunched over the crutches, she appeared ready to turn around and dash upstairs again, but Ingeborg touched her arm reassuringly. "Peter had his accident searching for you. Why don't we all sit down?"

Mrs. Hector appeared with a tray and Diamond noticed she'd put four cups and saucers on it. "I'll be in with the teapot directly," she said.

"And then you'll find something to do in the kitchen, won't you?" he said. "We need to speak to Belinda in private."

"She might be glad of my support."

"Perhaps, but we have to follow our rules and no one sits in on interviews unless they're solicitors."

"It's my own home," she said.

"Yes, and I'm sure you know of another room you can use for a few minutes."

She turned away, clicked her tongue and made for the door. "I'll fetch the teapot."

"Sergeant Smith will save you the trouble."

With that settled, and alone in the room with Belinda, he offered her the armchair, but she wouldn't take it, preferring one of the upright ones nearest to the door. "You look as if you've had a hard time," he said, plonking himself on another chair across the room from her and resting the crutches against a radiator. "We both have."

Belinda wasn't for bonding.

Ingeborg returned with the teapot and biscuits on another tray and used her foot to close the door behind her. "We shouldn't be disturbed now," she said. "There's a small TV in the kitchen and I found Jeremy Vine for her."

Once the tea was handed round, Diamond forced himself to be agreeable to the instrument of his undoing. "We've got some catching up to do, Belinda. I can't say enough how pleased we are that you're safe and well."

She refused to make eye contact. Or was too shy.

Ingeborg added, "You're going to help us understand what happened, aren't you? Let's start with the race. We know you didn't finish because your top with the race number was found in a field on Combe Down, some way from where the race went through."

Staring down into the teacup, she said in the faintest of voices. "I put it there."

"Under a hedge?"

"I didn't want it found."

"So you rolled it up and buried it under the leaves?"

She rested the cup and saucer on the chair next to her as if preparing to make a statement, but nothing came. Diamond wondered if she was about to get up and leave the room.

"We're getting ahead of ourselves, aren't we?" he said. "You started the race with everyone else. Why did you pull out?"

He shouldn't have spoken. He was ignored. Didn't even get a putdown. This would be strictly woman to woman.

He reached for a biscuit just to fill the silence.

Ingeborg had her own more subtle way of eliciting the story. "You enjoy running, do you?"

The answer was a sigh, a faint release of breath that came across as negative.

"Why did you do it, then—to raise money for the charity?"

The murmur she gave was probably a yes.

"With someone in mind?"

She mumbled something inaudible and lowered her head so much that her hair screened her face entirely.

"I didn't hear."

"My mother."

"She's a heart patient?"

"She died a year ago."

What can you say to that except the response Ingeborg gave?

"I'm so sorry."

She was pausing for respect when Belinda used the back of her hand to wipe away tears and added, "I was alone with her."

"At home? As her carer?"

"I lived there all my life until then."

The history was becoming clearer, the mother–daughter bond persisting into adult life. No mention yet of her father.

Ingeborg said in a soft tone, "You wanted to give some-thing back so you ran the race?"

The blonde hair shifted slightly.

Diamond watched and listened, took another biscuit and left the talking to his capable sergeant.

"That's a lovely way of saying thank you," Ingeborg said with warmth, as if the tiny movement of the head had been a full answer. "A big commitment, though."

"It took . . ." The rest was lost. Belinda was still talking to the floor.

"Took what?"

". . . took my mind off . . . off . . ."

"The grief. Of course. I mean as well as getting fit, you had to get sponsors. How much did the charity ask you to raise?"

"Three hundred and fifty."

"Obviously you managed it."

"Over two thousand." Spoken flatly, without a shred of self-congratulation, but at least a few more words had come and she'd lifted her head enough for her face to be visible.

"Awesome," Ingeborg said.

Diamond was in awe himself, at a loss to understand how this painfully shy young woman had raised such a sum. In the past he'd been asked by friends and people at work to pledge small amounts for personal challenges they were taking on for charity, some seriously demanding and some quite silly. He always paid up regardless. It was bound to be a good cause and you don't turn your back on somebody you know. But how many friends did Belinda have? Even if he was wrong and she had hundreds, he couldn't imagine her asking anyone to sign up.

The mystery was cleared up in her next utterance. "Crowdfunding."

Ingeborg smiled and said, "Of course. The internet is your job. You know how to get yourself a page on JustGiving and reach out to people you don't even know. But two thousand plus is still a marvellous sum."

"A burden."

"I beg your pardon."

"The responsibility."

"I understand. All those pledges mounting up and the sponsors trusting you to finish the race."

"Which I didn't."

"You pulled out halfway through. What happened, Belinda?"

She shook her head more emphatically and there was a real danger she would go silent again. .

Ingeborg was quick to say, "You'll feel better for explaining. Don't internalise it. I'll bet anything you were fit enough to run. You did the training, didn't you?"

"Mm."

"I'm trying not to put words in your mouth. You must tell us what went wrong."

Belinda clearly sensed that she was being edged towards sharing more than she intended.

"You know why it's so important to us," Ingeborg added. "I already explained and I think you understand."

Belinda raised her face and she was frowning as if, in fact, she didn't understand. Then apparently a new thought dawned and the frown turned to a look of shock and then horror. "Did he find someone else?"

"Who are we talking about here?"

"The man I escaped from."

A suggestion that hadn't yet occurred to Diamond. He'd been fixated on Belinda's story to the exclusion of everything else, even the mortifying mistake he'd made about the body in the quarry. He couldn't duck the fact that he'd forced his idiotic hallucination on his entire team. Or could he? Was she right to suggest Pinto may have attacked another woman? Was there a body down there after all?

He wanted to pursue this, but he could see that anything he said would destroy the delicate rapport Ingeborg was trying so hard to create. He was torn, feeling uncomfortable staying in the room and possibly inhibiting Belinda from speaking frankly, but needing to hear every word she said. Her story was inextricably linked to his own survival as a senior police officer.

"We don't know anything for certain," Ingeborg said, "but you can help by telling us your experience."

"There was someone else, wasn't there?" she said, still wide-eyed. "You're not telling me everything."

"I could say the same about you, Belinda."

"He terrified me. He was vile. I didn't know how to deal with it."

"Deal with what?"

"Comments about my body, suggestions, touching—trying to make it seem accidental."

"This was during the race?"

"Right from the start, when we were bunched in the pen."

"He touched you?"

"My bottom, more than once. The second time his whole hand was groping, clutching." The thought that another woman might have suffered the same and worse had broken the shackles of Belinda's shyness.

"That's sexual assault. What did you do—tell him to stop?"

"I was embarrassed."

"Anyone would be, but he had to be told."

"I turned my head and couldn't see him properly. He said, 'Oops,' or something as if it was accidental, but I knew it wasn't. I tried to move away and couldn't. We were packed in, starting to step forward and people were touching each other accidentally, but this was deliberate."

Animated by anger, she was speaking with absolute freedom now, vividly revisiting the incident. "I just wanted to get away from him, but when we crossed the start line and started to run, he stayed close behind. You know how you can sense someone's presence? I went faster, quicker than I wanted to run the race, overtaking other runners, and he kept up, and soon he started saying things."

"Chatting you up?"

"Trying to. About what a good mover I was and how he liked my action and crude stuff like that. I didn't know how to get rid of him. He started asking my name."

"Did he tell you his own?"

"If he did, I didn't hear it. I was in a bad state."

"Understandably. Can you describe him?"

"I tried to blank him out. I deliberately didn't look at his face. All I can tell you is he had a blue headband, yellow top and blue shorts. And he was a lot older than I am."

Diamond hadn't any doubt that the groper was Pinto, so the colours of the running kit came as no surprise.

"How long did this pestering go on?" Ingeborg asked.

"All through the first part of the race. Through Sydney Gardens and Bathampton and a long stretch beside the canal. It's a beautiful part of the course and I'd been expecting to enjoy it, but it's just a blur. My mind was totally taken up with that horrible man and what I could do to get rid of him. Running faster wasn't doing any good."

"He stayed with you all this time?"

"There were a few times when he seemed to go away but never for long. I'd sense him close behind me and the remarks would start up again. Was that a sports bra I was wearing and wasn't it uncomfortable with so much crammed into it? I was almost in tears. We came to a feeding station and I felt his hand on my back and he said he'd pick up extra water to share with me. I kept telling myself not to speak to him because it would only encourage him, but I blurted out, 'Leave me alone,' which he ignored, of course."

"Weren't there marshals to complain to?"

"Yes, but what was I going to say? 'This man is pestering me, and will you please ask him to stop?' Other women know how to deal with men who come onto them. I'm different. I can handle most problems, but not that."

"You're not alone," Ingeborg said. "It's difficult for us all."

"I'm not used to it. I don't go on dates, don't go out much at all. My parents divorced when I was four—I was their only child—and my father went to live in Spain, so men are outside my experience. What were you asking? About why I didn't report this man for pestering me? It's against my nature to share private things with other people. You can see the effort it's been telling you what happened."

"You're doing okay."

Doing remarkably well, Diamond thought. Partly this was thanks to Ingeborg's sympathetic questioning, but mainly the outrage that had needed to be expressed.

"Now I've started, it's easier. I want to relate to other people more and I know I should force myself, but it's not easy. Anyway, as we went under the Dundas Aqueduct and headed towards Monkton Combe I was already dreading what was to come."

"The Combe Down tunnel?"

"Yes. I know what it's like. I'd been in there once on a training run. It should be a fun part of the race, a change of atmosphere. There are lights at intervals and a nice breeze runs through it, but it's narrow and of course when you're inside you have to keep going for a mile. There's no escape. I was already heavy-legged from running faster than I should have done and a mile seemed a very long way."

"You must have done half the course by then."

"Much too fast and I was in a pitiful state. I was thinking I was going to collapse in the tunnel and what he'd do if I was helpless. It preyed on my mind."

"You were under huge stress."

Reliving it, she drew a sharp breath and brought her hands together with fingers intertwined. "I decided my only option was to drop out of the race and that's what happened."

"Where was this?"

"Before we reached the viaduct at Tucking Mill. You go over that and you're thirty feet above ground so you can't escape. We were on a winding footpath in the Midford Valley among trees and bushes. He'd gone a few yards ahead of me. I don't know why. To ambush me when we reached the tunnel perhaps. Anyway, I took my chance and

left the footpath and ran out of sight behind some trees.
Two other women in the race saw me and laughed, thinking it was a call of nature, I suppose. Actually I just threw
myself down and wept."

"But you'd got away from him."

"It was very emotional. I felt some relief, of course, but
I was devastated to have given up after all the training."

"Did you think of joining the race again?"

She shook her head. "I was sure he'd be waiting for
me if I did, and probably in the tunnel. I was terrified of going in there. I knew my race was over and I
needed to think how I would get home from there. It's
very remote."

"I know it," Ingeborg said. "I can't think how you'd get
out of there unless you went back the way you came."

"You mean the half marathon route? I couldn't do that,
facing all the runners as they came towards me, and their
comments. I suppose I could have waited until it was over
and they'd all gone past, but it would take a long time,
maybe another hour or more, and I was already shivering
and I needed to move from where I was. The sides of the
valley looked awfully steep."

"They are."

"I had a rough idea where I was. If I climbed the slope
to my right I'd be going towards Bath. Somewhere up there
was Combe Down. That's what I did. I started up the slope."

"Rough going, I'm sure."

"I got scratched, but I wasn't thinking about that. Every
step was taking me away from my tormentor."

"He didn't follow you, did he?"

"I couldn't tell, but the thought of him was driving me.
By the time I reached the top, I was spent. I flopped down
and tried to recover some strength. All kinds of negative
thoughts were running through my head, but now that
I'd got away from the man, I was shattered that I'd failed

to finish. All those sponsors had trusted me and I'd have to tell them."

"I'm sure it's happened before. The sponsors can't ask for their money back, can they?"

"But I didn't collapse or anything. I copped out."

"That isn't true," Ingeborg said.

"But it is. Let's be honest. I ran away. I'm going to have to admit it. Some of my sponsors follow everything on social media and I've been giving updates on my training and everything. As soon as the results were announced online they'd look to see where I came and find my name was missing. They'll believe I took their money by false pretences. How can I announce I quit because of some man who grabbed my butt? I was mortified. I still am."

"He assaulted you and you're not the first," Ingeborg said in a salt-dry tone Diamond knew well, holding back her impatience. "He's a predator. You were a victim, not a fraud."

"A fraud is what I feel like." She was getting breathless again and the tears were ready to flow.

Blatantly heading off more emotion, Ingeborg said, "What happened next? We don't know where you've been since Sunday."

Belinda's self-contempt ran deep. "I'm a coward. I wanted to hide from him, from everyone. Like I said, I got to the fields at the top and took off my shirt with the number and hid it. I had another layer underneath. Oh, and I untied the chip from my shoe and threw it away. I was thinking if I disappeared no one would know I'd failed."

"Did you have your smartphone with you?"

"What's that got to do with it?"

"Sat nav."

"I didn't think of that. It goes with me everywhere. That shows the state I was in."

"And then?"

"After I'd recovered enough to walk again, I made my way towards Combe Down village and came to a road."

"That would be Summer Lane."

"It was, and I saw a car drive by. I plucked up courage and waited for more to come along, hoping I would be able to spot a woman driver and wave her down and ask for a lift into Bath. I didn't want to be alone with a man, dressed as I was."

"Did you get lucky?"

"Eventually. A woman in a pale green Fiat. It had to be a woman's car. There were decals of purple flowers on the bonnet. She was so sweet. I told her I'd dropped out of the race and wanted to get back into town and she drove me straight there."

"Here, you mean? Spring Gardens Road?"

"No. I couldn't face being questioned by Mrs. Hector. I asked to be put down outside the Francis Hotel."

Diamond's self-imposed silence came to an abrupt end. "The Francis? You went to the Francis?" He couldn't have been more surprised if she'd been staying all week in his office in Concorde House. The hotel in Queen Square had been a second home to him when CID was based in Bath.

"It was about the only hotel I've heard of. I told them I'd been in the half marathon and needed to rest."

"They took you on as a guest just like that?"

"I offered a deposit using tap and pay on my phone. I looked like a scarecrow, but they were very understanding."

"You had no luggage."

"I said I'd be fetching it later. I just needed to rest, which was true."

"I bet you slept like a baby," Ingeborg said.

"Not really. I was deeply worried still and my brain was

fizzing, but at least I was resting my tired body. Late in the evening I used room service to get a meal and I did the same next day for breakfast."

"And that was where you were all this time?" Diamond said in exasperation. She could at least have fled to the Outer Hebrides instead of being under his nose. He shuddered to think what they would make of this at the disciplinary hearing he would surely face. "Didn't you hear we were searching for you?"

"It wasn't on my phone."

"I can't get over this. You stayed all week in the Francis?"

"I went out and bought some clothes and personal items on the Monday morning."

"Out shopping in Bath?" It was worse.

"I came back here as well."

"You couldn't have done. Mrs. Hector would have told us."

"She wasn't here. Every Tuesday morning without fail, she meets her friend Ivy in the cafe at Marks and Spencer for what she calls a chinwag, so I knew I could get in and collect a few things without being noticed."

"I can't understand why you went to all this trouble, staying hidden."

Ingeborg said, "She explained, guv. She was going through an emotional crisis. She needed space to sort herself out."

"I'm sorry," Belinda said. "I didn't expect anyone to miss me except Mrs. Hector and I didn't know she'd go to the police."

"We went to *her.*" He reached for the crutches. He'd heard enough.

"This man," Belinda said, "has he done this sort of thing before?"

"You did the right thing, escaping from him. Let's leave it at that."

* * *

In Ingeborg's Ka, he said, "What did you make of that?"

She started the engine. "Now we've met her, I understand why she acted as she did. The upbringing has a lot to do with it."

"Mother-dominated?"

"So much that I felt as if the mother was speaking. Mealy mouthed phrases like 'a call of nature.' She couldn't tell Pinto to piss off. She's never heard anyone say that. And yet she's brave, waving down the woman in the car and marching into the Francis to ask for a room."

"Desperation."

"I had to feel sorry for her. She tried so hard to do the right thing, raising that big sum for the heart charity. What do you make of her?"

"I'm biased, aren't I?" he said. "I went in wanting to feed her to the lions and my heart went out to her when she talked about Pinto trying it on. But now I'm out of there the old antagonisms have come back. Bring on the lions."

"You don't mean that."

"I do. Without meaning to, she dropped me in it."

"Speaking of which," Ingeborg said, "is your phone switched off? I had a text from Georgina telling me to make sure you read your mail."

"Oh Christ. What's she up to now?"

24

At 8:50 on Monday morning, Paloma drove through the gate at Avon and Somerset Police headquarters at Portishead with Peter Diamond as her passenger and brought the car as close as possible to the brown and cream main building. She said she wouldn't come in unless he wanted her support and he said he'd prefer to tough this out alone. They agreed she'd return in a couple of hours unless he phoned.

He didn't move. "Funny when you think about it," he said.

"What's funny?"

"The speed of all this. When I charge a lawbreaker, as likely as not it doesn't get to court. If it does, it takes anything up to six months. But I put a foot wrong and what happens?"

"You end up with a surgical boot," Paloma said. "Stop feeling sorry for yourself and think what you're going to say."

She got out, opened the passenger door and helped him out. He was in his most respectable black suit, white shirt and a sober tie.

"Think of it as truth and reconciliation," she said before straightening the tie and kissing him lightly. "Try not to get angry."

He limped inside.

At the desk, he said to the civilian receptionist, "DS Diamond reporting for the high jump."

Bemused, she looked at him and the crutches keeping him upright. "I'm sorry but I don't understand."

"The disciplinary hearing. Peter Diamond from Bath."

"Ah." She checked her computer screen. "Are you a member of the panel?"

"The main man."

"The chairman?"

"The fall guy." She still didn't seem to understand, so he said, "The one in the naughty corner."

"Oh." The sides of her mouth twitched in understanding. A smile wouldn't have been seemly on the dignified face of headquarters. "It's upstairs in meeting room two, but you're to wait outside to be called."

"Upstairs, you say. Where's the lift, ma'am?"

"Temporarily out of action, I'm afraid."

"So am I, as it happens."

"I noticed."

"I can't do staircases."

"That's unfortunate. We weren't informed in advance that you have a problem."

"It's not a problem at ground level."

"I'd better advise the chair."

"Thank you. Speaking of chairs, are there two I can use while this is sorted out?"

"Two?"

"One to rest the broken foot on. I've been cramped up in a car since seven-thirty. I was told there's a risk of thrombosis when I discharged myself from hospital." This was all true. The bit about thrombosis and discharging himself had been more true the previous week, but so what? When you play the sympathy card, you make sure it counts.

The receptionist asked a uniformed constable to fetch the two chairs. Then she phoned meeting room 2.

He was happy to lean against the desk and wait, especially as he was close enough to listen to her end of the conversation. "There appears to be a problem, sir. Detective Superintendent Diamond is here in reception, but he's on crutches and can't manage the stairs . . . No, it's not working. I'm told we're waiting for an engineer . . . In the foyer, sir. I've asked for chairs . . . No, not for the panel. For Mr. Diamond. He needs two in case of thrombosis . . . Oh, I will, at once." She switched off and told him someone would come down and speak to him.

The chairs were supplied and Diamond made sure they were positioned where they were likely to be noticed, under the plaque stating that the building had been opened by Her Majesty Queen Elizabeth II on June 2, 1995. He asked for water and was brought some in a paper cup. He was soon getting sympathetic smiles from people passing by. One woman asked if he was there on behalf of the disabled. She unzipped her purse and he realised she was about to drop a coin into his cup.

After a short wait, he was aware of someone coming downstairs and crossing the floor to speak to him.

Georgina.

She was in her number one uniform, all braid and silver buttons. The look she gave him wasn't friendly and neither was her opening salvo. "If this is your way of hitting back, it doesn't impress me in the least."

He said, "And good morning to you, ma'am. Pardon me for not standing up."

"I'm not amused," she said, "and neither is the Chief Constable."

"I don't see him."

"He's waiting upstairs in the meeting room."

"He'll have to wait until the lift is fixed unless he's willing to descend to my level. What's this all about, ma'am?"

"Isn't it obvious?"

"Not to me. I had a message and a phone call ordering me to report here this morning to account for my recent conduct."

Georgina noisily filled her lungs. "You drove me to this, Peter. I chose to overlook your indiscretions for years because you had successes bringing criminals to justice, but this time I can't cover for you anymore. Headquarters wanted to know why our overtime costs have shot through the roof and I was forced to confess that all those hours were wasted on a wild goose chase, searching for a missing woman who it turns out is alive and well."

"Belinda Pye?"

"As you very well know, I didn't authorise the search of Combe Down. You high-handedly arranged it behind my back. Twenty officers, not to mention dogs and vehicles."

"One dog. The other belongs to Paloma's neighbour."

"The dogs are immaterial. The man-hours are not. And on the very next day you had another fifteen officers taken from other duties."

"I told you about the second search. You authorised it."

"Only because you convinced me it could save the woman's life."

"She could have been trapped underground, or dead."

"She wasn't. And after you found she was alive, did you inform me? No. I was one of the last to hear, and no thanks to you. What was I supposed to say to headquarters when they asked if the operation was successful?"

"You could have told them the good news that Belinda was okay."

"You know full well that the money men here don't see it like that. They see Bath Central leeching funds. I'm blamed for failing to control the costings when the truth is that you're the problem. I can't cover for you any longer and that's why you're here."

"That's one mystery solved, then," he said. "What am I charged with?"

"Didn't they tell you? Insubordination. Reckless decision-making. Failure to communicate. Even your phone is switched off most of the time, so I can't reach you. I'm at my wits' end."

"Is that what you told them upstairs?"

"Not the last part. The rest is all documented and you know it's true, but I'll repeat it for the panel and you'll have an opportunity to defend yourself."

"I can hardly wait."

"It's typical, somehow, that you should be on crutches on the day the lift breaks down. Nothing is ever straightforward with you. It wouldn't surprise me if you could get up the stairs as well as anyone else."

"Is that also on the charge sheet?"

"Don't be sarcastic. Because of you the hearing will have to be downstairs. I came down to arrange the change of room."

"Good thinking, ma'am."

Georgina marched across to the desk to try her luck with the hard-nosed receptionist. A grizzled police sergeant joined them, a self-important twit, to Diamond's eye. He seemed to be responsible for the use of rooms on the ground floor. He was shaking his head a lot. Georgina flapped her hands a lot. The receptionist passed the phone to Georgina and she spoke earnestly into it. Her face was a study in frustration. Finally she stepped over to Diamond and said, "It appears no rooms down here are available until noon. The Chief Constable has another appointment, so the hearing will be put off for another day."

"So be it," Diamond said. "More man-hours, more travel expenses, but heck, who am I to complain?"

* * *

In Paloma's car on the drive back, he told the story of the aborted disciplinary hearing and finished with, "Sorry."

"What for?"

"I wasted your morning."

"It's Hartley you should make your peace with. He missed his morning walk."

"But you have a business to run. I appreciate this."

"You can do me a favour then. Come back to the house and join me for a spot of lunch."

"And face Hartley? I don't know if I dare."

"He's very forgiving. He'll lick you all over."

A mile or so farther along the road, the rain bucketed down. Diamond scarcely noticed in his satisfaction at the outcome.

Paloma said, "I was all set to offer words of comfort. It sounds as if Georgina needs more comforting than you do."

He smiled.

"What was she hoping to get out of this?"

"They could reprimand me or transfer me to another station. I doubt if they'd put me back into uniform or dismiss me."

"Does she really want that?"

"You'd have to ask her."

"I think it's a love–hate relationship. She wouldn't care to admit it, but she'd miss you terribly. I do have sympathy for her. I wouldn't wish to be your boss."

Halfway down the A4, he started thinking about the things Georgina had said. Man-hours had been wasted. And he should have informed her what was going on. He'd be the first to complain if his team failed to communicate. He took out his phone and switched it on.

"What do you know?" he said presently.

"What's that?" Paloma asked.

"Would you mind if we had that lunch another day? I'd be mighty grateful if you'd drop me off at Combe Down."

"Why?"

"Message from Keith Halliwell. They found a body in Vinegar Down Quarry."

25

Vindicated.

He hadn't hallucinated while dosed on morphine. A body was down there. Not Belinda's, obviously, so whose?

From Summer Lane, where Paloma stopped the car, he could see several four-by-fours and a crime scene van parked on the far side of Shepherd's Field near a wooded area. This had to be the copse containing the shaft entrance Halliwell and the search team had discovered at the end of the previous week. No one seemed to be about and it was still raining steadily.

"Let's go."

"We're going nowhere," Paloma said. "My car won't go through mud like that and you'll be no help when I get stuck."

He looked at the state of the ground and the tracks left by the vehicles that had made it to the top of the field, all four-wheel drives.

"Help me out, then."

"You're not aiming to cross the field on crutches, I hope?"

"Try and stop me."

"You haven't even got a mac."

"Don't wait," he said. "Someone else will see that I get home."

He set off at a speed that would have confirmed

Georgina's worst suspicions about his ability to climb stairs. Keeping out of the ruts left by the vehicles and going like a crane fly at a window, he managed without falling once. The action wasn't elegant. Single-minded intent got him there.

Through the trees ahead was a wide area marked off with police tape. On getting close, he saw that a mass of tangled ivy had been dragged away to reveal the hole that was the outlet to the shaft. The protective grille had been lifted and a rope ladder was in place.

He spotted some of his team in a Range Rover and banged the side with his crutch. A steamed-up window was wound down and Halliwell looked out at his bedraggled boss. "Didn't expect to see you, guv. Don't you have an umbrella?"

"How could I with these?"

"You'd better get in. We'll make room."

Ingeborg and Paul Gilbert slid closer to make a space on the back seat.

"Don't bother," Diamond said. "I won't be able to climb in. What's happening? Is someone down the shaft? Someone living, I mean."

"Stanley, with the guts man," Halliwell said.

"Who did you get?"

"Dr. Sealy."

"Him." Bertram Sealy was a complainer with an acid tongue, not Diamond's favourite forensic pathologist. His one redeeming quality was that his thoroughness couldn't be doubted.

Ingeborg said, "You're getting soaked, guv. You'll ruin that suit. We must have an umbrella in the back. Paul, why don't you see if you can find it?"

"Don't fuss. I'll survive. Stanley, you said. You do mean the lad I was underground with?"

"He discovered the body," Halliwell said.

"How was that? I called off the search."

"It seems he came back yesterday and went down for a look. He's not much of a talker, as you know, but he's the go-to person if you want to see down a quarry and it gives him status in the village."

"He found the body and called us?"

"Nothing so simple as that. Sod-all was done about it until this morning. The call came from that old guy you visited last week."

"Seymour Ramsay."

"Stanley must have spoken the word 'body' to someone in the pub last night and the news got back to Mr. Ramsay and he decided it was a matter for the police."

Knowing the personalities involved, Diamond had to agree that this was the likely scenario. "So what are we dealing with, Keith? Is this a fresh corpse or a skeleton? Clothed? Male or female?"

"Mr. Ramsay didn't seem to know. You'd think Stanley would have told him."

"I wouldn't bet on it."

"We'll know shortly, anyhow."

"Hasn't anyone taken a picture yet?"

"The photographer is sitting in the forensics van waiting for his chance to go down. Nothing can be rushed. It's dangerous down there."

"I'll vouch for that."

"Old Mr. Ramsay said the quarry has a sad history. There are stories of roof falls going back to the eighteen-hundreds. It was reopened about 1912 and then closed again a year later after a fatal accident."

"Did they get the guy out?"

"Don't worry, it's not *his* body. But the mine was too dangerous to work. The entrance was sealed and the ground levelled. The only access point is here."

"Not anymore," Diamond said. "There's another way into it—the tunnel I crawled along—linking Patch Quarry to Jackdaw. I told you I had a sight of the body ahead of me before I had my accident. I told everyone."

"I can see something," Ingeborg said. "Someone's coming up."

All eyes were on the shaft. A hand appeared and grasped the top rung of the ladder. Then a curved yellow object. Inside the hard helmet was the chubby, florid face of Bertram Sealy.

"It's either a hobbit or a groundhog," Diamond called out, getting in first with the abuse.

"Coming from a Long John Silver impersonator, that's rich," Sealy shouted back. "Where's your parrot?"

Diamond spoke to his team. "Someone better give the poor sod a hand out of there."

"No need," Sealy said. "I haven't finished. I only came up for a body bag. There's one on the back seat of my car if anyone here has a shred of decency and will fetch it."

Paul Gilbert had heard. He left the Range Rover and walked over to another vehicle.

"What can you tell us?" Diamond asked Sealy without much expectation of a helpful answer.

"Very little until I get the deceased to my dissecting table. The light is terrible down there. The cause of death is anyone's guess right now. As for the time, we're looking at several days, going by the aroma."

"We think about a week, the day of the half marathon," Diamond said.

"Makes sense. The deceased is dressed in running clothes."

"Good."

"What's good about that?"

"It confirms my own observation. I was down there in a side tunnel, got a partial view of her legs and saw the trainers she was wearing."

"She?" Sealy said. "Your powers of observation can't be up to much. I know it's dark down there but the runner I was looking at isn't my idea of a she."

"Male?"

"Nothing is certain in the strange world we live in now, but that's my assumption." He reached for the white plastic body bag Gilbert had fetched. "I'm never without one of these. I'll also need at least ten metres of rope and some muscle to help with the lifting. Lower one end of the rope through the hole. Can you arrange that?"

"Don't you think we should get some pictures of the body before it's moved?"

"Has the photographer shown up at last, then? Send him down. Send the entire police force down if you like. There's plenty of room at the bottom. It's just the shaft that's narrow." He dropped the body bag into the void and climbed down after it.

The photographer must have been listening because he left the forensics van, stepped over the tape and crossed to the shaft entrance. No attempt seemed to have been made to mark an access path. What with the rainfall, the clearance of undergrowth and the footsteps around, the crime scene was well and truly corrupted.

"Get yourself into a zipper suit and a hard hat, Keith, and see what's down there," Diamond said. "I won't be joining you."

"Sanity breaks out at last," Ingeborg said.

"I didn't catch that."

"It wasn't meant for your ears, guv."

He told Paul Gilbert to find the length of rope Sealy had requested and he was about to go closer himself for a look down the hole when Ingeborg said, "I hope you don't mind me asking . . ."

"What about?"

"How it went for you at headquarters."

She'd heard he'd been summoned to headquarters, of course. You can't expect an official roasting to pass without everyone getting to know and revelling in it.

"I'm still here, aren't I? Enough said?"

Not enough for Ingeborg. "Just a warning shot, then?"

"Postponed because of a technical issue."

"Cool."

"You think so?"

"Maybe what's happening here will make a difference." He'd put his trouble with the high-ups to the back of his mind. "How exactly?"

"The body being found. You were right to authorise the searches. It wasn't a wild goose chase."

"That's true."

She cleared her throat. "Would it be an idea to text Georgina, keep her in the loop?"

He saw the sense in that. "Smart thinking, Inge."

"You could sit in the forensics van and do it in the dry."

"Right now?"

"The sooner the better."

Without more prompting from his tuned-in sergeant, he made his way to the van and opened the door at the back, pushed aside a stack of overshoes and made enough room for his rear.

Back at Combe Down dealing with the corpse I saw down the quarry. May be late returning.

He resisted garnishing the message with a note of "I told you so."

His speed of texting wasn't the quickest. By the time he'd sent the message, the logistics of bringing the body to the surface were being discussed. Dr. Sealy had put his head out of the hole again. He'd decided the best solution was to strap the dead man to a rigid rescue stretcher and lift it vertically. He didn't want it swinging against the sides of the shaft, so a pulley was about to be fixed in place.

One of the younger policemen asked if the body would be wrapped.

"Squeamish, are you, son?" Sealy said. "Yes, I'm zipping it into the body bag. You won't miss your beauty sleep tonight." He disappeared from view again.

"What a jerk," Diamond said, back beside Ingeborg. "Where's Keith?"

"Still down there, helping to strap the body to the stretcher, I expect."

"He won't mind doing that. When the nerves were given out, Keith had already left."

A small crowd assembled around the shaft when the pulley started to turn. The mechanism jerked alarmingly at one stage as some earth was loosened under the supports and a few gasps were heard, but the job was done without more alerts. The stretcher and its load were detached from the winding mechanism and returned to the horizontal.

"Wait," Diamond said to the officers about to remove it to a mortuary vehicle. He limped across to the stretcher. "Hold it steady for a moment."

The tab on the zip was at the top end. He pulled it down far enough to see the face inside.

And gasped.

He zipped it up again as if the tab was red hot.

26

Diamond hated being humbled. He thrived on self-confidence and it was in short supply right now. After the accident and the disciplinary hearing he hadn't expected fate to kick him in the guts yet again.

Sodden, in his drenched, mud-spattered suit, he leaned on his crutches and waited for Bertram Sealy to re-emerge from the shaft. Sealy was the last person on earth he wanted to enlighten, but it needed to be done.

The first to show his helmeted head was Keith Halliwell. No one was nearby to help him transfer from the rope ladder to the surface. All interest was elsewhere now that the body had been recovered. He scrambled out on hands and knees, looked up and said, "You'll get pneumonia, guv."

Diamond wasn't thinking about his health. "You saw who it is?"

"The stiff? Some runner."

Halliwell didn't know. He'd never met the man. He may have seen his picture, but that wasn't the same.

"Forget it," Diamond said. "Help Sealy out of the hole."

A second hard hat had appeared. Halliwell went over.

"You're a useful fellow," Sealy said. "Why don't you give up this policing nonsense and do a proper job as my assistant?"

When this attempt at humour didn't get an answer, Sealy

switched to Diamond. "What are you waiting for, peg leg? I can't tell you anything I haven't already. From the look of you, I'll have you on my slab before long."

"I know who he is," Diamond said.

"Took a peek, did you? Some people have no respect for the departed."

"I can save time getting him identified. His name is Tony Pinto. He's an ex-con on parole. A violent sexual predator. I put him away years ago."

"No great loss to the world, then."

"How soon can you do the autopsy?"

"I'll have to look at my diary."

"Give it priority, please. He's been dead for a week and you know how important the first few hours of an investigation are."

"You're sunk, then, and the crime scene is a quagmire. Call me later."

A trip home for a change of clothes would have been nice, but a fast return to Concorde House came before anything else. He got a lift from Ingeborg and spent most of the trip sending a text to Bertram Sealy. That autopsy couldn't be delayed.

The team were grouped around the kettle when he got there. They deserved their break, but it couldn't last long. He told them to be in the briefing room on the hour, which was under fifteen minutes away.

A text came back from Sealy, which was quicker than he expected, but the offer of 3 P.M. on Tuesday was no good at all. He got through for a live call which was more of a blast than a conversation.

The muddy suit troubled him until the ever-resourceful Ingeborg visited the traffic section and charmed a police motorcyclist into lending her guv'nor a set of leathers. Getting into it was a challenge that he embraced. Zipped, sibilant with every movement and feeling more macho than Brando in *The Wild One*, he appeared before his squad as never before and got a reaction he didn't expect or deserve. Middle-aged bikers are nothing unusual, he told himself, so what are the sly smiles for?

He told them to get over it.

He could have said the same to himself. He was still in shock from learning that the killer he'd been pursuing was in fact the victim. Until he got his own thoughts in order, he wasn't ready to trade theories about how the death had occurred and why. The briefing would be all about action.

"I've twisted the pathologist's arm and the autopsy takes place at six P.M. tonight, with Keith in attendance."

This was the first Halliwell had heard of it. He'd known Diamond too long to complain. And in truth he wouldn't have expected any different. No one could remember Diamond attending a postmortem.

"As well as that, you're the admin officer dealing with duty rosters and the bloody budget. Keeping Georgina off my back, in other words."

Halliwell nodded.

"We'll use this as our incident room and, John, you're the office manager. Get it up and running as soon as possible or quicker."

Leaman, a borderline obsessive-compulsive, would have gone into a strop if anyone else had been named.

Diamond turned to Ingeborg. "I want a profile of Pinto from you. Every facet of his life. I'll speak to the probation officer, who was quite sniffy about releasing information and can't refuse now. We'll get the prison record, the current address, next of kin, his employment details and anything of interest from their supervision. Your job is to get the gen on everyone else who came into contact with him and draw up a list of possible suspects. Ex-cons, anyone he worked with, everyone affected by his pursuit of women, including angry boyfriends, of course, and possibly other runners he knew."

"Is that all?" she said with irony and immediately wished she hadn't.

"No. There's more. Get close up and personal with the Police National Computer and HOLMES. I'm relying on you to cover the field—and it could be a large one. Now, Paul."

DC Gilbert flexed. "Guv?"

"You get several jobs rolled into one. Basically, you chase forensics for information until we get it. We're off to a really slow start. It's over a week since the day we think he was murdered. You're the exhibits officer, the receiver and the indexer. Any problem with that lot?"

"I don't think so, guv."

"See Keith if you need backup."

He went on to delegate more duties to other staff. Already he was certain the team needed to grow by at least ten more officers. He'd get reinforcements from downstairs and square it with Georgina when she found out.

"Get to it, people." To show solidarity, he made an effort to get his own body on the move as well. The crutches undermined the macho look of the biking leathers.

From the quiet of his office he put through a call to Deirdre, his stonewalling contact in the probation service. When he announced himself, she said, "Before you say another word, Superintendent, I'm not allowed to say any more than I already have about Tony Pinto."

"But you are," he told her. "You're liberated. In fact, it's your duty. I'm conducting a homicide enquiry now."

She needed time to take in what he'd said.

"He's dead?"

"For over a week."

"Are you sure?"

"His body was recovered from a mineshaft this afternoon.

I saw him close-up. No question it was Tony." He allowed her a few more seconds. "You *were* his probation officer, weren't you?"

She'd refused to confirm this up to now. A whispered, "Yes."

"You told me he failed to report for his weekly appointment."

"I did."

"Well, then."

Untypically of the Deirdre he thought he knew, her voice was subdued, breathy with emotion. "This is dreadful. He was doing so well."

He didn't trust himself to comment on Pinto's rehabilitation. "So where was he living? All I have is a box number."

"Duke Street."

"He *was* doing well." Duke Street is one of the best addresses in Bath, a fine Georgian terrace close to the centre of town. "How the hell did an ex-con manage to get in there?"

"It was only a basement flat, I understand."

"Better than you or I could afford, Deirdre. You'd need a small fortune to pay the rent. And flats don't come on the market too often."

"Well, yes. I gather it was a private arrangement through a friend."

"Did you get some background on his situation? Did he have a job?"

"He didn't say."

"Or you didn't ask?"

"Oh God." She paused, apparently on the verge of tears. She tried to recover her official voice and didn't quite succeed. "Tony could be charming and evasive at the same time. My main concern was that he was keeping out of trouble and he assured me that he was."

"He would say that. Wasn't he tagged?"

The scorn in his question helped her recover some of the old Deirdre. "I told you before, he was judged to be no risk. We don't put everyone under surveillance. There were conditions attached to his parole and as far as I'm aware he kept to them. No nightclubbing, for instance. No unapproved travel. The first and only breach in his probation was the missed appointment."

"He must have missed a second by now. And we know why. He was killed on the Sunday they ran the half marathon. He was still wearing the kit. Are you looking at a screen with his details on it?"

"I am."

"I'll have the number of the house, then, and the flat, if it has one, and everything else of assistance, including his prison record, however spotless it is."

After ending the call, he levered himself to a standing position, stumped back to the incident room and asked Ingeborg if she'd boned up on Tony Pinto.

"It's underway," she said. "There isn't much to go on."

"Which is why you need to see inside his flat, which I just discovered is in Duke Street."

"With you on board, guv?"

"Nothing gets past you, does it?"

John Wood the elder, the man whose vision transformed Bath from cramped, timber-framed medieval to the gracious, spacious, cream-coloured city of local stone it became in the eighteenth century, had Duke Street high in his thinking. His *Essay Towards a Description of the City of Bath* proposed "a grand place of assembly to be called the Royal Forum of Bath" which would occupy the Abbey Orchard, twenty-five low-lying acres reaching southwards from the Abbey precincts to the bank of the River Avon. Duke Street was to be one of two access routes to this spectacular site of assembly rooms and promenades softened by the backdrop of leafy Lyncombe Hill. Sadly, in Wood's own lifetime the project fell victim to small-minded municipal officials and get-rich-quick developers, and in the next century Lord Manvers owned the land and did a deal with the Great Western Railway that blighted the area past redemption. All you see now is the mayhem of Manvers Street with its office blocks, a two-storey car park, pubs, shops, churches, student quarters and the railway station. The lone relic of Wood's great plan is Duke Street. Elegant Georgian terraces stand either side of a flagged pavement, the widest in Bath and open only to pedestrians.

Ingeborg found a space in the car park next to what was now known as the Virgil Building, formerly the main police station, now said to be a learning centre. Each time Diamond passed the place, he felt withdrawal symptoms, so he tried not to look. He needed anyway to give full attention to what he was doing with the crutches. Fortunately, Duke Street was only a short distance away, across South Parade.

"I'd dearly like to know how a jailbird can afford to live here," he told Ingeborg as they made their way there. "He wasn't a bank robber, for pity's sake."

The terrace was three storeys high. Three storeys and an attic, and that wasn't counting the basement. Iron railings and gates dissuaded passers-by from going down the steep stone steps—a long way down.

"This is too much," Ingeborg said. "You'd better wait up here, guv."

"You're joking, I hope."

He let her go first, and then started his own precarious descent going backwards using only one crutch and relying on the railing for balance. The spare crutch ended up beside Ingeborg at the bottom of the stairwell. He felt the pressure on his good leg right away and wished he was as slim as she was. With dogged determination and some swearing he reached the bottom. It had a strong smell of decay.

"I wouldn't want to do that every day, even on two legs," he said.

"Do you have a key?" she asked him.

"How would I?"

"Shame about that."

"It's an old-fashioned Yale lock. Use a credit card."

"Not one of mine, thank you." She emptied the plastic water bottle she was carrying, took a penknife from her pocket and cut a rectangular strip from it that she bent double. Then she slid the improvised tool downwards between door and frame and freed the latch.

The inside was larger than you would guess from the street. Georgian terraced houses are like books on a shelf, the spines a compressed indication of the large interior. The hallway stretched about forty feet, with five doors on either side, all closed.

"This can't all be his," Diamond said. "Any guess which door we try?"

"Better keep our voices down, guv."

"No point," he said. "We need help. Let's make ourselves known." He rapped on the first door to his left.

It opened wide at once, suggesting that the tenant had been waiting behind her door. A very large woman in a very large wheelchair. How large? XXL for sure. Do they have XXXL? She looked not much over thirty, but every other statistic was way beyond that. Above the chins and between the cheeks was a pretty face. Blue, intelligent eyes, neat nose and small, well-defined mouth. What was an outsize chair-bound woman doing in a basement flat? Best not to ask at this stage. Anyway, other matters were more pressing.

Before they spoke, she said, "I'm sure it's a good cause, but I don't have any spare change."

Those pesky crutches.

Ingeborg explained that they weren't asking for a donation. "We're trying to find Mr. Pinto."

"You mean Tony?" she said. "You've made a mistake,
then. This is my room."

"Which one is his?"

"Last on the left, next to the kitchen, but he isn't in. He
hasn't been home for over a week. Friend of yours, is he?"

"We're police officers making enquiries." She showed
her ID.

"I'll need my glasses to read that."

"It says I'm Detective Sergeant Smith and this is Superintendent Diamond. Who are you?"

She rolled her eyes and spoke in a mock-posh voice.
"Beatrice Henson, but everyone has always called me Beattie
and so can you. There's nothing seriously wrong, is there?"

"It sounds as if you know Tony quite well."

"He's the only one I do know and he's good to me."

"Friendly, then?"

"Not the way you mean. I can do without that sort of
nonsense in my situation. Tony is my rescuer. They march
in here, brazen as you like, as if they own the place."

"The other tenants?" Diamond said.

"Spiders, honey. Big ones, and not just in September.
That's one of the drawbacks of life below stairs."

"Nasty."

"Somebody told me they come out of the vaults under
the street."

"I didn't know about the vaults."

"Nobody uses them. They're damp and horrible. When
this place was built three hundred years ago or whenever
it was, everything had to be raised up because the ground
underneath was a swamp, being as close to the river as
it is, so Duke Street is built over vaults and that's where
the spiders come from. They make my hair stand on end.
Thank goodness Tony knows what to do."

"Traps them in a jar?"

"Stamps on them. I couldn't do that."

Diamond pictured Pinto doing it, no problem.

"I couldn't do it either," Ingeborg said. "I take them out to the garden."

"Where they die anyway, if they're house spiders," Diamond said, to steer this exchange to a conclusion. More important topics needed airing. "They can't survive long outside. I've got a cat who takes care of the problem. Keep a cat and you won't often see a spider."

"We aren't allowed pets."

"Shame," Ingeborg said.

Diamond got the conversation back on track by asking if Pinto was equally popular with the other tenants.

"I wouldn't know about that," Beattie said. "They don't speak much English, any of them. Come to think of it, he does go upstairs and sees them off in the mornings, which is rather sweet. They're all blokes. I'm the only woman down here apart from the ones Tony brings home."

"He's still one for the ladies, is he?"

She laughed. "Do you know about that? I hear him bring them in sometimes. I've got perfect hearing. When they come through the front door like you just did, I know about it. I can't always pick up the words, but I know the difference between a bloke's voice and a woman's and you don't expect ladies, as you call them, to be coming in here unless they're invited back. He makes them giggle and I hear it and think that's Tony up to his games again. What he gets up to after that isn't my business. I don't judge him."

"Do the other residents have lady friends?"

"They don't have the privacy for that sort of thing. Four or five to a room and maybe more."

Diamond glanced at Ingeborg and then at Beattie. "Migrants, are they?"

"I expect so, but they're not taking advantage and

claiming benefits. Quite the opposite. They work long hours, poor things, collected at seven every morning and driven off in a silver van that only gets back about eight in the evening. That's a long day if they're doing hard work and I think they must be because their faces show it. They use the kitchen at the end of the passage and make themselves some sort of meal and then by nine or nine-thirty everything goes quiet until next morning."

"You share the kitchen with them, I expect," Ingeborg said.

"No, my dear, I'm self-sufficient. I buy everything online and have it delivered. I have a fridge freezer and a microwave in here and I don't need to cook the old-fashioned way."

"Have you lived here a long time, Beattie?"

"Eight years this August. I didn't have to use the chair in those days, but my legs won't hold me up anymore. It's my own fault. Comfort-eating, it's called. People were friendlier when I started here, but they all left for one reason and another. The rents going up made a difference. I wasn't budging." She laughed. "They'd never get me up the stairs. I like it down here, apart from the spiders. After everyone left, the place was empty except for me for six weeks, which wasn't nice. I put on a lot of weight to cheer myself up. And then it filled up almost overnight with these foreign blokes. Before Tony, there was someone with tattoos and a shaved head called Alex who seemed to act as their foreman, if you could call him that. He had the room where Tony is now, up the corridor. He didn't ever have much to say to me."

"Who is your landlord?"

She laughed. "That's a joke."

"Why?"

"It's some agency in London and they keep changing their name. It was Howes and Watts when I first got here and two weeks later it was something else and one of the tenants called them Whys and Wherefores, which I thought was very witty. It's Zodiac now or something with the letter Z. I pay by direct debit and, fingers crossed, they haven't put the rent up in the past two years."

"So apart from when you find a spider, you don't see much of Tony?"

"Only his legs going up and down the steps. I know they're his because of the good strong muscles and the nice tan." She blushed at what she'd said. "Can't avoid seeing them, living in this room with a view of nothing else except the steps, and if he chooses to wear shorts that's his business. He's sporty, you see. He goes for runs."

"He was in the half marathon last week. Did you know?"

"Sunday, wasn't it? He left in the middle of the morning in his sky-blue shorts."

"Did you see him come back?"

"This is it: he didn't. Has something happened to him? Is that why you're here?"

"We're investigating," Diamond said. "Has anyone else come visiting since the day of the race?"

"Who do you mean?"

"A stranger. Someone who might have been interested in Tony and maybe wanting to see inside his room."

She shook her head. "You're the first I've seen, and I don't miss much."

"I can believe that, Beattie. Just to be sure, we'll check the room ourselves."

"I'll come with you. The chair just fits in his doorway."

"You'd better not. We don't know what we're going to find."

Beattie clapped her hand to her mouth.

"Stay in your room. We'll deal with it."

No sounds came from behind the other doors when they passed them. The rest of the basement seemed to be empty, bearing out the story of the early morning working party. Diamond strongly suspected modern slavery overseen by Pinto and he'd be alerting colleagues who dealt with trafficking. He felt sickened by the exploitation of vulnerable people.

At the end of the corridor, Ingeborg produced her piece of plastic and opened Pinto's door at the second swipe.

Diamond found the light switch and revealed a room no bigger than a mobile home and with the same attention to space-saving. At first sight, it was a sitting room dominated by a two-seater sofa bed in red upholstery. Floor cushions, a large shaggy rug, a Tiffany mirror, spotlights, a fully stocked wine rack, plasma TV, music system with loudspeakers—clearly Pinto's seduction salon. Yet it could easily convert to a breakfast room, with a hinged tabletop fitted to the wall and above it a cupboard probably containing crockery and food items. And there was storage for clothes in a fitted wardrobe. The wallpaper had vertical red and white stripes topped off with a pseudo-classical frieze that combined the tenant's known preoccupations—athletics and sex—showing naked runners, male and female, in the style of Greek vase painting. No detail had been left out. If anything, the details were accentuated. Some of the males had prodigious erections.

"What would his lady visitors think of this?" Diamond asked.

"They'd soon get the idea."

"Cosy?"

"Creepy is the word I'd use."

They started the search. "I'm looking for his phone," Diamond said, "and failing that I'll settle for his laptop and his wallet."

"Won't he have taken them with him?"

"In a half marathon?"

"Runners often carry phones."

"Nothing like that was with the body."

They checked every surface, every drawer, the backs of things, the tops of cupboards and wardrobe, and found no electronic device other than the TV remote and no paperwork other than a few shop receipts. The pockets of his clothes were empty.

"Disappointing," Ingeborg said. "Do you think his killer has been by?"

"And nicked the phone and things? Possible, but risky."

"If there was incriminating stuff . . ."

"We'll keep an open mind. Beattie hadn't seen anyone and I get the feeling she knows every time a visitor comes down those steps." He took another look inside the wardrobe. Pinto seemed to have worn nothing but sports kit, T-shirts, shorts, running jackets and tracksuits for all weather conditions. "I wonder where he bought this stuff."

"Argyle Street," Ingeborg said. "Two of the shop receipts were for John Moore."

"We'll take them with us."

On the way out, he said to the shut door, "All clear, Beattie. Any problem, give us a call."

The major incident room was a reality when they returned, twenty or more officers behind screens. John Leaman was in his element, crisscrossing between desks making sure that the computers were installed and working. He'd labelled every desk with a notice in large letters describing its intended use. The staff who knew him well had screwed up the paper and binned it. If you were the exhibits officer or the CCTV viewing officer, it was obvious enough. But he deserved credit for the speed of the operation.

Diamond's brain worked in a different way from Leaman's. He'd been playing Queen numbers in his head to get to the elusive mnemonic he wanted, and after deciding

"We Are the Champions" was no help, the right one came to him. "Get me ROCU, will you. I need to report something before I do anything else."

He was given a phone and spoke to a sergeant at Portishead who promised to pass on the news about the suspicious activity in the Duke Street house. If a basement stuffed with exhausted foreigners driven off each morning in a van wasn't organised crime, pigs could fly and the moon was made of green cheese.

The main players in his team apart from Leaman were known in incident-room jargon as the outside officers. They were given desks and computers, but most of their work would be off-site. Diamond limped across to Ingeborg and asked her to move her screen aside so that he could sit on her desk. She didn't complain. If he parked himself in a chair, like Beattie, he'd have difficulty getting up. He gestured to the others to come closer for a short briefing and filled them in on the visit to Duke Street. Leaman, emphatically an inside officer but who missed nothing, made sure he was near enough to join in.

"In short," Diamond said when he'd been through the details, "a main question was answered. How could Pinto have gone straight from prison to one of the top addresses in Bath? It seems one of the head honchos in Berwyn Jail did a deal with him. In return for a comfortable pad, he would see that the illegals in the basement caused no trouble and went to work each day. Easy-peasy for Pinto and he could still find time to go chasing women and bring them back for sex. I notified the Regional Organised Crime Unit a few minutes ago."

"Will they be taking over?" Paul Gilbert asked.

"Christ, no. We still have a homicide on our patch."

"But if it's linked to people-smuggling—"

Diamond closed him down. "How do we know that? We don't. Let ROCU make the case. Your job and mine remains the same, to get a grip on what happened on Combe Down, right?"

No one objected.

"First question: was Pinto killed there, or some other place?"

"Hold on, guv."

Diamond glared. Leaman was supposed to be setting up the room.

"That's not the first question," Leaman said.

The glare turned thunderous.

"Surely the first question is was he killed?"

Typical of Leaman to butt in, but he was the team's logic man, and his intellectual rigour had proved useful before.

"It can't be suicide, if that's what you're thinking," Diamond said. "The iron grille was back over the shaft when the search party got to it. Someone else had to be involved."

"Accident, then."

"How in the name of sanity is that possible?"

Leaman was unabashed. "He was pestering that woman Belinda, right? She quit the race and made her way to Combe Down. Fact, okay?"

"Okay."

"Pinto went looking for her—"

"Speculation," Ingeborg cut in.

"This is what we're doing, testing theories," Leaman said with a convenient sidestep. "Nobody here knows for certain what happened. If you don't want my ideas, I'll shut up."

Ingeborg gave a shrug. Everyone was used to being harangued by Leaman. You had to remember it wasn't personal.

"He got a sight of her in the wood, then lost her again. He found the shaft—"

"Just like that?" Ingeborg said.

"It's Combe Down, for pity's sake. The place has more holes than a slab of Swiss cheese. He lifted the cover thinking maybe she was hiding down there."

"Thirty feet down?"

"He didn't know how deep it was and neither did Belinda. He lost his footing and fell in when he was lifting the grille. Either it slammed back into place then or Belinda was somewhere nearby and saw what happened and closed it—which would explain why she panicked and went AWOL."

Ingeborg was the first to react. "It's not impossible, but it's bloody unlikely, John, as you well know. It's far more likely he was murdered. If you want to get rid of a body, a disused mineshaft is a good solution."

Paul Gilbert said in support, "Easy to do and difficult to find."

Leaman sniffed. "The boss found it."

"At a cost," Diamond said, tapping his injured leg and getting sympathetic smiles. He was always looking for ways to defuse the tensions Leaman caused. "Who agrees with Inge that this was more likely a murder?"

"I do, for one," Gilbert said, "and I wouldn't mind betting the postmortem confirms it. A knife wound or a bullet hole. You can't argue with that."

"We won't have long to wait, I hope," Diamond said, checking his watch. The autopsy would be into its second hour already. "Any thoughts on a possible motive?"

"Where do I start?" Ingeborg said. "He was a sexual predator. This could be someone who heard he was out of prison and wanted revenge for the attack on Bryony Lancaster, or it could be down to a new encounter."

"A woman he just met?"

"Or her boyfriend or father or some family member angry at how he'd treated her. We know he was back to his old ways."

"We're assuming he was, from what Beattie told us," Diamond said, sounding as finicky as Leaman.

"No, we heard from Belinda, and you saw for yourself. He was pestering her so much that she quit the race."

"Could Belinda have killed him, trying to fend him off?" Gilbert asked. "She's the only person we know for sure who was on Combe Down."

"I don't see how," Ingeborg said.

"You don't think a woman's strong enough?"

"I didn't say that. She couldn't have killed him because she wasn't there with him. He was still in the race when she was at Combe Down. He finished at least two hours later and then made his way there."

"Why?" Diamond said. "Did he expect to find Belinda still up there? Had they arranged to meet? I can't believe she would have agreed to that. Why would he have gone to Combe Down except to meet someone?"

"Does she have a boyfriend?" Gilbert asked.

"In the words of her landlady, Mrs. Hector, she's shyer than a limpet," Diamond said. "The boyfriend theory doesn't hold up, I'm afraid."

"Hasn't it occurred to any of you that he may not have been killed because of how he behaved with women?" Leaman said. "Look at it another way. He spent twelve years in prison. He must have made enemies in that time."

"Fair point, John," Diamond said. "Old scores to settle when he gets out, but why kill him on Combe Down?"

"Who said he was killed there?" Leaman said. "It's a great place to hide a corpse, we all agree, but the murder needn't have been done there. He could have been killed in Bath and moved there after he was dead."

"When you say moved, you mean driven," Ingeborg said, "in which case there will be tyre tracks."

"The best of luck finding the right ones," Gilbert said. "The field looks like it was used for a motocross rally."

"Not our job," Diamond said. "We're going to rely heavily on scenes of crime and forensics—which we all know will take an age, which is why the early progress has to come the old-fashioned way, through deduction. If John is right, and the body was moved to the shaft from somewhere else, the killer has local knowledge."

"And wheels," Gilbert said. "And the strength to do the lifting."

"I sense a sexist deduction coming on," Ingeborg said. "Let's hear it for the female murderer. We're not incapable of loading a body into a vehicle and dropping it down a mineshaft. Anyway, what if the victim was brought to Combe Down alive and forced at gunpoint to lift the grille and jump in?"

"He wouldn't necessarily die."

"With a thirty-foot drop he'd not be in good shape. Who's there to help? He wouldn't survive long."

"You made your point," Diamond said. "We'll keep the fair sex in the frame, along with the jealous boyfriends and the ex-cons. Back to work, everyone."

He limped across to the exhibits desk just as Paul Gilbert returned there. The task of bagging up material securely and making sure it had a valid chain of evidence would occupy the young man for days to come. "Did we give you the receipts we found in Pinto's room?"

"For food and clothes? Yes, guv. I dealt with them."

"Let me see the John Moore ones."

One of Bath's longest-surviving businesses, John Moore had been founded in the days when sportsmen wore baggy shorts reaching to the knees and sportswomen were still in long skirts.

Diamond read the first receipt through the transparent zipper bag. "He paid cash, I notice. Pair of trainers. Serious money. You get a proper fitting in a shop like that. Where do you go for your trainers, Paul?"

"Sports Direct."

"And try them on yourself, quick decision and pay?"

Gilbert grinned.

"Buying shoes will be a full-on performance in Moore's," Diamond went on. "They'll remember a regular customer like Pinto. First thing tomorrow, take a trip into town and see what they can tell you about him. Personal stuff. We're not interested in shoe sizes. What's that?" He'd heard a shriller sound than the humming computers.

"Your phone." Ingeborg raised a thumb in approval. For once it had been turned on.

He looked at the display. "Keith, from the mortuary." He jammed it to his ear, eager for the findings. "Is it over?"

"Only a tea break in the office, guv," Halliwell told him. "This could be a late night. We've done the photographs and the external examination."

"Is that all? What's the story so far?"

"Broken bones for sure, as you'd expect with a body falling down a shaft. Bruising and cuts, but nothing like a knife wound or a bullet hole. And he thinks there may have been a struggle, He's hopeful of getting DNA from under the fingernails. Did you hear that?"

"I did. I'm taking it in. No obvious cause of death, then?"

"Not yet. We'll find out later if some of the injuries happened before death."

"Make sure the clothes are sent to the lab as soon as possible. Sealy is quite capable of bagging them up and leaving them on a shelf until someone asks."

"Hey-ho," Halliwell said, "looks like they're going back in. I'll need to go. Do you want me to phone you when it's over?"

"Depends. I've had a long day. No later than eleven."

"Jesus, I hope it isn't that late. I had a sandwich for lunch and that's all. I'll be ravenous."

How anyone could be ravenous after witnessing an autopsy was beyond Diamond's understanding.

27

At 10 P.M. Diamond was at home and talking to his cat. An early night was indicated after the tiring day he'd had. Getting to bed in his disabled state was a slow process these days. The problem was that Raffles worked to his own timetable, wanting to go out at 10:30 and return a few minutes after. It wasn't wise for an elderly cat to stay out all night among younger toms eager to fight for territory. One orange tabby had come visiting several times through the cat flap and sprayed the kitchen, forcing Diamond to keep the flap secured overnight. He couldn't lift Raffles and shove him out of the back door, so it was down to persuasion, which wasn't working. Raffles sat eyeing him from across the room, indifferent to every appeal. More of a sit-in than a stand-off.

Twenty minutes later when the phone rang, Raffles hadn't budged.

In this battle of wills, Diamond had forgotten Keith Halliwell's offer to call.

"I hope I'm not too late, guv."

"Too late? No. What time is it?"

"I only just got in. The postmortem finished twenty minutes ago."

"Got you. And what was the cause of death?"

"Bleeding on the brain."

"He's sure?"

"There was nothing so obvious as a bullet wound or a stabbing."

"You told me that already. So what are we talking about here—a crack on the head?"

"Right." But there was a note in that one-word response that spoke of problems.

"You don't sound confident."

"The difficulty is deciding what happened before and after death. The brain injury killed him."

"You already said."

"But most of the damage was to the legs and pelvis because it seems they hit the floor of the quarry first."

Diamond felt a twinge from his own bad foot.

"The head wasn't such a mess," Halliwell went on. "Sealy shaved off the hair and found this injury to the back of the skull, a fracture."

"Blunt instrument?"

"No, he ruled that out. Hitting someone over the head produces a different kind of injury."

"More of a dent, I expect."

"Yes, usually circular, or else stellate—like a starburst. He called Pinto's a simple linear fracture, like if you drop a hard-boiled egg on the floor."

Diamond would have preferred not to be told about the egg so soon after supper.

"As he explained it," Halliwell continued, "our skulls are lined with bony plates and that sort of impact puts pressure on the edges and they snap and look like the cracked egg, see?"

"I can picture it, thank you."

"When he removed the brain, he found bleeding from the under-surface of the frontal lobes."

"Hold on. You said he was hit on the *back* of the head."

"This was from a secondary fracture at the front."

"Now you're losing me."

"The brain sits inside the skull surrounded by membranes and fluid, so it's not fixed in position. If it gets a big jolt, it will smack against the thin bone of the orbital roof and fracture it. He said this is called the contre-coup effect. It's not unusual in traffic accidents." Halliwell had attended so many autopsies on Diamond's behalf, he could be excused for trying to sound like the pathologist he wasn't.

"Can we cut to the chase, Keith?"

"He said it was typical of someone falling backwards and striking the ground."

Diamond's theories about the killing were being challenged. "Is that certain? We know Pinto had a fall, straight down the shaft."

"Yes, but a long fall like that produces horrendous injuries if it's head first. The skull and cervical spine are forced together and—"

"Spare me the details. If that didn't cause the injury and he wasn't bashed with a blunt instrument, what happened?"

"Like I said, a fall."

"Above ground, is that it?"

"You can't tell from the injury where it was done."

"You're starting to sound more and more like bloody Sealy. Was Pinto alive when it happened?"

"You can tell from the bleeding on the brain."

"I'll take your word for that—or Sealy's. I'm trying to arrive at a likely sequence of events, Keith. It's not impossible he was attacked above ground and killed outright and dropped down the shaft. But equally he could have got the brain injury from his head hitting the quarry floor, right?"

"Or the wall. The legs hit the floor first. That was obvious from the state of them. But the rest of his body felt the impact and you'd expect the head, being heavy, to strike something. It's surprising the skull wasn't more marked.

I suppose it could have been protected by an arm or the chest."

"Were there any other signs of a physical attack?"

"A cut and some bruising on the left cheek."

"I saw when I did the ID."

"Could have been caused when he hit the quarry floor."

"Do bruises still appear after death?"

"Even I know the answer to that one," Halliwell said. "I've been to autopsies where the bruise gets bigger as the day goes on."

"I've got the picture, I think," Diamond said to save himself from more titbits from the mortuary. "Is Sealy expecting anything from the lab tests?"

"Maybe, but don't hold your breath. He took clippings from the fingernails. There was slight bruising to the knuckles of the right hand. If there was a fight, there may be some of his attacker's DNA."

"That would be a bonus. You left him in no doubt we need those results as soon as possible?"

"He's aware of it."

"Okay, I've heard enough for now." Some gratitude was wanted here. "Well done, Keith. I appreciate this, as always. Did you get something to eat?"

"No, and I'm famished, but there's some liver in the freezer. I'll fry that with bacon and a couple of tomatoes."

The man had a cast-iron stomach.

When Diamond put down the phone, his cat had moved and was waiting by the back door. It was 10:30.

Raffles had won.

In the incident room next morning, a detective constable called Sharp was assigned to trawl through the CCTV footage of the Other Half. She would need to live up to her name. Picking out Tony Pinto from five thousand runners wasn't too difficult when you had his timing at various checkpoints, but Diamond wanted the race numbers of everyone who passed each camera within five minutes of him. Any who featured more than once would come in for special attention. The job would take days.

The man himself was in his office with a detective inspector from ROCU who'd shown him a card with the name Jones on it. Jones had the air of a man who could recite the Official Secrets Act like the Lord's Prayer. He'd insisted on a private room for the conversation. He probably had visiting cards with Smith, Brown and Robinson in his wallet as well. His true identity wasn't an issue with Diamond. If he wished to be coy, let him.

"Are you soundproofed?" Jones stepped over to the wall and tapped on the plasterboard.

"No one is listening, if that's what you mean," Diamond said. "We all bat for the same team here."

Jones moved to the window and looked down, as if some eavesdropper might be out there on a ladder.

Satisfied, it seemed, he sat opposite Diamond and struck a more positive note, but pianissimo. "You did the right thing, notifying us about the house in Duke Street."

"Doing my job."

An approving nod.

"Will you deal with it?" Diamond asked.

Jones looked wounded by the directness of the question. After a pause, he said, "Let's put it this way: we're aware of the situation."

Diamond pictured a POLICE AWARE notice stuck onto an abandoned vehicle at the side of the road. In no way did he consider the Pinto case abandoned.

"That's it," Jones continued, as if pleased by the form of words he'd used, "aware of the situation."

"I guessed as much." ROCU *would* say they were aware. Like every other department in the police service, they were over-stretched and short-staffed. They didn't keep tabs on everything. "So why are you here?"

"Just touching base," Jones said. "I gather you're interested in one of the tenants."

"Tony Pinto."

"Pinto," he said, and added, as if he knew the name, "Aha."

"It's more than interest," Diamond said. "It's an investigation into his death. I reported this to your lot because I'm suspicious he was involved in people-smuggling and modern slavery. I'm assuming he was put there to manage the day-to-day operation."

"Conceivably." Even this vague word was a stretch for Jones.

"If I'm right," Diamond said, "it's organised crime."

"People-smuggling? Certainly."

"That's why I reported it."

"Good man."

Diamond waited for more. Jones looked left and right as if deciding whether to test the walls again. "Without for a moment wishing to denigrate the people at the coal face such as your good self, we work from a different perspective."

"Okay."

"We focus on the high-ups, the people at the top. Identify, disrupt and dismantle. The Duke Street operation, if there is one, will have been masterminded elsewhere."

"Obviously. Was Pinto recruited in prison?"

"Why do you ask?"

"Because he's only been out a few months. He didn't ask for help finding a place to live. He moved straight into the bedsit in the basement."

"You're well-informed."

"I put him behind bars in the first place."

"There's some history with you, then?"

"I don't let it get in the way," Diamond said, sensing a trap. "Do you know all about him?"

"We have our people inside prison."

"Grasses?"

"I'm speaking of the RPIU."

"Never heard of them."

"Good. You can forget them again after I've told you. They're the Regional Prison Intelligence Unit. Any contacts he made will have been monitored."

"You know who the villains are, then?"

Jones didn't. Transparently, he'd never even heard of Duke Street until Diamond reported it. He trotted out another of his bland responses. "Bringing the ringleaders to justice isn't easy. It's all in the timing."

"What can I expect to see next?"

"That's a strategic decision."

"Simultaneous arrests?"

"Probably."

"Nothing in the near future?"

"I'm not at liberty to say. In the meantime, ROCU can't allow anything to compromise the progress we're making with our own investigation."

Diamond said with eyebrows raised, "How could that arise?"

"We look to you to soft-pedal. Pinto's death isn't high priority."

They were round to the reason for the visit. Finally.

"It's still a homicide," Diamond said. "Someone out there killed him and dumped him down a mineshaft."

"And you've got an excellent clear-up record. You'll catch up with your perpetrator when the time is right. As of now, we don't want the human slavery story all over the media. Softly, softly, as the saying goes." Jones ended the exchange by widening his eyes as if to say we're all in this together, aren't we?

Diamond, being Diamond, didn't bat an eyelid.

Alone again, he sat back in his well-padded swivel chair and pondered his next move. There was a chance Pinto had been murdered because of some failure in his duties at the Duke Street house. Working for traffickers was high-risk. As a minor player, he was dispensable, and he knew too much to be allowed to live. If so, this would have been a contract killing ordered by the high-ups Jones had spoken about. So what could Bath CID do about it? Catching the killer wouldn't be enough. It was only a step on the way to exposing the so-called masterminds. No argument: ROCU were better equipped to take that on.

But if the homicide was unconnected with the slavery scam, Diamond had a duty to track the killer down. He would investigate, even if it meant going back to Duke Street to eliminate the slavers from his enquiries. That was the way he worked, following up each lead until he got his man—or woman.

He reached for the crutches and moved out to the incident room. Everyone knew about the ROCU visitor. "Relax," he told them. "We're still on the case. Nothing is off limits except careless talk about people-smuggling. I'm not even sure he knew what was going on in Duke Street."

Ingeborg looked up from her keyboard. "Did he know about Pinto?"

"Probably not. Our Tony is small fry to them."

"He must have been small fry to the slavers. They haven't replaced him and they haven't moved the men to another location, or Beattie would have known for sure."

Leaman, hovering nearby as usual, said, "Why don't they just walk away?"

"The men in the basement? Isn't that obvious?" Ingeborg said.

"Not to me."

Ingeborg wasn't bluffing. Modern slavery was a scourge

on humanity she'd hated ever since first hearing about it. The visit to Duke Street had brought the evil closer and she'd made sure she knew how it functioned. "Debt bondage, for one thing."

"What's that, then?"

"Typically, they're allowed to earn a small wage at whatever menial job they do, but they're told they owe the slavers big money for smuggling them in and providing them with a place to live, so what they get is a pittance."

"All the more reason to escape."

"Escape to what? They're stateless. If any of them had passports, they'll have been taken by the traffickers. They're in terror of being repatriated. They have a place to live and the van still comes for them each day, so they climb in and go to work. They're conditioned to it."

"What an existence," Gilbert said.

"It's vile, and it's more widespread in Britain than you think. Nobody knows how many for sure. More than six thousand, anyway."

"How can anyone put a figure on it?" Leaman said.

"Reported cases."

"And how many are not reported?"

"Leave it," Diamond said. "Back to work, people."

Gilbert remained, obviously with something else to say. "I did as you asked, guv, called in at John Moore Sports this morning."

"Anything helpful?"

"They were shocked to hear he was dead. All the staff seemed to know him and he was well liked, chatty and cheerful."

"Especially with the women, no doubt," Diamond said.

"Nobody said."

"I did. Tony Pinto would score in a nunnery. I'm asking if you heard anything of use to us."

"They said he'd set himself up as a personal trainer."

"Nice work if you can get it. He was doing the same in prison, and now he gets to visit rich people in their homes. They work up a sweat on the bike and he tells them to keep pedalling."

"Spinning, guv."

Diamond missed the point and Gilbert didn't enlighten him.

"Did you find out who he trained?"

"One of their main customers. Very rich. Buys only the best kit. She couldn't speak highly enough of him."

"As a trainer, you mean?"

"That's what I said."

"Name?"

"Olga something. Russian."

A feature of recent times in Bath was the influx of oil-rich billionaires who had bought properties, but a Russian community had thrived here for over fifty years. The devout had their own Orthodox church in Alexandra Road. How many of the ultra-rich attended church was an open question, but clearly they patronised the sports shop.

"What's her address?"

28

Sydney Place makes up the two front sides of the hexa-gon of handsome terraces bordering Sydney Gardens, a green sanctuary in the heart of the city. The entire area was a concept of Thomas Baldwin, who had already designed some of the city's big-hitting attractions, the Pump Room, Great Pulteney Street, the Guildhall and the Colonnade. Sadly for Baldwin, the pleasure garden became a source of pain when he was found to have overreached his finances and was sacked as city architect, hounded into bankruptcy by a ruthless rival, John Palmer, who replaced him.

Only the first twelve houses of Sydney Place are Baldwin's. To anyone who knows his story they stand as a monument to a flawed visionary.

"Mostly flats," DC Paul Gilbert said prosaically after glancing at one of the door entry panels they passed.

"But what an outlook," Diamond said.

"I'm surprised at a Russian billionaire living in a flat."

"Unlikely. He'll have bought one of these houses outright. Possibly the ones each side as well."

Gilbert never could tell when his boss was kidding. "Why would he do that?"

"Security. Money on that scale brings its own problems and one of them is that you have to watch your back. Everyone knows that, Russians especially."

"How would he get rid of all those tenants?"

"How did he get to be a billionaire?"

They had phoned ahead and were admitted by a man dressed like a servant in a Chekhov play, in a pale-blue high-buttoned, loose-fitting linen suit tied at the waist. But the room they were shown into was English through and through, pure Jane Austen, the sort of place that would have earned orgasmic shrieks from the furniture expert on the *Antiques Roadshow*. Sheraton, Chippendale and Hepplewhite jostled for attention—chairs, armchairs, a reading stand, secretaire, card tables and even the corner piece known as a whatnot. "Mrs. Ivanova will join you for tea in a few minutes, unless you prefer a sherry," they were told in good English. "She is getting ready."

"Ready for *us*?" Gilbert said when the man had gone.

"For afternoon tea. We'd better sit down." There was no shortage of chairs. Sitting on any of them seemed uncouth, but Diamond had never had any problem being uncouth. Besides, he needed to sit. He was trying to manage without the crutches, using only a stick.

Gilbert remained standing, awed by the surroundings. He was simply begging to be wound up a little.

"Are your hands clean?"

Gilbert spread his palms.

"Turn them over." Diamond winced at what he saw. "God help us, Paul. You could grow radishes under those fingernails. Better hide them under your napkin."

"I don't have one."

"You'll be given one, Irish linen, nicely ironed and folded. Do you know how to use it?"

A worried shake of the head.

"You take it by one corner, shake it open, spread it over your lap and treat it with respect. Don't even think about using it to wipe your nose or your grubby fingers. You may have seen people tucking one under their collar. That isn't done at teatime. Wait to be served and don't drop any crumbs. One small square of sandwich only, which you don't lift open to see what's inside. Watch our hostess and make sure she bites into hers before you lift yours to your mouth. Take small bites and make it last. All things considered, you might do best to leave it on your plate."

"Are you sending me up, guv?"

"What do you think? Shall I tell you how to hold the teacup?"

The exchange was cut short by a large woman entering with three builders'-size mugs and a packet of biscuits on a tin tray. Not a napkin in sight. She was in a loud pink sweatsuit and white trainers.

Another servant, anyone would have assumed.

Just in case she wasn't, Diamond got up and Gilbert dipped his head respectfully.

"Please to sit. I am Olga Ivanova. You like Hobnobs?" Blonde, quick to smile, she handed the packet to Gilbert, who almost dropped it when he realised this was the lady of the house. "Take some and pass on."

There was mischief in that smile, but also some nervousness and maybe pain as well.

The manservant glided in with the sugar and glided out again.

"So," Olga said when they were all seated, "policemen come to my house. In Russia, this is not good. We have saying: When police come calling, get out chequebook. If cheque is no use, get out vodka. If vodka is no use, get out." She shook with laughter and then, seeing the blank faces, frowned and added, "Does not translate well, I think."

"You're not in trouble, ma'am," Diamond said. "We're hoping you can help us with an enquiry."

"Call me Olga please. I do not like this 'ma'am.'"

"Olga it is, then. We were told you have a personal trainer."

"I do not think so."

"A fitness expert who gives advice."

She shook her head.

"No?"

"No."

"Are you sure?"

"I am sure. He is not here this week, last week. No phone call. No message. I think I do not have trainer anymore."

"But you had one before?"

"Of course. My gorgeous Tony, three times in week. I don't know what happens. I pay him well, each time cash in hand. Now nothing."

"Tony Pinto?"

"You know?"

"I'm sorry to tell you he's dead."

Olga clapped her hand to her mouth and turned paler than the ceiling. There was no question she was shocked.

"We found his body at the bottom of a stone quarry last week."

A gasp. "That is why he stop coming?"

There was an opening for black humour here, but Diamond could see Olga's eyes reddening and welling up, so he just nodded.

"Someone push?"

"We're investigating, trying to find out."

"This is so sad. He is—was—lovely man, top trainer. I am getting much help from Tony. New treadmill, rowing machine, exercise bike."

Much help and much expense with it, Diamond thought. What was the betting that Pinto took backhanders from the sales team? "Are all these machines in the house?"

"My exercise hall downstairs. You like to see?"

He shook his head. "No need."

"Is boring, anyway," she said. "Fitness machines. My husband everywhere."

An interpreter would be helpful. "Your husband watches you training?"

"No, no. Photos, certificates, newspaper stories all over walls. Gold this. Silver that. Black belt. Ivanov win again."

"He's a sportsman?"

"All sports. Marathon. Lift weights, karate, football, swimming. Are you sportsman?"

"I played some rugby. I don't think it's popular in Russia. Getting back to Tony, did you get to know him well?"

She reddened. "What does this mean—get to know?"

"Did you talk much with him?"

"I am trying to breathe."

A pause to decide what she meant. Distressed as she was by the news of Pinto's passing, she seemed to be inhaling normally. Her problem was linguistic, confusing the present and past tenses. She meant there had been no chance to chat with Pinto during the exercise sessions. "How did you find him in the first place?"

"Where is this first place? I have not been."

Diamond took a deep breath. He was trying his best to keep things simple. "Did somebody recommend Tony?"

"My husband Konstantin I am thinking."

"Excellent. That's all I wanted to know."

"*Niet.*"

Everyone turned to see who else had spoken. The man in the serf costume had stepped back into the room, and it soon became obvious they'd got him badly wrong. He spoke in Russian to Olga in a tone of voice that scuppered all their assumptions. This guy couldn't be a servant. He had to be the husband. He must have been standing outside listening to everything that was said and wanted it corrected.

"I am sorry," Olga said when the tongue-lashing was over. "I make bad memory. My husband Konstantin tell me I find Tony in *Bath Chronicle.*"

Whereupon husband Konstantin sprang his second surprise, a grasp of the vernacular. "And I had fuck-all to do with it. I was out of the country on business. My wife got this absurd idea into her head that she would lose weight."

Feeling sympathy for Olga, Diamond said, "Sir, we're here about Pinto, not your wife. Did you meet him?"

"Not at the beginning. She chose to be secretive about him and this cock-eyed training regime. As a result, she was mugged."

"Literally mugged? You're not talking about all the fitness equipment?"

"Physically attacked. At Pinto's suggestion, she went out walking at night and was set upon by some thug and robbed of a gold chain. She could have been seriously injured."

"When was this?"

"Some months ago. I was away on business and I heard nothing of it until recently. Ask her. She'll tell you herself."

Diamond turned back to Olga. "Where did this happen?"

"In Great Pulteney Street," she said in a low voice. All the ebullience had drained away. "I am not hurt."

"Did you report it?"

"No. Like Konstantin say, I am foolish woman to go out alone. I make my own problem."

"If you were robbed, you should have called the police."

"Now I am telling you."

"It's a bit late, Olga. We needed to deal with it at the time." In truth, he was more interested in her experiences with Pinto than the mugging, but he felt compelled to ask, "Do you remember what your attacker looked like?"

"No. He hold me from behind like so." She mimed the action with a grasping motion. "Chain break and he is running off to car. Favourite chain I wear all day, every day."

"A birthday present I had made for her," Konstantin added as if to let it be known that he wasn't entirely unforgiving. "White and yellow twenty-four carat. Not cheap."

"What do you remember about the car?" Diamond asked Olga.

"I do not see. I am scared, run away. I hear car start and drive off. That is all."

It didn't need Sherlock Holmes to suggest a scenario. This was no spur-of-the-moment mugging. Someone knew that the rich Russian woman sporting a valuable gold chain went for evening fitness walks along Great Pulteney Street. Pinto had been well placed to tip off an accomplice or even do the job himself. It would have been simple to wait in the line of parked cars for her to come along and grab her from behind.

She hadn't finished talking about the incident. "I run down steps, fall down, cannot move, big pain in leg and shout for help."

"I don't know of any steps in Great Pulteney Street."

"Basement steps, guv," Gilbert prompted him.

"Got you. Someone's basement entrance?"

"And nobody there. Dark, smelly, dirty place. No chance I ever get out of here, I am thinking, but some person is hearing me."

"Bit of luck."

"Maeve."

"Who's Maeve?"

"Bloody fine Englishwoman pick me up and carry me home."

Difficult to believe as stated unless Maeve was Super-woman, but the general drift was clear. A Good Samaritan had come to the rescue. "Where did she come from? Does she live in the street?"

"Larkhall. She is training for Other Half."

Another runner, for Christ's sake. "Did she know you?"

"No. I am strange."

"Okay," Diamond said, trying to stay focused on the facts. "She happened to be jogging by and heard your cries for help?"

"And now she is true friend we sponsor for five hundred pounds."

Konstantin rolled his eyes, plainly unhappy she had parted with five hundred, for all their millions.

"For a good cause, no doubt," Diamond said in Olga's defence.

"Heart."

She pronounced it as "Art" and he tried to think of a charity for destitute painters.

"What's Maeve's second name?"

"Kelly."

"From Larkhall, you said?"

"Bella Vista Drive. She is schoolteacher."

"Getting back to your personal trainer, Tony Pinto, when did he start working with you?"

"Five or six months and I lose many pounds."

Pounds sterling were in Konstantin's mind, going by the exaggerated sigh.

"Is true," Olga said, doing her best to ignore her husband. "I can show you photograph. I was big fat woman. Tell them, Konstantin. You know I am burning calories like crazy."

"They're not interested in your weight problem," he said. "They're here about your trainer."

"Tell them I walk the half marathon, thirteen miles."

"You were in the big race?" Diamond said. "We were there. We must have seen you go by."

"Not unless you stayed to the end," Konstantin said. "She took longer than four hours."

"Four hours walking," Olga said.

You'd think the husband would have been proud she'd completed the course. There was bitterness between these two and most of it was coming from Konstantin. "Did you know your trainer Tony was in the race?"

"Of course I know. He tell me," Olga said, "but running. He is fast runner."

"I'm not sure that's true. He took as long as you did. What was your time?"

"Four hours fifteen minutes and some seconds."

"In that case, you finished ahead of him. He did four twenty-three. Do you remember overtaking him?"

She laughed at the idea. "I am walking and overtake Tony? Not possible. No, no, no."

Konstantin said, "Four twenty-three? Are you sure this was the right guy? He was supposed to be a fitness expert."

"Were you in the race, sir?" Diamond asked.

"Me?" He looked pained by the question. "It's for fun-runners."

Paul Gilbert spoke up for his school friend Harry Hobbs. "Some of them are better than that."

"That's a matter of opinion," Konstantin said. "The winner's time wasn't anything special."

Gilbert refused to let it rest there. "It's a brute of a course, more like cross-country in parts. You wouldn't expect fast times."

Olga gave her husband a told-you-so look. "You hear that, Konstantin?"

"I heard." He added something in Russian that drew a glare and a quick one-syllable response from Olga.

Diamond wasn't interested in their feuding. Konstantin's snide remarks were undermining the interview and could well be stopping Olga from speaking frankly about Pinto. "Were you in Bath on the day of the race?" he asked Konstantin. "You said you didn't run it, but were you watching?"

"I had better things to do."

"But you weren't abroad at the time?"

"I was here making conference calls if I remember rightly."

"Not cheering on your wife?"

"Give me a break."

Disgusted, Diamond turned back to Olga. "Where does everyone go after the race? Did you see Tony?"

Olga shook her head. "I go straight home. Shower, much drink, big pizza, long sleep."

"Did he phone? Wouldn't he like to find out if you went all the way?" In the split second before the words came out, he knew how crass they sounded and he stumbled over them, making the gaffe ten times worse.

Olga turned the colour of her sweatsuit and vigorously shook her head and Diamond, too, felt himself blushing.

Konstantin spoke a few sharp words to Olga in Russian and then swung back to the visitors. "She isn't here to be insulted. She's answered more than enough of your questions. You'd better leave now. I'll see you out."

"Is that Olga's wish?"

"It's mine. She is my wife and this is my house."

29

Outside, Diamond fumed, more angry with himself than with Konstantin. His self-respect had taken a kicking. "Bastard. I should have fronted it out, got heavy with him."

Gilbert didn't comment, so Diamond asked himself the question.

"Why didn't I? Because I was getting nowhere. She can't talk freely with him standing over her."

"What more could she have said?"

"I don't know, Paul. I just don't know. I needed to question her more closely."

"About Pinto?"

"We weren't there to talk about the weather." He released a long, angry breath that ended in a groan. "I messed up, didn't I, opening my big mouth about going the whole way? I was talking about the bloody race, not her sex life."

"Easy to do."

"What?"

"Slip of the tongue. It was on your mind already. It was on mine."

"Whether she slept with Pinto?"

"She wouldn't have told us if she had."

"Why should she? It's private to her if it happened but I suspect it didn't. He was on a good thing, getting regular fees as her personal trainer. Olga may well have had thoughts about bedding him, but from everything I know of Pinto, he's a one-night-stand man. What was that crude phrase you came out with when we were watching the race?"

"Love 'em and leave 'em?"

"That's not what I remember."

Gilbert grinned.

"But it's true. That was his attitude to women. He wouldn't have kept coming back three times a week. Olga was his meal ticket, not his mistress."

They got into the waiting police car. "Where to, sir?" the driver asked.

"Larkhall. Bella Vista Drive."

"Are you thinking the friend knows something?" Gilbert asked.

"I can't tell until we've questioned her, can I? If they're as close as Olga suggested, she knows stuff you and I don't."

"About Pinto?"

"More about Konstantin. From all we saw of him, he's the controlling type. Some of what we heard was emotional abuse. I was uncomfortable with it, so God knows what Olga was feeling."

"She isn't totally submissive."

"We can agree on that. I like her spirit, but he's doing his best to break it."

"He was pissed off that she'd hired a trainer."

"Stood out a mile, didn't it? He goes away on business and when he gets back the basement is stuffed with all the latest bodybuilding equipment and his wife is taking orders from a personal trainer."

"Could it be worse than that? Could he suspect that Pinto actually made out with her?"

"Even if it didn't happen? That would really get to Konstantin. Got to be faced. I can't wait to hear from this friend of hers."

* * *

The one good thing about Bella Vista Drive was the bella vista and there wasn't much of that, a glimpse of green hills through a slot between blocks of hideous butter-yellow stone. The housing was typical of the so-called urban renewal of the 1960s, packing-case terracing on two floors that could have been designed by a child with a pencil and ruler. The contrast with the palatial façade of Olga's street couldn't have been more extreme.

A postman told them which eyesore was Maeve Kelly's. Kids of school age were skateboarding in the street so there was a good chance school was out and she would be at home.

The young woman who answered the chimes was younger and prettier than any teacher Diamond could remember from his own schooldays. She confirmed that she was indeed Maeve Kelly.

The usual reassuring words about this being a routine enquiry got them inside.

Maeve's home was a box, but she had gone to unusual lengths to make it different. She had turned the living room into a game reserve inhabited by hippos in every form except the living animals, in ceramic, wood, bronze, resin, wire, plastic, glass, wool and satin. One fine beast of leather was large enough for a child to sit astride and another on a crowded wall unit was nine-tenths submerged in what looked like water but was actually transparent plastic. There were paintings, photos and embroideries.

"Don't ask," Maeve said. "They're a flaming nuisance. I was brought up in Zambia and I couldn't resist the big one as a reminder of home when I saw it in Harrods. My friends and family got the idea I was a hippo freak and I was inundated, every birthday and Christmas. I don't throw gifts away when people have taken the trouble to find them and this is the result. Have a seat if you can find one. Sling the stuffed toys on the floor."

Diamond made for a hippo-print armchair. "I grew up

with that Flanders and Swann song, 'Mud, mud, glorious mud.' Before your time."

"I know it well. All too well. I can't count the people who have sent me the YouTube clip."

Paul Gilbert had settled into a rocking chair with hippo armrests. "Isn't the hippo an endangered species?"

"Definitely if I have anything to do with it. How can I help you?"

Diamond launched into his prepared speech. "We just met your friend Olga, the Russian lady, and she told us how you rescued her when she was mugged."

"'Rescued' is putting it far too strongly. If that's what this is about, I'm no use to you as a witness. I came along too late to stop it happening. I was out for a run in Great Pulteney Street one evening and heard a cry for help and found Olga down some basement steps. Helped her home, that's all."

"And now she's your friend for life."

"She's a sweetie. I think she's lonely. Her husband's away a lot of the time."

"Not today. We met him."

"I've met him, too." There was a look that Konstantin might not have found flattering. "I can't help you find her attacker. He drove off before I arrived on the scene."

The mugging was of small interest right now, but Diamond didn't mind her thinking it mattered. "You were out running, you said."

"If you can call it that. Training, for the Other Half. You must have heard of it."

"We have."

"Trying to get fit. I'm not a serious runner."

"Did you run in the race? How did you get on?"

"I made it to the finish, which was all I needed to do. I owed it to my sponsors to finish, and that was a big incentive."

"Have you run it before?"

"God, no. It was my one and only. I got into it by accident, quite literally. It started with a Toby jug. I seem to be fated to be given presents I don't want. One of my work colleagues— I'm a teacher, did I say?—gave me this Toby jug."

"In the shape of a hippo?"

"Jesus, no." She laughed at that. "An old-fashioned Toby with the three-cornered hat. You know? To be fair to him I don't think it was meant for me. He was, like, giving it to the BHF in return for the baseball cap."

"You're losing me," Diamond said.

Gilbert said, "British Heart Foundation, guv."

"The baseball cap?"

"I'm telling it wrong," Maeve said. "My aunt supports the BHF in a big way and sent me this spanking new red cap with the logo and I don't wear them, so I took it to school and gave it to Trevor, who's losing his hair, and instead of being grateful he seemed to take it as an insult, as if I was mocking his baldness. I've never seen him wearing it. Fair enough, we all make mistakes. And yet he felt he had to do something in return. I don't know if I was supposed to be grateful. I can tell you I wasn't. He told me the jug was some sort of family hand-me-down he'd inherited and didn't need anymore."

"He was being honest."

"He's like that, tells it to you straight. Well, I was stuck with this thing that was meant for a good cause, and I couldn't dump it, so I got on my bike and set off for the nearest BHF shop and on the way—wouldn't you know it?—the bag split and Toby ended up in pieces on the road. The worst part is that I found out later the damn thing had been antique, really, really valuable. To cut the story short, I felt so bad about doing the BHF out of a big payday that I got myself sponsored and ran for them in the Other Half."

"Good on you."

"Taught me a lesson, didn't it?"

"Did Trevor know about this?"

"The running? Yes, he helped me prepare. He takes the kids for games, so he's well up on fitness, knows a lot about training and stuff, but he still doesn't know the reason why I took it up. I dread having to tell a porky if he ever asks me about the sodding jug. When he heard I'd signed up for the race he gave me some tips, quite useful."

"He obviously likes you," Diamond said.

"Trevor?" She pulled her arms across her front as if she felt a sudden chill. "You could be right. He hasn't asked me out or anything, but he looks out for me."

"How?"

"In school, he seems to time his visits to the staffroom to fit with mine. If any of the others say anything critical, even joking, he comes to my defence. I ought to be pleased, but I'm capable of standing up for myself. He's well-meaning and helps me with my training, so I can't tell him to piss off. A short time ago he moved into an upstairs flat across the street and I can't help thinking he chose it because I'm here and he can keep a fatherly eye on me."

"Fatherly?"

"It's not romantic for sure. I'm not his type at all. He wants someone serious-minded like himself, not a wacky woman with a house full of hippos."

"He knows about the hippos, then?"

"The whole school knows about them. We have a tradition that at the end of each school year, the leavers club together and buy their teacher a present. Guess what mine is, year after year without fail. Everyone in the staffroom falls about laughing."

Diamond was warming to this young woman. There are people in this world—and he was one—who are fated to provide amusement for their friends and colleagues and can't understand why.

"So you taught yourself how to run seriously?"

"Me and Trev both. Most of it's obvious. Anyone can do it if they're motivated, can't they?"

"You don't have a personal trainer, other than Trevor?"

She smiled. "On a teacher's salary? That's a joke."

"Have you met Olga's trainer, Tony Pinto?"

She tensed at the name. "Sure. He's often at the house."

"You know he's dead?"

"I saw on social media yesterday. Big shock."

So it was common knowledge already. The Combe Down grapevine had fruited.

Maeve said, "I haven't mentioned it to Olga. She'll be devastated."

"She knows now," Diamond said. "She hadn't heard until we told her."

"Is that why you're here?" She formed a word with her lips and no sound came out. At the second try, she asked, "Was Tony murdered?"

"He was found at the bottom of a mineshaft. He didn't get there by accident."

A gasp. "Who would do that? He was . . . fun to be with."

"Women liked him, that's for sure."

"Well." She blinked several times before a burst of words followed. "He knew how to make you feel special and not just in the obvious way through flattery. He could do it with a look and the tone of his voice and he had a great sense of humour, which makes a difference."

"Sounds like you got to know him."

Her cheeks flushed. "Only through Olga."

"But enough to be impressed?"

She made an effort to sound more controlled. "I'm sure it was a technique he'd used with other girls. You kind of knew it and still felt good inside because he was giving you his full-on attention."

"He had a reputation as a ladies' man." Listening to Maeve going on about that fuckwit's seduction routine was hard to stomach, even though the man was dead and dissected. "Do you know whether Olga slept with him?"

All the goodwill drained away and Maeve's voice became metallic. "That's a question for her, not me."

"I would have asked her, but Konstantin was present."

"What has this got to do with you or your investigation?" She sounded like the schoolteacher she was and Diamond was supposed to feel like a ten-year-old. Instead, he was weighing the significance of the way she'd spoken about Pinto.

"It could have provided a motive for murder."

She absorbed that. "You're not serious. You don't think Konstantin . . . ?" She couldn't bring herself to say the words.

"It's our job to explore every angle."

Maeve shook her head. "Well, you're wrong."

"You know for sure?"

"She would have told me." She frowned, questioning herself. "I feel sure she would have told me."

Feeling sure wasn't knowing for sure.

"They were on edge with each other when we were there, as if trust had broken down. Is that usual?"

"It is, now you mention it. He can be really sharp with her and she seems to take it as normal, but she laughs about him when he isn't there. She manages him well in her own way. I guess it's a price you pay if you marry a hard-headed business type. Wouldn't do for me."

"Has she ever spoken of violence?"

"You mean beatings? Not to me, she hasn't. If he hit her, she's strong enough to hit back, and she would. What's going on there is coercive control, which I suppose gets him results in his working life, so he brings it home as well.

I would find it intolerable, but Olga doesn't. Women have found ways of coping with men like that since the beginning of time. Some never do, unfortunately."

"He disapproved of her efforts to get fit."

"He can't have it all ways. He tells her she's fat and when she tries to do something about it, thinking it will please him, he's like, what are you playing at, you stupid cow?"

"She seems to have worked hard at the slimming."

"Really hard. She was too heavy to run far, so she took up walking and was out on a fitness walk the evening she was mugged. That didn't stop her. Instead of using the streets she found a circuit in Henrietta Park, close to where they live, and did laps. I can't walk at that pace for long."

"She must have got fit to have walked the Other Half."

"Yes, she kept quiet about that until after it was over, in case she failed, I suppose. I didn't even know she'd entered. You've got to admire her spirit."

"You said she'd hit back if Konstantin attacked her."

"I'm sure of that. She's got the upper body strength. I've seen her working out with weights. I wouldn't pick a fight with Olga."

"Strong enough to take out a pint-size guy like Pinto?"

"*Pint size?*" She didn't like the description.

"Compared to her."

She reached for a felt hippo and for a moment Diamond thought she would throw it at him. Instead, she kneaded it like bread. "Oh, come on. What are you suggesting? She liked Tony. She fancied him."

He followed up with a combination that would have floored anyone. "And if he didn't come across?" Before she had a chance to deal with the jab, he hit her with the uppercut. "And she discovered he'd screwed one of her trusted friends?"

Her look of panic said it all before she spoke. She was open-mouthed. "How do you know that?"

He hadn't for certain, not until this moment. He'd inferred it from her answers, dangled the bait and she'd swallowed the hook. "Your reaction when we spoke of him just now. You don't have to look so guilty, Maeve. Your sex life is your own and I'm sure he made you feel special."

The stuffed animal in her grip would burst at the seams any second. "It was a one-off. A couple of drinks in a bar on Wellsway supposedly to talk about my running and he'd pre-booked a room. I had no idea he wanted me." She shook her head, remembering. "The thrill of finding out was overpowering. I wouldn't have hurt Olga for all the world."

"I believe you."

She dropped the hippo and ran her fingers through her hair. "Does she know? Who would have told her? Tony himself? How cruel is that?"

"If he did," Diamond said, wanting to calm her now that he knew, "he paid for it with his life. But this is only me speculating. All angles, as I said just now."

"When was he killed?"

"After he finished the race. He was still wearing the kit."

"But the finish is far too public for anyone to kill a man. Where was the body found?"

"Combe Down."

"The race goes past there, but where they finished is two miles north of there, easily. Did he go back for some reason?"

"It seems so."

"And was murdered somewhere near the mineshaft?"

"That's our supposition, unless the body was driven there."

"Could Olga manage that? I guess she could. But how would she know about a mineshaft on Combe Down?"

"She'd just walked the course," he said. "She may have

gone there previously to practise. How far is it from Sydney Place? Two miles, you said?"

"Will you question her again?"

"That's likely."

"You won't tell her I did it with Tony?" she said, and then added with a stricken sigh, "I suppose I can't stop you. What an idiot I was."

30

Messages were waiting when Diamond got back to his desk. His staff knew the best way to get his attention wasn't by phone or online. Sticky yellow Post-it notes were arrayed across the top of his computer like Widow Twankey's laundry. Some he glanced at and screwed up. When the sorting was done, three were left. Keith Halliwell had left one, so the big man limped over to his deputy's desk.

"How was the Russian lady, guv?" Halliwell asked.

"On the large side. I can say that, because she's larger than me. You wouldn't want us both in your balloon. But I liked her, which is never a good sign. I always seem to get on well with the guilty party."

"Capable of killing a man and throwing him down a mineshaft?"

"Without a doubt. And the same can be said for the husband, except he's thinner than my wallet and fit as a butcher's dog. He runs marathons, real ones. You wanted to see me, your note said."

"It's a follow-up on the autopsy from Dr. Sealy."

"A postscript to the postmortem?" When Diamond played on words, it was a sign of positivity. "Helpful, I hope?"

Halliwell wasn't saying yet. "He sent off the usual samples of tissues and body fluids for testing by the lab."

"And the results are back already? I can't believe this."

"They aren't. But you know what he's like. He leaves nothing to chance. He keeps a second set of samples himself in case of disputes or something going missing at the lab. It's a way of covering himself."

"Typical Sealy."

"It's paid off this time, because he kept some of the hair he shaved off the back of the scalp to reveal the fracture."

"What use is that?"

"He had an idea of what he might find. Under a microscope certain hairs were shown up as stained."

Diamond smiled faintly. "Don't tell me Pinto dyed his hair."

"No. These were grass stains."

"Grass?"

"When the head hit the ground it picked up traces from the turf. He analysed it under infrared and found cellulose and chlorophyll and all the main constituents in grass. He checked with the lab and grass staining was also present on the T-shirt. Do you see the point? The fatal fall must have been above ground. There's no grass growing inside a stone quarry."

"Smart," Diamond said, but in a voice drained of admiration.

Halliwell joined the dots. "So now we know the fight, the incident, or whatever we call it, happened above ground."

"And killed him?" There was a momentary hiatus while Diamond absorbed this. He pulled a disbelieving face. "I've hit my head many times playing rugby and I'm still here."

Halliwell's first thought was disrespectful. He rightly sensed that this wasn't a moment for levity. "I guess it comes down to the force of the impact."

"And we're a hundred per cent sure there's no chance he was bashed from behind, as we first thought?"

"Sealy says so. We can forget it."

"But was he in a fight?"

"Apparently. Some kind of punch-up, because of the secondary injuries like the bruising on the face and hand."

Halliwell was ahead of Diamond on the implications of all this and he seemed to be waiting for Diamond to reach the same bleak conclusion.

The big man looked as if he, too, was about to fall flat on his back.

Finally, he said, "We'll never get a murder conviction from a fall. Manslaughter at best. What it boils down to is homicide, but not murder."

Anticlimax had deflated Diamond like a punctured beachball. He gazed the length of the incident room at the team and the civilian staff beavering away at what they believed was a murder enquiry.

Eventually, he said, "I can't face them yet, Keith. I'll need to take this in properly."

"We still have a duty to investigate, don't we?"

He shrugged. "Can't call it off now." Shaking his head, he hobbled back to his own desk and sat hunched and inert, staring at the empty screen. Minutes passed before he picked off another of the Post-its. He read the words without fully taking them in. They were from Samantha Sharp, the DC he'd assigned to trawl through every official video of the race. She'd written: *Sir, if you would like to see, I have footage of Pinto at the drinks station and the 10K point.*

Her desk wasn't far away. She was staring fixedly at her screen. Too fixedly. She knew her message had been seen. She just couldn't know if it was one of those he'd screwed up and binned.

It was next to impossible to get enthused anymore, but he was here among his team and he had to act normally or come clean. For the present he wouldn't say anything about downgrading the investigation. He'd break it to them at tomorrow morning's briefing.

He crossed to where DC Sharp was scrolling through

images from one of the fixed cameras. Mind-numbing work. She was the newest on the team, in her twenties, tall, with dark brown hair in a thick plait. She'd come with a recommendation from the inspector she'd worked for in traffic.

"You found him, then? Good spotting."

"His kit stands out from the rest, sir," she said, eager to make the right impression. "Hold on, I'll pull up a chair for you. Then I'll get the first sequence up."

"The start? I don't need to see that. Can I see the next one, whatever that is?"

"No problem. I've bookmarked his appearances."

In no time at all her screen was filled with runners taking bottles from tables. "This is the first drinks station, Dundas Aqueduct. I'll pause it when he appears. There."

Eerily alive, more animated than anyone else on the screen, Pinto, in his polka-dot headband and yellow T-shirt, was in line at a table where there was some congestion. Immediately ahead of him was a woman Diamond recognised as Belinda Pye. She looked even more under strain than when he'd met her. Pinto seemed to be saying something, but of course there was no sound. Just as Belinda was reaching for a bottle, she turned her head sharply and looked over her shoulder.

"Did you see that?" Diamond said. "Play it again. I think he goosed her."

"He what?"

DC Sharp didn't know the term or didn't approve of it, making Diamond feel he belonged to the generation that had condoned or ignored the whole range of inappropriate handling of women from hugging to coercive sex. He might deplore the action, but the word condemned him.

"Can you re-run it?"

Sharp played the few frames again and Belinda's startled reaction was obvious.

"What did you call it, sir?"

"Groping. Didn't I say that? She told me this happened a number of times in the starting pen and during the race."

The film moved on and so did Belinda. She hadn't waited to drink at the table, as most did. With the unopened bottle in her hand she got into her stride again. Pinto was the fresher and wouldn't have any difficulty catching up. He grabbed two bottles, glanced up at the marshal behind the table, a short, swarthy man, and did a double take. They both appeared transfixed, as if the video had been paused, but others in the shot were moving.

"Odd," Diamond said. "What's going on there? The marshal didn't give him lip for touching her, did he? Can we play it again?"

He watched the sequence closely. Nothing seemed to have been said by either man. If anything, panic was written on the marshal's features, not reproach.

"They know each other."

"Looks like it," DC Sharp said.

"Now what's happening?"

Pinto moved out of shot, and other runners replaced him. The marshal turned from the table as if about to reach for another stack of bottles and instead darted to the left and was lost to view. How frustrating it was that the camera was fixed and didn't follow him.

"He's off."

"What was that about?"

"I'd love to know."

As more runners came into shot, the table rapidly emptied of bottles and after a short delay when people were clustering there, another marshal stepped in with fresh supplies.

"Okay, you said you have footage of them going through ten K."

The computer-wise DC Sharp soon had it ready to roll.

A camera sited on a narrow stretch between low walls gave a view of runners passing over the mat that by electronic wizardry took information from the chips attached to their shoes. A timing display along the foot of the picture was showing 56 minutes and rapidly changing seconds.

"Do you know where this is?" he asked. "I can see the remnants of railway sleepers."

"Tucking Mill viaduct, not long before they entered the Combe Down tunnel."

"Ten K is six miles, give or take?"

"A bit over."

"Can you slow it up? I'll never be able to pick him out." She said, "I know when he appears."

"You did well to find this."

"I had his time at ten K, so it was easy. He stands out anyway. Here we are. Belinda comes into the picture now and he's only two-tenths behind her." She changed to slow motion.

"I see him, the tosser."

Belinda's laboured running was apparent and Diamond remembered her telling him she'd gone faster than she planned because Pinto had been so close behind. At this stage the man was still moving easily.

"She got away from him by quitting the race soon after," Diamond said. "She wasn't going to risk the tunnel."

"Good for her."

"It wasn't easy. She's not used to dealing with predators like him."

"Not many of us are, sir."

"Yes, but she had an unusually sheltered upbringing, a one-parent family, I believe. Lived all her life with her mother and became her carer. Worked from home on a computer. No social life to speak of. When her mother died, Belinda made this effort to get sponsored and run for the heart charity and she was devastated at pulling out.

We can look at all these runners and we have no idea of the stories behind them."

"He'll have had a story, too," she said. "Where's he from?"

"Prison. A fifteen-stretch for using a knife on another young woman. Waste no sympathy on Tony Pinto."

She nodded. "I've yet to find him at the other points where cameras are placed. He seems to have slowed right up or taken a rest because his finishing time is really slow. Do you think he went off course to look for Belinda?"

"Can't say for certain. Keep at it and we may get some answers."

He reached for his stick, braced his good leg and picked his way back to his own desk.

The final Post-it note simply read: *Call Mr. Jones.*

He'd left it until last to give him time to remember who Mr. Jones might be. He'd known a few Joneses in his time. This one hadn't bothered to leave a contact number. There were surely some in Bath Police, but he couldn't think of any in Concorde House. The wording was more of a command than a request. There wasn't a high-up in Concorde House or headquarters called Jones.

The penny dropped. Mr. Mysterious from ROCU.

Somewhere in the Himalayan range of paper spread across the desk was the business card with Jones's personal number. Much burrowing in the foothills caused minor avalanches and didn't uncover anything. He rolled his chair away and tried to see what had fallen on the floor. Then he remembered using one corner of the card to scratch an itch on the back of his neck. Perfect for the job. Where had he put the damn thing after that?

Somewhere handy.

Got it. Under the mouse mat.

"Mr. Jones? Diamond from Bath."

"Oh?"

"You asked me to call."

"But how can I be sure it's you?" The opening move in the silly game of secrecy.

"You remember. The house in—" He was about to say Duke Street when he was drowned out by a sound like Niagara Falls that he later decided must have been Jones taking a huge, shocked breath between his teeth.

"For the love of God," Jones said. "You'll undo months of patient work."

"You want me to prove my identity."

"In a word, yes."

A "yes" was an achievement.

"What am I supposed to tell you—my mother's maiden name or the name of my first pet?"

"I recognise your voice now and I've seen where you're calling from. We can proceed. Have you progressed that investigation you spoke of?"

"Not a lot," Diamond said. "Softly, softly, you said."

"We're on the same wavelength, then. This is better."

"How about you? What's the progress on your side?"

"That's not up for discussion," Jones said, "except . . ."

Diamond waited. He pictured Jones looking left and right to see if there was danger of being overheard.

". . . after tomorrow you could be in a position to steam ahead."

"Right." The fact that Diamond and his team were at full steam already needn't be disclosed. Jones liked to believe he inhabited a secret world, so he could remain in the dark. "Tomorrow, you say?"

"Did I? Slip of the tongue. Better if you forget this conversation."

"That won't be any hardship." The call ended.

It didn't take much detective work to divine the next move by ROCU: a dawn raid on Duke Street to make arrests and close down the modern-slavery scam. If his informant had been anyone else but Jones, he would have had questions to ask. What exactly was Pinto's part in the operation? Had someone replaced him? Where were the men employed? What was their nationality? What would happen to them next? Who was pulling the strings?

With no more Post-its to deal with, he was forced to return to the depressing here and now. He'd announce to the team tomorrow that the case they had sweated over for days had been downgraded from murder to manslaughter. He'd be able to tell them at the same briefing that the slavery racket had been stopped and arrests made. Some consolation, anyway.

That evening he met Paloma for a meal in the Ram at Widcombe, a dog-friendly pub where Hartley the beagle could be taken, provided he was supplied with things to chew to distract him from shredding the table legs or their own shoes. Paloma had filled her handbag with rawhide knots.

She sensed even before they found a table that Diamond had taken a body blow.

"Are you in trouble with the top brass again?"

"I could be."

Once seated in the lounge area, small and separated by a glass partition from the more generous-sized bar, and with drinks in front of them and the dog working his teeth on the treat, Paloma demanded to know more.

"What it comes down to is that I've wasted hundreds more man-hours for no result."

He could rely on Paloma for a sympathetic hearing. She cared about his misfortunes and humiliations and usually had the wit and wisdom to put them in perspective. He explained about the autopsy report and the significance of the secondary fracture in the skull. "I'm not even sure the case will come to court if we get our man. The Crown Prosecution Service will almost certainly throw it out. They know a smart defence lawyer will treat it as manna from heaven."

"Is it totally certain he was killed by falling backwards?"

"Dr. Sealy is the expert. We've got to believe him."

Paloma held out her hands in appeal. "Does it matter? This Pinto guy was no great loss to the world. He's dead now. Whoever was responsible may deserve to get away with it."

He shook his head. "If we think like that, making value judgements on offenders, we're playing God. My job is to catch the killer, not judge him."

"But what if your killer turns out to have been a decent person who was driven to it by Pinto's foul behaviour?"

"For example?"

"Belinda."

"Oh, come on. She didn't do it. She was exhausted. She couldn't have pushed him over if he was a cardboard cut-out."

"Does she have a father?"

"No."

"Boyfriend?"

"Belinda? No."

"In that case you're looking for someone else with reason to pick a fight. The Russian woman? She's strong enough to take him on."

"Olga liked him. She couldn't get enough of him. He was her personal trainer."

"The husband, then. He can't have been overjoyed that she fancied her trainer."

"Konstantin?" He nodded. "You're right. He's in the frame, but I thought we were talking about decent people. He's a bully."

"All right. Any of the slave labourers, the men living in appalling conditions in that basement?"

"They're prisoners. How could any of them have done it?"

"Desperation."

"I said how, not why. They're driven to work every morning and I don't think work is up on Combe Down."

"Where are they taken, then?"

"I'm expecting to find out in the very near future." Taking a leaf from the Jones book of secrecy, he checked in all directions including the exposed beams above him to make sure no one was eavesdropping. "Keep this to yourself or I'll certainly be out of a job. A raid on the Duke Street house is being planned."

"So at least some good will come of your efforts. That's reason to be cheerful, Peter."

"It's not my operation. It's being handled by a regional crime team who specialise in people-smuggling."

"Would they have known about Duke Street without you?"

"Probably not."

"That's a success you can chalk up, then."

She was right. He wouldn't chalk it up anywhere, but he'd know in his own mind that his information had helped uncover a disgusting misuse of wretched, exploited people.

The food was served—Cumberland sausages swimming in thick gravy with red fried onions and mash—and his spirits revived a little. "Thanks."

"What for?" Paloma said.

"The moral support."

"Ah." She smiled. "For a moment I thought you were thanking me for the meal. I was going to say I didn't know I was paying. Moral support comes cheaper than sausages and mash."

They spoke of other things, mainly a TV period drama series she was having difficulty with as costume adviser. The award-winning director wanted to dress her actors in cage crinolines in the 1880s after the bustle had come in. For Paloma this was a resignation issue that could affect her professionally. Diamond felt her pain and talked like a politician about red lines. She seemed to appreciate his support. He reflected that points of principle don't have to be matters of life and death. It's all a question of scale.

After the plates were cleared and coffee was served, the talk turned back to his own disappointment.

"What will you do about your murder investigation?" Paloma asked.

"Basically, call it off," he said. "My first obligation is to the team. I must let them know and I'm not looking forward to it."

"A meeting?"

"Tomorrow morning. Then I must speak to Georgina. She wasn't keen on this from the start. It's got to be faced."

"You're a policeman. You can't know about brain injuries any more than I can."

"Tell that to Georgina when she looks at the overtime claim."

"Was Pinto killed instantly by the fall?"

"I can't answer that. Like you say, I'm a cop. But I doubt whether Sealy could tell you either."

"Sometimes people go into a coma, don't they? And die later?"

"You hear about them living on for years."

"I'm talking about an interval of no more than a few minutes. I wonder how long it takes for a bleed on the brain to kill someone."

"Paloma, I appreciate what you're saying, but I'm not the best person to ask."

"This is my point, Peter. You've been assuming he died instantly, but there's a good chance he didn't. His attacker didn't call an ambulance and didn't go for help. Pinto was moved and dropped into the mineshaft to get rid of the evidence, right?"

"Yes."

"Well?"

"Well what?"

"Don't you see what I'm getting at? You've made a big assumption that isn't necessarily true. Think out of the box. If he wasn't killed the moment his head hit the ground, it would have been obvious he was still breathing. The person who attacked him finished him off by dropping him down the mine. That's premeditated and that's murder, isn't it?"

31

Diamond had set his alarm and was up before dawn.
A rare event.

He didn't waste time showering or shaving. A swish
of tap water took the sleep from his eyes and a squirt of
deodorant completed his grooming. Unshaven jowls were
standard among the younger members of his team.

If he'd read the runes correctly (the runes being the
hints from the ROCU man who called himself Jones),
the wretched slaves living in the Duke Street basement were
about to be liberated and he intended to be there when
it happened, regardless of operational secrecy. So Raffles
was fed earlier than usual and breakfast for Diamond was
a banana eaten in the car on the drive in from Weston.

The Lower Bristol Road was blessedly clear. The only
problem with such an early start was the dazzle from the
rising sun.

His first thought was to use the pull-in at the top end
of North Parade Road opposite Duke Street, but when he
got near, it occurred to him that this was precisely where
the transport for the working party was likely to park, so he
motored past, did a U-turn and ended up with his nearside
wheels on the pavement in nearby Pierrepont Street. A
short way farther up, two police minibuses had done the
same and he could see heads inside.

He'd read the runes right.

He sat at the wheel and tried not to doze off, wishing he was in radio contact to get a sense of what was planned. He should have got tough with Jones and insisted he had a right to be here as head of the murder enquiry. Would it have worked? Probably not. Jones, like God, worked in mysterious ways, and, like God, he issued commandments.

An hour later, nobody had moved. Clearly this raid wasn't going to follow the usual pattern of a forced entry with a battering ram ("a five-pound door key") when everyone in the house was asleep. The traffic increased, people walked by on their way to work and Diamond stroked his bristles and reflected that he could have fitted in that shave and shower or better still had another hour in bed.

And then everything happened.

Two squad cars came from nowhere and turned up North Parade Road.

One of the minibuses started up and headed in the same direction.

Diamond flung open the door, stepped out, remembered his stick just in time, made his way as best he could around the corner and tried to appear like one more nosy member of the public wanting to check the action.

Give ROCU their due: the operation was neatly planned. The stretch of North Parade Road from Pierrepont Street to the bridge was already taped off and guarded by armed officers. Traffic from both directions was halted and backing up. The pull-in Diamond had rashly thought of using was occupied by a silver transit van trapped between the two flashing police cars parked diagonally at front and rear. The minibus had halted laterally, preventing anything from entering the taped-off section. Armed officers were scrambling out and taking up positions either side of the terraces that fronted Duke Street.

In the centre of North Parade Road, a man was lying

handcuffed with one officer holding him down and two others training their assault rifles on him.

The police guarding the scene were some of Bath's authorised firearms officers. Diamond didn't need to produce his warrant card to get past.

He approached the van and spoke to a constable he recognised.

"Are there people inside?"

"A lot, sir. Twenty or more crammed in, poor devils. They look done in already and they're supposed to be working a twelve-hour day. We'll be transferring them shortly to a minibus."

"Foreign?"

"Trafficked."

"Any idea where from?"

"Whichever language it is, I don't recognise it."

"Who's the guy in cuffs?"

"The driver, British. Small fry, we think."

"Is there a gangmaster?"

"If there is, we haven't got him yet."

"Was anyone with them when they walked out to the van?"

The constable shook his head. "It's weird. They could have escaped, any of them, and they didn't try."

"That's down to conditioning," Diamond said. "Their brains work differently from yours and mine. It wouldn't surprise me if they've been living in that house for days without a gangmaster."

"I don't get it."

"They don't need to be whipped into submission like slaves picking cotton. They believe working for a pittance at the waste-disposal place is better than being sent back to the hell they came from, so they go to work and return from work and eat and sleep and start the same cycle again."

"I'd make a run for it."

"You don't know what it's like where they came from."

"That's for sure."

"How do you come to be involved in this? You're not from ROCU."

"They're running the show, sir, but they used our armed response team. We were notified last night. Very hush-hush."

"I can believe that. Is anyone left in the house where this lot were living?"

"I saw a team from Bristol go in. It's a big operation. Simultaneous raids at several addresses."

He stepped up Duke Street to the house and this time had to show his ID. "Are you from ROCU, sir?" the sergeant with the Heckler & Koch asked.

"Working with them." A stretch of the truth, but forgivable, even if Jones might not agree. "Who's inside?"

"The search team and one very large lady in a wheelchair. I can't think how she fits into this."

Diamond couldn't think how Beattie fitted into anything. "She doesn't know it, but she's the respectable face of the scam, living in the first flat you come to. She's sharp. She'll make a key witness."

"They're taking her to headquarters. They've sent for a taxi with wheelchair access. I'm looking forward to seeing the driver's face."

"The small problem of getting her up the steps? Do they know they'll need some kind of hoist?"

"Like a crane?"

"Be kind." Diamond looked over the railings into the basement. "Will I get shot to bits if I go down there?"

"They finished their check for suspicious persons, sir. There was just the wheelchair woman. They're waiting for the crime scene unit now. If you like, I can radio to say you're coming down."

"Please do."

Steadier with his footwork than the last time, he picked his way down the steps and got the musty smell he recalled from the previous visit. Almost every bit of rubbish blown through an open-ended street in Georgian Bath ends up in basement wells. Mouldering paper and plastic anchored in dust and leaves was heaped up at either end. A few hardy weeds had sprouted from cracks in the stone. No one from this flat had cleaned up in months, even though there were three wheelie bins along one side.

After stepping through the open door he didn't get far. Beattie was occupying most of the corridor. "Another one of them," she said with distaste and then saw who it was and changed her tone. "Oh, it's you. Did you arrange all this, smashing doors down and treating the place like it's some cop show on the TV? I don't know what the landlord's going to say."

"Not my doing, Beattie," he said, which wasn't strictly true. "You'll get a nice taxi ride out of it."

"What's it all about? Has one of the tenants misbehaved?"

"Nobody knows for sure. They want your opinion."

"I told you everything I know when you were here last time. They're all good blokes."

He told her he would see what else he could find out, giving him a reason to squeeze past the chair and move along the corridor to where three of the search team were in conversation outside the damaged open door of Pinto's room.

"Found much?" he asked, eager to know whether their search had yielded more than his and Ingeborg's.

"Sod all, really," one said. "This was obviously the gangmaster's drum, as you see."

"The alleged gangmaster," another said.

"Fuck that. He's dead. He was killed running the half marathon. I can call him what I bloody like."

"Pity he's dead," the second man said. "We'd have got a load of information from the tosser, wouldn't we Jimmy?"

"He was smart enough not to leave his phone or wallet here." Jimmy had a voice and believed in using it. "He must have owned a laptop or some such. Without phone records and card transactions we'll never get a case to stick. None of that stuff was on his person when he was killed, so where is it?"

Just what Diamond was here to find out.

Jimmy's words hadn't been aimed directly at anyone. They were more of an appeal to the gods in general—or whichever god looks after frustrated policemen.

Diamond was no god, but he had a suggestion. "Has anyone checked with the marathon organisers?"

"What would they know about it?"

"They're sure to have some unclaimed bags."

"Why would he leave a bag with them when he lives so near? The runners' village was barely a stone's throw from here."

"Safer," Diamond said. "He wouldn't trust the people here."

"We can mention that to the boss."

Diamond looked through the doorway at the seduction salon, as he thought of it, where Pinto had entertained the women he brought back. To his eye, it was as sexy as a car crash, but it was Pinto's private knocking shop as well as his office, sitting room, music room, bedroom and breakfast room. The scumbag had spent a large amount of his time here. Surely it held more clues. "Mind if I step inside?"

Jimmy shrugged. "I guess one more set of shoe prints is neither here nor there."

When Diamond had last been here, he and Ingeborg had done what the search team had done—looked for the hardware that stored the data so vital to modern evidence-gathering. Pinto must have had access to the internet to function as a gangmaster.

Try a different approach, he told himself.

Instead of searching for equipment that wasn't here, why not look more closely at things that were?

Modern slavery was a world-wide twenty-first-century crime utilising con-tricks that had worked since Eve was persuaded to pick the forbidden fruit. The gangs recruited vulnerable people in places abroad where they had no hope of betterment and offered them jobs and places to live in more advanced countries where casual labour was in demand. The traffickers demanded a fee, of course, and the transport was basic and illegal. On arrival, the victims were taken to open a bank account to receive their wages. They were issued with debit cards that the slavers took over. As the cash flowed in, it was creamed off. Any objections were met with the answer that the rent had to be funded and the debt repaid.

All the unfortunates under Pinto's charge would have gone through something similar. He must have controlled twenty or more bank accounts. Each came with its password, pin and security number. Remembering so many details wasn't possible. Put them on computer and you run the risk of being hacked and losing the lot.

Diamond had trouble managing his own account data along with all the other passwords and pins he needed to function. He kept his in a notebook he was always updating.

What was Pinto's system? Surely more devious than that. Yet he'd need to keep a record somewhere. He'd be an idiot to keep it on his phone.

The only paper items found in the room had been the receipts from the sports shop.

Was anything noted on some surface you wouldn't expect?

He looked inside the wardrobe and the crockery cupboard. Pulled the folding table from the wall and examined the underside. The edge of a door might have been a smart place, but Pinto hadn't used that.

What was his secret?

It had to be somewhere here in this basement.

Beattie's room?

Unless she was a genius at bluffing, Beattie had no active role in the slavery operation and it was unlikely Pinto would have asked her to take care of anything. However, it was not impossible that he'd gone into her room on some pretext and lodged stuff out of sight and out of her reach on top of a cupboard.

He spoke to the guys at the door. "Have all the rooms been searched?"

"All except one." Jimmy lowered his voice. "We'll get in there shortly."

"While she's at headquarters?"

A nod. He didn't have to tell them their job. They'd know where to look.

What else, then?

Having checked every conceivable piece of furniture in Pinto's room, he was left studying the walls.

And now he saw what had been so easy to miss.

"Jimmy, you might like to photograph this."

The striped wallpaper was topped by the frieze with the nude runners of both sexes chasing each other endlessly around the room. The pink figures were enclosed between narrow bands of a repeating Greek meander pattern in black on a sand-coloured background.

Just above the lower band, in small, neat letters you wouldn't see unless you got close up, was a long line of words and numbers, several hundred. They went around three walls, so neatly done that they seemed to be part of the pattern.

"Cool," Jimmy said. "But what the fuck is it?"

"It looks to me like his record of all the accounts under his control. Each guy's name followed by the bank, account number and pin."

"I've been staring at that fucking wallpaper and all I saw was bollock-naked people."

"You would," Diamond said and added tactfully, "Anyone would."

"I don't know how you thought of it."

He didn't answer. He'd stepped over to the fourth wall, the one with the door. The frieze along here was empty of writing—or almost so. A number had been written just below the light switch in the same minute hand and the same black ink: *50598*.

"Any thoughts what this might be?"

"Search me," the sergeant said. "A pin number?"

"They're usually four digits."

"Phone?"

"If it's a local number, they're six digits, aren't they?"

"I'm stumped, then."

"It seems to be here by the door as a reminder before he steps outside." He scratched his unshaven chin. He was trying to dredge up a conversation tiptoeing on the edge of his memory and refusing to make itself known, an insight Beattie had unexpectedly provided. Not from today. Must have been when he was here with Ingeborg. He'd been impressed at the time because it had been a snippet of local knowledge he hadn't heard about in more than twenty years of living in Bath. Suddenly it mattered.

There had been some connection with Duke Street. But how it linked up with the number under the light switch was a mystery known only to Diamond's unconscious.

"Thanks, anyway." He left the room and started up the corridor to where Beattie still awaited her taxi.

She was chuntering on about the outrage of the dawn raid. "They won't let me lock my door," she told him. "They said they have a search warrant for the whole basement. I don't want strange men going in my room when I'm not here and opening my underwear drawer. I'm a law-abiding woman. How can I be a suspicious person when I'm stuck in this chair all day?"

"I'll make sure they respect your belongings," he said.

"If I find anything gone, I'll sue you."

There's gratitude, he thought. "Did Tony visit your room before he went out to run in the Other Half?"

"What are you suggesting now?" Beattie said. "You lot with your dirty minds take my breath away."

"That's not what I meant, Beattie. He could have left some of his valuables in your care, or even his phone. I'm sure he trusted you."

"Are you calling me a thief now? I've got nothing of Tony's. God knows I'd tell you if I had."

"But did he visit your room just to let you know what was happening?"

"Will you listen?" she said. "The only time Tony Pinto has ever been across my threshold is when I had an unwelcome visitor."

"Oh? Who was that?"

"A spider, silly."

"Ah." But the "ah" in this case wasn't downbeat. It was the "ah" of enlightenment, a Eureka moment. That elusive conversation at the back of his brain had come back to him and of course it was the spider invasion. They came from the vaults under the street, she had said. Duke Street was built on a raised platform over vaults that elevated it by five metres above marshy ground once thought to have been uninhabitable.

Thanks to Beattie's eight-legged visitors he believed he knew why Pinto had written the five-digit number on his wall.

"I'm coming by." He edged around the back of the wheelchair and left Beattie muttering to herself. Without another word, he passed the armed officer on duty at the basement's main door and stepped into the walk-out area nobody had bothered to clear of leaves and rubbish. Being so far below pavement level, this shaft was shadowy as well as smelly. Before anything was built, this would have been ground level, the swamp Beattie had spoken about. The grey stone walls were part of the foundations supporting the street above.

The space below the street had to be searched. Years ago, the residents would have stored their coal there and may have stowed a few unwanted pieces of furniture as well.

The stout wooden door was half hidden by the wheelie bins. He dragged them aside and found what he was expecting: the entrance to the vault secured by a strong hasp and staple and a heavy-duty shiny brass padlock.

A five-digit combination padlock.

He rotated the disks to get 50598 and the shackle sprang up. One mystery solved. The door groaned on its hinges.

The vault's interior was cold, pitch black and smelt rank. He took out his phone and found the torch function. The beam picked out a massive limestone arch over a flagged floor. Beattie had been right about the spiders. Generations of webs like filthy net curtains hung from either side. But the centre looked clear to walk through, suggesting somebody had come this way not long before.

He turned the beam of light in all directions before taking a few shuffling steps, prodding the flagstones with his stick. Ahead, the archway opened up to a stone passage that crossed laterally. He didn't need to go far. Just behind the base of the first archway his light picked out a plastic storage box and through the transparent lid he could see a laptop, an iPhone and a stack of bank cards held together with a rubber band. Enough data to employ the computer forensics geeks for months.

And two knives.

The vault was Pinto's office storeroom.

He shone the light across the rest of the space to check for more and was startled by a movement on the far side. A large rat had emerged from under what looked like a folded tarpaulin, its eyes caught in the beam for a second before it raced away and out of sight.

This wasn't a nice place to be. Diamond had found what he came for and wouldn't be staying much longer, but out of a sense of duty he crossed the floor for a closer look and uttered an untypically genteel "oh, no" at the feel of a cobweb draping itself around his face. In the act of brushing himself down, he made things worse by dropping the phone. Fortunately, the light stayed on. He had to go on one knee to pick it up.

Then he went rigid.

Ahead, caught in the beam a little more than a yard away, a hand was poking out from under the tarpaulin, the fleshy underside chewed to the bone.

32

"I won't ask how you came to be in the wrong place at the right time."

Puffed up by the overnight success of Operation Duke Street, Jones from ROCU was seated in the comfortable armchair in Diamond's office for what he called a debriefing.

Diamond had no intention of being debriefed, a term he'd always thought unfortunate, so he didn't comment. If Jones wished to expose himself, so to speak, that was his choice.

"But it's a good thing you were," Jones added after one of his long pauses. "My lads would certainly have found that box with the laptop and the phone when we made a wider search, not to mention the body, but you saved us valuable time and I'm grateful for that."

"Do we know who it is?" Diamond asked.

"The corpse? One of the slaves. His name was Vasil, according to the others, and he attempted to escape months ago. He's listed on the wall with the rest in Pinto's room. They all knew he'd been killed. Pinto kept reminding them, to discourage anyone else from escaping. It was a rule of fear. He called himself the Finisher because he'd finish anyone who stepped out of line."

"So they're talking to you?"

Jones gave the smile of a seasoned interrogator. "You need to know how to get people like that onside. You tell them their cooperation will be taken into account when their applications for asylum are heard."

"Where are they from?"

"Albania. We had to ring round to find anyone able to act as interpreter. Got there in the end."

"What's wrong with Albania that made them want to leave?"

"Where shall I start? Horrendous unemployment. Poverty. It was a Stalinist country until 1992 and vast numbers left when they got the first chance. About three million stayed on and ten million are living abroad. The economy has never really caught up."

"I'm not even sure where Albania is."

"Think north of Greece and south of Serbia and you won't be far wrong. It's a Mediterranean country with a good long coastline they try to promote for tourism. Ever heard of the Albanian Riviera?"

"I'm not much of a traveller."

"Stunning beaches, I'm told."

"Not much of a beach boy either."

"You're a miserable bugger, Diamond. Did anyone ever tell you that?"

"All the time. What happens next?"

"Most of the victims need medical treatment and counselling. Some of them were living rough in Tirana before they got here. Others were on the run from the police. They're desperate men. They'll be housed while their claims are processed."

"And Tony Pinto was the gangmaster?"

"The cog in the machine that failed to function, which is why he ended up dead."

"Was he Albanian himself?"

"Some of his childhood was spent there, but he'd lived most of his life here."

"Where did he go wrong?"

"Two more of the group escaped, or tried to, only a few days ago. One, a man called Spiro, was picked up later by the police in Reading. We don't know the fate of Murat, the second one. After it happened and the news of the escape got back to the mafia who ran this racket, Pinto's fate was sealed. He was being monitored pretty closely and was caught out, so he had to go."

"Orders from the top?"

"Without a doubt."

"Do you have evidence of that?"

"We will. We've barely started transcribing all the data we seized."

"How was the killing done, then?"

Jones had been talking freely up to now. Hubris loosens the tongue, even of a tight-lipped ROCU man. But the directness of the question made him hesitate and glance at the door to make sure it was closed. "What I am about to say is for your ears only. You need to understand that Duke Street was just one outpost of a vast international empire and only a handful of boss men had any idea of the full extent of it. Pinto was answerable to his controller in Bath and that was as much as he knew."

"And who was the controller?"

"A Russian guy called Ivanov."

"Konstantin Ivanov?"

"You've heard of him?" Jones frowned. "You're better informed than I thought."

Diamond could have added that he'd met Konstantin and had suspicions about him, but that would be the next thing to a debriefing.

"Until yesterday," Jones went on, "Ivanov was living with his wife at a grand address in Sydney Place, a beautiful nineteenth-century terrace facing Sydney Gardens. Bath's billionaires' row. Kings and queens lived there when it was first built. Now it's mostly expensive flats, but he and his wife occupied the entire house, bought by an anonymous company based in some tax haven." The narrative flowed more easily again. "His cover story is that he's one of those filthy-rich oligarchs who prefer to live outside Russia. Money-laundering is behind it, for sure. He buys top-of-the-range properties in Bath and rents them out. The Duke Street house is one such. The top two floors are used only occasionally by high-earning footballers who pay the rent and ask no questions about what happens in the basement. The ground floor flat isn't occupied."

"And Konstantin Ivanov oversees the modern slavery in Bath?"

Jones nodded. "What is more, he prides himself on his fitness. Marathon running, martial arts, wrestling. Do you see where I'm going with this?"

"Did he run in the Other Half?"

"No, and this is my point. You'd expect him to have taken part. His wife Olga was in it. She speed-walked the course. And who do you think they employed as Olga's personal trainer? The organisation had recruited Pinto from prison, where he had become super-fit in the gym and quite a fitness fanatic. But in Bath he was under-employed, just seeing off the slaves early in the morning and checking them in at night. What is that saying about idle hands?"

"The devil finds work . . . ?"

"That's the one. To keep him occupied, he had to make regular visits to Sydney Place and supervise Olga's training. We're not sure about Olga. She doesn't seem to have played an active part in the slavery operation, so she wasn't arrested yesterday. Ivanov was. He denies everything, of course, but we have his phone and hard drive and we'll nail him. The DNA evidence will prove he killed Pinto."

"Ivanov?"

"No question. He was in dire trouble himself if he didn't take decisive action."

"How did he do it?"

"Karate. He's a black belt. There's a framed certificate in their basement gym. The cause of death was a brain injury from a fall, as you know. There seems to have been a short fight, if you can call it that. Pinto was a fit man, but I doubt whether he had the slightest idea how to defend himself."

"And where did this fight take place?"

"On Combe Down."

"Where the mineshaft is?"

"There, or thereabouts."

"Do you also know when it happened?"

"Late afternoon or early evening, long after the race was over. Pinto was one of the last to finish because he ran off course chasing some girl he flirted with." Jones was coming down to earth and getting more matey. "The man was a goat. He couldn't get enough. She quit the race to get away from him and he followed."

"Belinda Pye."

"You know the name?" he piped in surprise.

"I've interviewed her," Diamond said, peeved at being patronised. Peeved, also, that ROCU knew details of the case he and his team had worked so hard to discover.

"Did they have sex?" Jones asked.

"No. She got away, but she was so traumatised that she went off the radar for days." He checked himself. He didn't need to tell Belinda's story right now, even though her experience was vivid in his memory. "What interests me is why Pinto went back to Combe Down after the race was over. All most runners want to do is rest up."

"He hadn't exerted himself," Jones said. "He could have run it much faster. It must have been the pull of the girl. He had unfinished business with her."

"More than two hours after he'd lost contact with her? I find that unconvincing."

"There is another explanation."

"Okay."

"He was under orders. Ivanov had instructed him to report there at a certain time."

"That's more likely," Diamond said. "It explains why Ivanov was there—which would have been my next question."

"Ivanov has no alibi. He was supposed to be in his office in the Sydney Place house dealing with business matters, but of course his wife was in the race, so she can't vouch for him. He's the killer. He'll plead manslaughter, but we'll be able to show it was premeditated."

"How?"

"Phone evidence. My people are going through Pinto's call history—and Ivanov's—as we speak."

"You've got it buttoned up, then," Diamond said.

Jones prised himself out of the chair. "I know this is disappointing for you and your team, but it's crime on a scale you could never have known about. We at ROCU have the advantage over you fellows working at the coal face, but we do appreciate the work being done locally. Do you play golf?"

"No."

"I wouldn't mind meeting you again some time. Incidentally, my name isn't really Jones. One of these days when we're both off duty I'll tell you what it is."

Diamond was tempted to say it was Smart-arse, but he refrained. Inside he was seething, but his contempt for the man and his tinpot theory mattered less than pushing ahead and really cracking this case.

Alone again at his desk, he gathered all the information he had about the Other Half—the race-pack information, sponsorship rules, description of the course, the coloured map, the list of finishers and times at all the checkpoints. He turned on his computer and went to the race website and studied the photographs the organisers had posted. He was trying to reconcile Pinto coming in after four hours when he should have got round in two or less. Even if he *had* lost time chasing after Belinda, he should have finished sooner. He was a fitness freak, for God's sake.

There was a limit to the amount of time the head of CID was willing to spend poring over details. After twenty minutes he'd had enough, so he took everything into the incident room and asked the efficient DC Sharp if she'd completed her searches into Pinto's race at each checkpoint.

"Almost, sir," she said.

"'Guv' is what most of them call me," he said. "What they call me behind my back I can't tell you, but 'guv' sits better with me than 'sir.' What's your problem with the checkpoints?"

"He keeps up with the rest until Dundas Aqueduct. You'd expect him to get there with some of the people who started at the same time and he does."

"You showed me."

"But then we lose him."

"He ran off the course, we think."

"Yes, and I've looked for him at the next checkpoint after the two tunnels, but he misses that. He must have rejoined the race towards the end." On the wall beside her was pinned a large-scale 1:25,000 Ordnance Survey map of Bath on which she'd highlighted the entire half marathon course in yellow. She placed a fingertip on one of the southernmost points and moved it upwards. "Here's the first tunnel. If he stayed above ground and went over Combe Down, he could have taken a short cut through Lyncombe Vale and cut out a large loop."

The short cut was obvious when she showed it.

"And still taken four hours? It doesn't make sense. Can you bring up the clip of him finishing?"

"This is the problem, guv. I've been through the footage any number of times and I haven't found him." She went back to her computer screen, found the video of the finish and used the pointer icon to accelerate the action. "The race time is shown at top right."

"Okay. He finished in how long?"

"Four hours, twenty-three minutes, twenty-six seconds. He ought to be obvious."

Runners in various states of exhaustion were crossing the line. He saw the ostrich with swollen legs go by. "Four hours, three minutes. That's when I gave up myself and stopped watching. Move it on."

After a few more plodded through, a sturdy, smiling blonde woman approached the finish with her arms going like piston-rods beneath conspicuous well-contained breasts.

"She's walking," Diamond said. "It's Olga." He couldn't hold back a smile of his own. "Show me again."

Exuberant, confident and with a touch of self-mockery, Olga crossed the line again.

"Back to work."

DC Sharp stopped the action at 4:23:26. "This is where we should see Pinto, but we don't." In slow motion, she ran the film through the next few seconds. First, another fun-runner came through with a polyester Royal Crescent curved across his shoulders. "He's got so much superstructure you can scarcely see the guy immediately behind, but you do get a glimpse on one frame. Here."

She had stopped the film again and the head and shoulders of the second runner definitely didn't belong to Tony Pinto and wasn't anyone Diamond recognised. The height was about right, but the physique was heavier, the face broader, the mouth wider and the kit was different, the cap and T-shirt black. The time was correct at 4:23:26.

"Run it on a bit longer."

She worked the mouse again. "I must have watched this fifty times over thinking I missed him. If you can see him, you've got X-ray eyes."

"This is all I need," he said.

She blushed. "Sorry, guv."

"I was talking to myself, not you. You've done all you can and done it well. It's up to me to make sense of this."

That evening he took a taxi to Lyncombe. Paloma had promised to cook. An appetising aroma was drifting into the hall from the kitchen.

She looked him up and down. "How are you on your pins?"

"Fine. I could almost manage without the stick."

"Don't you dare. In that case, I'm going to ask a favour."

"You left the veggies for me to do?"

She shook her head. "They're done. It's Hartley."

"Oh?" He'd forgotten about Hartley. "You're still in charge of him?"

"Yes, and he's being a pest tonight. He's so restless. I had to shut him in the office. He had his walk earlier but I think he may need another."

"No problem."

"Are you sure? He'll pull on the lead."

"He's just a scrap. He's not going to pull me over. What time are we eating?"

"Take as long as you like. It's a beef and ale casserole in the slow cooker and I can serve it whenever we want."

"I caught a whiff of something special as soon as you opened the door. You know what? I can tell you why Hartley is playing up. The smell is driving him crazy."

"It's not for him. As well as the ale there's half a bottle of Rioja in it."

"A drop of booze won't hurt him."

"Take him for his walk, Peter, and we can argue later."

He collected Hartley and clipped on the lead. He was about to go out of the door when Paloma handed him a small plastic bag.

"What's this for?"

"There speaks a cat owner. On your way, guys."

It was an open question who was being taken for the walk. Hartley set off at a fast trot, helped by the downward slope, head down and ears almost brushing the pavement, straining to get to the limit of his retractable lead.

Lyncombe Hill is paved on one side only. Ten-foot walls front the road on the other side, guarding large properties, so everyone uses the pavement on the side where two-storey terraces stretch down most of the way. Hartley hadn't got far when he met quite a procession of men and women, twelve or more, toiling up the gradient from the opposite direction, mostly a few yards apart from each other.

Diamond's first thought was that a train had come in and they were commuters on their way up from the station. On getting closer, he decided they didn't have the tired look of office workers. Nor were they out for an evening on the town. Soberly dressed, the women mostly in heeled shoes and skirts and the men in suits, they had a sense of purpose about them—and that was all he could tell.

Being a cat owner, as Paloma had put it, he didn't foresee what happened next. He was so interested in the advancing cohort that he forgot about Hartley. The excited beagle was already among the skirted and trousered legs. A sudden interest in a lamppost and the cord tightened behind the heels of a frail silver-haired woman with a stick, across the shiny black toecaps of a stout man and under the heel of a younger woman in stilettos.

"Watch out," someone shouted.

Everyone watched out, including Hartley. To give the

small dog his due, he stopped and looked round at Diamond.

The elderly woman felt the cord move against the back of her ankles and screamed.

Diamond yelled, "Hartley!"

A blonde woman who wasn't in the tangle acted swiftly. She ran forward, reached down, grabbed Hartley around the chest, scooped him up and averted mayhem.

Mortified and shaking his head, Diamond stepped forward. "I can't tell you how sorry I am," he said to the people disengaging themselves. Hartley was immobilised, but because he was off the ground the long cord of the lead had ridden up the back of the elderly woman's legs and revealed a white lace slip. She didn't seem to have noticed.

"Excuse me." Diamond moved around the back of her to slacken the cord. She said something he didn't understand. The stout man spoke, also in a foreign language.

Order was restored, the cord reeled in. Diamond reached out with his free hand to collect Hartley and found himself face to face with Olga Ivanova.

"What on earth did you find to say to her?" Paloma asked later, when the casserole was served and he'd given his account of the incident.

"I forget the actual words. I felt like a horse's arse at the time. I can't blame Hartley for what happened. I didn't see the problem coming. Olga's husband, Konstantin, is in custody on suspicion of murder and she was on her way to chapel, to pray for him or herself, I suppose. That's where all these people were heading in their formal clothes."

"They'll be from the Orthodox church," Paloma said. "They have a chapel on Lyncombe Hill they use for Vespers, or whatever the evening service is called. How did she react to you?"

"She was as surprised as I was, but she wanted to talk when she recognised me. There wasn't time, unfortunately. She would be late for the service, so I arranged to meet her tomorrow. She's staying with Maeve, her friend. The house in Sydney Place is off limits while ROCU look for evidence."

"Is Konstantin your murderer, then?"

"Some people think he is."

"But you don't? Have they caught the wrong person? How awful."

"It's not so awful as you might suppose. Konstantin is a trafficker and a slaver and deserves to be banged up for the rest of his life, but I don't believe he killed Tony Pinto."

33

The next morning was a Saturday, but there was no weekend lie-in for the senior members of the murder squad. They had all been summoned to a 7 A.M. briefing. And when they heard the boss sum up his conclusions about the case in his brusque, workmanlike way, they were at first puzzled, then disbelieving, but ultimately won over. There could be no other explanation. Diamond himself had always been a pragmatist with the rare ability to see through the cleverest of deceptions. Justice was about to be served.

By 7:30, they had their orders and were on the road. Soon after 8, three unmarked cars parked in a Larkhall side street close to Bella Vista Road, where Maeve Kelly lived and Olga Ivanova was temporarily her guest. The glare of the early morning sun made the yellow stonework of the block more offensive to Diamond's eye than he remembered. With Detective Sergeant Ingeborg Smith at his side, he walked the rest of the way to the small terraced house.

"She'll be emotional for sure. Her life has hit the buffers," he warned Ingeborg. "She might get physical and she's strong, which is why I asked you to come with me."

"How about Maeve?" Ingeborg asked. "If it comes to a fight, will she wade in?"

"They're friends, so it's possible, but I'd say she's too smart to get involved."

"Your impressions of women aren't always reliable, guv."

"Why did you ask, then?"

He stepped up and rang the bell.

Maeve, dressed in a blue tracksuit, opened the door. She was barefoot, blinking in the bright light, but not altogether surprised to see Diamond on her doorstep. "You're early."

"I don't think I fixed a time."

"At the weekend, eight-fifteen is early. I think she's up and about. You'd better come in."

As soon as they were shown into the strange, cluttered living room he wished he'd told Ingeborg in advance about the hippo collection. He didn't want to spend time on explanations. Good thing she had the sense to say nothing. "This is Sergeant Ingeborg Smith, I should have said."

Maeve gave Ingeborg no more than a glance. Her blue eyes, wide, tormented by her personal demons, fastened on Diamond. "Olga still doesn't know."

"Doesn't know what?"

"About me and Tony in that grotty pub. Do you need to tell her?"

"I'm sure she's got other things on her mind."

"I feel so mean. She's suffered enough and she's being incredibly brave."

"We'll see how this develops. Before she comes in, there are a couple of questions for you. You told me you finished the race."

"The race?"

She was so fixated on her disloyalty to Olga that she could think of nothing else.

"Get with it, Maeve. The Other Half."

"Oh."

"I didn't ask who else you saw during the run."

"Thousands of people."

"Any you know?"

"I wasn't counting. At least a hundred."

An answer he hadn't expected until he remembered she was a schoolteacher and would have been cheered on by the kids she taught. "Was Tony Pinto one of them?"

Her face tightened at the mention of the name. "He started ahead of me. He would have been in a different pen. No, I didn't spot him."

"At some stage in the race you must have overtaken him. He finished long after you did."

"I told you I didn't see him."

"The official results say so." He was interrupted by sounds from upstairs. The cheap 1960s house had narrow joists and a thin ceiling. "Did I hear voices?"

"She talks to herself a lot," Maeve said, but there was no disguising her own startled expression. "Poor darling, she's going through hell. I don't know if she heard you come in. I'll go up and see." Seizing the chance to cut short the questioning about Pinto, she was through the door before she finished speaking.

Diamond exchanged a disbelieving look with Ingeborg. "Sounded to me like more than one voice upstairs."

"How many bedrooms are there?"

"In a place this size? Two, maximum."

They both heard Maeve clearly, and then Olga's deeper response. Two voices only. Possibly Maeve had spoken the truth about her stressed-out visitor talking to herself.

Diamond took out his phone and checked for texts. "Everyone's in place. All exits covered."

They heard the two women come down the stairs.

Olga appeared first, wearing a borrowed white housecoat and light grey slippers with hippo faces. She'd brushed her hair and fixed her make-up and didn't look as if she was suffering. After Ingeborg was introduced, they busied themselves removing hippos from chairs for somewhere to sit. Maeve, not wanting to be in the same room, offered coffee and fled to the kitchen.

"She is fantastic friend," Olga said.

"When we met last night, you said you wanted to speak to me," Diamond said, keen to get on.

"That is true."

"So?"

"I am homeless lady now, house full of people in white suitings. Nobody tell me when I can go back."

"They're checking for evidence. It's a large house, but I should think they'll be finished soon. If you need extra clothes or anything else personal to you, make a list and we'll have them brought over. You were questioned, I was told, and you claim to know nothing about your husband's criminal activities. I find that hard to believe, Olga."

She looked back at him without blinking, as if deciding whether she was being insulted. "Listen, I am God-fearing lady, speak only truth. Konstantin he is typical Russian husband, say shit-all to me. You know. You meet him."

"Didn't you ever ask him about the house in Duke Street and what went on there?"

"Konstantin buy nice houses to rent is all I know."

"Your trainer Tony Pinto lived there."

"Tony come to Sydney Place, my home, okay?"

"He was the gangmaster and Konstantin was his controller and you say you didn't know what they were up to?"

"I say this many times over."

"All right. You claim to be innocent. Let's move on. You invited me here this morning. What else do you want to say to me?"

She nodded. "Konstantin is prisoner, yes?"

Diamond's eyes switched briefly to Ingeborg. The exchanges had been civil so far. Everything could be about to change. "He's under arrest and being questioned. If he's charged, he'll appear before a magistrate and then a judge."

"Big trouble, yes?"

"That depends what he's accused of. He'll have a chance to defend himself."

"You lock him up how long?"

Keep it impersonal, he told himself. "I don't lock him up. I don't deal with him. The judge decides these things."

"How long?"

"Do you understand? I don't decide."

She pressed him harder. "What is punishment for trafficking?"

"If he's found guilty under the modern slavery act, you'd better prepare for bad news, Olga. It's going to be prison."

"How many years?"

"That will be at the judge's discretion." She wouldn't understand what he meant, but the obfuscation would soften the blow.

"For life?"

He tried to look as if the possibility hadn't crossed his mind. "That would be the worst possible outcome."

"Worst for Konstantin." Olga's chest started shaking and she rocked back in the chair, arms flapping like a hen vainly trying to take flight. The only things that flew were several hippos from the table beside her.

Hyperventilating? An epileptic fit? Diamond looked to Ingeborg for assistance.

Then Olga found her voice and laughed heartily. "Worst for Konstantin, best for Olga."

She was rejoicing in the prospect of her husband being banged up for years.

"What will you do?"

"I stay here in Bath. Enjoy myself." She was fitting in the words between bursts of belly laughs.

"That may not be possible. Your house could be seized if it was bought with laundered money."

"No problem. I buy another. Great Pulteney Street is nice."

"Can you afford it?"

"Sure. I have money in bank, my money, clean money. Why do you think Konstantin marry me? My daddy he is capitalist pig, top businessman in Russia, has many companies. I ask, I get."

"Won't you be lonely?" Ingeborg asked.

"What for, be lonely? I have friends. Friends at church. English friends like Maeve."

There was another sound from upstairs like a chair being moved.

They all went silent. And now heavy footfalls crossing the bedroom floor removed all uncertainty.

"Someone's up there," Diamond said.

"Is Maeve, I think," Olga said.

As if on cue, Maeve stepped into the room with a tray of steaming coffee cups. "Did I hear my name?"

"Who's upstairs?"

Diamond didn't get an answer and didn't expect one. He'd see for himself. He almost knocked the tray from Maeve's grasp in his hurry to get out of the room and check. His damaged foot pained him but didn't stop him from taking the stairs two at a time. He crossed the landing to the bedroom above the living room and immediately saw a window fully open, the stay unfastened, the curtain flapping in the breeze outside. Below the sill was a chair that must have been put there to climb out.

He went straight to it and looked down. In the time he'd taken on the stairs, nobody could have got far. He was expecting to find someone hanging from the sill or clinging to a downpipe or even standing on the small square of lawn at ground level.

He was wrong.

Across the street was Keith Halliwell.

Diamond called out, "Did anyone jump for it?"

Halliwell shook his head.

"Then how the hell—"

He didn't get the question out. He was silenced by a sharp hit from behind. His right kidney took the force of it and before he could react to the pain, he was gripped in a tackle as ferocious as anything he'd ever felt in his rugby-playing days. He was dragged back from the window, flung on the bed and pinned to it. A forearm pressed his face into the bedding and a massive hand grabbed his arm and jerked it upwards behind his back until he yelled for mercy.

34

"M urat!"

The word meant nothing to Diamond. He had almost passed out from shock, suffocation and the near certainty that his arm had been wrenched from its socket.

"Murat!" The voice was Olga's and she was bellowing her disapproval in words he took to be Russian. They needed no translation.

Diamond's attacker got the message and acted on it, relaxed the hold, removed the shoulder choke, released the suffering arm and rolled off the bed.

Diamond still couldn't move. He lay winded, wounded, inert and angry with himself that he'd stupidly walked into the trap. The open window and the chair beneath it had so taken his attention that he'd not checked to see if anyone had been waiting behind him poised to attack.

Ingeborg's voice broke through the ringing in his ears. "Are you okay, guv?"

Dumb question in the circumstances, but what else could she have said?

"I'll let you know." He tried to extract his face from the bedding, felt an explosion of pain in his neck and flopped down again.

"Maybe if you roll the other way," Ingeborg said.

He wasn't willing to try.

"Who the hell was that?" he managed to say.

"I've no idea."

Then Maeve's voice joined in. "Murat is Olga's boyfriend. He must have thought you were up to no good, coming up the stairs like that."

Boyfriend? Olga was a married woman.

As if she read his thoughts, Maeve said, "He's a lovely guy. A gentle giant really."

"Really?" Diamond said with as much irony as he could express with his face flat to a mattress. Giant, yes. Gentle, no.

"He's staying here, helping Olga get over her shock of being made homeless. I'm sure he didn't mean to hurt you."

Now Olga spoke some words in English. "He is professional wrestler."

Diamond needed no convincing of that. At the cost of more pain spreading from neck to shoulders, he managed to roll over as Ingeborg had suggested. She propped a pillow under his head.

"Try that, guv."

He could see them now, the three women and his tall assailant standing over him like witnesses at an autopsy. The image was so disturbing that he wriggled into a position against the headboard that left no doubt he was a living being.

"Is he Russian?"

"Albanian," Olga said.

Albanian. A memory stirred in Diamond's befuddled brain, but he wasn't ready to make connections. It was easier to listen than speak.

"But I speak to him in English."

That was English? You could have fooled me, Diamond thought.

Big Murat gave a nod. He didn't have any difficulty understanding her. The pair were intimate companions.

"We meet in St. John's," Olga added.

Diamond was no wiser. Could be anywhere. She might as well be talking about the capital city of Newfoundland.

Maeve filled in some details. "The Eastern Orthodox church, St. John of Kronstadt. They're so hospitable. They gave him a place to sleep. Before that, he was living rough, poor man."

The truth was coming together in his head now. Murat had been one of the two Albanians who escaped from Pinto's basement prison in Duke Street. One had been recaptured and the other was unaccounted for.

Maeve added, "Now that Konstantin is out of it, Olga has invited Murat to move in with her."

Simple as that. To a smart woman like Olga, there's no such thing as a setback; there are only opportunities.

"Why did he attack me?"

"He thought you were a Border Force officer, I expect."

And I should turn him in as an illegal immigrant, Diamond felt like saying. He was getting his head straight. But there was a more urgent matter to be settled than Murat's status. "Help me up," he told Ingeborg, offering his good arm and swinging his feet to the floor.

The room started spinning. He took a deep breath and stabilised himself as much by force of will as the blood flow to his brain. He moved to the open window and looked for Keith Halliwell.

Keith wasn't in the street any longer.

"I'm needed downstairs."

"You're not safe to move yet," Ingeborg said.

"You go first. I'll steady myself with a hand on your shoulder."

With reluctance, she allowed herself to be used as a prop. They got to ground level and he stood unaided.

"You can't take anyone on in this state," Ingeborg said.

"Watch me." Brave words, but he knew she was right.

The terrace opposite was a mirror image of the building

they were leaving. He crossed the street, taking in as much reviving air as he could. And when he reached the door of the house that faced Maeve's, it was ajar, so he pushed it fully open and stepped inside.

The first person he saw was Halliwell. With him was a small, smiling man in a pink long-sleeved shirt and tight white jeans.

"This is Mr. Franklin, the landlord and owner of the house, guv."

Mr. Franklin had spent some holidays in Spain, going by the framed posters of bullfighting all the way along the hall. His bright-eyed, darting look suggested he was eager for some action on his own premises and expected Diamond, the limping matador, to make the moves that would achieve the coup de grâce.

Diamond looked away from him. "And?"

Halliwell pointed at the ceiling.

"Has anyone spoken to him?"

"Like you ordered, we waited for you. I've got John Leaman watching the rear of the house and young Gilbert is out front."

"Are we certain our man is up there?"

"Gilbert saw movement at a window."

"He will have watched the two of us cross the street. He'll know it's showdown time. I'll go up and speak to him."

"You look as if you've been in a fight already," Halliwell said.

Ingeborg said, "He has."

"Yes, and I came off second best." He was already on the stairs, driven by his strong desire to see this through to its conclusion. His brain had snapped into full conscious-ness. The throbbing and the soreness in his body were unimportant at this stage. Halliwell and Ingeborg were close behind him.

He'd learned his lesson and wouldn't charge into the

front room of the small flat. Instead, he paused on the landing and spoke with all the consideration he would employ when visiting a sick friend in hospital.

"Trevor?"

After some hesitation came, "I'm in here." No hint of aggression.

"The house is surrounded. We're police officers."

"I guessed you must be." A door was opened. "You'd better come in." Broad-shouldered, muscled, but only average in height, Trevor, the PE teacher, stepped back to allow them inside. He was dressed in a black T-shirt that on his torso looked as if it was a boy's size, black jeans and a red baseball hat with the British Heart Foundation logo.

Diamond knew the face. He'd never met the guy, but the features were familiar. The cavernous, troubled eyes, wide mouth and oversize teeth. A thrilling moment of certainty. Theory confirmed as fact.

For a suspected killer, Trevor was remarkably hospitable. "I don't have chairs for everyone, but you're welcome to sit on the bed." Mr. Nice, it appeared.

And Diamond cooperated, too, and with gratitude, by letting the side of the bed take the strain.

But every cop knows—like every fighter—that you don't drop your guard just because your antagonist does.

"We'll check you over first." He gestured to Halliwell to make a body search.

Trevor didn't object.

While the pat-down went on, Diamond took stock of the small bedsit and the set-up wasn't as he'd expected. In fact, there was no obvious set-up at all. No surveillance gear. No camera, telescope, binoculars. No gallery of secretly taken photos of Maeve. The pictures on the wall were entirely of sports teams and action studies of professional athletes. A collection of medals on ribbons. Glass-topped computer desk and rotating chair. A two-shelf bookcase stuffed with paperbacks. No room for anything else.

"You take the chair," Diamond told Trevor. "These two are happy to stand. They spend their time sitting in front of screens."

He passed up the offer, opting instead to face the music from an upright position.

"What is it with the BHF cap, Trevor? Here you are wearing it at home and I was told you didn't think much of it."

He reddened enough to match the scarlet baseball cap. "Who told you that?"

"Maeve Kelly."

"That I don't think much of my cap?"

"That's what she told me yesterday."

"She's wrong. I wear it all day when I'm here."

"She hasn't seen you in it."

"Because I wouldn't wear it to work. I look after it. You can't trust anyone." He put both hands to the peak and made sure the angle was right before pressing his fingertips against the soft fabric behind.

That small gesture was a revelation. He was drawing comfort from the cap, fondling it like a living thing because it came from Maeve, regardless that it was the catalyst for the chain of events that led ultimately to a violent death.

"Maeve gave it to you and you presented her with a gift in return."

"How do you know about that?" Trevor said, blushing again.

"A valuable Toby jug. She told me."

"What did she say about the jug?"

"That it was very old, one of the first to be made."

"She said that?" He was pathetically ignorant about the true reaction of the woman who meant so much to him.

He changed his mind about standing. He grasped his computer chair, wheeled it closer to Diamond and sat in it, within touching distance. He was hearing something encouraging and unexpected—that Maeve had appreciated the value of his eccentric gift.

Or so he convinced himself.

Diamond didn't need to disillusion Trevor. He was getting an insight into the heart of this case. He could see in the moist brown eyes how completely the guy was infatuated. No need to hurt him by revealing Maeve's disrespect for what she'd called the sodding Toby jug or that she'd accidentally smashed it and been on a guilt trip ever since.

"I knew she'd find out its true worth at some stage," Trevor said in a hushed voice as if he was talking about Mother Teresa, "but she never said anything. She may have donated it to charity. They're not daft in these shops. They spot antique items. Maybe they told her its value. She's very public-spirited. She raised a four-figure sum for the BHF by running in the Other Half."

"And you coached her."

"Is that what she told you? A slight exaggeration. It didn't amount to much. Running is something I know a lot about, so I offered a few tips, that's all." He touched the talisman cap again. "She really said I coached her, did she?"

"Words to that effect, anyway. Whatever advice you gave, it worked. I heard she ran the full distance."

"All credit to her, yes."

"You weren't running yourself?"

"Not this year. I've done it before."

"You know all about the Other Half, do you?"

"Sport is my thing."

"Obviously. Sport and Maeve. Twin obsessions."

Trevor reacted to the last word by bringing his hands together in his lap and tightening them so hard that the knuckles turned to ridges of ivory.

"Let's face it, Trevor," Diamond went on. "You can't get

her out of your head. You don't want to. Ever since she gave you the cap you're wearing, you've idolised her. It's why you live here, across the street, why you follow her about. I was prepared to find you're a voyeur, but I've changed my opinion. You're not a stalker either, not in any unpleasant way. When you follow her anywhere, it's from a wish to protect her. Am I speaking sense?"

Trevor didn't answer.

"You do follow her sometimes, don't you?"

"She's safe with me," he said.

"I don't doubt that for a second. But God help anyone else who tries it on."

Trevor flattened his palms against his beefy thighs and stared down.

"Such as Tony Pinto?" Diamond said. "Bit of a tomcat, sniffing around sports girls for a few months now. You knew about his reputation, I'm sure. So did I. I can tell you, Trevor, I despised the guy. I didn't shed any tears when I found out he was killed."

Trevor looked up, frowning, thrown by the last remark.

Diamond had genuine sympathy for the lovelorn loner he was gently and methodically dismantling. "When Pinto made his move on Maeve, it all happened quickly and at the worst possible time. On the day before her big race, he turned on the charm, offered expert advice on how to run and gave her more than just advice, in a bedroom upstairs in that squalid pub where he was drinking with her. Made you mad. I'm guessing now, but you weren't far away at the time, were you?"

Trevor emitted a sigh that was as good as confirmation.

"The waiting must have been painful for you. Where were you—inside the pub, or standing out in the street?"

Now he took a deep breath, remembering. "I didn't go inside until after they came out. She would have seen me. The seating area wasn't much bigger than this room. Then

I spoke to the barman, like Pinto was my friend and we had a bet over whether he'd . . ." He couldn't get the words out.

"Made out with her?"

He lowered his face again. "The arsehole had hired an upstairs room in advance."

In Trevor's mind all the blame was heaped on Pinto. Maeve was still Snow White.

"The next hours must have been hell for you."

He made no response, suspicious, perhaps, that he was being lured into admitting he planned the killing.

Diamond chose not to press him. They would go over this again in an interview room before he made his statement.

"The next day, instead of accompanying Maeve on your bike during the race, you followed Pinto and watched him chat up another woman who was clearly unsettled by him. Am I right?"

This time he spoke a clear, "Yes."

"The young woman decided to quit the race rather than enter the mile-long tunnel with Pinto. He went after her and fortunately she got away. Was that because you tackled him on Combe Down?"

He nodded.

"Tell me about it."

"You seem to know it all."

"You're the only one who knows how he ended up where he did."

Trevor straightened in the chair. No doubt he'd rehearsed this a hundred times, trying to make sure he gave it the best possible gloss—not easy when you've killed a man and disposed of the body. "He was crossing a field on the side of a hill. I left my bike at the side of the road to follow him. He turned round and there I was, a few steps behind him. Like you say, I was mad. Angry, I mean. I hadn't slept at all. I called him names. I wanted to hit him, I don't mind telling you, but it wasn't much of a fight. He slung a punch or two and so did I, not enough to hurt him. He had a longer reach than me. But when he aimed another punch and missed my chin, I put both hands against his chest and pushed him and he fell back like a skittle and cracked his head. It was stone where he fell, with only a thin covering of turf. I could see straight away he was out to the world."

"Dead?"

"He didn't move. Is that what you want to know?"

His version chimed in with what Dr. Sealy had said about the linear fracture suggesting Pinto had fallen backwards and hit his head.

"I want to hear the rest, Trevor—what you did when he was lying still."

"It's weird. It should have been satisfying, knocking him out, but it wasn't. All I'd done was shove him in the chest. I wanted him to get up and I'd throw a real punch at him, but he didn't. I stood over him and he didn't move. After a bit I started to walk away. Then I thought better of it. What if I'd killed him? I went back and felt for a pulse at the side of his neck. There wasn't any. I didn't panic exactly, but I knew I'd be in deep trouble if he was found. I decided to get the body out of sight. There was a copse at the edge of the field and I dragged him there, thinking I'd cover him with bracken and stuff. After I got him there, I saw this iron grille almost covered in weeds and I knew what it was."

"A ventilation shaft."

He nodded. "We've had school trips to Combe Down to teach the kids about the old mines. I've seen a covered shaft before. I managed to lift the grille and dropped him in. That's it, really."

No, it isn't, Diamond thought. You don't want to tell me the rest because it implicates you even more. "Bad luck for you that we found him down there. We were searching for someone else—Belinda Pye, the young woman he was pursuing."

"So how did you get onto me?"

"It wasn't easy," Diamond said. "There was nothing obvious to connect you to the killing. And you made our job more difficult by making it appear that he finished the race. Covering your tracks, you thought. We studied the video of the finish, the exact time he was supposed to have crossed the line. Pinto's name appears in the results, but the runner wasn't Pinto, it was you, trying to hide from the camera behind some fun-runner with the Royal Crescent on his back. Your number wasn't visible, but your head and shoulders were, briefly."

"I thought I was out of shot."

"But registering a time?"

"And I did. He's in the results."

"And there had to be an explanation," Diamond said.

Trevor waited to hear it, still wanting to give nothing away.

"You were carrying Pinto's chip. The timing system is electronic, so every runner has to wear one. Before you dumped the body down the shaft, you removed the chip from his shoe. With that, you could masquerade as a competitor. You took a short cut through Lyncombe and joined the stragglers completing the last section of the race and carried the chip across the line, right? The electronics showed Pinto finished, so what happened on Combe Down was neatly erased as far as anyone could tell. But I've studied the video and it was definitely you."

Trevor felt for the baseball cap again and pushed the peak higher up his forehead. "In a strange way, I'm relieved it's over. What happens next?"

"We take you in as a suspect and get a statement from you. A confession is your best option."

"Concealing a body is a serious crime, isn't it?"

"Serious, but not the worst."

"I didn't intend to kill him."

"You've made that clear."

Diamond nodded to Halliwell, who told Trevor to stand up. He cuffed him and said, "Let's go."

Paloma joined Diamond that evening for what he called a painkiller—a therapeutic pint in his local, the Old Crown at Weston, a dog-friendly pub where Hartley seemed to know he was appreciated and lay on his side as if to announce that all shoes and chair legs in this sanctum were safe from his attention.

"So Olga comes out of this best," Paloma said after she'd heard the story of Diamond's day. "She escapes from Konstantin, who is the real villain, and ends up with the gorgeous Murat."

"Gorgeous he is not," Diamond said. "He left me with one good arm and a pain in the neck that isn't going to go away for the rest of the week."

"But you won't turn him in?"

"My battered body tells me to lock him up and throw away the key, but I guess not. He was trafficked. If I reported him, the taxpayer would have to pay for his keep while his asylum application was considered. Allowing him to move in with Olga at her expense is a better option."

"And Trevor. What will happen to him?"

"The police have some discretion in dealing with first-time offenders who make full confessions. Have you heard of out-of-court disposals? They're a way of dealing with someone without prosecuting them and saddling them with a criminal record. I said nothing to him about this, but I'll speak to Georgina."

"The other baddy in this case, apart from Konstantin, was Tony Pinto, as you said from the start."

"And there's a twist," he said. "Pinto liked to be known as the Finisher, striking fear into everyone under his control.

As it turned out, the real Finisher was Trevor, and in more than one sense."

"He finished off Pinto," Paloma said. "What else?"

"He finished the race. He hadn't run the course, but he finished and carried Pinto's microchip over the line."

"Neat."

"I think so."

"Clever old you." She swirled the gin and tonic in her glass and watched the movement of the floating slice of lemon. "That leaves only one thing to be settled."

"What's that?" His face changed rapidly from a look of mild enquiry to strong suspicion that something personal was about to be said.

But he was reassured. "Hartley," Paloma said.

At the sound of his name, the small dog raised his head to look at her.

"His owner, my neighbour Miriam, will be back from Liverpool at the weekend. She's arranged the care package for her mother. I'm going to miss him. The house will seem empty without him."

"Maybe you should get one of your own."

"A dog?"

"Or a cat."

"Funny," she said. "I was thinking along the same lines. How would you feel if I made an offer to Raffles?"

"To move in with you? Yikes!" he said. "He wouldn't stand for that. I'd need to come with him."

She laughed. "Would that be such a bad thing?"

RUNNING INTO WRITING

I am sometimes asked if I'm a runner. I must confess that I'm not even a fun-runner. I can think of a thousand things that are more fun. Paying my income tax is more fun. It's true that I've written several books with running as a theme, but I am pathologically incapable of doing it myself. I get the stitch if I go a few yards. As a youth, I tried. How I tried, shambling and shuffling through the streets of suburban Whitton after dark, being questioned by the police (this was long before jogging became respectable), attacked by dogs, tripping over paving stones and running into lampposts when my glasses steamed up, all the time convincing myself I was training and would soon amaze the world. And on the day of reckoning I staggered in last in the school cross-country race. All my memories of running are painful. But I owe my career to it.

In 1948, my father took me to the Olympic Games. I was eleven, an impressionable age. The excitement, the atmosphere in the stadium and the achievements of great athletes like Emil Zátopek and Fanny Blankers-Koen stayed with me all my life. I dreamed of being a runner myself. I still do. Eventually I found my own way to participate by *writing* about athletics. I discovered a rich seam nobody else had mined: the history of the sport. A new magazine was desperate for articles and published me. Overnight I was billed as The World's Foremost Authority on the History of Athletics; in truth, I was the world's only authority. By 1968 I had the confidence to publish a book on great runners of the past called *The Kings of Distance*. It was well received. It doesn't get better than this, I thought. Will I ever write anything else of book length? Realistically, no.

Then, by some quirk of fate, an advert appeared in the press in 1969 announcing a first crime novel competition. The prize was £1000, more than my annual salary as a teacher. Encouraged by my wife Jax, who is a keen reader of crime fiction, I submitted a whodunit about a Victorian long-distance race and called it *Wobble to Death*. With a catchy title and an unusual setting that worked within the convention of a puzzle story, it won the prize.

Barely believing in myself as a crime writer, I needed to find subjects other than running to use as backgrounds for detective stories. I played safe and embarked on a series that was set, like *Wobble to Death*, in the late Victorian period and featured various popular entertainments such as pugilism, the music hall, the seaside and table-turning. After five years I was able to retire from teaching to make my living as a professional writer.

I still couldn't see myself making a career out of Victorian whodunits. The sport of running remained a passion and I returned to it in a contemporary novel. In the 1970s, athletics was undergoing huge changes. The old code of amateurism was being displaced. For years, so-called shamateurs had received backhanders from promoters of a sport that was a good money-spinner. With the extra incentive of cash payments came temptations to cheat by using drugs. It was an open secret that athletes were improving their performances with sophisticated chemical and biological aids. State-sponsored athletes from the Eastern Bloc had for some decades achieved unbelievable records. In the free world there was evidence of hormone injections and the use of blood transfusions to gain lucrative advantage.

I decided to air some of these issues in fiction. Enter Goldine Serafin, a gifted and attractive American woman who would challenge for three gold medals at the next Olympic Games, due to be held in Moscow. *Goldengirl* (written as Peter Lear) was about the marketing opportunity this presented and the moneymen, crooks and cranks who homed in on the unfortunate athlete to exploit her. The novel became a bestseller. Even better, it was bought by Columbia and filmed with the beautiful Susan Anton in the starring role and a cast that included James Coburn, Curt Jurgens and Leslie Caron. The bad news was that in real life the Russians marched into Afghanistan and the Americans boycotted the Olympics in protest, so *Goldengirl*, the film, never went on general release.

But these were heady days for a wannabe athlete. I was commissioned to write the official centenary history of the Amateur Athletic Association, encouraged by Harold Abrahams, the 1924 Olympic sprint champion, who was a family friend, an unofficial uncle to our children. After his death in 1978 I was invited by the actor and writer Colin Welland to supply some memories of Harold for a film project that would become the Oscar-winning *Chariots of Fire*.

Fortune favoured me again when June Wyndham-Davies, a TV producer, read a review of *Waxwork*, the eighth book in the Sergeant Cribb series, and persuaded Granada to buy the rights and screen it in prime time on the Sunday before Christmas 1979. Starring Alan Dobie as Cribb, William Simons as Constable Thackeray and Carol Royle as the convicted murderer Miriam Cromer, this pilot production was so successful that a series was commissioned using all of the books. I was thrilled when one of the best scriptwriters of his generation, Alan Plater, took on *Wobble to Death*.

The episode was filmed in Manchester Free Trade Hall, an early Victorian building remarkably like the Agricultural Hall, Islington, where the original six-day races had been run. The weird form of entertainment was made believable and compelling by a cast including Kenneth Cranham and Michael Elphick.

Sergeant Cribb's investigations came to an end with the TV series. Together with Jax, I wrote six original screenplays for a second series and used up the stock of ideas that might otherwise have become novels. Several "stand-alones" followed and then a trilogy featuring Bertie, the Prince of Wales, as an inept amateur detective.

In 1991 I foisted the burly, belligerent Peter Diamond on to the city of Bath's murder squad in *The Last Detective.* He resigned straight away and then surprised me by returning in *The Summons* and staying in the job for nineteen books over twenty-nine years. He was middle-aged in the first, so I don't like to think how old he must be now. As for his cat Raffles, one thing I have learned as a crime writer is that you can murder anyone, but you never kill the cat.

Writers are often asked where they get their ideas from. Tough question, but the inspiration for *The Finisher* is clear. The book comes fifty years after *Wobble to Death.*

Running has undergone seismic changes since the Victorian event I wrote about in 1970. I have mentioned some of the bad practices that plague modern athletics, but there is one development we can all applaud—the rise in popularity of "Big City" marathons. People in the thousands run distances that were regarded fifty years ago as only to be attempted by specialists. The trend began with the New York City Marathon, first run in 1970 with a field of 126. By 1980 this had grown to 14,000 and by 2019 more than 50,000. The figure for the London Marathon, instituted in 1981, is over 40,000.

In *The Finisher*, the half marathon known as the Other

Half is entirely fictional. The real Bath Half is one of the most popular city races in Britain and takes place each March over a fast, flat course attracting almost 12,000 runners. It is always over-subscribed. There is also a full Bath Marathon usually run in August over a demanding course that includes the two railway tunnels described in the book. I couldn't resist using the tunnel of death in my narrative. I am grateful to the management teams of both races for details of their organisation.

Many accounts of marathon-running have been written by brave people who don't consider themselves as athletes yet attempt and achieve feats I can only dream about. I found Phil Hewitt's *Keep on Running* and *Outrunning the Demons* particularly helpful. Alexandra Heminsley's *Running Like a Girl* and Bryony Gordon's *Eat, Drink, Run* give honest and fascinating insights into the challenges they overcame as women runners.

For the Bath setting and the lore of the stone quarries, I did some mining myself, of *Around Combe Down*, by Peter Addison and "A Brief History of the Stone Quarries at Combe Down," by David Workman, in the *Journal of the Bath Geological Society*. The true story of the tunnel of death can be found in Diana White's *Stories of Bath*. The map of the course at the front of this book is the work of Saffron Russell and her mother, Jacqui Lovesey. Finally I wish to thank my friends David Dell and Yury Tereshchenko for putting me right on some Russian terminology. Any flaws are my own.

Peter Lovesey
www.peterlovesey.com

Continue reading for a preview of the next
Peter Diamond investigation

DIAMOND AND THE EYE

1

"Mind if I join you?"

Peter Diamond's toes curled.

There's no escape when you're wedged into your favourite armchair in the corner of the lounge bar at the Francis observing the last rites of an exhausting week keeping a cap on crime. Tankard in hand, your third pint an inch from your mouth, you want to be left alone.

The stranger's voice was throaty, the accent faux American from a grainy black-and-white film a lifetime ago. This Bogart impersonator was plainly as English as a cricket bat. His face wasn't Bogart's and he wasn't talking through tobacco smoke, but he held a cocktail stick between two fingers as if it was a cigarette. Some years the wrong side of forty, he was dressed in a pale grey suit and floral shirt open at the neck to display a miniature magnifying glass on a leather cord.

"Depends," Diamond said.

"On what?"

"Should I know you?"

"No reason you should, bud."

No one called Diamond "bud." He'd have said so, but the soundtrack had already moved on.

"I got your number. You're the top gumshoe in this one-horse town and you're here in the bar Friday nights when you're not tied up on a case. What's your poison? I'll get you another."

"Don't bother." Diamond wasn't being suckered into getting lumbered with a bar-room bore who called him bud and claimed to have got his number.

"You'll need something strong when you hear what I have to say." The bore pulled up a chair and the voice became even more husky. "Good to meet you, any road. I'm Johnny Getz, the private eye."

"Say that again, the last part."

"Private eye."

Against all the evidence that this was a send-up, Diamond had to hear more. "*Private eye?* I thought they went out with Dick Tracy."

"Dick Tracy was a cop."

"Sam Spade, then. We're talking private detectives, are we? I didn't know we had one in Bath."

"What do you mean—'one'? I could name at least six others. The difference is they're corporate. I'm the real deal. I work alone."

"Where?"

"Over the hairdresser's in Kingsmead Square." An address that lacked something compared to a seedy San Francisco side street, which was probably why the self-styled PI added, "The Shear Amazing Sleuth. Like it?"

There was a pause while the conflict in Diamond's head—contempt battling with curiosity—raged and was resolved. "What did you say your name is?"

"Johnny Getz."

"How do you spell that?"

"Getz? With a zee."

Diamond sighed. "Is it real?"

"Sure. You heard of Stan Getz?"

"The jazz musician. You're not related?

"I should be so lucky."

"It was his real name as far as I know," Diamond said. "Is yours your own?"

A shake of the head. "In my line of work, you gotta make a noise in the world."

"You play the sax yourself?"

"Nah. I'm talking publicity." He took a business card from his pocket and snapped it on the table like the ace of trumps. "*Johnny Getz. Gets results.* How does that grab you?"

Diamond had a pained look, and not from being grabbed. "What do you want with me, Mr. Getz?"

"Johnny to you."

"Mr. Getz. I keep first names for my friends."

Johnny Getz took a moment to reflect on that. He refused to take it as a putdown. "What do I want? I want your help with a case."

"Don't even start," Diamond said, seizing his chance to end this. "I'm a police officer. We don't get involved outside our work."

"This *is* your work. It's got your name all over it."

"What the hell are you talking about?"

"*Police, do not cross.* The break-in at the antiques shop in Walcot Street last Sunday night. The owner is away. You know about this?"

"I don't hear about every crime that happens on my patch."

"The cops have sealed the place."

"If it's a crime scene, they would."

"Fair enough, except I need to see inside."

"Why?"

"My client wants to know what was taken."

"And who is your client?"

"The owner's daughter."

"Has she spoken to anyone?"

"Several times. Your people tell her jack shit. They say they want to deal with her father."

"That's understandable if he's the owner. Where is he?"

"Nobody knows. The best guess is he's buying more stock. From time to time he gets wind of a house clearance, hangs the 'closed' sign on the door and goes looking for bargains."

"No one else runs the shop while he's away?"

"He wouldn't let the Bishop of Bath run it."

"One of those."

"You got it."

"Why isn't the daughter content to wait until he gets back?"

"You want the truth? She doesn't trust cops."

"Careful what you say, Mr. Getz."

"I'm telling you why she hired me. She hasn't a clue how much was stolen. Not all of you are angels. Some are light-fingered and if it isn't a cop who walks out with a valuable item, it could be a scene-of-crime person. Who's to know if the thief took it?"

"I've heard enough of this horseshit."

"I'm accusing nobody. I'm telling you what's on my client's mind. The longer this goes on, the bigger the suspicion."

"The owner could be back today or tomorrow. He'll know what's been taken, I presume."

"Sure—but he won't know who took it."

"Neither will you, for that matter. There's more to this. Who reported the break-in?"

"My client. She came past the shop, saw it was closed, checked the door and found it had been jemmied, the wood splintered around the lock. She reported it right away."

"This was when?"

"Monday afternoon. Two thirty-five."

"She didn't go inside?"

Getz shook his head. "She didn't know if the perp was still in the shop."

"She'd heard nothing from her father about going away?"

"He wouldn't have told her. He's like that."

"I'll tell you something for nothing," Diamond said. "I've known cases where the thief turns out to have been the person who reported the crime."

"Now you're slandering my client."

"You slandered the police. And here's something else for you to get your head around. The break-in may never have happened."

Getz frowned and fingered his silver magnifier.

"The damage to the door could be a con, done by her father to defraud his insurance company. That happens."

"We don't know if he was insured."

"Find out, Mr. Getz. Tell your client to quit racing her motor and leave us to do our job."

A pious hope, but it ended the exchange and allowed Diamond to finish his drink.

2

Diamond had treated me like something he'd trodden in, but I expect no different from a cop. They can't take competition. I'd found the fat slob and he'd listened and there was a brain behind the bad-mouthing, no question. He was interested. I had a line into the pig pen.

Would he stir himself and get on the case? Not yet. Everything about him screamed idle bastard. We all know the police are cash-strapped and undermanned and only 5 percent of burglaries get solved, so if you want action you need to kick ass.

Early Monday morning (early for me is around 10 A.M.), I called Ruby to fix another meeting. She offered to come at once. Tomorrow, I told her. Didn't want her thinking she was my only client.

When she showed up next afternoon, I made sure there was a shoulder-high stack of files on my desk and the red light on my phone was flashing. She wasn't to know I'd sent voicemail to myself.

I wasn't the only one putting on a show. She was in a long black dress more fishnet than fabric, matching tights and shiny pointed shoes. Her amazing red hair had turned black, or so I thought before I saw it was hidden under an eagle's nest of a wig. Velvet choker studded with jet beads. Murderous dark-rimmed eyes and purple lips like she'd just emerged from the bat cave. What was all this in aid of? The last time we'd met, she was dressed like Daddy's little helper.

"Do you want to get that, Johnny?" she asked, meaning the phone.

"They can wait," I said, more laidback than a poolside lounger. "This is your time, Ruby."

Her eyes gleamed under the beetle-black lids. "Have you got something for me?"

I didn't move my feet off the desk. "You could say so."

She waited and I kept her waiting. I let her take stock of the bookshelf behind. Funny how so many of my favourite writers have better names for sleuthing than their creations. Karin Slaughter, Ann Cleeves, Jonathan Gash, James M. Cain, Joe Gores, Martha Grimes, Will Carver, Christopher Fowler, Magdalen Nabb, Candace Robb. When any one of those guys advertises for clients, I'll be the first to hire them to find my missing Maltese Falcon.

"Speak to me, Johnny, for God's sake." Today she was more hyper than ever. "What's happened? I can take it."

"Chill, babe," I said. "We're one step on the way, that's all." I picked up my phone and thumbed in a number. "Up to now, the break-in has been handled by the cops in uniform. You don't want that. This is a direct line to a chum of mine called Pete." My thumb was poised over the green.

"Who's he?"

"The law."

She turned whiter than a steamed plaice. "A policeman?"

"Detective Peter Diamond. The chief of CID. This isn't his case, but I filled him in on the facts and he's our best hope of getting inside the shop."

"No." She raised both hands like I was Dracula moving in for a bite. "I don't want the police involved. That's the whole reason I came to you."

"Easy, babe," I said. "I'll be calling the shots, not Pete. I'll make sure of that."

"You don't understand."

"But I do," I said. "Think about it. You brought in the cops yourself when you saw the shop was broken into. They moved in and sealed the place. If I'm going to find your dad I need to see inside."

"It's not the way I planned this."

"Yeah, but get real. Trust me, Ruby, this is what we must do."

She chewed on that for a moment and seemed to get the message. "Are you going to speak to him?"

"Better if you do."

"Me?"

Was I kidding myself when I thought for a moment the black wig stood on end?

"Call him sir," I said, passing the mobile towards her. "He'll appreciate that."

She wouldn't take hold of the phone. "I won't do it, Johnny."

"Tell him who you are. You're worried out of your skull about what happened, you think it's possible your dad was in the shop when it was raided and is being held by the robbers."

"Is he? Please God, no," she said.

Jesus, I thought. This dame is dumber than she looks.

"I made that up, about him being kidnapped. It's what you tell Pete. We need to ramp this up to get him on side. How's his health?"

"Daddy's? Okay, I think."

"That isn't what you say. You say Daddy could die without his medication. You want to get into the shop to see if the pills are in the desk drawer where he keeps them. Is he on medication?"

"Not as far as I know."

"Pete needs to be told how urgent this is, okay? Lay it on thick."

Funny how fast the spooky goth turned into the virtuous maiden. "I don't tell lies, Johnny. I can't. What you're saying isn't true. I could get in trouble, lying to the police."

There was no changing her mind. "Want me to make the call? No problem." I touched green and got through to Diamond at once. "Pete? Johnny Getz, about that matter we discussed in the Francis. My client is with me and it sounds like really bad news, I'm afraid."

"Get lost, Mr. Getz."

Jerk. Good thing Ruby couldn't hear his end of the line.

"It's like this, Pete. Yesterday was her birthday." I noticed Ruby's eyes widen in surprise. She had a lot to learn about the tricks of my trade. "Her dad always calls her on her birthday, wherever he is. He's never missed. Yesterday, zilch. No phone call, text message, email. She's in a state of panic here or I'd put her on to speak to you. Between you and me, we have a wandering father job, to misquote the great Dash."

I waited for his brain to crunch through the gears.

"If you haven't read Hammett, that's your loss," I went on. "I'm sorry for you. In words you understand, this looks like a misper situation."

"You're talking bollocks, Getz," he said.

"Have you been inside the shop yet?" I asked him, knowing how unlikely it was.

"Weren't you listening the other night?" he said. "It's someone else's case."

"It's yours if the old man has been topped."

Ruby made a sound like an emergency stop.

"What was that?" Diamond said.

"My client. I'm speaking in front of her. I'm saying we should prepare for the worst."

"Pure supposition," he said. "I've heard enough of this."

"Hang on, squire," I said. "The young lady is talking about taking her own life."

"I'm not surprised when you're feeding her this bilge." A long, thoughtful pause. He wouldn't want to be responsible for a suicide after being warned it was coming. The police hate being caught with their pants down and I was giving him no choice. Finally, he said, "All right, I'll put her mind at rest, but only to get you off my back. Ask her to meet me outside the shop at three this afternoon."

"Cool. I owe you one, Pete."

"You can start by calling me Mr. Diamond."

I put down the phone and did a mental victory roll. From now on, he was Pete and I was Johnny.

Ruby's eyebrows had lifted like a drawbridge.

I passed on the good news. Didn't get the hug I deserved, but she'd come round to my plan, in spite of all. "I wish you hadn't told him so much that isn't true, like the stuff about my birthday and me threatening suicide."

"Young lady," I said, "I'm a private eye, not the Pope. Truth-telling isn't in the job description."

"But it wasn't my birthday and he could easily catch us out."

"He won't even try. It's unimportant. We got what we wanted, didn't we?"

"Yes, and after listening to you, I'm dreading what we'll find."

The antiques shop was at the end of Walcot Street, close to Beehive Yard, where the Saturday flea market pulls in the crowds. Other days it's quiet, if you know what I mean. The traffic still makes one hell of a racket. I found Ruby waiting outside, checking her phone. She'd done another quick change, washed off all the black muck, liberated the do and put on tracksuit trousers and top. "I'm thinking he may ask me to squeeze into one of those white forensic suits you see on TV," she said, eyes gleaming.

I cottoned on. This lady got her kicks by dressing up.

"You can hope," I said, "but it's unlikely. They've had all week to lift the prints and collect the DNA." I could have told her this was a simple B and E, not murder, but I didn't. You don't downplay a case to a paying client.

No sign yet of my new friend Pete. I'd be pissed off if he let me down.

The big shop windows and the doorway between them were boarded up and a police notice had been screwed to the front, like they expected a long closure. Already there was graffiti across the chipboard. Kids with aerosols can't resist a blank surface. This was a well-drawn burglar in mask, flat cap and striped shirt, with a bag over his shoulder marked SWAG. Being Bath, you'd call it street art.

"Daddy would hate this," Ruby said.

"People knowing he's been done over?"

She nodded. "He's a very private man. And so proud of his shop."

"Who lives upstairs?"

"He owns that, too. It's where he keeps the stuff he hasn't valued yet."

"Anything worth stealing?"

A frown spread over her pretty face. "Mainly ceramics and fine furniture. He doesn't deal in tat."

"Is this the first break-in he's had?"

"Small objects get shoplifted from time to time, but nothing as drastic as this."

"Hold on, Ruby. Until we get inside, we won't know how much has gone."

"I meant this is the first time anyone has forced the door."

A cop car pulled up at the kerb and the back door opened for the big dick to heave himself out. Too idle to walk, obviously. He was in a light trenchcoat like he expected rain and he stuck a hat on his bald head, a brown trilby. One more fancy-dress freak, I thought. Join the club, pal. "I agreed to meet the young lady," he told me. "I didn't invite you."

Friendly.

I looked him up and down like he'd crept from under a stone. "How would she know who you are? She doesn't talk to any hobo who comes up to her in the street."

"Any more of that and you can wait outside." He produced a key and poked it into the padlock. "I didn't get your name, miss."

"Ruby Hubbard."

"And what's your father's first name?"

"Septimus."

"Unusual."

"He's Seppy to his friends."

When he got the temporary wooden door open, we could see where the real lock had been jemmied. Nothing subtle about it. We stepped inside, all of us. Pete had said his piece about me being unwelcome and wasn't making an issue of it. In point of fact, he needed me. These days, it isn't smart for a senior cop to be alone with a young woman.

"Can anyone see a light switch?"

The boarded windows made the place darker than a beetle's ass. Ruby, who was no birdbrain, used her phone as a torch and found the switch.

As antique shops go, this was high class. Windsor chairs in front to keep you at arm's length from the breakables. Chests and tables behind, covered with crockery, silver and glass, with a back row of display cabinets, big items like sideboards and grandfather clocks against the wall. Whoever had broken in could have had a field day. They hadn't.

Ruby walked towards the far end, giving the once-over to some funky items that probably appealed to diehard collectors: three shiny suits of armour; a rocking horse; a doll's house; an ancient Egyptian coffin half covered by a bearskin rug; a penny-farthing bike; several busts of Roman emperors; and a stuffed lion grinning like it had just made a meal of a stuffed antelope. She said she couldn't see anything missing. Her mood was improving. "I was expecting mayhem."

"Don't get your hopes up," I warned her. "It was still a forced entry. Something will have gone. Does he keep money here?"

"Very little, as far as I know. People pay by cheque or card."

Pete had moved over to a corner formed by the bend in a wrought iron staircase. A massive ship's figurehead of a crowned Neptune was attached to the banisters and below was a mahogany desk topped by a land-line phone that was an antique itself, a wire in-tray filled with paperwork and a row of reference books arranged like a defensive wall. A magnifying glass. A china ashtray with two squashed cigar butts. A coffee mug with the words VINTAGE IS THE NEW COOL. The dregs had dried and left a stain inside.

"His lookout point," Ruby said, stepping closer. "He can see all he wants from here."

"He sits here?"

"All the time. He doesn't go up to customers unless they welcome it. He believes in leaving them to wander until they find something that interests them." She looked down at the only space left on the desk. It was the shape of a square outlined by dust. "His laptop is missing."

"Doesn't he take it home with him?"

"Not to my knowledge."

Pete shrugged. He wasn't getting into a state about a missing laptop. "Forensics will have taken it for checking. You said he takes credit cards. They'll also have taken his payment machine for evidence of recent transactions. I'm surprised he doesn't have CCTV."

"He's against it on principle. He calls it Big Brother."

The head of CID wasn't interested. Something had caught his eye. "There's a safe here."

I glanced down at a grey metal combination thing not much bigger than a microwave and still coated with some of the aluminium flake the SOCOs use to show up fingerprints. "I wouldn't call that a safe. It's small enough to carry away."

"I don't advise you to try. It will be bolted to the floor."

I let him know I was no idiot. "Is the report in from forensics?"

"You're joking. But I was told the safe was open and empty when they first got here."

"It shouldn't be," Ruby said, turning as red as her hair. "He kept small items of value in there."

"Such as?"

"Jewellery, for one thing."

"Doesn't look like it was forced," I said.

"They'd need the combination, wouldn't they?" she said.

For Ruby's sake I kept my mouth shut about some of the methods crooks use to persuade safe-owners to tell all. I bet the same thought was going through Pete's head.

"Do you know precisely what he keeps in there?" he asked Ruby.

She blinked nervously. "No. Why should I?"

He sighed. "It will help if we know what's missing."

"I'd have said, wouldn't I?"

Probably not, I thought. Young Ruby doesn't trust the fuzz any more than I do. We only need them to do the donkey work for us.

"Want to look upstairs?" Pete said.

We followed him up, past a notice that said *PRIVATE*. Ruby had said this was where the spare stock was kept. Portable stuff mainly, pictures, toys, chairs, footstools, things like that. You wouldn't want to lug a sideboard up those winding stairs. The only big item I could see was a shabby old sofa with a back rest at one end.

"What that?"

"The chaise longue?" Ruby said. "Sometimes he works late and sleeps over."

Almost everything else was covered in dust sheets or boxed up in cardboard. Most of the china and glass was in bubble wrap stored in tea chests and cartons tidily arranged in rows. An army storekeeper couldn't have made a neater job of it. I'm sure we all sensed right away that nothing had been disturbed up here. Thieves wouldn't go to the trouble of wrapping everything up again.

"I get the impression they knew what they were looking for and it wasn't any of this," Pete said, speaking for all of us.

We returned downstairs.

I saw Pete looking at his watch. "Seen all you want, Miss Hubbard?"

She thanked him.

I wasn't letting him off so lightly. "Give us your two cents' worth, supremo. What's happened to Ruby's dad?"

"Who knows? I'm assuming he wasn't here when the break-in occurred."

"So where is he?"

"Have you checked his home?" He turned to Ruby. "Where does he live?"

"Odd Down." There was a catch in her voice. "He isn't there. I've been to the house several times and I can see the mail heaped up on the doormat."

"He's away a lot, I was told."

"Buying antiques, yes, but never for more than a day or two."

"You reported the break-in a week ago, but you didn't tell us your father was missing."

She shook her head. "I thought he must be on one of his forages, as he called them."

"No one will take any notice unless you report it officially."

Hearing Pete talk to my client like she was twelve years old, I saw red. "She's reported it now and you'd better get your finger out, pal, or we talk to the press."

"Is that a threat, Mr. Getz?" he said. "If you want to help Miss Hubbard, you'll do well to keep your mouth shut."

Ruby said, "Please, Mr. Diamond, I'm really worried about Daddy."

"I'll inform the Missing Persons Unit."

"Can't you deal with it yourself? I'd much rather put my faith in you."

"Not my job." He lifted his stupid hat an inch off his head. He was about to leave. But before turning away, he glanced down. "What's that?"

"What?" I said.

"The white marks. They weren't here when we arrived."

We all looked at the dark-stained floorboards, now marked with a trail of powder spots stretching all the way from the stairs we'd just come down to the stuffed lion.

"One of us trod in some chalk, by the look of it," I said.

"It must be me," Ruby said. "Neither of you went right up to the end where the lion is."

"Could I see under your shoe?" Pete asked her.

Holding my arm for support, she lifted each foot in turn, bending her legs behind her for him to see the soles of her trainers.

"Got it," he said. "Do you mind?" He curled his hand under the toe of her left shoe and prised out a chip of something wedged between the rubber ridges. "Plaster, by the look of it, but where's it from?"

He released her foot and marched off, all masterful, to the end of the room where the lion and other objects were. "Hey ho, someone clobbered Julius Caesar."

Ruby and I hadn't a clue what he was on about until we

joined him and saw for ourselves. The bust of one of the Roman emperors was lying on its side in a mess of dust and bits. Not much had broken off, mainly half the laurel wreath and part of the shoulder.

"How did we miss this?" Ruby said, and then covered her mouth with her fingers. "Did I knock it over?"

"You'd know if you did," Pete said. "They're plaster of Paris and heavy, several kilos for sure."

"It looks recent," she said. "The broken-off bits are really clean."

"Must have been done by your cack-handed scene-of-crime people," I told Pete.

He was quick to challenge that. "They wouldn't have left it like this. It was the thief, more likely. Our people may not even have noticed. The three of us didn't when we came in."

"It's their bloody job to check," I said and the blame game was well and truly on.

"Check what?" he said. "Only the owner knows what's in the shop and what isn't. Their job was to do the obvious stuff, lift any prints on the front door and the safe. They'll have taken the laptop away. Anything else is guesswork."

"You're seriously saying they wouldn't make a full inspection of the place?"

"It's a pesky break-in, not a murder scene."

Which was when both of us were silenced by Ruby giving a gasp and saying, "Oh my God!" She was on her haunches, studying the damaged bust. "Are these bloodstains?"

"Where?"

Pete and I both bent to look. She was pointing to a small crop of brownish-red stains near the base of the thing and smaller than ladybirds. I counted seven.

Not much doubt what Ruby was thinking. She was ashen.

"Is that all there is?" Pete said, trying to be the voice of calm.

"Anything on the floor?" I said. If there was, it wasn't obvious.

Together, we lifted the bust to one side. No more spots.

"He could have covered the stains with something," Pete said. We pushed aside the lion, which was fixed on a wooden plinth the size of a door. No more stains.

"The coffin, then," he said. "Grab the other end, Getz." He dragged off the bearskin and dropped it behind him. The man-shaped mummy case was solid considering it was so old, but the painting on the outside had faded and flaked off badly, which I guess was why it ended up in the antiques shop and not a museum. Originally the whole surface must have been covered in Egyptian symbols.

Mine was the top end. The lid had been carved into the shape of a lifesize figure, face up in a headdress and with crossed arms. Bits of paint remained, like the whites of the eyes. When I bent close to get a grip, an upside-down eye glared up at me. I don't easily get spooked, but this made my flesh creep.

"Heavy," I said. I couldn't lift my end of the thing. Close to nine feet long, it must have been hewn from a single log.

"Try sliding it," Pete said.

That almost brought on a hernia. With Ruby's help we shifted the brute a few inches. The floorboards underneath were a different colour than the rest, but there were no more bloodstains.

"Nobody's moved this bozo in years," I said.

Pete stood back, hands on hips, like a bowls player studying the lie of the woods. "It shouldn't be as heavy as this."

"Something must be inside," I said. "Maybe they hid the loot here and meant to come back. Shall we look?"

He didn't need persuading.

We bent to it. The lid was solid and bulky, but easier to shift. Any fit guy could have done it on his own. What we hadn't decided was where the fuck to put it.

Naturally Pete wanted us to know he was in charge.

"This way."

He tugged his end of the lid towards him and stepped back without looking and his heel struck one of the remaining Roman busts. The emperor rocked on his base like the tenth pin in a strike, toppled over and hit the floor with a mighty thump. Bits of plaster slid everywhere.

"Shit."

I was pissing myself laughing.

Meanwhile, Ruby had stepped up to the coffin and used her phone to shine a light inside.

She took a huge breath and screamed.

You wouldn't have seen bigger eyes if a cartoon artist had drawn them. She backed off and couldn't find words. All she could do was point.

Pete and I dumped the lid, darted to the coffin and looked inside. The smell got to us first and then the sight of the dude lying at the bottom dressed in modern jeans and sweatshirt, socks and trainers, and as dead as last week's news. No mummy, for sure, but I had a nasty feeling he was someone's daddy.

Other Titles in the Soho Crime Series

STEPHANIE BARRON
(Jane Austen's England)
Jane and the Twelve Days
of Christmas
Jane and the Waterloo Map

F.H. BATACAN
(Philippines)
Smaller and Smaller Circles

JAMES R. BENN
(World War II Europe)
Billy Boyle
The First Wave
Blood Alone
Evil for Evil
Rag & Bone
A Mortal Terror
Death's Door
A Blind Goddess
The Rest Is Silence
The White Ghost
Blue Madonna
The Devouring
Solemn Graves
When Hell Struck Twelve
The Red Horse

CARA BLACK
(Paris, France)
Murder in the Marais
Murder in Belleville
Murder in the Sentier
Murder in the Bastille
Murder in Clichy
Murder in Montmartre
Murder on the Ile Saint-Louis
Murder in the Rue de Paradis
Murder in the Latin Quarter
Murder in the Palais Royal
Murder in Passy
Murder at the Lanterne Rouge
Murder Below Montparnasse
Murder in Pigalle
Murder on the Champ de Mars
Murder on the Quai
Murder in Saint-Germain

CARA BLACK CONT.
Murder on the Left Bank
Murder in Bel-Air

Three Hours in Paris

LISA BRACKMANN
(China)
Rock Paper Tiger
Hour of the Rat
Dragon Day
Getaway
Go-Between

HENRY CHANG
(Chinatown)
Chinatown Beat
Year of the Dog
Red Jade
Death Money
Lucky

BARBARA CLEVERLY
(England)
The Last Kashmiri Rose
Strange Images of Death
The Blood Royal
Not My Blood
A Spider in the Cup
Enter Pale Death
Diana's Altar

Fall of Angels
Invitation to Die

COLIN COTTERILL
(Laos)
The Coroner's Lunch
Thirty-Three Teeth
Disco for the Departed
Anarchy and Old Dogs
Curse of the Pogo Stick
The Merry Misogynist
Love Songs from a Shallow Grave
Slash and Burn
The Woman Who Wouldn't Die
Six and a Half Deadly Sins
I Shot the Buddha
The Rat Catchers' Olympics

COLIN COTTERILL CONT.
Don't Eat Me
The Second Biggest Nothing
The Delightful Life of
a Suicide Pilot

GARRY DISHER
(Australia)
The Dragon Man
Kittyhawk Down
Snapshot
Chain of Evidence
Blood Moon
Whispering Death
Signal Loss

Wyatt
Port Vila Blues
Fallout

Bitter Wash Road
Under the Cold Bright Lights

TERESA DOVALPAGE
(Cuba)
Death Comes in through
the Kitchen
Queen of Bones

Death of a Telenovela Star
(A Novella)

DAVID DOWNING
(World War II Germany)
Zoo Station
Silesian Station
Stettin Station
Potsdam Station
Lehrter Station
Masaryk Station
Wedding Station

(World War I)
Jack of Spies
One Man's Flag
Lenin's Roller Coaster
The Dark Clouds Shining

Diary of a Dead Man on Leave

AGNETE FRIIS
(Denmark)
What My Body Remembers
The Summer of Ellen

TIMOTHY HALLINAN
(Thailand)
The Fear Artist
For the Dead
The Hot Countries
Fools' River
Street Music

(Los Angeles)
Crashed
Little Elvises
The Fame Thief
Herbie's Game
King Maybe
Fields Where They Lay
Nighttown

METTE IVIE HARRISON
(Mormon Utah)
The Bishop's Wife
His Right Hand
For Time and All Eternities
Not of This Fold

MICK HERRON
(England)
Slow Horses
Dead Lions
The List (A Novella)
Real Tigers
Spook Street
London Rules
The Marylebone Drop (A Novella)
Joe Country
The Catch (A Novella)
Slough House

Down Cemetery Road
The Last Voice You Hear
Why We Die
Smoke and Whispers

Reconstruction
Nobody Walks
This Is What Happened

STAN JONES
(Alaska)
White Sky, Black Ice
Shaman Pass
Frozen Sun
Village of the Ghost Bears
Tundra Kill
The Big Empty

STEVEN MACK JONES
(Detroit)
August Snow
Lives Laid Away
Dead of Winter

LENE KAABERBØL & AGNETE FRIIS
(Denmark)
The Boy in the Suitcase
Invisible Murder
Death of a Nightingale
The Considerate Killer

MARTIN LIMÓN
(South Korea)
Jade Lady Burning
Slicky Boys
Buddha's Money
The Door to Bitterness
The Wandering Ghost
G.I. Bones
Mr. Kill
The Joy Brigade
Nightmare Range
The Iron Sickle
The Ville Rat
Ping-Pong Heart
The Nine-Tailed Fox
The Line
GI Confidential

ED LIN
(Taiwan)
Ghost Month
Incensed
99 Ways to Die

PETER LOVESEY
(England)
The Circle
The Headhunters

PETER LOVESEY CONT.
False Inspector Dew
Rough Cider
On the Edge
The Reaper

(Bath, England)
The Last Detective
Diamond Solitaire
The Summons
Bloodhounds
Upon a Dark Night
The Vault
Diamond Dust
The House Sitter
The Secret Hangman
Skeleton Hill
Stagestruck
Cop to Corpse
The Tooth Tattoo
The Stone Wife
Down Among the Dead Men
Another One Goes Tonight
Beau Death
Killing with Confetti
The Finisher

(London, England)
Wobble to Death
The Detective Wore Silk Drawers
Abracadaver
Mad Hatter's Holiday
The Tick of Death
A Case of Spirits
Swing, Swing Together
Waxwork

Bertie and the Tinman
Bertie and the Seven Bodies
Bertie and the Crime of Passion

SUJATA MASSEY
(1920s Bombay)
The Widows of Malabar Hill
The Satapur Moonstone
The Bombay Prince

FRANCINE MATHEWS
(Nantucket)
Death in the Off-Season
Death in Rough Water
Death in a Mood Indigo
Death in a Cold Hard Light
Death on Nantucket
Death on Tuckernuck

SEICHŌ MATSUMOTO
(Japan)
Inspector Imanishi Investigates

MAGDALEN NABB
(Italy)
Death of an Englishman
Death of a Dutchman
Death in Springtime
Death in Autumn
The Marshal and the Murderer
The Marshal and the Madwoman
The Marshal's Own Case
The Marshal Makes His Report
The Marshal at the Villa Torrini
Property of Blood
Some Bitter Taste
The Innocent
Vita Nuova
The Monster of Florence

FUMINORI NAKAMURA
(Japan)
The Thief
Evil and the Mask
Last Winter, We Parted
The Kingdom
The Boy in the Earth
Cult X

STUART NEVILLE
(Northern Ireland)
The Ghosts of Belfast
Collusion
Stolen Souls
The Final Silence
Those We Left Behind
So Say the Fallen
The Traveller & Other Stories

(Dublin)
Ratlines

REBECCA PAWEL
(1930s Spain)
Death of a Nationalist
Law of Return
The Watcher in the Pine
The Summer Snow

KWEI QUARTEY
(Ghana)
Murder at Cape Three Points
Gold of Our Fathers
Death by His Grace
The Missing American
Sleep Well, My Lady

QIU XIAOLONG
(China)
Death of a Red Heroine
A Loyal Character Dancer
When Red Is Black

JAMES SALLIS
(New Orleans)
The Long-Legged Fly
Moth
Black Hornet
Eye of the Cricket
Bluebottle
Ghost of a Flea

Sarah Jane

JOHN STRALEY
(Sitka, Alaska)
The Woman Who Married a Bear
The Curious Eat Themselves
The Music of What Happens
*Death and the Language
  of Happiness*
The Angels Will Not Care
Cold Water Burning
Baby's First Felony

(Cold Storage, Alaska)
The Big Both Ways
Cold Storage, Alaska
What Is Time to a Pig?

AKIMITSU TAKAGI
(Japan)
The Tattoo Murder Case
Honeymoon to Nowhere

AKIMITSU TAKAGI CONT.
The Informer

HELENE TURSTEN
(Sweden)
Detective Inspector Huss
The Torso
The Glass Devil
Night Rounds
The Golden Calf
The Fire Dance
The Beige Man
The Treacherous Net
Who Watcheth
Protected by the Shadows

Hunting Game
Winter Grave
Snowdrift

*An Elderly Lady Is Up
  to No Good*

ILARIA TUTI
(Italy)
Flowers over the Inferno
The Sleeping Nymph

JANWILLEM VAN DE WETERING
(Holland)
Outsider in Amsterdam
Tumbleweed
The Corpse on the Dike
Death of a Hawker
The Japanese Corpse
The Blond Baboon
The Maine Massacre
The Mind-Murders
The Streetbird
The Rattle-Rat
Hard Rain
Just a Corpse at Twilight
Hollow-Eyed Angel
The Perfidious Parrot
*The Sergeant's Cat:
  Collected Stories*

JACQUELINE WINSPEAR
(1920s England)
Maisie Dobbs
Birds of a Feather